PEACEWEAVER

The Story of Eadgyth Ælfgarsdottir

Judith Arnopp

Published in 2011 by FeedARead

First Edition

A CIP catalogue record for this title is available from the British Library.

With thanks and appreciation to The Cwrtnewydd Scribblers, Rachael Thomas, Brenda Old, Iris lee, Margaret Williams and Sue Moules for their undwindling support. Thank you for listening. Also to my sister, Cherry and my husband, John, for their belief in me.

About the Author

Judith Arnopp lives on a Welsh smallholding and is mother/stepmother to seven children. Always passionate about her writing Judith graduated from the University of Wales, Lampeter in 2007 and is now able to devote herself to writing full time.

Peaceweaver, is the tale of Eadgyth, queen to both Gruffydd ap Llewelyn of Wales and Harold II of England. Her second novel, *The Forest Dwellers*, follows the lives of a family dispossessed from their home to make way for King William the Conqueror's New Forest. *The Forest Dwellers* is a nail biting tale of oppression, sexual manipulation and revenge.

Judith is currently editing her third novel, *The Song of Heledd*, the tale of Heledd and Ffreur, Celtic princesses from the land of Pengwern, a dynasty destined for disaster.

Set against a backdrop of seventh century conflict the author has taken fragments of the 9th century poem, *Canu Heledd* and filled in the gaps to form a fiction of what might have been.

Prologue

CHESTER 1070

We watched him ride past today, the one they are calling *The Conqueror*. Eadgytha and I saw him pass through the city gate and, although he is just a man, I buried the faces of my young sons in my skirts to shield them from the sight. Thus concealed, they escaped the gaze of the squint-eyed king as he clattered by and did not see the splendour of his retinue throw a gaudy splash of colour across the sombre street. Around us the crowd stood silent in the rain and, although I am tall and feared that the hatred surging in my heart would knock him from his mount, he did not notice me

The crowd dispersed slowly, muttering against the ravages of the Norman dog who, having laid waste to the south and north of England, now turned his attention to Chester, our place of refuge and the last Saxon stronghold. Many have been slaughtered and homes destroyed, leaving ruins to smoke beneath the sulky sky and the destitute to huddle in the darker places of the street.

A ragged old fellow snorted and spat greenly into the mud where the Norman king's horse had trod, 'God's curse be on ye gutter shite.' he cried in cracked tones, shaking his feeble fist in the air. I patted his arm in mute sympathy before we turned away.

'Why are you trembling, Mother?' asked Harold as we hurried back to our lodging, heads bent against the driving rain.

'Your mother is chilled, that is all,' replied Eadgytha, hastily taking the child's hand. 'We have stood too long in the rain, come, hurry along, Harold, make haste, Wulf.'

We climbed the steep castle hill, inhaling the acrid stench of smouldering fires newly quenched by sheeting rain.

Too close to the stronghold for comfort now it is in Norman hands, we need to move on. Chester is no longer a safe refuge for any Saxon, let alone women such as we.

Indoors the fire has sunk low. Eadgytha stoops to feed it a few meagre sticks before warming a little goat milk for a nourishing drink. Then we sit, knee to knee, before the hearth while the twins play with swords fashioned from two sticks. Anwen bursts through the door accompanied by a flurry of wind and leaves.

'My, 'tis cold out there, my ladies. I've managed to find a few things for supper, 'tis nothing to drool over but better than nought. I'll get it going right away so we can dine and get ourselves early to our beds.'

She throws vegetables into a pot for broth while Eadgytha and I, chilled more by circumstance than weather, begin to discuss our options. There are few places of refuge left in all of England, the invasion having been thorough. No Saxons are content beneath the Norman rule yet most, eager to save their necks, collaborate, quelling their hatred to meekly bear the yoke.

A few have rebelled, some rally to the call of Hereward, known as the Wake, in his hiding place in the Fens. Perhaps we should join them there but it is a far off place, haunted by the dispossessed and the marshes are fraught with mischievous sprites; besides, neither of us knows the way and there is no man now to protect or guide us. We cower here in this dark place, two women alone. Our household is scattered and we are forced to look to ourselves. It is not easy for women such as we to live in obscurity, raising our children and scratching a living from the dirt.

Eadgytha's sons are far away and her daughters are … well, we know not where. My family is scattered also; my older sons are across the dyke with their Welsh kin and my brothers are lost.

We make an odd pairing, Eadgytha and I, but we have only each other now. Of all the women in the land, we are the two that William of Normandy most desires to lay his hand upon. If captured, he will put out our eyes and cut off our noses. If we are lucky we may be shut away in a religious house but, if he lays hands upon my infant sons, he will show them no mercy but will kill them straight. There are none in this stricken land who flee King William more diligently than we, for Eadgytha the Gentle Swan was, for twenty years King Harold's mistress.

I am named Eadgyth too and I was Harold's queen and mother to the Ætheling, Harold Haroldsson, who tumbles in play even now with his brother upon the dusty floor.

Part one
Exile

Mercia 1056

Clad in my new saffron yellow gown, I held out my arms and turned full circle. 'How do I look?'

'Fat,' replied Morcar rudely, sending Edwin to the floor in a fit of giggles.

'Morcar.' reprimanded mother, 'you are cruel. 'tis nought but baby fat and will melt away as she grows. You'll be forced to eat your words when she grows to womanhood. You are beautiful, daughter, and do your father proud.'

As always it was snug in mother's chamber although, outside, the world was ice locked. It was Christmastide and we were at my Grandfather Leofric's hall in Mercia where rolling hills cupped us gently so that I felt safe; unlike the terrain of our East Anglian home where the world has no edge but spreads like endless waters to the horizon. I was always warm in those days before sadness and fear touched my life.

Even when the wind blew strong across the heath and mud lay in frozen ruts there was comfort to be had within doors. I recall great fires roaring in the hearth, a full belly and the red shiny faces of the bards as they strummed their lutes, singing for their supper. Father, leaning back in his chair, bellowing with laughter at something somebody had said and my brother, Edwin, feeding his dog titbits from his trencher while mother, smiling and proud of her well run household, pretended she did not see. My father was rich and his hall a fine one. My brothers said there were finer and richer halls but I chose not to believe them; they were boys and I had learned early that boys often lied.

The walls of my Grandfather's house were hung with bright tapestries and the scarred mead benches, laden with festive fare, gleamed in the torchlight. Smoke curled over our heads while, underfoot, the dogs snatched and snarled at scraps discarded in the straw. My Grandfather, Leofric, was the Earl of Mercia and wed in his youth to the notorious Lady Godgifu whom, legend said, had ridden naked through the town of Coventry. Morcar had once had the temerity to ask our father if the story was true but he had clipped his ear and sent him howling from the hall. When I broached the subject with my mother in the privacy of her chamber she threw scorn upon the idea.

'Well, I know none who would dare ask her. Your grandmother, when she was in good health, was a severe old lady, I am sure she would never have stooped so low. Twas no doubt just a story made up for the delectation of men for 'tis said she was very fair in her day.'

When I knew Grandmother Godgifu, she was confined in her chamber, lost in some half lit world, neither alive nor dead, where none could reach her. I still wonder sometimes about the truth of the tale and try to imagine the bent crone that I knew, riding upright and radiant, bare-rumped upon her palfrey. The days when she could have revealed the truth are long gone now and my parents with her; those rosy winter feast days are gone too, slipped into the past with the other good things. Those warm childhood days, with servants to carry out my every whim, ill prepared me for what was to follow and I was not ready to be lurched into womanhood in my thirteenth year when Father fell foul of King Edward and, stripped of his lands, was exiled.

'Exiled.' I cried 'What do you mean exiled? Why does Father not just tell the king he is sorry? He can't let his pride deprive us of our homeland. I don't want to leave. I want to stay here at home.'

Mother looked strained and pale and, although I realised that she probably was as loath to leave as I, still I allowed my tongue to flap on. Wearily, she looked down at her hands.

'Do not rant Eadgyth, it is unseemly, remember who you are. Your father is accused of treason so we should praise God that King Edward has seen fit only to exile him. He has slandered the king, claiming him unfit to rule and so we must take flight to Ireland.'

Throwing my arms in the air and pivoting on my heel, I wrenched dramatically at my hair. 'Ireland.' I wailed, 'Oh Mother. We can't go there. I've heard 'tis an outlandish place where the rain never ceases. And the Irish. They say they are an ungodly race. Mother, there must be something to be done. Where is Father now?'

Morcar stood sulky by the central fire that was dying from want of fuel, picking up a log he tossed it into the embers.

'He has departed already and awaits us at port. There is nothing to be done, the king is a fool and a coward and Father was right to say so. Edward knows the earldom should stay in our possession but he is too afraid of Godwin to enforce it. He should have kept them down when he had the chance and never have let them back from exile. Father has the right of it but the king is too lame to back him up in the face of Godwin's strength and so thinks to replace us. I say 'tis a shame when a fool rides the throne but worse indeed when that fool is a coward also.'

'Morcar.' reprimanded mother 'That is enough. Curb your tongue. Eadgyth, I will not argue with you now, just do as I bid, for heaven's sake. I have more important matters to attend to. Tell Anwen to pack your things, we leave at daybreak.'

Anwen, more friend than slave, had been with me since childhood. We had grown together and now she served the role of my own personal servant and companion. As she flew about the room tossing things into a travelling box, I questioned my brothers further about the reason for our plight. Edwin's determination to prove himself able to follow in Father's footsteps had made him a fine source of political information.

'So, tell me,' I said, 'what is the cause of all this upset? Are the Godwins truly so evil?'

'Not evil, no. Just ambitious and ruthless. Old Godwin was used to having things his way and his sons flourish under him now they are grown. I must admit that they have done England some favours. Edward is no warrior-king and Godwin provided the military strength and leadership that he lacks. Our country has floundered for years beneath Edward's rule; he is a weak and feeble king, much like his father Ethelred was in his day. Since old Godwin dropped dead at Eastertide Edward's puny attempts at leadership have been at the expense of the rest of the Saxon nobility. And the earldormen, are further displeased by the way he insists on filling his court with Normans.'

I raised my eyebrows, surprised.

'Why does he do that? I didn't think anyone liked Normans.'

Morcar laughed.

'You are not wrong there, little sister, but Edward was brought up in exile in Normandy and once he had finally gained his rightful throne he began to fill his court with the friends he had made across the channel. The Godwins didn't like that any more than the rest of us and sought to prevent Norman influence from growing too strong. In a shrewd move they somehow managed to persuade Edward to marry their sister which, I'll admit, did keep him from a Norman marriage, but now the Godwins themselves grow too dominant. Even though the old man is dead and their brother Swegen dishonoured, it is Harold and his brothers, Leofwine and Gyrth, that stand to take over where the old man left off and as for Tostig …'

'Well, if there was ever mischief in the making it's him.' interceded Edwin, 'and now we are ousted from the picture, the Godwins will have rule over the whole blasted country from north to south and all because Edward can't or won't control them.'

Collecting my psalter I lay it with my other few treasures on my bed for Anwen to pack.

'But didn't you say that they had been banished before? How did Edward find the guts to do that if he is such a coward?'

Edwin and Morcar glanced at each other, each waiting for the other to reply; finally Edwin spoke up again.

'That's a good question. They were banished before and, God knows, they should have been made to stay away. There was a massive fall out with Edward when some of his fancy friends visiting from Normandy fell into a dispute with some locals in Dover. Some of them were killed or injured, I do not recall the details, and Edward ordered Godwin to carry out retribution. When Godwin refused, Edward exiled the lot of them and even had their sister, his own wife and an anointed queen, thrown into a nunnery.'

Astounded, I stopped petting Stella, my greyhound and turned back to my brothers.

'But, what had she to do with it?'

'Oh, probably nothing at all, although I have heard that she meddles in Edward's affairs. There is little doubt he did it out of spite; Edward can be an unpleasant fellow for all his pompous piety.'

I pondered upon what I had learned while I ate a rough and ready meal before embarking upon our journey. It seemed that Father had gone too far and, in raging at Edward of injustice and accusing him of cowardice, his lack of diplomacy and use of blasphemy had offended the saintly king and sealed our fate. As a consequence my family were doomed to live out our lives in a state every man dreaded … exile.

Looking back, I now scorn the girl that railed so hard against her fate; the weak tears that I shed that day were those of a child. In my ignorance I believed that eviction and exile were the worst things that could befall me. Had I known how wrong I was I would have saved my tears.

IRELAND-1056

At daybreak I was helped onto my mare and we rode, chilled and miserable, from our home to the coast where a ship bobbed at anchor waiting to take us across the seas. As despondent as I was, the sight of the sea thrilled me. My brothers said it was just a little choppy but the waves tossed our small ship about so that one moment we crested the wave and the next plunged down unto the depths. It was my first experience on board ship. I clung to the side feeling the salt air whip my hair from its cap; laughing I turned to make comment to Edwin but found instead my father, who was furious.

'Get thee behind with the women!' he cried, 'are you a fool?' and, forced to obey, I slunk back to my mother's side.

Huddled in the makeshift tent beneath the mast, I tried not to listen while mother and Anwen heaved over leather buckets and wept that they were dying. It was a long, weary voyage; our only food the coarse stuff that made up a seaman's diet and brackish water with which to quench our thirst.

Morcar and Edwin, allowed the freedom of the ship, had a better time than I and their faces were soon burnished to gold by the sea winds.

'I was born to be a seaman!' declared Edwin as he fell to learning how the sailors navigated the longship across the choppy waters but I was glad when, at last, a cry came that land was in sight. Gulping in mouthfuls of fresh air, I clutched the side of the ship with both hands, eager to see land again but Ireland was so swathed in mist that I was unable to discern where the sea ended and the shore began.

King Diarmaid's court was a dank, cheerless place. The mist and the rain billowed in sheets, crept up through the wooden walls and trickled down through the leaky thatch. One by one we were beset with chills, Anwen, just as sick as we, shuffled about our miserable dwelling in her outdoor clothes, her nose dripping as she dosed us all with warmed honey and wine. Mother wept, night and day, yearning for her cosy chamber, her fleet of servants, an appetising meal and her sumptuous fur-trimmed wardrobe. She swore we suffered some evil Irish malady that lurked in the loathsome bogs about our temporary dwelling. While we endured the torment and I mourned the loss of my dog Stella, Father spent his time interred with Danish and Irish chieftains, plotting against his king.

The Welsh, ever ready to harass the Saxon throne, had joined with us against Edward. In better days Father had hated the Welsh, cursing them as savages and thieves but, in his exile, he clasped them to his bosom and called them brother. Years before I was born the Welsh king had slain my uncle in battle but now it seemed Father had forgiven him and for the first time I heard the name Gruffydd ap Llewelyn spoken without a curse.

He broke bread now with Magnus, the son of the Norwegian king, a man he had disdained during his days as Earl. Magnus, like his father Harald Hardrada, was a huge man, towering over everyone around him; one day I met him as I was coming from the privy. I made to creep past but he barred my way and greeted me with glee, grasping my shoulders and planting a wet kiss on each of my cheeks. I did not understand what he said but I knew it was an expression of his approval. He smelled of ale and woodsmoke and when he laughed, which he did often, he displayed large yellow teeth.

I do not think he was a bad man, just rough and untutored in gentler manners but he overawed me nonetheless. His men were just like him, coarse and loud, drinking long into the night until they fell senseless and spent the night on the floor. But, for all their uncouth ways, they seemed somehow more alive than other men. I think they liked women for they never failed to bellow with pleasure should they encounter any of the ladies of the household and they made free use of the serving maids, none of whom seemed to object. After a while Mother and I learned not to mind them and once I even saw mother blush prettily at something Hardrada whispered into her ear when my father wasn't looking.

The Welsh and the Irish, I noticed, were gentle spoken, their voices soft like the breeze in the treetops or gentle rain tinkling from the roof. When I was in their company they were courteous, making way so I could pass by and calling me *Cariad*, although it was not until later that I learned what it meant.

Sometimes the company sang; the Welsh bards wistfully of lost battles and lovers and the Irish gaily of bygone days. The Norwegian songs were sung with gusto, brave tales of bitter battles and valiant defeats.

I grew sneaky during that time and, listening behind doors, witnessed behaviour I had never seen before and heard words that had never been used in my Saxon home. No longer sure if my father were a good man or not, I was confused. He seemed at home with these rogues, as my mother called them. I worried that he was playing into King Edward's hands, turning his sons into traitors and destroying any chance we had of a pardon. If his plans failed then we would never be allowed to return home and what should we do then? Remain here, spending the rest of our days in this wet and dreary place, forced to adjust to the strange customs of its people? Did Father truly trust these men? Were they really his friends?

He seemed to believe they were so and I could do nothing but place my faith in him. Surrounded by enemies as I was, I had yet to learn that an enemy can become a friend just as easily as a friend becomes an enemy.

Part Two
The Dragon's Flame

Winter-1057

I screamed, pleaded and begged him to take me with him but he was as immovable as a stranger. Father shrugged off my clinging hands and sold me, like a brood mare, in marriage to his old enemy Gruffydd ap Llewelyn. I was his pawn; a bargaining tool to ensure that Gruffydd would keep to their agreement and help him in his fight against the Saxon king. I had spent a lifetime hearing him denounced as a murderer and a thief but now, in order that the alliance between them be sealed, I was expected to welcome him as my husband.

The ceremony was taken in haste. 'Mother.' I entreated, but she refused to look at me and I had no choice but repeat the reluctant vow beneath Father's malevolent glare. Bundled, weeping onto the ship I assumed we all returned to England but, after a brief stop on the coast of *Cymru*, Father's ship sailed away leaving Anwen and I alone with the Welshmen on the shore.

We ran down the beach to stand ankle deep and watch the ship disappear around the headland. Edwin raised his hand in a brief farewell but my father did not watch or wave God be wi' ye; that congenial man with the laughing red face was gone and I would see neither him, nor my mother, ever again.

All around us people rushed about in the incessant rain, calling to each other, their Welsh tongues too rapid for me to decipher. Pack ponies were laden with bundles and boxes that had been dumped on the beach and we were given a tiny white pony to ride. At least, I believed her to be white beneath her muddied coat. Men rode forth, sent by my new husband with messages to other chieftains.

How strange it seemed to call that man 'husband;' Gruffydd was past fifty and, to my thirteen years, he was ancient. He was not tall but sturdily built, his long stringy hair that had once been black was worn caught up in a tail at the nape of his neck. I did not know then if he were kind or otherwise for we had never spoken a word except for the exchange of our hasty marriage vow. All I knew was that I did not want him as husband.

Anwen's native tongue was Welsh and she valiantly tried to interpret the conversation that batted around us but her quick voice made my head buzz all the more.

'Oh, do hush, Anwen,' I said at length, 'it brings me no comfort.' And so, we stood, two bedraggled children in the rain, waiting for someone to lead us to warmth and shelter.

It was nigh on noon when we mounted our ponies and left the port to trail inland on an upward path through a blanket of rain. My cloak was soon wet through and my hands that clasped Anwen's waist grew numb. I am shamed to say my nose began to drip and so despondent was I that I left it so.

On and on we travelled, our wooded path often seeming to terminate suddenly only to reveal itself again as a sharp twist in the trail took us ever higher into the hills. The mist-shrouded terrain loomed threatening from the edges of the path, giving no clue as to our location and it was dark before we reached our resting place.

Never had I seen such a welcome sight. The glowing firelight from within the ringed enclosure cheered me slightly as I was helped, stiff backed, from my pony

A dark haired boy, just a few years my senior, led the ponies away while we were ushered inside to thaw our hands and feet and slurp the hot bowl of watery soup that the Welsh called *cawl*. Gruffydd, who had ridden on ahead, was seated at the hearth with his *teulu,* the household knights that accompanied him everywhere, ready to die for him should the need arise. They barely looked up as, cold and dripping, Anwen and I joined them at the blazing hearth.

The only furniture consisted of crude stools and benches set about a rough table and rough mattresses on the earthen floor. Smoke sulked from the central fire, seeking escape through the insufficient thatch, making the windowless place cheerless. Surely this could not be the home of the king of all *Cymru*. In my halting Welsh I asked the old woman, as she ladled *cawl* into small wooden bowls. She showed us her gums and cackled in amusement. 'Nay Lady, 'tis the property of one of Gruffydd's thegns.'

My mistake was batted around the Welsh contingent and their laughter lilted like music. They were not unfriendly but I felt alienated nonetheless and swallowed a sob. I wanted my mother and father, I was so lonely and homesick that had even Edwin or Morcar come into the room I should have rushed to them with outstretched arms.

When the door opened again, bringing in a hail of cold wind everyone cursed as the fellow struggled in with my box. I beckoned Anwen and we sought a dark corner where she helped me change from my wet things.

There was no privacy from the rest of the company but I made the best of it and, when the time came, snuggled with her beneath a fur covering on a straw pallet in one corner while the rest of the household snored around us. Gruffydd and his men sat up long into the night, drinking and conspiring in whispers before the fire.

Anwen's cry of surprise ripped into my uneasy dreams as she was dragged from the warmth of my bed. A masculine curse sent her scrabbling away and I realised, with some fear, that my lord had come.

He climbed in beneath the furs beside me; grunting and cold and immediately began to fumble at my clothes. He was malodorous, still damp from the trail and reeking of mead. Although I knew what it meant to be married and had seen enough rutting dogs to know it wasn't a delicate procedure, it was the closest I had ever been to a man.

His huge, cold hand began to creep up my inner thigh and I tried to clamp my knees together but he wrenched my legs apart. Mortified, I tried to wriggle away but he grasped my jaw and snarled, 'Be still,' and so I lay still and, in the midst of the sleeping household, reluctantly surrendered.

Cold, miserable and bruised the next morning I huddled on my pallet wrapped in blankets while the horses were made ready. We breakfasted on coarse bread and goat milk but my stomach craved something hot. I avoided Gruffydd's eye and was not a little relieved when he and his huscarls rode out early. We were left with just a small escort to guide us.

The young man, who appeared to have been left in charge, introduced himself as Rhodri. He smiled and bowed his head as I emerged from the hut and then Anwen helped me to fasten my cloak before I prepared to mount my little mare.

'How pretty she is now all brushed free of mud.' I exclaimed, not missings Rhodri's flush of pleasure at the compliment.

'She is the best we have, Lady,' he said, 'bred of the finest native ponies and this one selected especially for you.'

Stroking her soft pink nose and appreciating the thought that had gone into the gesture I warmed towards him.

'I thank you for that, Rhodri. If she has no name already, I think I shall call her Glimmer, for last night on the trail, as it grew dark and my eyes heavy, all I could see was her mane glimmering in the gloom.'

I looked upon his strong-boned face and honest, dark eyes and recognised a potential friend. He returned my smile briefly before turning to issue orders to load up the pack horses. Then, leaping onto the back of his mount he signalled for the party to move out and we proceeded on in single file along the narrow mountain track. I wished I was as able as Rhodri in the saddle for, while I bumped and slid about on my mare's broad back, Rhodri's leather clad torso moved in perfect unison with his horse.

No that Gruffydd no longer rode with us, I noticed a different, lighter mood. The rain had stopped and some of the company began to sing as we climbed higher into rocky terrain. I have since learned that there is not another race on earth who can sing as well as the people of *Cymru* and, as I listened to their lilting voices, with the countryside sparkling all around me, I began to feel a little better. The sunlight illuminated the lingering raindrops and mirrored the bright blue skies and mountaintops in the surface of the lakes. Eagles soared above us, keening in the frigid air and, although the cold made my nose tingle, the sun was warm upon my back.

At noon we broke our journey, pausing on a swathe of green where a leaping waterfall disturbed the surface of the lake. Far out on the mere, waterfowl glided, tranquil as the day. Anwen and I stretched our legs and strolled to the edge of a nearby wood while the servants lit a fire and prepared food. The voices of the company, still strange to my Saxon ears, followed us as we moved away from the camp. Bright shafts of sunlight sliced into the gloom and, as we made our way discreetly between the trees in search of privacy, a shout halted us and Rhodri ran up behind us.

'Do not go deep into the wood, Lady; seek the cover of the undergrowth here and I will guard you. Bears and wolves lurk in these mountain forests and it does not do to wander off alone and there's nothing one of our bears likes more than a plump, Saxon princess for his supper.'

I blushed but said nothing as he turned his back discreetly and whistled between his teeth to conceal any sounds we made. More than a little alarmed at the prospect of becoming a bear's supper, I cast anxiously about me as Anwen and I squatted, making dark puddles on the forest floor. We made the business as brief as possible before strolling with Rhodri to rejoin the rest of the party. In East Anglia and Mercia there were no longer any bears but here, it seemed, I must learn to be wary of new dangers.

The company were relaxed, breaking into small groups to eat a small repast. I felt almost content squatting close to the fire watching the slow roasting small fowl that had been felled with arrows as we travelled along the way.

Rhodri produced some skins of wine and some small, wizened apples and nuts and the conversation rose and fell as we replenished our appetites. We tarried too long and, by the time we had finished, the sun had passed its zenith and we knew the warmest part of the day was over.

While the servants doused the fires and tidied up the remains of the meal, I remounted and we continued the journey. The gentle singing and the rhythmic motion of the pony lulled me into semi-consciousness. I don't know if it was the singing or the effects of the food I had eaten but, with my eyes half closed and my hands loose on the reins, I was ill-prepared when a bird flew up suddenly in front of my mare and she reared, knocking me from the saddle.

Anwen's scream alerted the rest of the party as I fell heavily to the ground. I was only momentarily winded and, feeling foolish, I sat up just in time to see Glimmer darting off into the distance while various members of the party tried to catch at her trailing reins.

Rhodri appeared, as if from nowhere, at my side.

'Are you hurt, Lady?' he asked and, behind him, I saw Anwen's horrified face and the sight of her I made me giggle. I shook my head clear and smiled up at them.

'I am perfectly all right,' I assured him, 'I should have paid more attention to where we were going instead of allowing myself to all but fall asleep. It is entirely my own fault.'

Taking Rhodri's proffered hand I staggered to my feet but, once upright, my head swam and my knees immediately gave way again. Rhodri broke my fall but, no lightweight, I fell half on top of him in the drying mud where, supporting me in his arms, he said.

'It seems you are not all right, Lady, do not rush to get up, we do well enough here. Anwen fetch your mistress a drink, there is a skin of mead fixed to my saddle, and we will allow her to take time to recover. We must wait until they recapture your pony anyway, she could be half way to home by now.'

I felt foolish sprawled upon the ground in Rhodri's arms but, I confess, it was not an altogether unpleasant experience. I could smell his horsey odour and see where his soft beard was trying to sprout upon his cheeks. As we half lay there he asked me questions about my childhood and family. I told him about my parents and and he laughed when I mentioned my two dreadful older brothers. But, when I went on to tell him I was just thirteen years old, he snorted and I saw his jaw tighten, as if he were angry.

It may have only been a tumble from a small pony but it took a full half hour for me to feel recovered enough to rise. Glimmer was led, shamefaced, toward me and I stroked her gentle muzzle to renew our friendship and show that there were no hard feelings. Once I had remounted and we were on our way once more, the lingering memory of Rhodri's protective arms and the way his breath had hushed gently upon my face comforted me as we approached what was to be my new home.

My first view of Rhuddlan is one that will stay with me forever. The mountain terrain gave way quite suddenly and I found that we were travelling downhill toward an area of marsh and mudflats. There, ringed by *Cymru's* mountainous heart, Gruffydd's *llys* stood proud and stark upon Twthill; a wooden fortress amid the marshy estuary beyond which I could glimpse the sparkling, open sea.

We followed the track through a tiny settlement that clustered about the fording place on the river; ragged children, knee deep in the water, ceased their play to watch us ride by. As we splashed across, women collected their washing from where it had been drying on the bank and stood, hand to brow, watching as we passed. The gatekeepers noted our approach and the wooden gate swung back ready to admit us at the top of Twthill.

As we passed into the stronghold the sudden cessation of the wind came as some relief; my hair, that had blown free of its confines to whip about my face, dropped to its customary place on my shoulders and my cheeks began to sting as the warmer air licked my frozen skin. Within the walls all was hustle and bustle; folk darted about scattering poultry and small children as they went. A rangy looking mongrel came to sniff at us as we dismounted but unimpressed, he lifted his leg against my travel box and trotted off in search of something more interesting. Rhodri shouted to a passing boy to lead the horses away while we sought the comfort of the hall. As he guided me through the throng the people jostled each other for a glimpse of their new princess.

It was mercifully warm within, the central fire was blazing and servants were scurrying to seek refreshment for the travellers. As I unfastened my cloak I looked about me with some pleasure. Bright torches illuminated the dark corners revealing rich tapestries that lined the walls to exclude the drafts. Although not so grand as those in my father's hall, they were fine enough and a welcome surprise after the squalor of the previous night's lodging. A man and a woman all swathed in furs hurried forward to greet me and drew me closer to the warmth of the hearth.

'Welcome to Rhuddlan, My Lady. My name is Llyward and I am the Lord Gruffydd's chamberlain and this is my wife.' He bowed low over my hand before gesturing his wife forward to make her greeting.

'Welcome, Lady, I am Tangwystl and it is my pleasure to serve you. Come, take a seat at the Lord's table. You must come to me should there be anything you require that we have not thought to provide.' Truly all I wanted to do was sleep but Gruffydd's people were eager to greet me, even though I was a Saxon. They put on such a hearty display of welcome that refusal would have seemed churlish.

Bards emerged from nowhere and began to tune their lutes and mead began to flow as, suddenly ravenous, we devoured whatever Gruffydd's cooks placed before us. Everyone gathered to make merry, even the lowliest slave was eager to welcome the proud Saxon princess who, in her husband's absence, was placed at the head of the table. All assembled, it seemed, could sing or recite a ballad or pluck music from a harp and soon my belly bulged beneath my gown and my eyes grew heavy from the warmth and lack of sleep. As the company quietened a minstrel stepped forward and stroking his harp began to sing. I could not understand every word but his voice was rich and full and I sat back in my chair letting the beauty of the language wash over me.

The heat and the mead made my eyes heavy and Rhodri, from his place further down the board, noticed my exhaustion and nestled his cheek on his hands to signify that I should go to sleep. Determined not to give in to my weariness, I smiled defiantly and shook my head, pulling myself straighter in my chair. Looking benevolently upon my newfound people I was, for the first time since I had left my father's hall, relaxed and almost happy. The revelling grew louder and I tapped with my fingers to the rhythm of the music. At my feet two hounds, over excited by the furore, slobbered and growled over some scraps. I pushed at them with my foot to send them away and, as I did so, my slipper came free. Afraid that the dogs would steal it, I stooped down to retrieve it and, while I was engaged beneath the table, the music suddenly dwindled and a voice roared across the hall, silencing the festivities.

'What in God's name goes on here? Am I come late for the Christ's mass or is it ever your habit to make so merry in my absence? You, minstrel, shut up and get ye from my sight and you, cook, fetch me that platter. I am starved and have journeyed all the way from hell only to find you all revelling, drinking my mead and feasting upon my best hogs. Where the hell is my wife, bring her forth to me.'

It was the first time I had seen Gruffydd since our wedding night and I was reluctant to face him; in fact I realised now that I had, for the last few hours, been trying to pretend he did not exist. Slowly I raised my head from beneath the table, my veil askew and nervously made my presence known.

'God's teeth, madam!' Gruffydd roared, 'What do you beneath the table? Are you in your cups?'

'N-no, my lord, I did but lose my slipper,' I stammered, my throat dry. He was filthy, his cloak coated with the mire of the road and his face black with soot. He approached the table and threw himself in the chair beside me.

'Straighten your cap.' he said, taking a huge bite from a shank of meat, 'Ye have servants to fetch your slippers for you now and don't be getting too comfortable in my chair.'

It seemed to have grown colder in the hall, the music was stilled and the company muted; even the fire, it seemed, burned less bright. Llyward took his place at Gruffydd's side and engaged him in conversation so that my husband's back was turned from me. His companions, as travel stained as he, slotted themselves in where they could along the board and dove into the remaining food. They talked loudly about the settlement they had burned and the men they had slaughtered. Along the table Rhodri no longer looked in my direction but studied his trencher and I saw Anwen hurrying from the hall in the direction of my sleeping quarters.

The faces that had beamed up at me a short while since now no longer glanced my way and heads were kept low. The bards stood idle and, taking my courage in both hands, I cleared my throat, interrupting Gruffydd's conversation.

'My Lord, can we not ask the bards to strike up again? They sing so fine a song.'

Turning to me with a scowl he replied curtly.

'If the bards play I will not hear Llyward's report.'

'tis a shame to break up the party though, Lord, I was enjoying the entertainment.'

He swivelled back, his frown more quizzical than before.

'Your party, Madam, is inappropriate. You can make merry another night, this night my men and I talk of war.'

'The festivities were not planned, my Lord. We did not expect you. I thought not to look for you until Thursday.'

'Obviously,' he replied, hawking and spitting into the rushes. 'Unfortunately for you I completed my business early, burned the Saes in their beds and gained myself two days o' idleness, although to be sure, I'm a stranger to the luxury. I meet with your father again come Tuesday.' Expanding into his favourite subject Gruffydd raised his voice to encompass the whole company.

'While I harry the borders, Ælfgar and Magnus will invade the eastern coast. Harold and his lap dog, Edward will know not which flank to defend against us.' He laughed horribly before taking another draught from his jug, then he rose and, after wiping his mouth on his sleeve, grasped my wrist.

'Anyway, the night is over, your mistress and I are to our bed. I'll speak with you further on the morrow, Llyward.'

Gruffydd, with a curt jerk of his head, sent Anwen scurrying from the chamber; she gave me a compassionate look before leaving me to Gruffydd's mercies. Looking about the room, I saw it was warm and the bed piled with furs, there were even a few books on the table set close to the fire and a lyre propped against a chair. Wine and wafers were on the night table and a single torch burned, illuminating the room just enough to shield my blushes. Maybe tonight would not be so bad, I thought, perhaps the discomfort of the dwelling had prevented him from showing gentleness the last time.

Gruffydd pulled off his boots and flung himself backward onto the bed, letting out a gusty sigh. I began to loosen my braids and, as I did so, risked a shy smile at him over my shoulder.

'God's grief, madam. Would you stop fiddling with your hair and get yourself over here, I don't have all night.'

I dropped the comb and hurried to stand before him. He looked me up and down before pulling me onto his knee and burrowing his face in my breast, inhaling my scent. Gasping at the shock of his rough face against my skin I hardly had time to compose my thoughts before he picked me up and dumped me onto the bed, pulling my nightgown up to my chin. His attentions were brisk and thorough but mercifully short. I lay rigid beneath him until he rolled onto his back and began to snore, leaving me to fight back tears.

I awoke in the morning in an empty bed. Outside my window the mist lay heavy, obscuring both sea and mountains. I dressed myself and crossed the yard to the cooking hall where I found Anwen gossiping with the other servants, when she saw me she leapt up from her stool before the fire.

'Oh, my pardon, Lady, I thought you to be sleeping still. I was fetching your breakfast and got talking,' she said handing me a cup of spiced mead,

'Careful now 'tis very hot.'

'I thank you, Anwen,' I said, sipping the hot, sweet liquid, 'Mmm, that is most welcome.'

Drawing closer to the hearth, I held out my hands to the flames. A young servant girl dandled a baby on her knee.

'Tis a dank and dark day. I for one won't be sorry to see the end of winter. I can barely recall what the summertime feels like.' Leaning forward I poked the babe experimentally in the tummy and pulled a face at her; she grabbed for my hand and gurgled up at me, a bubble of milk at the corner of her mouth.

'Aw, dear lil' one,' gushed Anwen at my side, 'Maybe you'll have your own young ones soon, Lady.'

'Mmm, maybe,' I replied and, wondering if a babe would result from the indignities of last night, I dipped my face into my cup to hide my blushes.

'And a grand day that will be too.' chimed in Envys the cook, chopping a large onion and tossing it into a pot, 'tis long since we had any little princes running around our feet. Why young Rhodri'd be the last I do believe.'

'Rhodri was a child here? Where are his parents now then, are they still in service here?'

'Why L-Lady.' stammered Envys in confusion, 'He… he is the Lord Grufydd's son, did no one think to tell ye so? He was the last child born to my Lord's first wife, she died in childbed giving life to him. 'tis a miracle the poor wee bach survived at all for they rarely do without their mam… rarely do.'

She shook her head sorrowfully at the plight of all motherless babes until, astounded, I blurted out.

'Rhodri … is Gruffydd's son?' I could scarce believe what I was hearing. 'You mean the Rhodri that was my escort here from the coast?'
The two men were nothing alike, Gruffydd was so rough-edged and worn and cross and, Rhodri so kind.
'Are you sure?'

I looked from Tangwystl to Envys, half suspecting that they played some jest.

'Course I'm sure, Lady, didn't I help raise him when he was left motherless… and his brothers too?'

'Brothers?' I repeated dumbly, 'He has brothers? How many brothers?'

'Two, Lady; the Lords Owain and Meurig, they that rode in with your husband last evening. Did you not know about them?'
Plumping down on a stool I looked up at them all.

'No, I did not. It seems I know nothing at all about my husband or his family. Please enlighten me.'

I pulled up a stool and indicated that she should sit beside me and she lay down her knife and wiped her hands on her apron before joining me at the hearth. Her bottom overflowed the tiny seat and she folded her arms beneath her ample bosom before embarking upon her story.

'Well, Lady, 'tis a long tale to be told and I shall try to tell it well for you. Jiw Jiw. Fancy you not knowin' you'd inherited a full-grown family. Now then, let me think. Years ago, oh I know not how many, my Lord Gruffydd rode with his army to war against Hywel ap Edwin of Deheubarth. Well, one day he burned the stronghold at Pencadair to the ground, slaying the villagers and any they found alive there. Hywel managed to escape with a few of his followers but his wife was taken hostage and they do say that when she was brought before Gruffydd, instead of slaying her, he fell instantly in love with her instead and took her for his own. Bronwen the Fair they called her, begging your pardon Lady, if it should offend you but she is long dead now and no threat to you at all. This all happened when Lord Gruffydd was younger and…different. Ah, he was a pleasant man then, fond of the lyre and the harp; he often sang at gatherings in the hall. Oh, he'd the voice of a god, Lady.'

The stories were growing more unbelievable as they went on.

'Sang? The Lord Gruffydd sang? I do not believe it. What more surprises have you for me this morning.'

'Oh, tis all true Lady, he has not always been as he is now. In his youth he was much like young Rhodri, genial and kind … and handsome too; 'tis the harshness of life and its disappointments that have made him seem cruel. Why I remember, in his lady's time, the hall full of music and gaiety, 'twas a happy *llys* then when the children were small … until Rhodri's birthing that is. Everything changed then.'

'I see,' I murmured, trying to picture Gruffydd in the manner Envys described him. I failed for I had never seen him so much as smile pleasantly, let alone sing and the word 'pleasant' just did not fit the Gruffydd I knew.

'Twas a sad day, the day she died. The morning had dawned with sunshine and blue skies so, after breaking his fast, my Lord Gruffydd announced he was going to take advantage of the weather and go off for a days hunting. Soon after he rode away my Lady's pains began and, by the time my Lord returned at nightfall, his Lady lay dead and her newborn child despaired of.'

I passed a hand across my forehead, at once able to understand Gruffydd's misery the better. 'We feared he'd run mad at first, Lady. He rode out from the *llys* at once and nobody saw him for days and days and, when he did return, he was like a wild man. He wouldn't eat, wouldn't sleep, just drank jug after jug of mead and spoke not a civil word.'

'And has spoken scarce few since I'll be bound.' spat Anwen, who had tended my bruises and formed an ill opinion of my lord. 'All these tragedies were long ago and, King of all *Cymru* or not, 'tis no excuse to treat my Lady as he does.'

Fidgeting in my chair I frowned,

'Hush, Anwen. I thank you for telling me Envys. I feel better for knowing of his sorry past and, although I know him not and cannot begin to replace his first wife, perhaps it will cheer him if more children do come, for all men want as many children as they can get, do they not?'

The women drifted back to their chores leaving me to stare into the flames wondering about the long dead woman who had stolen Gruffydd's heart. Looking down at my own dumpy figure I imagined her to be tall, elegant and fair, the complete opposite to myself. I did not love my husband and could not imagine ever doing so but he was the only one I had and my mother had made sure that I was well schooled as to my duties as a wife. My primary role was to provide sons for my Lord. Childbirth was a risky business and the begetting of children unpleasant in the extreme but it was a task that I was, nonetheless, determined to fulfill.

More than once during the next few years I was forced to remind myself of that vow, for Gruffydd continued to prove an uncompromisingly harsh partner. As my grasp of the Welsh language improved so I began to settle in better. Refusing to resort to my native Saxon I persevered and, with Anwen always there to prompt me or supply a new word, I soon found myself beginning to join in fully with the gossipy afternoons when Gruffydd was away.

For the majority of the time he was away campaigning against the Saxon, Earl Harold of Wessex and, during his absence, I was able to relax into my new life, secure in the certainty of an undisturbed night's sleep. I had few household duties to perform for Llyward and Tangwystl ran Rhuddlan perfectly so all I had to do was endorse any decisions or changes that they proposed. Most of our grain, and that of north Cymry, was shipped in from Anglesey and the land about the stronghold was tilled for oats and turnips. Inside the enclosure we farmed pigs, sheep and poultry. Although the usual effects of illness and cold took its toll it was, by and large, a happy settlement, well run, affluent and secure. Should outsiders threaten us those living or working outside piled into the safety of the *llys*; outside dangers were scarce however and during my time there we saw no trouble and war kept away from Rhuddlan ...until the end.

While their Lord was away the children of the llys came out of hiding and ran tumbling in the rushes that were strewn upon the great hall floor. I liked to see them scampering about and gathered the elder siblings about me to teach me the most popular welsh songs and poetry. In the long winter evenings when the meal was over we gathered about the fire and listened to stories. Sometimes the marvellous tales of Arthur, or the *Dream of Rhonabwy,* or sometimes the tales of the old princes and the history of the land of which I was now princess. Rhodri's white face gleamed in the torchlight as he told of a fearful battle that had taken place here in Rhuddlan, hundreds of years ago, between the Welsh under Caradoc, king of north *Cymru* and the Saxons under Offa, King of Mercia. Rhodri leaned close, relating in hushed tones the sorry tale of a battle lost.

'After a drawn-out battle our armies were defeated with dreadful slaughter and Caradoc and many chieftains were slain. Such of our people as escaped the Saxon swords perished in the marshes from the influx of the tide and those who were taken prisoner were massacred, without any regard to their age or sex.'

He picked up his harp and began to stroke his fingers over the strings. The sound shimmered around the hall and we all leaned our cheeks upon our hands and settled down to listen to his stirring song.

Whilst Mother Wales, as she tears her wild tresses,
Weeps o'er the urns of her mightiest sons.
Beauty's rose dies at Caradoc's disaster,
Terror and panic his battlements climb;
Whilst his arch-minstrel, lamenting his master,
Makes Morva Rhuddlan our dirge for all time.

Saxon though I was, I empathised with the moist eyed company as they heard again the tragedy of Caradoc and his people, unleavened by time. The ties of kin are strong in *Cymru,* every door is open to a countryman in need and everyone seems related to each other either by blood or marriage. Hardship was a trouble shared and every household held a *croeso* for those facing misfortune and in all my time in Wales I never saw a single beggar.

The fire had sunk low in the hearth and a servant struggled in with logs and tossed them on to replenish the flames, sparks leaping into the air. Tangwystl signalled to a girl to refill the cups and I took a long draught of mead, leaning back in my chair.

'Ah,' I said 'how rich we are to live in a land where the brotherhood is strong.'

'Tis not always so, Lady,' said Llyward, 'why even in your good Lord's youth there was strife. When Lord Gruffydd reached manhood he suddenly decided to leave his father's house. From the innermost reaches of *Cymru*'s heartland he began to attack and harass all those who ruled about him. He did not stop until he had slaughtered all who stood before him. Once in a position of real power, he attacked, like a marauding bear, the neighbouring princedoms until all of *Cymru* was beneath his rule. Your Lord is the first to unite all of Wales and, since overthrowing the kings of Deheubarth, Gwent and Morgannwg, he had every right to call himself a king.'

I wondered at that; for all Gruffydd's power he was nevertheless known only as Prince. It slowly became clear that, sickened by the division of his country into small, undefendable cantrefs, he had vowed to unite the land as one nation, the better to fight the Saxons. For all that, his people did not love him; they were loyal because he was strong. His uncompromising ambition made him impossible to love and Gruffydd was a man with no real friends. In my time with him I learned that even his sons, Owain and

Meurig, feared rather than loved him and Rhodri, I am certain, felt nothing at all.

Shortly after discovering Rhodri's true status I had teased him about it. 'Rhodri.' I called with a giggle when I saw him enter the hall, 'Come and kiss your mother.'

In truth, my adolescent fancy meant I was only glad to see him and sought to share his company but, to my dismay, he walked stiffly toward me, bowing coldly over my hand and leaving an empty kiss on my wrist.

'You are not my mother, Lady,' he said, so that none but me should hear, 'and I would thank you not to pretend to be such.'

'Rhodri.' I exclaimed, 'I did but jest; of course I am not your mother nor should I want to be. I just thought it amusing that my stepson should be just a few years my senior. I imagined you would share the joke with me.'

His eyes were shuttered.

'There are some things, my queen, that I cannot jest about and my lady mother is one of them.'

'Oh, do forgive me, Rhodri.' I cried, close to tears, 'I did not think. I am ignorant and have been ill-prepared for this marriage. It came as no little surprise to learn I had step-sons. Why did someone not sit down and tell me of the family I was to marry into?'

Rhodri warmed slightly, shrugging his shoulders and shaking his head.

'I don't know, 'tis just Gruffydd's way. He expects everyone to do just as he says whether they like it or not. He probably thought it immaterial that you be told anything. Anyway, I wish you not to think of me as your stepson, nor even as Gruffydd's son. He has never openly shown me any acknowledgement. I'm more like his groom than a son and that's the way I'd rather it stayed.'

1059

Gruffydd's activities on the Welsh-Saxon border ensured that I remained largely undisturbed by his presence. He came and went, sometimes with minor injuries, sometimes in a bluff good humour and sometimes as sour as lemons. While he was in residence I was forced to suffer his attentions in the bedchamber but, after a while, I learned to disregard them and think of something more pleasant until it was over. If sometimes those thoughts were of my stepson Rhodri, well, I have no excuse but my youth and loving disposition. I did not see my growing affection for Rhodri as a sin and certainly saw no need to confess it to Father Daffydd when I took confession in his small wooden church. Rhodri was young and entertaining and my husband old and harsh and, moreover, I was more often in Rhodri's company and so grew to know him well. It was no fault of mine that I must bed with an old man and there was nothing in the rulebook to suggest that I should enjoy it. Perhaps it was my own lack of sexual fulfilment that delayed matters or perhaps it was my tender years, but it was not until late in 1058 that my womb first quickened with Gruffydd's child.

I kept the news to myself, swearing Anwen to secrecy until we were sure, and then, one night before he had time to get his leg across me, I told him he could expect a son in the spring. He greeted my announcement with a grunt and immediately quit the chamber and thereafter avoided my bed altogether; a consequence that made me regret not telling him sooner.

For six months I was able to enjoy the luxury of having the bed to myself. All day, if I wished, I could lie dreaming a young girl's dreams and think of my coming child and the difference he would bring to my life. That he would be a son I had no doubt and I planned to call him Leofric, after the grandfather I had so loved. He would be tall and fair, with eyes like the sky. I pictured him as a newborn when, coated still with womb grease, I would first hold him in my arms. I imagined him as a small boy, flaxen haired and comical, and later, a man grown, riding to war in leather and steel. I spent my days lost in dreams until the morning the birth pangs began and reality reared its head.

I woke early and lay staring unseeing into the absolute darkness wondering what it was that had disturbed me. An unspecific sense of unease hovered somewhere above the bed but I could determine nothing alarming in the chamber; straining my ears in the dark all I could hear were the usual night sounds of the *llys*. A dog barked and a curt voice cut across the night calling for silence and a far off door slammed. Then the frigid black silence resumed and my sense of disquiet grew stronger. At length I swung my legs over the side of the bed and rinsed my mouth with the mead that stood each night upon the nightstand. As I shifted to a more comfortable position I felt a gentle pop in some internal region and my inner thighs were swamped with a warm, sweet smelling fluid. Looking down in surprise I realised that my child had decided to put in an appearance. The delivery was not expected for another month and the birthing chamber not fully prepared.

I called for Anwen and then lay back, smiling to myself, eager to greet my new son but also afraid. As if to cement my fear, a vigorous tightening of my stomach chased my smiles away. The tightening grew stronger until at last it became a real pain located at the base of my spine. I whimpered and stirred my lower limbs trying to shift the discomfort and, when the feeling abated, rose and took a taper to ignite the tallow candles that stood close to the bed. Where were the women? My mouth was dry and I took more mead from the cup swilling it around my mouth before swallowing. I could hear Anwen hollering for Tangwystl and the scurrying feet of the slaves as they hastened at her command.

In a short while the fire had been stirred back to life and the torches lit. They hurried about, locating linen and setting the midwife's tools ready upon a low table; potions, salves and a birthing bowl and swaddling bands for the infant. I perched on the edge of the bed trying to ignore the increasing intensity of the birth pangs. To distract my mind from the immediacy of what was going to happen to me I watched the huge shadows cast by the flare of the torches of my attendants, ducking and diving on the chamber walls.

The fat midwife, the same who had attended the birthings of Bronwen the Fair, clucked into the room like an old hen and began to lift my nightgown. 'That's it, bach, lie back and let me feel your belly, I can tell then if all be well with the babe and judge how long we have to wait. There's lovely. Well done, bach.'

She pursed her moustached lips as her hands, which were dry and cold, probed gently at my distended stomach. Then she stood up and, to my surprise, squeezed each of my nipples and grunted in satisfaction when a bead of watery milk dripped onto the sheet. Pulling my shift demurely over my knees again she said,

'Tis early days yet, *Cariad*, you must rest and keep calm. I'll keep close by so you give me a call if you need to.'

Anwen took her place by the bed and gripped my hand, smiling encouragement. 'Oh, Anwen,' I murmured in disbelief, 'she says it will be ages yet but I am in sore pain already, do you think she may be mistaken and the birth is imminent?'

'Old Lois knows her business, remember she's been birthing the *llys* for twenty years or more. She told me she is preparing a brew of mother's milk, motherwort, belladonna and malmsey to ease you in the later stages. Come, do not fret, Lady, you are strong and will easily bear the pain.'

I was not so sure and, as the band tightened about my loins again, I gasped and gripped the wooden post of the bed, gritting my teeth and puffing hard. The women in the chamber, seemingly unmoved by my plight, sat diligently spinning, maintaining a light-hearted conversation to help the time pass. The braziers were kept well fuelled and the draughty windows muffled until the heat in the chamber grew to stifling proportions. I thought I would suffocate but Lois insisted that the night air was fatal for both mother and child and that they must be kept warm at all costs.

When the pain grew too great I was dosed with Lois' potion and some property within the concoction, either the herbs or the strong spirits, made me feel relaxed and drowsy and really rather silly. I floated off into a strange sleep in which my dreams were haunted by the past. My mother, father, Morcar and Edwin drifted in and out of my consciousness and, at other times it seemed Gruffydd were there and he was angry, shouting at me about something. I cried out more than once against him until Lois soothed my fears with more numbing drink. I sweated and twisted on the bed, detached from my companions and unreachable through a haze, isolated and imprisoned by fear and pain.

When I felt I could bear no more Lois heaved herself from her stool by the fire and urged me onto my knees. My body felt leaden and solid, an immovable object ungoverned by my brain but, with the help of Anwen and Tangwystl, I heaved myself onto all fours and hung above the bed panting like a stricken cow, my braided hair dangling from my ears. I felt Lois behind me and my nightgown was pulled up and my nether regions exposed to allow her to examine the child's progress,

'Not long now, bach,' the old woman encouraged, patting my bottom, 'when the next pain hits you can push him out.'

It was more comfortable to be on all fours and, with the weight of the child removed from my spine, I managed to take a quick look about the chamber. The sewing women in attendance seemed smug in their pain free serenity and Anwen and Tangwystl cruelly matter-of-fact in the face of my suffering.

After a while I became aware of another pain, the sensations expanded in waves and I tried to breathe with them. I cried for my mother until the agony encompassed my very being while my body laboured to expel the child. I strained, hanging onto the twisted length of cloth that Lois had tied to the bedstead. With face distorted and teeth gritted, I pushed to rid myself of the interloper. Then the pain receded suddenly and I collapsed face down onto the mattress. Anwen was at my side bringing more milk and mead but, before I could drink, the assault began again and I tossed the vessel away making a dark stain upon the linen.

I reared up, my knees parted and my head back, shrieking, teeth bared and twisting like a mad woman. While my mind begged respite from the labour my body seemed to take control and forced me onward in the struggle for life until again I was briefly released from the vice like grip.

Barely noticing the cool touch of the cloth with which Anwen bathed my forehead I rested, panting for breath, awaiting the next attack. Now though I became aware of a new sensation through the pain; something hard was pressing upon my person as though I needed the privy. Reaching a hand down I felt my child's head, hot, sticky and pulsing with life between my legs and I was instantly refuelled with energy. When next the irresistible desire to push came I put my chin to my chest, gritted my teeth and screamed aloud with fearsome determination, then twisting myself around, I watched my son, followed by a stream of bloody liquid, flop onto the mattress behind me.

In truth, now that it is over, I do not care to think to much about the birth, I have blocked it out of my mind for it was painful and I toiled long and hard to bring him forth. Gruffydd, who was away for my lying in, arrived a day or so later and when I heard, from my chamber, the sounds of his return, I sat up eagerly and called Anwen to me.

'Fetch me my comb, Anwen, I would look my best when I present my husband with his son.' She combed the tangles from my hair and I smoothed my shift before sitting upright on my pillow with my son in my arms. It was sometime before I heard the clump of Gruffydd's footsteps and the chamber door flew open. When my husband finally stumbled into the chamber my carefully constructed smile faded and I sank back deflated on my pillows.

He was drunk, staggering and ugly, drunker than I had ever seen him and his condition, so early in the day, appalled me. Without so much as a glance in my direction he slumped onto the edge of my bed and sat with his head bowed and shoulders sagging. I realised then that it was not drink alone that palsied his hands and reddened his eyes. Never in my life had I seen a man so defeated.

'What has happened?' I cried and, when I received no reply, I grew fearful and cried again. 'Gruffydd, tell me, my Lord, what has happened?'
The silence stretched on until I reached out to touch his shoulder, 'Gruffydd?' I said again more gently, 'Please tell me what ails you?'

He raised his head and looked at me with a face haggard and full of despair. He tried to speak but could not seem to find his voice.

He cleared his throat before croaking, 'Tis my son, Owain.' He stopped and ran a gnarled hand through his hair, swallowing deeply before continuing:

'A day or two ago, we were skirmishing close to Brecknoc, nothing more than that, just a skirmish, 'twas no more'n we've done a hundred times. We thought we'd seen them off. We'd chased a small band of Saxons for five mile or so but, on our return, as we laughed together at the ignominy of their flight, an arrow was let loose from the hills and struck Owain in the chest. He dropped like a stone and didn't live more'n a few moments after I got to him; right in his heart the arrow had lodged. He held onto my hand, told me he was sorry and then he died, just like that... sudden, no time for goodbye.'

It was the first time we had spoken to me intimately, as an equal. Gripping my hand, his jaw set, he silently asked for comfort but, young as I was, I did not know the words to console him. Appalled at his naked misery I was not equipped to help him and the opportunity to breach the gulf, that lay wide between us, passed.

Looking down at my sleeping son, I realised with a pang that even he, the fruit of our loveless union, could do nothing to ease Gruffydd's loss of a son born by Bronwen the Fair. I awkwardly stroked his hand, noting the contrast of his huge calloused fingers against my smooth skin. Our fingers remained entwined for a brief few moments before he snatched his hand away, stood up and abruptly quit the chamber; our chance of conciliation gone. He had not so much as glanced at our child.

'What about naming him Llewelyn after Gruffydd's father?' I asked the company that gathered at the hearth, 'That should not displease him should it?'

'I thought you'd decided on Leofric after your own grandfather?' Rhodri exclaimed playfully, 'Can't you make up your mind to anything?'

'Gruffydd wouldn't hear of it,' I complained, 'He said I could choose any damn name I cared to just so long as it wasn't that of a damned, murdering Saxon.'

Laughter rippled in the company in appreciation of my mimicry and Rhodri leant forward and offered the babe his finger who took it in his firm grip.

'Hmph, doesn't surprise me. I don't think he will approve of Llewelyn though. Didn't he fall out with his father? I don't know if they were ever reconciled or not so it might be best to stick with something neutral.'

'Well yes, there was a family quarrel but he seems to attract foes, twill certainly narrow our options if we're to select a name from his tally list of friends.' Another babble of laughter trickled about the hall.

'What about ...Rhodri, after his step-brother?' suggested Anwen slyly. She had guessed my secret long ago but I knew she would never betray it for all her teasing.

'No.' said Rhodri, 'Not that, Gruffydd wouldn't like that and don't suggest Owain or you will have us all hung. My brother seems to have assumed the attributes of a saint since his death. I think you should choose something innocuous like Maredudd or Idwal. We don't have any enemies with those names, or any friends either so I see no reason why he should object.'

'Oh, I like Idwal, Rhodri; it is lovely. Yes,' I said, looking down at my sleeping son. 'That is it. Idwal ap Gruffydd you shall be, my lover.'

The child thrived and grew apace while I continued, happily undisturbed by Gruffydd's advances. The day of my churching came and went and, when Idwal was just one month old, at Gruffydd's insistence a wet nurse was found and the first ties between mother and son were severed.

Anwen found a girl from the village whose own child had perished and she was glad to nurse Idwal, if only to relieve her own aching body. Her name was Heulwen, which in the Welsh means 'Sunshine' and, never in all my life, have I known anyone with a less sunny disposition. I did my best to befriend her and bring her out of her sadness but, the loss of her child had merely enhanced her bleak nature, and she shuffled, hunch-shouldered about her duties. I was heart-broken at having to stop nursing Idwal; it was hard to lose the close bond that was just beginning to form and see his hungry tears comforted by another woman.

As she nursed him I watched and envied her sore dugs and milk-stained bodice but, dutifully, I said nothing in protest; instead I tried to set my mind to other concerns.

Owain's death hit Gruffydd hard but, whether grief had tempered his aggression or there was another reason outside the scope of my knowledge, an uneasy peace was reached with the Saxons at this time. The truce with Earl Harold, at King Edward's approval, altered many things. My grandfather, Leofric, had died and my father was reconciled with King Edward and reinstated in Mercia. Gruffydd was content to have regained the disputed lands along the border with England. The need for war was momentarily appeased which meant that Gruffydd was home much more.

Instead of spending his days making war, he spent them hunting or administering his duties as king. He did not seem to dwell outwardly upon the loss of Owain but his authoritative presence at the *llys* dampened the congenial atmosphere that prevailed when he was from home. His close proximity meant that he spent many more nights in my bed and, much to my discomfiture, even the odd rainy afternoon.

As a consequence Idwal was just three months old when I suspected that I was with child again. This time I told Gruffydd the news straight away and, as I had hoped, he immediately ceased to visit my chamber, leaving me again in blissful solitude.

It was May, our large retinue was relaxed and happy as we traversed ancient pathways where blossom frothed thick in the hedgerows and birds and small mammals busied themselves with their young. We were on our way to a wedding, the journey was a lengthy one but Gruffydd was determined not to miss the nuptials of his favoured man.

The first place of note that we came to was Chester; a town set precariously upon the border between Saxon England and *Cymru*. Gryffydd's domain terminated at its wooden gate and the fortified settlement was ever vulnerable to spies and traitors from both sides of the divide. They exported salt, cloth and slaves and imported pelts, cattle and fish. It formed part of my father's Mercian holdings and we planned to spend a few days enjoying the rare pleasures Chester had to offer. We had no towns in *Cymru* and my women and I had spent weeks planning our shopping.

The streets teemed with life; shopkeepers, beggars, prostitutes and urchins jostled together, drovers cut through the throng driving sheep to market and rich merchants on horseback cursed at the crowd, slashing about them with their whips. The market place was packed with folk so a page walked ahead clearing a path for us. I found a stall selling fine disc brooches and I purchased one, set with an amber centre as a wedding gift for Alys. Tangwystl bought a fistful of coloured braid and Anwen some fine woven cloth to make a tunic for Idwal.

Our spending frenzy sated, we lodged at the abbey overnight and, in the morning, journeyed on. We planned to stop at smaller holdings along the way, for it was a long journey to the splendid *llys* at Dinefwr in Gruffydd's domain of Dehuebarth. Of course, the wedding feast of Gruffydd's henchman was not the only reason for our journey. Gruffydd always had another agenda and it seemed had scores to settle with dissenters in the south where an old feud had flared up again.

'There is no rest for Princes.' he declared, 'no holi days for me and, while my lowliest subjects are free to make merry on feast days, I must toil away to ensure their continued security. Why. I am more slave than Prince and there is always some upstart wanting to usurp my position.'

'And he should know since he himself has usurped every other bugger's seat,' mumbled Anwen darkly at my side and I shushed her, fearful that our Lord would overhear.

Scouts were posted both ahead and behind and several to the right and left of our cavalcade. Gruffydd rode at the front leaving me with Anwen, Tangwystl and Heulwen who, with her charge strapped to her front, clung to her pony's saddlepad in some discomfort, unused to travelling on horseback. Rhodri alternated between accompanying us and checking with the rear guard of the party. Ahead, I could see Gruffydd waving his arms around expansively as he talked with his half-brothers, Bleddyn and Rhiwallon. Meurig rode behind, seeming strangely isolated without his brother, Owain, beside him. I smiled at him and tried to engage him in conversation but his answers were taciturn and I soon left him to his own thoughts. It was a good journey, the weather remained fair and, with *Cymru* basking in the sunshine, everyone was in the best of spirits.

The *llys* at Dinefwr, to which we travelled, belonged to Gruffydd but the custodian, Rhys ap Rhys, was a good friend and staunch ally. His wedding to the daughter of a rich Saxon was the result of Gruffydd's alliance with my father. The bride was barely out of her teens and her name was Alys. Her family had lands in Mercia but I did not think I had ever met her. I wondered if she felt ill-used to be married to a Welshman for she had probably been raised, as I had, to distrust and loathe the race that dwelt beyond the dyke. Although I had no love for my husband I had learned to love his countryman as if they were my own. I felt like a Welsh woman now and hoped that Alys would come to feel the same.

The branches of the trees hung so low on each side of the path that they almost touched my cap as we passed beneath them. The heads of the ponies dipped and nodded as they strained to carry us up the last steep track that led to the *llys*. Twisting a way round the side of the hill, the path eventually took us to the summit and we clattered through a wooden gateway into the shelter of the palace. Rhodri helped me to dismount and I stood for a moment, stretching my back as I surveyed the busy scene. My legs were stiff and my buttocks numb from the journey so I was glad of the distance we had to walk to the great hall. The sound of hammering from the blacksmith's shop paused as we passed by and the smith touched his forelock in greeting. A young slave smiled shyly as she scurried past with a basket of fresh baked bread, hens scuttling from her path. There were people everywhere, grooms rushing to take the horses and children grubbing in the dirt while their mothers stood, hands on hips, to watch the new arrivals. Since our wedding I had been kept close in Rhuddlan and these people of *Cymru* were eager to appraise Gruffydd's queen.

'Rhys.' Gruffydd bellowed, when he caught sight of our host, striding out to greet us.

'Well met, fellow.' Rhys replied, slapping Gruffydd's shoulder before turning his attention to me.

'And this is your lady wife? Delighted, Lady, to meet you,' he said, his voice booming about the echoing hall. He was a big fellow with a big laugh to suit and in his presence I felt my spirits lift. I warmed to him, certain he was a good man. After a similar elated greeting with Meurig, Bleddyn and Rhiwallon, the men walked off together leaving Anwen to help me remove my cloak.

A servant bustled up bringing us refreshment and I sipped a cup of mead as I looked about me at the splendid hall. Tangwystl, having made enquiries as to our lodging, joined me at the hearth;

'They have put you in the best room, lady, far from the sounds of revelry should you wish to retire early of an evening. The Lady Alys, it seems, is lodged close by and seeks an audience before her nuptials tomorrow.'

'Oh, how lovely. Yes I am most eager to make her acquaintance. Come,' I said, putting down my cup, 'let us go to her at once. '

Alys leapt from her stool and stood uncertainly as we were shown into her chamber. She was about fifteen, her face was pale and strained and I at once empathised with her prenuptial fears. 'Lady Eadgyth,' she said, sweeping out her gown into a deep curtsey

'No, no, Alys' I said, the Saxon words feeling strange upon my tongue. 'You do not need to curtsey to me, I hope we shall be friends.'

'Oh, Lady.' she cried, 'how refreshing it is to hear a civilised Saxon tongue again. All around me all I hear is the heathen Welsh.'

I sensed, rather than saw, Tangwystl's displeasure at her words and sought to soothe the air.

'I know how you feel, and it was so with me at first but, believe me, you will soon learn to understand and then to speak it. Once you have got the best of it you will find 'tis a beautiful language.'

'It doesn't sounds like it to me, Lady.'

Noting Alys' red-rimmed eyes and trembling lower lip and recalling my own despair at being forced to marry Gruffydd, I sat down on the settle and pulled her beside me.

'What do you make of Lord Rhys? He seems very jovial.' I asked but Alys pulled away in alarm.

'He is a monster lady, he has no Saxon at all and when he speaks, his tongue is foreign and his eyes don't look honestly into mine but linger … here.'

She indicated her generous bosom and the disgust on her prim little face suggested that, unless she quickly learned some harsh lessons, the union would not be a happy one.

'It is hard at first, Alys, I don't deny it, but I would recommend that your try to accept things as they are. Truly, once your children come, so will happiness follow. I too found it difficult at first to see any joy in my union with Gruffydd but I am happy now I have Idwal and … between you and me, there is another child on the way already. Look how lovable my son is,' I said, beckoning Heulwen to bring the babe forth. Alys peered at the flushed sleeping face of my child and her expression softened.

'You are fortunate indeed to have found contentment but I fear the intimacy, Lady, in fact I fear even the shortest conversation with Lord Rhys. He is a stranger to me. How can I lay with a stranger? In truth, I had expected to be allowed to wed another, the son of my father's neighbour and a man I have known since childhood but, suddenly, the plans were altered and my wishes as nothing. I was sent here. Since my lady mother died, my father is not the caring parent he was.'

'Fathers do change once we reach a woman's state,' I agreed, remembering my heartbreak the day my father had left me on the Welsh shore, 'but it is up to us to make the best of things. Look at his wonderful *llys* you will have the running of, why 'tis a girl's dream. You will want for nothing. There will be fine gowns and jewels and the best food to eat. I predict a long and happy, fertile union Alys … truly I do.'

Later, as I lay sleepless in the guest chamber, realising that the girl was probably weeping into her pillow, I prayed that my words would prove true.

The day of the wedding arrived and the hall was wreathed with garlands of flowers and herbs were strewn upon the floor to sweeten the rushes. The company, clad in its finery, stood and cheered when Gruffydd and I entered the hall. We bowed our heads to them graciously, Gruffydd, for once, looking almost handsome in his fur-trimmed tunic. About his neck a thick torque gleamed in the firelight and he had trimmed his beard and washed his hair. He looked every bit the king that night and, knowing I looked every bit a queen, I sought his approval. A curt nod was all I received when he saw me in my new sage and yellow gown with a delicate circlet of gold balanced upon my shining dark hair. Rhodri, however, made up for his father's lack. His eyes lit up and he skimmed across the room to take my hand and make his bow. The kiss that he left upon my wrist sent a dart of delicious agony through my body.

'Lady,' he murmured, 'you are beautiful.'

He was right, I was beautiful that night; in the fourth month of pregnancy I was vibrant with good health and for once it did not matter that I was plump. My eyes shone and my skin glowed with expectant happiness. I loved the company and, at that moment, I loved my life.

The actual wedding ceremony had taken place earlier in the afternoon at the small wooden church that stood at the base of the hill and now, the piety over with, the good people of the *llys* prepared to celebrate extravagantly. We sat expectantly while an army of servants paraded into the hall to place laden platters and pitchers of mead on the tables and the bards struck up a lively tune. Alys sat beside her husband, her huge eyes contrasting sharply with her stark white face; I sent her a comforting smile and she returned it waveringly. I prayed to God that Rhys would be gentler with her than Gruffydd had been with me on our wedding night. He didn't seem a cruel man, in fact his warmth was a little overwhelming, but you could never tell the secrets that a man reserved for the privacy of his bedchamber.

Meanwhile the company was merry. Bards played, the wine flowed and the maidens danced. Gruffydd and Rhys beside me, grew drunk, slopping wine on their finery and, as the night progressed, their banter grew more and more obscene. They roared with laughter, almost rolling together beneath the table and my hopes for a gentle deflowering for Alys faded.

Meurig, alone at the end of the table, watched the proceedings, slowly imbibing cup after cup of mead. I saw him watching his uncle, Bleddyn, making not inconsiderable progress with a pair of serving wenches but he made no effort to join them. As the evening wore on I ate much too much and my under garments began to feel uncomfortable. Gruffydd and Rhys had disappeared from the table. I could see Rhys laughing in a corner with Rhiwallon and some young retainers but my glance shifted to where Rhodri was trying to master the steps of a dance. His comical attempts to keep rhythm made me splutter with laughter, which, in turn, made me realise I was overfull and needed the privy. Placing a hand beneath my tunic I caressed the small bulge of my stomach, I felt content and confident of the future. Swilling the dregs of my mead cup around my mouth, I looked about for Anwen to accompany me. The men, when they needed to relieve themselves, were expected to go outside to the midden but, set discreetly in one corner of the hall, were several screens and behind each screen was a pot for the comfort of the ladies. Full of wine and cheer and still laughing, I swept behind a screen and immediately stopped dead, shocked rigid at what I saw there. My laughter turned bitter in my mouth.

My Lord husband, with his finest breeches crumpled about his royal knees, was servicing a comely servant maid. Her skirts over her head, she was bent forward with her rear end thrusting out, while Gruffydd humped her from the rear.

So engrossed were they in their activity that they did not so much as notice my presence and I spun quickly on my heel, staggering from the sight and lurching back into the main hall. The music and laughter seemed an assault upon my ears now and, almost retching as I gasped for breath, I clutched at my stomach while tiny bright lights danced in the periphery of my vision. Unable to shake the sight from my eyes, I grabbed at Anwen, who had witnessed the scene also; she was gabbling and gasping at my side, clearly as disconcerted as I. Certain that I would faint, I clutched tighter at her arm, mortified to feel vomit rising in the back of my throat.

'Lady, come with me,' said an urgent voice at my elbow and Rhodri was there, leading me dazedly across the hall in the direction of my sleeping bower.

He ushered me gently to my chamber, making crooning sounds in his throat to sooth me as if I were a child. There, he helped me to lie upon the bed and began to remove my slippers; then, sitting beside me, he chaffed my fingers, looking, questioningly, into my eyes. 'Go and make my Lady's excuses,' he said to Anwen and, as she scuttled from the room, he gripped my hands trying to prevent me from sitting up. 'Lie still, Lady,' he said, 'and tell me what happened.'

I struggled to sit up and, for a while, so great was my shock that I just sputtered and stuttered but I eventually managed to blurt it out.

'Your wretched father, Rhodri.' I raged, anger replacing the nausea at what I had seen.

'I caught him humping that maid, the one with the black hair …the one with the enormous dugs, you must have seen her.'

'No, Lady, I don't believe I have,' he replied calmly, 'but do go on. He was humping her … where? In the ladies privy?'

'Yes, Rhodri, the king, your father, was humping a slut in the privy.'

Rhodri's face was inscrutable. I was quivering with anger now and he relinquished my hand and rose from the bed, pouring me a drink from the pitcher on the table.

'Try to calm yourself, Eadgyth …' he said, using my Christian name for the first time, then, after a pause, he added, ' I had not supposed you would care.'

I spluttered into the cup.

'Care? Of course I care. Oh, not that he was doing it, I suppose, but that he was doing it there. And with her. Why anyone could have seen them. Has he no shame? And why with a woman like that when he has the pick of *Cymru*? God's grief but men are disgusting.'

He took my cup.

'Not all men, Lady,' he replied and I was suddenly very grateful for his support.

The humour of the situation struck me as the ridiculous scene I had witnessed became vivid in my mind again. I let out a snort of laughter. It came from nowhere, surging up from my belly and erupting from my mouth. It was quickly followed by a stifled giggle.

'He looked like a rutting billy goat,' I looked up at my confidant, my lips twitching and tears springing to my eyes. I put my hand to my mouth and emitted a high-pitched peal of laughter that ignited a similar instinct in Rhodri. When Anwen re-entered the chamber two minutes later, Rhodri and I were sitting on my bed clutching each other while we howled with ungodly laughter.

Unfortunately the fourth month of pregnancy cannot last and soon my body began to bloat and digestion became a problem. I lightened the size and frequency of meals but still it persisted. The intention had been to stay a month at Dinefwr and then return to Twthill but continuing insurrection in Deheubarth meant that Gruffydd was forced to stay. Had I paid more attention at the time I should be able to relate in detail the problems that beset him but I was caught up with the excitement of my coming child and thought of little else. It was toward the end of summer that Gruffydd, realising that the last trimester of my pregnancy approached, agreed I should begin to journey back in small stages so that I could be safe at Rhuddlan when the child came.

Expectant women were advised against many things, the consumption of pork and ale and, of course, horseback riding. However it was decided that a slow journey with lengthy stops along route should do me little harm and it was late August when I made my farewells.'God be wi' ye, Alys,' I said, as we embraced, 'Remember to entreat your Lord to bring you to us in the spring and we can spend all of the next summer together.'

'I will, Eadgyth and do not fail to send me word as soon as that babe arrives.'

In many ways Alys had taken the place of my family and, for all I loved my Welsh companions, it was good to have a Saxon friend with whom I shared a similar background. When I looked back and saw Dinefwr dwarfed by distance I felt sad to be leaving my friend but glad to be riding away from the oppression of Gruffydd's company. I turned my thoughts toward home and the long journey ahead, calling to Rhodri to strike up a song.

At first things went smoothly; we rested at Hay and Dinas Bran and various smaller settlements before arriving in Chester three weeks after our departure from Dinefwr.

Anwen and I again took advantage of the shops, buying ribbons and laces and a pair of fine slippers for my swollen feet. As we set off on the last leg of our journey we remarked upon the curious mix of blue grey skies and pink wisps of cloud. Heulwen, who saw bad omens in most things, distrusted it and warned of evil portent but we laughed at her superstition, glad to be nearing the last leg of the journey and eager to be home.

The sun climbed higher and, as it did so, the cloud in the distance thickened, piling up like duckdown on the far off mountaintops. We stopped for refreshment on rising ground and, as we ate, watched the wading birds in the flooded valley below. Anwen fussed and cosseted me, asking if I were comfortable and, as the day had grown chill, ensuring I was warm enough. Rhodri tended the horses while I watched Idwal at Heulwen's breast and afterwards took him on my lap to relieve his wind while his nurse partook of some food herself. I blew raspberries on his fat red cheeks to make him giggle and then I removed his napkin so he could stretch his legs for a while in the fresh air. His limbs were stout and strong with rolls of fat at the top where they joined his torso; not content to stay still, he kept trying to escape, crawling bare arsed from the blanket. Heulwen, not at all pleased that he had become so mobile, constantly retrieved him and lay him on his back again.

When we set off again the first spots of rain had begun to fall, large, sparse drops but, by the time we had travelled a further five miles, it was raining in earnest. The ponies held their heads low to avoid the driving force of it as it beat its way beneath our clothes and stung any part of exposed skin it happened to fall upon.

I glanced behind to see Anwen with her head down and her cloak pulled about her ears and Heulwen with my babe clutched to her chest in much the same manner.

'We must stop and shelter, Lady,' Rhodri yelled at me, 'there is an old abandoned lodging not far ahead, it is rough but it will have to do, it will be better than nothing. I shall send a couple of men to clean up and start a fire for when you arrive.'

I nodded, too drenched to mind where we sheltered, and Rhodri spurred his mount to the rear of the small, straggling cavalcade. We made haste then, cantering along a track obscured by rain and dark and, when we arrived at the abandoned lodging, we found that a portion of our party had fallen behind. Rhodri, Anwen, Heulwen, a few retainers and I had somehow left Tangwystl, her maid and members of the *teulu* with the packhorses somewhere along the road.

Inside, the thatch was patchy and leaked in one corner. It was little better than a hovel but a small fire struggled for life in the centre of the room, promising some comfort. I squatted inelegantly with my hands stretched toward the meagre flame as smoke eddied around, making me cough.

'Not long now, Lady, and we'll be warm,' said Rhodri, spreading a dry blanket for me to sit on. ' Here, take off that wet cloak and wrap yourself in my blanket, it is dry.'

'I wonder where my baggage has got to and why the rest of the party were waylaid. I hope they have taken shelter and not come to grief.'

'I will send out a search as soon as 'tis light, Lady, do not fret, we will do well enough here. Have some rye bread and a cup of milk, t'will hold you 'til supper.'

'Ooh, supper,' I teased, 'what have we, Rhodri, roasted mutton and turnips?'

'Nay, Lady, we have some cheese and onions, a store of nuts and I think I saw berries and apples growing along the way, although I doubt the apples will be ripe.'

Anwen handed Idwal to me who proceeded to grab at my hair and face. Then she took my wet tunic, cloak and stockings and hung them on some sticks she had arranged by the fire.

'This reminds me of that awful lodging we had in Ireland, Anwen, do you remember how ill we all were and how desperately Mother wanted to go home? At least we are in better straits than we were that day.'

'I try not to think of that, Lady. Are you warm enough? Are you sure? Here let me tuck the blanket about you better.'

'God's grief, Anwen. I am pregnant, not invalid. I do well enough, sit and rest yourself, for heaven's sake. Rhodri, if we take some unripe apples and cook them they will make a warming nutritious food … if only we had honey.'

Anwen stood up, putting a hand to her back that was stiff from so long in the saddle.

'I have honey, Lady. I carry it always to wear on my face at night to smooth my complexion. It is in my saddle bag.'

'Anwen, you are a treasure. God bless your vanity. Now if I weren't too lazy to carry my own belongings I should never have lost them and we should have a host of warm clothes and tasty morsels to eat.'

With the men of the *teulu* seated a little apart from us, we told each other tales until the dark crept in from the corners of the hut and the fire shrunk low. Then, wrapped in coarse travelling blankets instead of fine furs, we slept fitfully until first light. Leaving Anwen to prepare breakfast and two men to guard us, Rhodri rode out to discover the fate of the rest of our party.

Heulwen tidied our things together while Anwen took the remnants of our makeshift meal outside to feed to the birds. I, crook backed from a night on the floor, strolled around in the watery sunshine thinking dismally of mounting my pony again for another day in the saddle. In truth I longed for a day abed although I would never admit it to the others.

My lower back was an agony of knotted muscle and my thighs were chaffed raw from the wet ride of the previous day. I thrust my arms upward and made a big circle in the air, stretching and easing my aching shoulders. I had mislaid my comb with my baggage and my hair was a mass of tangles. I called to Anwen as she returned from the privacy of the nearby woodland.

'Anwen, my hair feels awful. Would you see if you can comb it through with your fingers and form some sort of a braid of it? Oh, I will not be sorry to see home; think of the jugs of warm water and the roaring fires in my chamber and these garments can go straight on the midden, look at them. Mired to the knee and I have even managed to get a large rent in the skirt. Should anyone come across me now I'd not be taken for a princess of Wales.'

My hair somewhat tidied and my face washed on the corner of a blanket dipped in the brook, I sat on a fallen log and waited for Rhodri to return. At length he appeared, emerging from the woodland alone and worried.

'Rhodri?' I queried, ' is there no sign of them?

'No, Lady, I can only think they took a different path and will find their own way. I am reluctant to spend more time searching for them but thought to send the men back for a further look and to see if they can pick up their trail. I know this country and think we shall do well enough, the four of us.'

It is only in retrospect that this suggestion emerges as a singularly stupid idea. The armed men of the *teulu* were sent back to search for the others and we went on alone, confident in Rhodri's ability to protect and get us home safely. The dank day made little effort to brighten and we travelled on through light, misty rain for most of the morning. As before we stopped around noon for sustenance and then continued our journey. We were about half way from the settlement where we planned to pass the night and I anticipated an evening spent in the hospitality of one of our own.

Everything smelled of rain; wet grass, wet heather, wet alder, wet horse and I began to grow impatient with the weather.

'It's August for goodness sake.' I cried, 'surely we can expect to see sunshine for at least some part of the day.'

But, as if in answer to my protest, the rain grew heavier and a good deal wetter. Soaked through again, my hair dripping in rat's tails about my face, I cursed the day I had suggested we travel back to Rhuddlan. Had I stayed with Alys I should be warm and dry in her sumptuous palace not here, freezing like some bedraggled hedge drab.

The mountain track we traversed was steep and narrow so no conversation could be exchanged and my spirits grew grim as my body grew more tired. Ahead of me I could see Rhodri's straight back moving in time with his pony as it nimbly followed the broken path. Behind, Idwal was whimpering into Heulwen's bosom and Anwen came along in the rear, every so often calling out to me to assure herself of my well-being.

Rhodri had just reached a plateau and his pony was climbing into a clearing when I heard a cry behind me, followed by a rumpus of scrambling and screaming. I turned abruptly. Heulwen's pony had missed its footing and slipped on the steep uneven slope. Idwal and his nurse had, fortunately, been thrown clear but the pony continued to slide helplessly, straight into the path of Anwen's mount. Both ponies, unable to manoeuvre on the wet slope, collided and went down and, in their struggle to halt their chaotic slide down the hill, Anwen was dislodged from her saddle. I heard the sickening snap of bone as her mount rolled heavily across her leg.

Forgetting my ungainly size, I leapt from the saddle before Rhodri could forestall me. Heulwen was sitting up and I could hear Idwal's fretful cries so, knowing they lived, I ignored them and rushed to help Anwen. As I drew close, the ponies found their footing and lurched to their feet, galloping away into the wood. Anwen lay unmoving in the mud.

'Anwen, Anwen.' I panted, kneeling at her side. 'Oh God, Rhodri. She is dead.'

He knelt beside me and felt beneath her bosom. I remember thinking irrationally that she would be mortified had she known of his intimate exploration, then he lifted each eyelid.

'I think she lives Lady. But I know not for how long. Her leg is broke and she has banged her head, look at the swelling here.' He stood up and looked about him desperately in the relentless rain.

'God damn me for a fool.' he cursed, 'I should never have allowed us to become separated from the others.'

There were five of us. One man, three women and an infant; one woman was unconscious, one heavily pregnant and the other carried in her arms the precious son of the king. We had just two ponies and were miles from any holding. In the end I sat on Glimmer with Idwal strapped to my back, for it was impossible to strap him to my belly.

Heulwen took the other mount, supporting in her arms the unconscious Anwen, her leg held straight in a makeshift splint. Rhodri held the bridle and walked, casting about him through the gloom for a sign of shelter. It seemed an age later when he spotted a cave on the side of the wooded hill, half hidden by brambles and bracken.

Our refuge was not cut very deep into the rock face but it provided shelter from the wind and rain and still allowed enough light to enter so that we could light a fire and see to our patient. Rhodri decided we should meddle no further with Anwen's leg, it seemed the splint was holding and should continue to do so until we could find a medicine woman. We bathed her bruised head with some water that trickled in through a fissure in the rock and then I took Idwal on my lap and examined him from head to toe to ascertain that he was unharmed. Heulwen looked dazed; the side of her face was plastered with mud but she was otherwise none the worse for wear. When I handed her charge back to her, he latched on to her breast, suckling long and hard until they both drifted off to sleep.

'I am deeply sorry, Lady, 'twas my arrogance got us into this mess.'

'It isn't your fault, Rhodri. How could you ever have foreseen anything like this?'

'I don't know, but a man should be prepared for anything. Can you imagine what Gruffydd will say when he finds out? He will have me hanged.'

I lay my head back against the cave wall. Pain surged at my temples and my eyes were sore, my body felt as though I had swam the millrace. I must have wrenched myself when I leapt from my horse for fingers of pain wandered around my midriff. Suddenly, dragged back from my reverie, I became aware of Rhodri standing above me, blocking out the light from the cave opening.

'Oh, did I fall asleep? I am sorry, Rhodri, to leave you to fret alone.'

'You weren't asleep long. I didn't intend to wake you. Why don't you try to nod off again?' I stretched out my limbs and groaned as the feeling surged back into them.

'God's grief. I ache from head to toe. Have you had time to think yet what we are to do? We can hardly travel all the way to Bistre with Anwen in that condition. Has she stirred at all?'

'Nay, Lady, only to snore like a drunkard. I have seen something similar before. I fear she is in a deep state of sleep from which she will not waken until she is ready … or maybe never even wake at all.'

I sighed and crawled across the floor to where my dear friend lay, her face pale and deathlike in the fading light. Closing my eyes tight, I sent up a prayer to God, I did not pray often, outside of church, but this situation was dire.

'I will have to ride to Bistre for help at first light. You will have to stay here, it should take me no more than a few hours to get there and back if I take no rests. Will you be alright if I do that, Lady? I doubt things can get much worse.'

Fear plunged its burning dagger deep as I looked up at him, tears springing from my eyes, my mouth gaping in horror.

'Oh, My God.' I screamed, clutching at my nether regions. ' It can get worse, Rhodri, it can get a whole lot worse.' I wailed, for I had discovered that the back of my gown was soaked and that I sat in a sweet smelling puddle of birth fluid.

I had long imagined Rhodri's hands upon my body but the circumstances in which his touch became reality I had never dreamed of. My pains began soon after the birth waters were released. We had no proper supply of water, no potions, no midwife and very little dry fuel for the fire. Rhodri remained calm, as he ever was, in the face of my panic. He did not try to staunch my tears but, instead, nestled me to his metal studded tunic and I found a strange comfort there, my tears ceasing of their own volition. The labour pains, I now realised, had been gathering in strength for a few days and, now that I acknowledged them, they soon became unbearable.

Rhodri knelt beside me and rubbed wherever I indicated required attention. Fidgeting and unable to find a comfortable position, I was so grateful that he was there, never losing patience but offering me sips of wine and constantly stroking and soothing my rigid body.

This had been going on for sometime when Heulwen woke from her slumber and squeaked at the shock of finding us engaged in such intimacy. When she realised I was in labour she staggered over to help and immediately upset my cup of wine that had been set beside the fire to warm.

'Go away, woman.' snapped Rhodri, 'see to the babe and Anwen, but stay close, I will call you if needs be.'

Looking up at him through my sweat-dampened fringe as he massaged my distended stomach, I realised, through the fog of pain, that he loved me. The expression on his face was not one of disgust or even fear at the danger we were both in, but one of supreme contentment. I remembered the salves and potions the midwife had applied at my first lying in and acknowledged that none of them had relieved or calmed as Rhodri soothed me now. I tried to speak but, as I did so, a pain came again, distracting my thoughts. As it abated I felt the beginnings of an impulse to bear down and expel the child from my womb; this labour was progressing much faster than my last.

When the urge grew too strong to resist, I signalled to Rhodri and, putting my arms about his neck, pulled myself into a kneeling position and placed my forehead against his, puffing hard I looked into his eyes. He was my life line and I felt that, if I lost eye contact with him for one moment, then all would be lost but if I maintained it, if he continued to hold and help me, then all would be well. Despite the fact that I was giving birth to a royal prince, half way up a wooded valley in a cave that was the winter home of hibernating mammals, I no longer felt afraid.

I strained and pushed, moaned and gyrated my hips and, all the while, he guided me, never once becoming too tired himself or stopping for a drink or a piss. Heulwen crouched beside Anwen on the other side of the fire with Idwal in her arms but we were oblivious to her presence. I had been pushing for some while before I felt the head lurch suddenly into the birth canal. Panting like a hound, I waited for the next pain and when it came and I felt a vice had been placed about my middle, I pushed and cried out aloud as the child slid, wet from my body into Rhodri's waiting hands. Collapsing forward with my arse in the air, I caught my breath and then turned myself over to greet my child. Rhodri wiped him and wrapped him in his tunic before offering him to me. I looked upon my second son and then up into his half brother's eyes and was glad; everything, as absurd as it seemed, was as it should be.

Rhodri squatted close to the fire, adding fuel to the dying embers and, every so often, he glanced to where I sat happily suckling my child. Catching my eye he smiled, a smile of gentle regret.

'What?' I asked, when I saw his wistful expression, 'what is it?'

'Oh, you know, Eadgyth, don't you? You know I wish that he were mine, and you were mine and we were far away from Rhuddlan and Gruffydd. I'd be happier were I a penniless woodcutter and you my wife, living in a hut where our children played in the dust.'

I pondered that happy scenario for a while and then, with a wry smile, whispered,

'I wish that too Rhodri but it can never be. Even were I widowed, we could not be wed. In the eyes of the world I am your mother or as near as makes no difference.'

He ducked his head to tend the flames again,

'It has been hard to watch Gryffydd use you so badly; you were a child when you came to him and he a man old enough to be your grandfather. He didn't let that stop him though did he? He paid your tender years no mind? I should like to kill him, to ring his blasted neck and watch him die, slowly for the way he has treated you … and for that matter, that way he has treated me for all these years.'

'Rhodri.' I sobbed, my euphoric afterglow of birth plummeting. He dropped the stick with which he stirred the fire and threw himself down beside me. He took hold of me, dropping kisses on my dirty face and on my sweaty hair, only to draw back and release me when we heard Heulwen clumping back up the path after relieving herself in the wood.

I was churched and fully recovered from the ordeal of the birth before we met again. I had seen him from my bower as he went about his business and I watched him sparring with the grooms and flirting with the maids. I felt cut off from him, as if the emotion that had flared between us had been quenched.

Recalling the long ago afternoon when he had helped me choose Idwal's name I decided to christen the new child with the second name he had suggested. Maredudd had been the name of Gruffydd's grandsire on his mother's side so I could see no obvious objection to the choice.

Although we had sent him news of his son's birth, Gruffydd remained in Deheubarth and sent no word in return. We knew that he was dealing with his old adversary, Cynan ap Iago, whose father had been killed by Gryffydd's hand. Now, grown to man's estate, the son sought vengeance for his father's murder. The sinner, that had of late grown so strong in me, wished him luck. Gruffydd's business affected us not at all at Rhuddlan, we did not mourn his absence and the *llys* resumed the relaxed, happy atmosphere it usually enjoyed in the Lord's absence.

It was the morning of my churching and Tangwystl, who had taken over some of Anwen's less arduous duties, helped me into a new gown and over tunic. Anwen had spent many hours stitching it. The kirtle was of sea green and the tunic a pale sky blue and I knew it suited me well. It was an exciting moment when we fastened the shoulder clasps and brushed out my hair to fall, dark upon my shoulders. During the pregnancy it had thinned and dulled but now it had begun to thicken and the comb slid through it, making it crackle and stand out until Tangwystl smoothed it with a piece of silk. Anwen, her broken leg propped on a footstool, sat with the children before the fire.

'How do I look? ' I asked her.

'Oh yes, Lady, you look fine. Motherhood suits you well, I remember you looked the same after Idwal's birthing.'

'I think it is more than evident I am now a mother of two,' I said circling my thickened waist in despair.

'Nay, Lady. It suits you, 'tis a woman's form you bear now and there is a new self-assurance about you that is attractive; as if a new dimension has been added.'

I crossed the room and dropped a kiss on Anwen's head. 'Thank you, Anwen, you are such a good friend to me, whatever should I have done without you all these troubled years?'

She shrugged off my gratitude while I smiled at myself in the looking glass, then I called to Heulwen, who collected the children and followed Tangwystl and I from the chamber and into the sunshine.

Standing outside the church door, a soiled being, the priest blessed me, declaring me cleansed and fit for the company of men once more. After making my confession and sending up some hasty prayers, I left, feeling reprieved. How marvellous it felt to be free of my chamber.

The autumn sky was bright and a sharp wind blew in off the sea scattering yellow leaves about the churchyard. I sucked in the fresh air as we strolled about the settlement, my small laughing group of women and children hurrying along behind. The people of Rhuddlan surged forth to welcome me back among them and congratulate me on the birth of another prince. Then, thoroughly chilled and hungry, we returned to the great hall where refreshments would be on offer and a welcome fire in the hearth.

Rhodri was lurking near the door with an expectant glint in his eye. He was looking remarkably clean, his hair was brushed back and his untanned forehead, where his fringe usually flopped in his eyes, contrasted sharply with his brown cheeks. I had the impulse to ruffle his fringe and pull it down into his eyes again. Without the usual growth of dark beard his jaw seemed square and strong and his lips invitingly moist. He seemed both different and the same and my newfound confidence leeched away in the face of this familiar stranger.

'Lady,' he bowed slightly, leaving a chaste kiss on the back of my hand, 'tis good to have you back among us.'

Following him into the hall, I said nothing, letting my eyes revel for a while in the sight of him. He looked very young and, as I followed him into the hall, I blurted out, 'How old are you, Rhodri?'

With raised brows he turned and replied, 'I am nineteen years, Lady.'

His dependability and self-assurance had made me suppose him older. Taking the cup of mead that he offered, I sat upon a stool and reached to take Maredudd from Heulwen's arms.

'Will you not greet your brother, Rhodri? He has much to thank you for … as do I.' He came close and squatted down beside us, offering the child a finger which the babe clutched, his digits miniscule beside Rhodri's.

'He has grown Lady. Although 'tis little more than a month since I saw him, I would not take him for the same child. His hair is darker I believe or perchance thicker.'

'He thrives upon his mother's own milk, that's why he's growing like a weaner. I never saw such an appetite,' interjected Anwen, who's chair had been carried down to the hall. I saw Rhodri's eyes flicker to my breast and his brief, hot glance brought a rush of warmth to my own face. Dipping my head, I let my veil fall forward to hide my blushes.

'I see no harm in nursing him myself in his father's absence; it cannot inconvenience Gruffydd at all and it keeps Heulwen free to see to Idwal's needs.'
Rhodri retrieved his finger and stood up.

'He is a fine child, Lady, his father will be proud and 'tis a fine name you have chosen.'
My smile was brilliant; he did realise why I had chosen it. Relaxed, I let him see the full force of my feelings and beamed upon the company like an idiot as they roared a toast unto the health of the new prince.

Rhodri and I were unable to find time alone but at first that didn't matter, as long as I was near him I was happy and I honestly did not plan a carnal affair.

There were too many risks for one in my position and, besides, Rhodri did not want to foist a bastard onto his own father. I knew our feelings for each other were wrong, even to steal the little innocent loving that we did at that time was sinful but I had known such little joy in my life and I was still so very young.

I am making excuses but, if the truth be told, a few moments in his company filled me with enough joys to compensate for the miseries heaped upon me by his father. It sounds ridiculous to say so and I can only blame my youth, but his voice turned my stomach upside down and the slightest touch sent the strength from my limbs.

Anwen was a godsend; both a chaperone and a conspirator, she allowed us quick snatches of intimacy that left me heady but satisfied… for a while. Like most good intentions, they did not last and things swiftly grew out of control.

In the privacy of my chamber, Idwal and the babe slept and Anwen sat on her stool overseeing Heulwen as she folded linen and smoothed my gowns and put them away in the clothes press. Rhodri and I sat, almost touching, by the fireside whispering silliness, every so often allowing our hands to accidentally brush or our knees to meet. The air grew thick with our lusty longing and, accordingly, Anwen came to our rescue.

'Heulwen,' she said, 'help me to the privy and then send down for some more wine will you. We wont be a jiffy, Lady.'

The moment they were gone we were up and in each other's arms, his lips on my neck and his hands at my breast. Devoid of breath, I panted as he explored the contents of my bodice and then, hearing a noise, he released me and I sat down abruptly on my stool.

'Eadgyth.' he groaned, 'I have to have you soon. I can think of nothing else.'

'I know,' I replied, sounding as though I had been running, 'but we can't, what if there should be a child?'

'There are ways to avoid it, I have spoken to Ogwen, the wise woman in the village, and she says there are ways.'

'I am afraid, Rhodri.'

'Of Gruffydd? He is far away. He would never suspect anything like that of us, he thinks me still a boy and, such is his conceit, he would never dream that you might betray him.'

'I didn't mean I was afraid of Gruffydd. It is damnation that troubles me. What we plan is incest, Rhodri. Adultery and treason. A three fold sin against God, we could burn for it.'

He stood up and pulled me to face him.

'Isn't it better to burn in the hereafter than to burn like this now … say you will come to me, Eadgyth, say I can have you.'

I pulled away.

'I can't, Rhodri. I can't plan it. Don't you see? I want to be with you and, if it should come upon us sudden, I could perhaps succumb to the sin, but I cannot sit here and plan it with you in cold blood.'

He was still for a moment and then continued as if I had not spoken.

'Anwen will help us, I have already spoken with her. If you can put yourself in her care she will bring me to you when the time is ripe.'

This was too intense, I tried to back away, it was all too real and too frightening, the enormity of what we proposed, the risk we took even being alone and talking like this together. Dragging my eyes to meet his I nodded silently and he pulled me from my stool into his arms again, planting an almost brutal kiss on my dry lips.

'I will send word,' he said, 'look to Anwen for guidance.'

I turned away to stare into the flames. I heard him leave the room and, as the door closed and Maredudd stirred in his cradle, I did not move. There are no excuses, although I constantly seek them in my mind, there is no escaping the fact that we sinned, against Gruffydd, against the church and against God. But, I tell you true, if I had known how sweet that sinning would be, I would never have fought against it for so long.

The chamber was warm; Anwen was closeted behind a screen in the far corner where she promised to be both deaf and blind to everything. Rhodri had fixed a stout lock upon the inside of the door and there was a small table with wine and wafers and a pile of furs and cushions upon the bed. Long after dusk had fallen I stood with my heart banging like a war drum listening as Rhodri drew the bolts. He came up close behind me and my knees threatened to give way as he slid his arms about my waist, burrowing his face in my hair.

'Eadgyth,' he murmured, '*Cariad*, I cannot believe we are really here.'

'Well, here we are.' I replied, my voice husky in the semi-darkness.

I could have run away but, even then, things had already gone too far; already I had sinned enough to deserve incarceration in a nunnery. Knowing I should draw back, it seemed I heard Morcar's cynical voice in my head, '*Might as well be hung for a sheep as a lamb,*' and so, turning into the axis of his arms, I raised my face for Rhodri's kiss.

He did not hurry, his lips were languid and his tongue firm as it probed mine. Every thought was driven from my head other than the delight of him. I forgot my position, my children and my husband and traded all that I had for a few short, sweet hours in his arms.

He pulled the cord at the neck of my bed gown sharply and, loosening the gathering about my neck, let the fabric trickle down my body to lie, in a puddle, about my feet. Then he stood back and looked at me, appreciation writ clear upon his face.

'No, don't,' I protested, 'I'm too fat.'
He laughed softly,

'Oh, Lady, you are not fat. Envys the cook is fat. You, Lady … are magnificent,' and, as he spoke, he began to stroke my breast and, just as he had soothed away the pain of my labour, so he now rubbed delight into every inch of me.

The soft light of dawn was leavening night's dark before I heard Anwen stir in her corner and Rhodri, his hair tousled and his beard fresh upon his chin, crept away. Like a sluggard, I lay abed for most of the day, reliving every instance of the precious night. When I finally rose and went down to supper I was certain that everyone would see that I had changed in some indefinable way.

In February we learned that Gruffydd had chased ap Iago back to Ireland and expected no more trouble from him. The news came from Alys who had sent news of the birth of a daughter whom she had named Eadgyth in my honour.

She said that Gruffydd had stayed at Dinefwr with them for the past few months and planned to travel home soon. It was typical that I should learn of his plans through another; I imagined him at Dinefwr, continuing his dalliance with the black haired wench no doubt. Not that I cared for, cushioned in my fool's paradise, I was happy that he should do as he wished, just so long as he remained far, far away from Rhuddlan.

Toddling all around now, Idwal was the darling of the *llys*. Heulwen began to wean him and, his teeth being fine and strong, he began to eat solid food and, quite often, inedible things that would have been best left undiscovered upon the floor.

We had some fine kid shoes fashioned for him and he loved them, laughing in glee as he stomped about in pursuit of the dogs. Rhodri made a great fuss of the children, throwing Idwal into the air and catching him again. I could not bear to watch lest he fall, but the toddler loved it, shrieking with delight and snatching at his brother's hair as he flew past.

Rhodri shrunk from acknowledging my children as his brothers but I refused to let him forget it. Everyday, at the back of my mind, was the knowledge that Gryffydd would, one day, return and Rhodri would no longer be able to treat his father's family as his own.

The April sun was unusually warm and someone suggested we ride to the coast for the afternoon to gather shellfish. We all bundled into cloaks and Anwen and Heulwen fetched bags while Rhodri saw that the ponies were saddled.

Twthill was splendid in the sunshine, *Y Ddraig Goch,* the red dragon banner, snapped in the breeze above the palace as we rode sedately toward the sea.

Including the children, we were a company of twelve and we made a gay party as we sang and laughed, the roar of the sea drawing us toward our destination.

A bracing wind blew in from the west and the surf rolled up the golden sands, the sky devoid of all but the lightest cloud. Settling myself, out of the wind on the beach with Anwen and Heulwen, I watched as Rhodri took Idwal down to the water's edge. I smiled to see them wading, hand in hand, through the shallow water. Every time a big wave came Rhodri hoisted the child up into his arms to save him from a soaking. Idwal's high-pitched laughter floated up the beach and mingled with the cry of the gulls that soared overhead. The rest of the party sat in groups, somebody had lit a fire and others had hunted for cockles and oysters to cook. Heulwen shaded Maredudd's delicate head from the glare of the sun with her kerchief and I lay back and looked at the sky, feeling so happy that I wondered I did not simply float away.

When I awoke everyone was gathered about the fire and Rhodri was nowhere to be seen. I got up and whispered to Anwen that I was going into the sand dunes and to keep everyone away. I lifted my skirts and wandered barefoot across the warm sand until I was out of sight of the main party, then I raised my gown and squatted, urinating copiously on the ground.

As I stood up Rhodri emerged from the opposite direction,

'I would have coughed,' he teased, 'but I thought it would startle you.'

'Did you see?' I demanded.

'No, of course not,' he lied, taking my hand and leading me further into the dunes, away from the laughter on the beach to a sheltered nest where the maram grass grew upon the sandy mounds. Pulling me to my knees he began to loosen my gown.

'Rhodri. What about the others? We may be seen.'

'No, trust me, we wont; it is quite safe. Besides they won't dare disturb my lady at her toilette.'

He eased me back into the sand and, after a moment, I relaxed to enjoy the warm kiss of the sun upon my breasts while his eager fingers crept up my skirts to discover further secrets. I was easily won and my knees moved apart to grant him easier access. His fingers grew moist and a moan escaped me as he transferred his lips from my mouth to my breast where, depriving Maredudd of nourishment, he pulled gently, suckling like a babe.

We forgot about the others on the beach and, afterward, lay naked in the sun, the sound of the surf and the gulls lulling us into a happy dream. That afternoon of sunshine with him was the absolute zenith of my life's happiness. When I emerged from the dunes, some half an hour later, my breasts were still burning from his kisses and my hair was scat about my head like a wild woman's. My gown was creased and daubed with damp patches but I descended from those dunes like a goddess.

'Lady.' cried Anwen when she saw me, 'you fell asleep again. I followed you after a while to make sure you were well and you were sleeping like a baby. Look at your gown all scat asunder.' she lied, brushing at the sand that clung to my damp skirts while I twiddled the ends of my hair and stared about me in a happy trance.

It was sometime later that I saw Rhodri slip back into the group and we both liked to think that nobody noticed. We would have liked to stay feasting on the beach, drinking wine from the skins brought from the *llys* but, when the pile of empty shells were piled high about us and the sun had begun its descent into the west, we collected our things together and made our way back home.

It was not until we had trotted over the bridge and into the *llys* that we realised Gruffydd had returned. Still mired from the road, he was sprawled in his favourite chair by the hearth, the men of the *teulu* gathered about him. He let out a huge roar as we entered, 'And where the hell have you all been gallivanting.'

I wanted to vomit for I knew, as I stood there with Rhodri's seed still damp upon my thigh, that come nightfall, I must lay with his father.

It was a cruel four months. Once more in the uncomfortable role of stepmother, I found myself tongue tied and embarrassed in Rhodri's presence. When I saw his angry eyes linger on the marks that Gruffydd's roughness left upon my neck, I felt shamed at my betrayal of him.

Since his return my husband had taken to coupling with me nightly, he was relentless in his attentions and now that I knew how sweet love could be, it was harder to bear.

I lay, convulsed with disgust beneath him as he strained to a climax, throwing back his sinewy neck, his haggard face suffused with blood until, sweating and noxious, he dropped down upon me. I turned my face from him, hardly able to wait calmly for his withdrawal.

All sympathy I may have previously felt for him had ebbed away and I felt no guilt for my adultery. I was fearful of being discovered and felt no small terror for the incestuous nature of our alliance but, deep down, I was convinced that such, sweet passion could surely not be wrong.

Gruffydd's attentions began to take their toll and I took less care of my appearance. The only comfort I found at that time was in the brief glance of support that Rhodri occasionally managed to cast in my direction. I became so steeped in misery that I thanked God with all my heart on the first morning that I vomited and knew that I was again with child.

Relieved that his visits to my chamber would now cease, I lost no time in seeking out Gruffydd to give him the news. I found him with the farrier examining the damaged foreleg of his favourite warhorse. When he saw me he raised his eyebrows but said nothing, forcing me to wait in the farmyard while he completed his business.

'Well, well, Madam, and what is it that brings you from the comforts of your hall?'

I drew him away from his companions and spoke rapidly.

'I came to you in some excitement, Lord, to tell you that, come February, you can expect another son. I have suspected such for sometime but this morning was made sure.'

Hoping the assumed confidence was convincing, I heaved a secret sigh of relief when he nodded, non-committal as always,

'Fine, good. I trust you will look to the child and keep yourself well then, Madam.'

I made to walk away but, as I reached the pigsty, he called after me, 'tis soon to tell, is it not?'
Dread bubbled in the pit of my stomach.

'Nay, Lord,' I lied, 'not for someone with Anwen's knowledge, she is skilled at such things and knows the workings of my body better than I know them myself.'

Hurrying back to the hall through the milling bailey, I counted back the weeks to the last time I had lain with Rhodri; it all seemed so long ago. Could the child be his? I counted again. It could indeed. Indeed it could. Once more I struck off the weeks on my fingers to be sure. If it came later than January it was Gruffydd's, any sooner and the chances were it was Rhodri's.

Instead of flushing with shame as I should have done, I was flooded with joy. My chin at a jaunty angle, I strode back to the hall certain that the burgeoning life within me was the issue of our union in the sand. I was glad and cared not at all that we were setting the cuckold's horns squarely on the old man's head.

Back in the hall, I asked Envys if she had seen Rhodri.

'He has ridden out Lady, to the woodcott at the edge of the forest; it seems there is a fine litter of hounds born and he wishes to replenish the blood of our stock. He should be back by dusk, is there anyone else I can send for?'

'No, no. I just wondered if he were about, that's all, my mare had a grass seed in her eye and I wondered if the poultice he told me of had helped it heal.'

Envys turned back to her chopping board, a tune on her lips and a sway to her ample hips. I hurried to my chamber and found Anwen tidying the bed. The coverings were twisted and soiled and she tutted as she bundled them up for washing. Unable to keep the delight from my voice, I burst out,

'There will be none of that for the next few months Anwen. I am to have another child, perchance in February but … maybe in early January.' I blushed as she dropped the bundle and hobbled across the room to take my hands,

'Oh Lady, tis a good thing, twill keep that man from your bed and restore some of the lost apples to your cheeks an' that's the main thing. We must be grateful he has ploughed your furrow so soon or twould have been the devil's job to explain.'

I paused, considering the implication behind her words.

'Do you think I will go to hell for what I have done, Anwen?'

She sat on the edge of the bed, still gripping my hand.

'Nay, Lady, do not worry over such a thing. What you have done is not really a sin, not in my book. You have just done what we are put on earth to do. Celebrated your youth and love of life with someone you love. 'Tis surely no sin to celebrate God's gifts and, if no one finds you out, no one shall suffer, so where is the harm? My mam always said that love spreads love and joy spreads joy and, judging from your face these last few weeks, misery spreads misery too.'

Although she believed what she said, I knew she was wrong. I had sinned and in the depths of my mind I knew that punishment awaited me, in one form or another.

'I need to tell Rhodri; he should hear it from me. Oh, in truth, Anwen, I just need to see him and tell him face to face. I do not want him to hear of it from others. Oh, if I cannot see him soon I think I will die.'
Anwen put down the sheet she was folding and came to me, rubbing at the top of my arms, bolstering my courage.

'Well, nobody ever died o' wanting, Lady, but just to be sure, I will arrange a place for you to meet but we must be cautious; even though you and Rhodri are loved far more than Gruffydd.'

That night after dinner, Anwen and I, muffled against the night chill, made our way to the stable where Rhodri was changing the poultice on Glimmer's eye. When he heard us he dropped what he was doing and regardless of Anwen's presence took me straight into his embrace.

'I have missed you, *Cariad.* I thought I should perish of misery if I did not see you soon. How are you, really? You are so peaked looking it breaks my heart to see you so miserable and alone.'

Holding my face in his hands, he kissed me long on the lips and then, as he pulled away, let his hands trickle over my torso, skimming my breasts and hips.

'Rhodri, I have something to tell you,' I murmured, trapping his hands so as not to yield to desire.

'What is it, Sweeting?' he mumbled, his lips buried in my neck.

'I am with child, Rhodri.'
His head snapped upright, his jaw tensing and the lazy lust of his eyes instantly extinguished. He pulled away,

'The bastard lost little time.' he snarled.

Behind us Anwen's feet rustled in the straw as she twisted and turned, keeping a look out in all directions. Reaching out to him again, I stroked his cheek.

'My lord,' I whispered, half laughing, half crying at his ingenuity, 'the deed may well have been yours.'

He seemed so young as I watched reality drench him like cold water. Stillness fell upon the stable; the only sound the rhythmic chomping of the horses at their hay.

'Oh God, what have we done? Oh my *Cariad*, if he should discover it …'

'How can he, Rhodri? He has been busy upon me every night. He is no midwife, only we shall know the truth. If the child comes in January it will be ours and I can claim 'tis but come early but … if 'tis later… 'twill be his.'

Rhodri looked down at my stomach and placed a hand upon it.

'I am torn. I want to be glad. I want it to be mine. I want it so badly. Oh, *Cariad*, 'tis hard to sit back and watch that man play husband to my sweetheart, let alone father to mine own son too.'

Anwen stirred in the doorway, 'We must go, Lady, before the watch is set,' she warned.

I looked down upon his dark head as he placed a wet kiss upon my wrist close to the place where my heart's blood pulsed beneath the surface.

'Take care, *Cariad*,' he said, 'I will be hereabouts, waiting and watching, but I know not when we can be together like this again.'

'Think you we will ever meet like this again?'

'Oh, do not doubt it and, in time to come, these troubles shall seem as nothing. When 'tis all over and the child is here, we must leave, take the young ones and ride away from all this and make our lives elsewhere. We will go to Ireland, we cannot live like this any longer.'

Silently, with tears tearing at my throat, I nodded and then, clutching Anwen's arm, we hurried back to the hall through the lilting rain.

My body was cumbersome but, freed of Gruffydd's attentions, my spirits were better than they had been. Four months into my pregnancy, my relationship with Rhodri was restricted to polite conversation and eye contact. We shared no intimacy but, sometimes, the silent messages that he sent across the crowded hall were so loaded with meaning that I wondered others did not intercept them.

The brimming mead cups probably helped, for the evenings were riotous and the entertainment grew more ribald as the year progressed. Without the activity of war to quell their spirits, Gruffydd's men grew fractious and undisciplined. The sound of debauchery that wended its way to my sleeping bower often kept me awake into the small hours but I was able to lie abed for as long as I wished in the mornings so it did not rob me of sleep. I preferred to break my fast in my chamber, for, in the mornings, the hall often remained littered with the debris of the previous night and the stench was nauseating.

The night that the end began is difficult for me to speak of, the terrible memories are clear in my mind but the words are reluctant to be spoken. However, I will try to explain.

I woke from a light slumber and sat up, groping for the cup that was usually at my bedside. It was empty and, when I called to Anwen, she was not there and I remembered that she had been summoned to help with a difficult birthing. Wrapping myself in a cloak, I quit the chamber in search of a drink. I don't know why I did not call out for someone, I just didn't think to, so used was I to Anwen being close by. I ducked through the doorway into the hall and began to make my way through the debris, stepping over comatose bodies, careful to avoid the puddles of puke.

One of the wolfhounds came to sniff at me but I ignored him and he soon slunk away again. The cooking fire was deserted so I made my way to the food hall beyond. As I picked my careful way over sleeping bodies and discarded mead cups, a familiar sound startled me and, instantly alert, I looked across to the far corner.

There, in the dim light, my husband was engaged with two females. I can find no way to describe what I saw without resort to some indelicacy, but he was busy between the legs of a young girl and another knelt at his feet.

I tried to back away, to creep off, hoping my intrusion would go unnoticed, but then, I recognised the black head that was buried in his lap.

'Heulwen.' I gasped, and staggered backward, seeking an escape. My head was reeling and, disorientated, I stumbled into the table, sending jugs and plates crashing to the floor.

The hounds leapt up barking. The sleepers in the hall began to stir and Gruffydd scrambled up, his women grabbing for their clothes while my husband struggled with the lacing on his breeches.

For a heartbeat we all stood staring speechlessly at each other until, bending forward I let loose a stream of vomit into the rushes. Heulwen burst into tears, clutching her gown to her bosom … the bosom that had nourished my sons, and fled. The other girl, who appeared to be scarcely out of childhood, was slower to quit the room and Gruffydd was forced .to hasten her sulky departure with his boot.

'Well, Madam, why are you prowling about at this time of the night?' he demanded. Momentarily speechless, I soon found my voice.

'What do I do?' I hollered in tones to match his own, 'What do I do? I do but fetch a drink, what is it that you do, my Lord?'

'Tis none of your business what I do woman. Now, get ye back to your bed, I owe you no explanation.'

'Oh, yes you do, Gruffydd. That woman, that seemed so engrossed in your genitalia, is in my employ. She works for me as a nurse to your children. How dare you place my sons at jeopardy by keeping her from her duties. I care not what you do, my Lord, in fact I am glad for you to take your satisfaction anywhere just so long as it isn't in my bed, but do not think to intrude upon the queen's household again. Find your whores elsewhere.'

Our voices were loud and people had begun to gather by the hearth.

'I am the king here and you, Madam, are here to do as you are bid. You are my property, bequeathed by your father into my care.'

'And you call this care do you, Gruffydd? Inflicting your nauseous attentions on me, your unwashed stench would offend a pigmaid and in the bedchamber your lack of finesse is nothing but a chore. I am glad to be done with it.'

He struck me then, hard across the cheek and I fell on hands and knees onto the soiled rushes. Wiping the blood from my mouth, I glared up at him, letting him see the full force of my contempt.

'How brave you are my Lord…' I began but a kick deprived me of further speech.

There was a deathly silence in the hall, nobody dared move or interfere but, suddenly, Anwen was there at my side, helping me to rise.

'Shame on you.' she cried at Gruffydd, 'What man are you to rend your Lady so?'

He ignored her as if she hadn't spoken and, shaking with anger, I stood before him with Anwen at my side. The top of my head barely reached his chin but, looking him in the eye, I gritted my teeth, almost choking on my loathing.

'I will be quitting your hall, Gruffydd, just as soon as horses can be made ready.'

Drawing back his fist, he made to assault me again but he found his arm pinioned from behind.

'Strike her again and I will kill you.' came Rhodri's voice, deadly calm in the silence.

Gruffydd twisted free of his grip easily and stood unwary, his puzzled eyes flashing from my bloody face to Rhodri's ashen one.

'And what business is it of yours, you ill-born piece of shite?'
Rhodri flinched at the insult and, as if to test the situation further, Gruffydd grabbed me by the hair, forcing my head down close to his fetid crutch.

'What if I should strike her again, Boy? What if I should kick and punch her, rape her here in the hall

before this company? What would a half-baked brat like you do about it, eh? What would any of you do?'
There was no reply. The company stood sullenly. He glared at his son. Rhodri did not move.

'I would kill you,' he said, 'without hesitation and without the slightest displeasure.'
Gruffydd leered a dreadful smile.

'And you can fight me can you, boy? You would risk your life defending my woman because I choose to beat her a little?' he laughed, looking about, trying to rouse some support from the tense crowd. Nobody moved until Rhodri spoke again.

'She isn't your woman, Gruffydd, she is my woman and the child she bears is mine also.'

Movement flurried about the hall but still nobody dared to intervene. Gruffydd loosed my hair and I stood up, a hand pressed to my aching back as I inched away from what had become a murderous situation. His bloodshot eyes flicked about the room and I saw that none but Gruffydd was taken by surprise.

Although we had thought ourselves so cunning, our relationship had, all along, been common knowledge among our friends at Rhuddlan.

I felt my face scorch red and my heart hammered as my eyes swivelled back to the drama. The situation was fraught with danger. Gruffydd was staring at me, a tremor of anger in his jaw; he had recognised the truth of his son's words too.

'You bitch!' he cried, lashing out full-fisted and smashing my teeth together. Bright lights flashed in my head and the world about me grew dark.

Through a fog of semi-consciousness, I realised that Gruffydd and Rhodri were fighting, I could hear their grunting breath punctuating the clash of their swords. Clutching at a table for support, I staggered to my feet and, shaking my head to clear my vision, focused on the scene before me.

Gruffydd's men were grouped at one end of the hall, watching the fight with some pleasure. The rest of the household were huddled at the other end. Tables had been overturned and the dogs barked from the perimeter of the room. Anwen tried to restrain me but I shrugged from her arms and staggered forward,

'Gruffydd!' I cried, 'My Lord, stop. Think what it is you do.'

'The time for thinking has passed, Madam,' he panted, swinging his blade and bringing it down with stunning force to meet Rhodri's. My sweetheart was no swordsman; his father had always denied him the instruction that was his due. His face was pale, his hair wet with sweat and, with a wrench of fear, I saw that blood was seeping through the sleeve of his jerkin. He was hurt. I licked my lips, frantically thinking of a way to calm the situation.

'Please.' I cried again, 'think what you do, Gruffydd. We have not injured your heart. 'Tis but your pride that is hurt, nothing more. Punish him no further, punish me instead.'

Attacking with a flurry of short, swift blows which Rhodri just managed to block, Gruffydd growled, 'That pleasure will come later, woman,' and deftly parried a thrust, leaping just in time, clear of Rhodri's sword.

Losing my control and letting the full force of my contempt show in my voice, I said clearly,

'And what would Bronwen say? Would she cheer you on as you seek to splice her son in two? 'tis vengeance for her death you truly seek, isn't it,

Gruffydd? You never could forgive him could you? You were never man enough to overcome that misfortune. Leave him alone. You are a coward. For God's sake man, he is your son.'

Sweating heavily and using all his strength, Gruffydd shoved Rhodri backward, sending him tripping over benches and onto the floor; then he turned and strode across the room toward me.

When I saw him coming I cowered, on my knees, certain that I breathed my last. A gasp snaked about the room and it seemed an age that I crouched there with my arms clasped over my head, praying for my soul … but the expected blow never fell. Just as I thought my life ended, Rhodri leapt up and, speeding across the room, raised his weapon and drove his blade into his father's back.

I saw the look of stunned surprise on Gruffydd's face but, the blade had glanced off and not stuck fully home. He twisted around to face his assailant.

Rhodri's sword clattered to the floor and I watched as he stood, unarmed, before his father's wrath. Ignoring my screams Gruffydd raised his weapon and, with a furious cry, plunged his sword down deeply into his son's heart.

The horror of that December night sent me whirling into a nightmare of grief. For a long time I wanted to die too and, had I been so offered, I would have exchanged all of my tomorrows for just one more chance at yesterday.

I raged against fate until Anwen despaired of my sanity and my own body, traumatised by my anguish, was forced to expel my child early from the womb. The birth was sharp and fast; the suddenness of her arrival thrusting my women into a whirl of activity.

My heart, that wished only to cease beating, was salvaged from utter despair by the timely arrival of a daughter.

On that cold morning when, through the curtain of my grief, I examined her nailess fingers and wrinkled skin, I knew she was not premature. She was no daughter of Gruffydd, she was Rhodri's.

Her hair lay dark upon her tiny skull and her damp lashes were like ebony stars upon her cheek. There was nothing of my husband in her and I was fiercly glad. All of Bronwen the Fair's sweet charm had passed into Rhodri's daughter and I knew she would be like him in every way.

Each pull at my breast tightened the strings that she wound about my heart, her tiny request for attention drawing me back from death and giving me a reason not to die …not just yet.

I nursed her myself for as long as I cared to; from now on I could look to my children's needs. Anwen told me, with no little satisfaction, how she had slapped Heulwen soundly and sent her squawking back to her father's house in disgrace.

'You are a good, loyal friend to me Anwen,' I said, 'I thank you. That trull will get no good word from me.'

Without my endorsement Heulwen's days would probably end in whoredom but I was too raw to care or to realise that she had probably been given her little choice in her actions. Confined to my chamber, I shut out the world and clutched my children tight, for they were all I had.

Idwal and Maredudd were both intrigued and bemused with their sister and sat on the bed to watch as she nursed. It was her Christening day and they were thinking of suitable names.

'Angharad?' Awen suggested.

'That was Gruffydd's mother's name, but I feel it is too much of a mouthful.'

'Call her Anwen.' cried Idwal, and Anwen began to tickle him,

'Sweet talker.' she cried, unhindered by his screams, 'you can't name a princess after a servant.'

'Oh, Anwen,' I cried, shocked out of my lethargy, 'you are more than a servant, you are my very best friend.'

Our eyes met over Idwal's head.

'Thankyou, my lady.' She murmured, cradling my son on her knee, her chin resting on his head.

Life goes on, as I have since learned, but with the soreness of loss still livid even fleeting contentment filled me with guilt that, in the small consolations of everyday living, I should come close to forgetting Rhodri. When the children were sitting quiet again, I shifted the babe to my other breast, watching as the fresh supply of milk trickled from her lips.

'I have a name for your sister already,' I said, 'I believe I shall call her Nesta.'

'Oh, Lady, tis a lovely name, a good Welsh name, a name fit for a queen.'

'Yes,' I agreed and the children's voices faded as my mind drifted away to a tranquil place, where the April sun had beaten down upon a nest of sand.

Unable to leave my chamber I grew used to the guard outside the door but I was, nonetheless, afraid. Within my chambers, with only my women and children for company, dread lay like a stone in my stomach.

Each morning I woke wondering if it were my last and each footstep outside my door became that of an assassin. The crime I had committed warranted death and I knew without doubt that Gruffydd would not be lenient.

Under Welsh law Gruffydd could do as he wished with me and there was just one thing stopping him from having me killed or cast off; his dependence upon my father. He could not risk the peace treaty for, the moment the alliance was broken, he knew that Earl Harold and his fighting men would descend upon Rhuddland with the might of England behind him.

Gruffydd was an angry man. The wound that Rhodri had inflicted on him proved to be superficial, although I prayed otherwise, and he had not even taken to his bed. He was soon striding about the *llys* as if nothing had happened.

Screened by the shutter, I watched him with loathing in my soul. Time would never dim the abhorrence we bore eachother. Instead it grew in strength and when, in my dreams, I relived that last awful night of Rhodri's life, I would wake to a burning hatred and lie awake, plotting Gruffydd's death in the dark.

I wanted it to be a long and lingering end and I wanted to look into his eyes as the last vestige of life drained from him. Oh, I knew I sinned and should seek absolution but I was not repentant. There was little doubt that, ultimately, one of us would destroy the other and I had no intention of letting it be me.

Each dawn in fear of the hereafter, I begged forgiveness from God, but every night the dream returned. Father Daffydd warned me against the self-detriment of hatred but I could not help it, I detested Gruffydd with such an all-consuming fever that I could barely contain it. I no longer considered myself his wife; I grieved for Rhodri as his widow, and knew myself to be alone in a frightening world.

Father Davydd was the one male visitor to my chamber, the only man I could now call 'friend' and, together, we spent many hours wrestling with the question of my sin. Unknown to me he spoke to Gruffydd, seeking his consent for me to attend my churching. The ceremony was long overdue and Gruffydd, unable to argue against God's representative, grudgingly gave his permission. I took a deep, shaking breath, quit my seclusion and walked into the outside world.

I did not want to face the people of the *llys* for I feared they would brand me a whore so we waited until the mid-day meal was over and the household quiet. Then we bundled the children into warm clothes and Anwen accompanied us to the small thatched church in the corner of the settlement.

The children were restive and naughty and I bribed them with promises of a long walk in the fresh air if they were good while I did my business with the priest.

The church door was richly carved with vines, birds and flowers and I stood examining it for some time before I finally pushed it wide and stepped inside.

It was dark within and the sharp contrast with the brightness of the day momentarily blinded me.

'Ah, here you are, Lady.' cried Father Daffydd when he heard my step upon the slate floor, 'Come you in, daughter, and we will pray together.'

My steps dragging, I approached the altar, reluctant for him to see me and, as I had feared, when the light of his candle illuminated my face, his shoulders deflated and he let forth a sigh.

'The sin is still with you, child.'

'I feel no sin, Father.' I had told him this a thousand times in the last weeks but he refused to listen. Crossing himself, seeking forgiveness for my depravity, he continued.

'Only the most determined of sinners refuse to admit their offence. I cannot believe that you see no sin in incest, in adultery, in wishing for the death of your husband, the king. Come, admit your transgression and seek absolution so I may cleanse you of it.'

Anwen was scolding Idwal for something near the church door, his feet scuffed on the floor as he tried to avoid her clutches.

'Has God abandoned me then because I loved?' I whispered, 'If He truly cares for my soul I do not understand why I cannot feel God's presence, Father. Why is He not helping me? My heart is sick unto death. Sometimes I cannot breathe for grief. I am suffocating with the guilt and for the hatred I feel for his murderer. I do not understand why He should want me to suffer like this. Should not Gruffydd be here confessing his sin instead of I?'

The priest sighed, looking down upon my bowed head as, on my knees, I wept.

'Everyone saw Rhodri strike Gruffydd first, I cannot condemn a man for striking another down in self defence, I should have half the country doing penance were that the case. Your sin is not an uncommon one, child, but a sexual union unblessed by God and His church is fornication, no more, no less and you must first confess and ask absolution.'

'And what of Gruffydd's fornication, Father, with his slaves and kitchen sluts? Does that not require absolution too?'

'That is between your husband and his confessor; he does not come unto my church. My concern is with you, child, I can help you if you will only admit the error of your ways.'

I let my head drop onto my hands, I had heard all his arguments before. I was tired of hearing them and, today he was determined to override my protests. He was aided, perhaps, by the unseen presence of God in that small dark cell, for suddenly I weakened, unable to fight him any longer, and gave in.

'Bless me, Father, for I have sinned,' I whispered, my voice hoarse with relief.

Father Daffydd let out a gusty sigh.

'And what is the nature of your sin, child?'

'I loved another, not my husband, I took carnal pleasures with him, my actions brought about his death and now I wish my wedded husband, his murderer, dead.'

'I absolve you, child, in the name of the Father and the Son and the Holy Spirit; now, go home and love your children and make peace with their father.'

I looked up at him, startled at such leniency, 'Is that all, Father?'

I had expected a harsh penance. He patted me on the head, 'You have suffered enough, child, and so have I with the hearing of it. You are a good girl and ill-equipped to deal with the trials God has seen fit to send you but, remember, He sent them for a reason. In your future life, my child, love moderately. Those that love moderately, love long.'

Relieved to be let off so lightly, I sent up a hasty prayer before the altar and left the church, Anwen limped along with Nesta swaddled in her arms and I slowed my pace to match her halting one, allowing the children to stop to examine small curiosities on the way. I felt in some way lighter since I had made confession, as if the heavy burden had been relieved a little.

Back in my prison I spent my time thinking. As the nights began to draw in, a deep sorrow began to replace some of the sharp pain of loss. The bitter north wind began to blow and the trees gave up their leaves to collect in corners about the settlement. They were dark days and although it was cold, I longed for the outdoors, to feel the wind in my hair and the rain on my face. The tolling fear that I had beat within me at the beginning of my confinement receded, leaving only tedium in its place.

Bored with inactivity, I began to believe that had Gruffydd intended to bring retribution against me he should have done so by now. I railed against my incarceration, no longer fearing death and wishing only for my freedom, I leant from the tiny window, drinking in the brisk winter air and wished I were a bird so that I could fly away. Sometimes it seemed that even execution would be better than to spend my life like a rat in a trap, there were days where the misery became so acute that I longed for death. And then, like a blow in the dark, came news of my father's death.

I remembered the father I had once loved but I did not mourn him. Dutifully I knelt and prayed for him at my lectern, lost myself in the memory of my childhood, thewarmth of my father's hall. So, when I heard the door close softly, I was startled and spun around to find Gruffydd standing in the shadows.

It was the first time we had faced eachother since that night and now I knew he had come to kill me. I said nothing, my heart hammering against my ribs, making my breath grow short.

He looked haggard in the leaping torchlight and, for the first time, I realised that the events of the past months might have been as cruel to him as they had me. We stared at eachother for a long moment, our mutual hatred shimmering like a livid thing between us until, from behind the curtain that screened off the sleeping platform, Nesta stirred and wimpered in her sleep. I made to go to her.

'Be still,' Gruffydd snarled and I froze, my eyes riveted to his face.

He began to pace about the room, picking up items from my table and putting them down again, his movements deliberate and slow. At length he came and stood close before me, so close that I could smell his tainted breath. I averted my face as he leaned nearer.

'You, Madam, are now without a father's protection,' he gloated. I kept my gaze on the window, my chin high and made no reply. He began to walk in circles around me, looking me up and down, his loathing of me apparent in every movement.

'You, madam,' he continued, 'are a slut and a whore and I will break you. Rest assured, your death will be both prolonged and painful.' I swallowed, disdaining to let him see I cared. 'When the screaming stops and you are finally dead, madam, you will receive no Christian burial. No, instead I will hang you high, like the traitor you are, and watch as the crows of my kingdom strip the flesh from your rancid bones. I will have your women and your children watch you die, and while your bones bleach in the sun, I will poison their memories of you. I will sell your bastard into slavery and I will make your sons hate you and feel shame for having been cursed with such a mother.'

It was difficult to draw breath. I could feel it rasping through my closed throat, sobbing tears not far away. Hatred tore at my mind so that I wanted to scream at him to stop, to take my dagger and thrust it deep into his gut, to claw out his eyes and laugh as the carrion feasted upon his remains.

'What say you to that, my fine whore?'he whispered, gripping my chin and pulling my face up to his. I closed my eyes against him, refusing to allow him to see my dread.

My lack of response was too much for him and he suddenly changed tack, thrusting me hard against the wall and wrenching my head back by the hair, his face inches from mine, his breath full in my face.

'I asked you a question,' he roared. I felt my neck would break; his body was thrust against mine in a grotesque mummery of our former intimacy.

Opening my eyes, I returned his stare and, my voice croaking through the restricted air passage, I spat the words at him.

'I say, that as the life drains from me, I will curse you Gruffydd. So that all that is now yours will perish, your strongholds will fall, your treasures will be lost and your people will turn from you. Your country will founder and never again rise to power; your countrymen will be vassals forever more. That is my curse, Gruffydd ap Llewellyn, and I will die willingly that it be so.'

His eye twitched as he drew away from me, the blood draining from his face and I knew I had penetrated the very nub of his superstitious fears.

He let go of me so abruptly that I dropped at his fee and, before he quit the chamber, he drew back his foot dealt me a stunning blow in the side.

He walked and as he slammed the door behind him away I managed to sit up and let loose a bitter laugh. A laugh that eddied and echoed about the room, spilled from the window and followed him into the night.

I harboured no doubt that he would keep his word and I found that, although I had so lately wished for death, my life was precious after all.

My prayers altered and I begged God to allow me a just a few weeks longer with the children. I had no hope for reprieve for who was there to save me?

Nest was fidgety with a head cold. She constantly rubbed at her nose with her fist, spreading the snot round her face and creating the additional problem of chapped cheeks.

One after the other the children had been ill. It was the coldest winter for many years and we spent as little time as possible away from the warmth of the fire. Prolonged confinement made the children argumentative and tetchy and, more than once, I regretted the self-imposed ban on nursemaids.

I asked Tangwystl to examine the young girls of the *llys* to see if there was one to whom I could entrust the children. She brought many girls too me but none were suitable until, in the end, she introduced me to one named Maude.

She was a timid child, extraordinarily plain and hampered with a palsied left side and, therefore, unlikely to attract male attentions. Her strange sideways gait meant she was awkward around the chamber but I liked her cheerfulness and admired her refusal to be inconvenienced by her crippled state.

Maude had steel in her heart and I knew that together with Anwen they would make formidable guardians of my children after my death. Idwal and Maredudd were wary of her at first but, once they had listened to her stories and realised her affliction wasn't the result of a devil's curse, they took to her and I gained some time to myself.

My life had shrunk. Wrapped against the cold in woollens and furs, a tear never far below the surface, I felt dead already. Although I was but eighteen years old and had scarcely begun to live, my time on Earth was almost over.

With my demise imminent I realised that I had never really lived, life had just happened to me. Apart from those few nights in Rhodri's arms I had made no choices, never been allowed to decide my own path. There were so many regrets, so much left unsaid, deeds left undone, places left unseen. Aching to live, each night I dreamed of Rhodri, felt his touch and his warm lips upon my skin, and in the morning, woke again bereft.

The cold that crept through the wattle walls of my chamber froze my frigid spirits further. My world was ice locked, the water left in my rooms for washing was solid each morning and the roaring fires and braziers did little to combat the cold that gusted beneath the doors, stirring the tapestries and snuffing the candles.

Most nights there was feasting in the hall but I was glad to be excluded from it. I was unwilling to be in Gruffydd's company, even at some remove. The bitter hatred that had pervaded the *llys* since the night of the killing was so strong that you could almost taste it. Discontent ruled at Rhuddlan now. I ate separate from the household. Food was brought to my apartments and I was grateful that Envys smuggled the choicest morsels beneath a cloth to tempt the colour to my cheeks. The gesture of support was great comfort and I wished I could thank her personally. I could only hope that the empty trays that I sent back to the kitchenhall evidenced my appreciation.

Nest was almost a year now and gloriously chubby; she pushed her food into her mouth, munching each morsel with stolid dedication.

The boys at three and two years old were becoming a handful but their noise at least leavened the loneliness a little. Christ's mass arrived and, for the first time, I was to be absent from the feast. Gruffydd instructed Anwen to accompany the boys to the table and they were in high excitement as they donned their best clothes, chattering about the bards and tumblers who would be present.

I listened to their footsteps pattering away and, faced with a solitary Christ's mass eve, memories of past celebrations flooded back, making the festive fayre stick in my throat.

The lilt of the harp found its way through the walls to where I lay on my bed and I could not help but recall Rhodri's skill with the instrument and remember his rich, Welsh accent as he sung for us all.

Despite the pain it brought I remembered the scene; as he told his tales of Carodog while the company did their best to drain Gruffydd's mead hall dry. Finding some comfort in the misery I travelled further back in my memories to other feasts in the far off days at my father's hall; the loud, jubilant revellers stripping the flesh from the roasted sucking pigs, the wine that had flowed and the riotous games and dancing that had followed. But on this night I could only hear the music of the revels and was allowed no part of it, just as I was allowed no part in life.

When the sounds of the roistering grew torrid I knew that Anwen and the children would soon return and, almost as the thought passed through my mind, the door opened and the children, protesting loudly all the way, were herded into my chamber.

The boys were rosy from over-indulgence and exertion; excitedly they related the events of the evening to me as we readied them for bed. They were joyous from the revel but, as I leaned over to kiss Idwal, he took my hand and held it fast in his.

'We missed you, Mother,' he said. Tears swam in his eyes and I realised with a jolt that he knew far more about my circumstances than I hoped. Mustering a cheery smile, I ruffled his hair.

'Oh, I had a fine time here in the warm with the babe,' I lied before bidding him good night.

His heavy eyes soon closed in sleep but I lay awake, listening until peace fell at last and I knew that Gruffydd and his men lay drunk about the hall.

Screams tore into my dreams, wrenching me from sleep. I sat up in my bed, reaching for my wrapper and yelling for Anwen, who was already leaping from her pallet. We hurried from the chamber together, colliding with Tangwystl who was tearing along the corridor in her night shift.

'What is happening, Tangwystl?' I cried.

'We are under attack, Lady, you must gather the children and prepare to leave. My Lord Gruffydd has ordered the household to flee to the western mountains.'

'Flee the *Llys*? Leave Rhuddlan? Are you sure? Who is it attacks us?'

'They say tis Harold o' Wessex, Lady, they are already upon us and have fired the stables and the grain store. Hurry, Lady, and get thee to the horses.'

That name sent the blood draining from my body as I grabbed my fur cloak, tying it with shaking hands over my nightclothes. Anwen was already bundling the children into their outdoor things and Maude was flinging our clothing into a sack.

'Come,' I cried, 'we must away. Forget the clothes.' Then, grabbing Nesta, I fled the chamber with the women and children in my wake.

Outside all was chaos, flames leapt and danced in the black sky and the air was filled with choking smoke. Horses were screaming and I knew that some of them had not been saved.

Men and women sped about, seeking escape, and I saw Envys, her mouth wide, waddling through the mire with her skirts held high above her fat knees.

Another scream, louder than the rest, and a man ran from the barn to throw himself into the slush of the farmyard in an attempt to quench the flames that engulfed him.

There was nothing I could do to help him and my duty lay with my children. Barely able to see through the smoke, I scanned the scene, unsure of where to run. Father Daffydd was gathering women and children to him in the churchyard, offering them the protection of his cloth; he was praying loudly to comfort the stricken.

I began to run toward him but, suddenly, one of Gruffydd's henchmen grabbed my arm. He was dressed for battle, half of his face obscured by his helm.

'Over here, Lady, mount up and prepare to ride out when you hear the order, don't look back and stop for nothing.'

The ponies he indicated were poor muddy creatures, they pranced about, pulling at their tethers, unsettled by the tumult. I wondered where Glimmer was but then, just as quickly, thrust the thought away.

Anwen helped me into the saddle and handed Nest up to me and then set Maude on her mount with Maredudd before her. I wrestled with the reins, securing a better grip, and looked up to see Anwen mounted and wrapping her cloak about Idwal's thin frame, the better to shield him from the cold. Idwal's eyes were huge, his face corpselike, all colour washed from his lips.

I smiled at him encouragingly. 'Do you have your sword, Idwal?' I asked, 'twill be a fine adventure and you may need it.'
He nodded earnestly and freed his arm from the cloak, indicating his wooden sword strapped to his waist.

'Good boy,' I said, 'now hold on tight, it may be a wild ride.'
He nodded again and my heart turned over in sudden fear for my children, so vulnerable and afraid. Then Gruffydd's voice cut through the commotion and, as the gates opened, the small cavalcade leapt into life and thundered through the gates and down the hill toward the river.

Hoof beats were drawing nearer and, knowing our pursuers were close, I kicked my pony mercilessly and we sped on, the icy wind cutting at my cheeks. Beneath my cloak Nesta clung to me although she made not a sound, and all the while I prayed for our safe deliverance.

Urging my mount faster through the steadily falling snow, I risked a glance behind me and could see horseman galloping, as recklessly as I, along the treacherous road. At the river crossing, where we were forced into single file, my horse's hooves slipped in the slushy mire but he regained his footing. As hard as I tried, I knew I was falling behind the rest of the party so I dug my heels into the pony's side again, desperate to catch up.

The foothills loomed before us, Tangwystl and Llyward were far ahead with the *tuelu* but Anwen and Maud rode a little in front of me, crouched forward, their cloaks flapping behind them. I heard Gruffydd shout something but I could not distinguish his words and, too late, I saw Maude's pony leaping over an obstacle. I gathered my reins belatedly but he mistimed his jump, clashing his foreleg into the fallen bough. As he began to fall I fought to keep my seat but, hampered as I was with Nesta, I flew over his head and landed heavily on the ground. Curling my body to protect the child, I rolled to the side of the trackway and struck my head upon something concealed beneath the snow.

The horse fell heavily beside me and then scrambled to his feet to stand, his reins trailing and his leg hanging useless. Dazed and winded, I tried to sit up and, as my head cleared, I heard Anwen's voice cry out in panic. I thought she was turning back for me and I tried to scramble up but, as I gazed blearily through the driving snow, I saw the indistinct figure of Gruffydd. His horse sidestepped and pranced in the snow for a brief moment before I heard his voice for the last time.

'Leave her.' he cried and, seizing Anwen's bridle, they galloped off into the hills.

Nest was whimpering and shivering with fright. I tried to scramble to my knees but they would not hold me. I held her close. 'It is alright,' I whispered, 'Mother's here,' but I knew it was far from alright and that I was in worse straits than I had ever been.

I looked for somewhere to run and saw in the distance that the squalid huddle of huts outside the *llys* walls were burning and that more flames leapt within the stronghold walls. Rhuddlan was vanquished and, as I watched through fogged eyes, the destruction of my home and heard the screams of the dying, I knew that Gruffydd had lost all and that my fate now lay in the hands of the Saxons.

Our pursuers approached. They almost rode past the place where I cowered in the snow but one of them saw me and drew to a halt, signalling to his companions to stop. The leader jumped down, leaving the reins dangling, he stooped and grabbed my hair, pulling my head back to look upon my face.

'Well, wot 'ave we 'ere?' he said, his Saxon tongue strange to my ears. His face was pushed close to mine and I could smell his unwashed body. 'A wench fer th' takin, boys and a foine lookin' one too. Let's tek 'er back wiv us, I'm damned if I'm gonna rut wiv 'er out 'ere in the snow.'

He gripped my upper arm and pulled me to my feet where I swayed dizzily from the blow I had received to my head. I wrestled weakly against him until he twisted my arm, snatching Nest from me and throwing her to the ground. I screamed and fought him, kicking and scratching, trying to gouge his eyes but my soft boots made no impact on his leather leggings and he easily overwhelmed me, pinioning my arms to my side. He shoved me against his horse,

'Come along, missy, show some willin' now, like a lady,' he said and, through the light material of my nightgown, I felt his hands on my body.

Nesta was crying in earnest now and I struggled, wanting to get to her but his arms held me fast, he lowered his face toward me but I whipped my head away, feeling his wet mouth slide across mine and the harshness of his beard scrape across my face.

'Noooo.' I screamed, as soon as my mouth was free, 'Get off me.' and, of a sudden, he was gone, struck down from behind. Finding myself suddenly freed, I slumped to the ground while my attackers grabbed their mounts and thundered back toward the blazing settlement.

I was on my hands and knees, the snowy biting cold through the thin cloth of my night gown. I looked up, blinking through the falling snow.

A horse, splendidly caparisoned, reared above me, his breath dragon-like in the frigid air. He pranced, snatching at his harness while his rider, swathed in furs and sitting tall in the saddle, curtailed his restiveness with a gauntleted hand.

I scrambled to where Nesta was bawling and cradled her to me; she was wet through, cold and shaken from her fall but we were trapped. I sent up a desperate prayer, awaiting our fate.

Thrusting his sword into its sheath, the fighting man took off his helmet, his hair falling in golden waves to the fur collar of his mantle.

'Come, Madam,' he commanded, reaching down his free hand to help me mount.

I hesitated, wildly weighing up my options. His expression was level and calm, his mouth framed by sweeping moustaches and his body richly clad. There was no doubting who he was, for he could be no other and, recognising defeat, I reached for the proffered hand and scrambled up before him onto his horse.

My head was level with his chin and, with both hands on the reins, his arms encircled Nesta and I in the warmth of his body, his hot breath whispering close to my ear.

At his signal, the horse leapt beneath us and we galloped away east, toward the Saxon border. Through a mist of tears, I saw Rhuddlan, that for five years had been my home, smouldering in the snow. Further off toward the coast further leaping flames bore witness to Gruffydd's blazing fleet of warships.

All was lost. I was escaping Gruffydd's punishment but at what cost? I wept, not for myself, but for my friends who were dying there, for the love I had known there and for the life I was leaving forever. But, most of all, I wept for my sons who, with every passing moment, were being taken further and further from my reach into the fastness of Snowdonia.

Part Three
The Fighting Man

Night was falling on the third day before we clattered into the yard at Kingsholm. Our arrival broke the evening hush and all was hubbub for a while. Children and dogs tumbled from within and curious members of the household appeared in their wake. Harold dismounted and lifted me down, steadying me while I found my feet after the long ride. My arms were numb from nursing Nesta and I smiled at a young female who gestured that she would take her from me. Handing the reins to a waiting groom, Harold said to the assembled household,

'You can address her in Saxon, she isn't a heathen; this is the Lady Eadgyth, daughter of Ælfgar and wife of the Welsh king. She will be lodging with us for a spell. You, Æthel, take her inside and see to her needs.'

He whirled off into the dusk as I followed the women into the lodge. It was pleasantly warm within after the bitter cold outside, the walls were hung with rich tapestries and cushioned chairs were pulled up close to the roaring hearth. The luxuries of the Saxon palace surpassed the more spartan comforts of Rhuddlan but I still yearned for the far off halls of home. Æthel smiled at me.

'You must be exhausted after such a hard ride, shall I show you to your chamber and have food sent to you there?'
The thought of a warm bed and dinner was more than I could resist so I nodded and reached for Nesta again;

'It's alright, Lady, I will bring her, we will be right behind you.'

How strange it seemed to hear the rhythm of Saxon speech again, the round vowel sounds sounded strange to my Welsh attuned ears. Music issued from somewhere within the palace confines but I was shown into a side room and, when I saw the sumptuous chamber with its roaring fire and the side-table laden with food, I was overcome. I plumped my bottom onto the nearest stool and let Æthel bring food to me, uncaring of what I ate or drank. There were apples, tangy and sweet, and nuts, rich pastries and a game pie. I ate as if I had not eaten for a twelvemonth and Nesta, when she stirred, saw the food and fell upon it too.

'What is this place?' I asked, once my appetite was quieted. Æthel looked up from my feet where she was engaged in easing off my slippers

'Kingsholm, Lady, near Gleawanceaster. Tis King Edward's hunting lodge. The king and his court are here for Christ's mass celebrations, it is a favoured palace of the royal family.'

I put down my knife and watched Æthel as she regarded the slippers with some disgust before throwing them onto the fire.

'The King is here? He sent the army forth into Wales from here?'

'Yes, Lady, the King and Earl Harold have been talking of little else all through the celebrations. King Edward is right glad to have struck the enemy so hard.'

The Enemy. That was *me*, I recalled with a start.

'I see,' I said, although I didn't really. I did not understand how it had been possible for Harold and his troop to have ridden so freely into Wales and all but murdered the king's household in their beds.

'We must find you some fresh garments, Lady. How came you to be abroad in your nightshift?'

I looked down at myself, muddied and mired from the mad ride.

'Your army came upon us unawares as we slept. We fled the burning *llys* with little warning; the rest of our party rode into the mountains but I fell from my horse and was captured.'

'Gracious God. 'Tis lucky you have your child with you madam and she is unharmed. You must not be worried for your safety now, Earl Harold does not make war on women and children.'

I pondered upon the fate of the children of Rhuddlan that I had seen running from Saxon swords. I recalled the screams of the women as they fell victim to Saxon lusts and then I remembered Idwal's stricken expression as we prepared to take that last ride.

'My sons were carried off by their father, into the mountains.'

Æthel sat up.

'Oh, Lady, I knew not that you had sons. I am certain they will be safe with their father, for every father values his sons above all else.'

She continued to wash my muddy feet and legs while the memory of Gruffydd's disdain for Rhodri reared wraithlike before my eyes. I hoped he would not vent his hatred for me upon his children.

'I will pray that your words are true, Æthel,' I said as I climbed into the high wooden bed, 'but their father is quite unlike other men.'

When Nest and I snuggled down into the soft linen for all my exhaustion I could not sleep at first. I watched her eyes grow heavy, her lids drooping, closing and opening again but, over come by the comfort, I could not stay awake long enough to see her fall asleep.

Hours later I was roused by a loud knocking on the chamber door and I heard Æthel in conversation.

'She sleeps still, Lord, you must come back later.'

'But tis past noon, woman, she has slept for hours.'

'Tis the trauma, Lord. Wrenched from her bed as she was and then falling from her horse and captured, only to be dragged across country on horseback. She told me all about it, tis no wonder she sleeps still.'

'You, my girl, are too argumentative for your own good but I suppose you speak true. I trust you will send her to me should she wake?'

As Æthel turned from the closed door she saw me watching her and put a finger to her lips.

'Sssh, twill do him no harm to bide awhile. Did his knocking wake you, Lady? Did you sleep well?'

'Yes …' I said, pulling myself up gently so as not to disturb Nest who lay beside me, her face rosy with sleep, '…like the dead.'

'She is a rare beauty, Lady, she will break some hearts when she is older.'

I sipped the drink that Æthel offered me before replying. 'She is like her father'

'Gruffydd? Goodness, I held a very different picture of him in my mind.'

Remembering to whom I spoke, I corrected my line of thought. 'Oh, I'm told he was different in his youth. Our old cook Envys …' I said, swallowing my sorrow as I recalled that she was probably dead, 'told me some fine tales about his youth. It seems he was both a musician and a scholar before he turned to warfare.'

Æthel held out some gowns for my inspection.

'Shame he didn't stick to singing then, Lady. Good folks, both sides of the border, have suffered around here for Gruffydd's blood lust. We found these gowns, Lady, they used to belong to Queen Edith but she says you are welcome to them. I think you are of a size, although you might be a touch broader across the shoulder. Come, wash your face and hands and we will try them on. Earl Harold wishes to speak with you when you have broken your fast.'

Harold was alone when I was brought before him. He turned and looked me up and down.

'Ah.' he cried, 'the Lady Eadgyth, I hardly knew you in your clothes.'

I blushed and lowered my head, curtseying but not too lowly, remembering I was a queen to his Earl.

'Earl Harold,' I murmured, 'I thank you for your hospitality.'

'Now look,' he said, 'don't be formal with me; I don't like it. My name is Harold so please address me as such. I suspicion you think of me as an enemy, well

I'm not, your brothers told me to fetch you back, should I have the chance.'

'My brothers? Why ever should they do that?'

'War is an unpleasant thing, Lady, and they wanted you out of it. 'Course I couldn't promise 'em anything but there you were and so I brought you … and your daughter too. 'Twas just a piece of luck.'

'Whether I wanted to come or no.' I exclaimed; annoyed at the assumptions he was making. 'I am not my brothers' property, Lord, any more than I am my husband's.'

My cup clashed as I replaced it on the table making Harold look up, surprised at my ire.

'We assumed you would want to come. You are Saxon aren't you? Why should you wish to stay on the heathen side of the dyke? Good Lord, things aren't going to be pretty there ye know. All Gruffydd's possessions are forfeit, 'tis only a matter of time before he is captured and killed. His men turn against him.'

I thought briefly of the gentle folk I had lived with in *Cymru*, people who fought for their perceived rights, people who grieved for past defeats but determined to fight on anyway.

If love and compassion for one's countrymen and empathy with the land of one's birth were heathen impulses, then the Welsh were indeed heathen. The idea of Wales, war torn and defeated, sent a twist of dread into my guts; fear for my sons sickened me.

'Which men?' I asked when I was sure I would not vomit.

'tis not for me t' name names, Lady, but we were able to ride unchallenged through both Powys and Gwyneydd. There is much discontent beneath your husband's rule, are you unaware of that?'

Remembering the surly faces of the household when Gruffydd was near by, I wondered for the first time how widespread discontent was outside Rhuddlan. He was a harsh leader, I knew that, but he had united all Wales and fought to control and protect the country from its enemies. There was no denying that the good of Wales lay at the heart of all his callousness. At what cost had that protection come though? I recalled the stories of his conquest of neighbouring princedoms, of his reckless justice. I remembered the smell of death on his clothes when he came home from campaigning and I knew that Harold spoke the truth. I turned to him with tears on my lashes.

'But what of the people of Rhuddlan? They did not deserve to die? They were good people. They were my people. Why did you order your troop to deal so harshly with them? With the women and children … who could do you no harm?'

Harold straightened his jerkin and came closer, fixing me with his thick lashed blue eyes.

'Had you seen the burned out homesteads along the border, Welsh and Saxon alike, you would not ask that, Lady. I have ridden into settlements where there remained not a creature living or unmolested after your Lord's troop has passed through. You would not ask, Lady, had you seen what I have seen. You know not what that man is capable of'.

His chin jutted forward in righteous indignation before he continued. 'I have seen much death in battle, Madam, but in Gruffydd's Wales, I have seen things done unto his own people such as I never wish to see again.'

Flustered, I sat down and got up again, walked a short distance away and then the same distance back to face him again.

'You mistake me, Lord,' I said, turning from him to look deep into the flaming hearth, 'I have more cause to hate Gruffydd than you can ever know, if I were to come upon you with your sword raised o'er his head ready to make the killing blow, I should take the weapon from you only to make the final strike myself.'
Harold raised his brows questioningly, while I continued.

'I will do nothing to prevent you in your campaign against Gruffydd and you have my blessing. But I do protest most strongly, Lord, if you ride against the people of Wales and against my children who are even now in their father's custody in Snowdonia.'

'Your children?'

'My sons, Idwal and Maredudd are in Gruffydd's keeping. Deal with him as you will, My Lord, but bring my boys back safe to me.'

I asked Æthel to draw me a bath, unusual in winter, but my body felt bruised and battered after my adventures and I felt the need to freshen myself before I met with the Saxon king. Muttering of the strange heathen ways of the Welsh, the women brought jug after jug of hot water and began to fill the tub. The shutters were closed, the torches lit and the fire in the hearth was built up high. Stripped of my clothes, I lowered my body into the steaming waters and lay back, letting the warmth ease away the worst of my anguish. Æthel and Mary scattered dried flowers and herbs into the water, the aromatic mist swirling about the room, lifting our mood a little.

'Well, I've never, in all my days, known a lady take a bath in January,' commented Æthel as she poured a jug of water over me and began to scrub my back. 'You are never intending to do your hair as well, Lady, surely. You will take a chill and die, you just mark my words.'

'Just look at it, Æthel, I cannot greet the king with hair like straw. I will not come to harm; in Wales they bathe in the rivers and sea when the weather is clement.'

Æthel snorted.

'Yes, well I can believe that but you are not Welsh are you? I suppose my grandmother was right when she said that if you lie down with dogs you get up with fleas.'

I laughed, my first since goodness knows when.

'Do you not know any Welsh folk, Æthel? They are not heathens at all. Some of their habits and traditions are different to ours but, most of them are good, honest sorts.'

Æthel snorted, her expression disbelieving.

'I suppose there must be some good Welshmen, Lady, but I can't say as I've ever met one and, if you want my advice, I'd keep your good opinion of 'em to yourself when you have audience with the King. You'd do well to remember you are a Saxon lady now and try to put off all the Welsh ways you have acquired.'

Shaking out a sage green gown, Æthel turned to where I sat drying before the fire. 'Is this one to your liking, Lady?'

'That will do, Æthel, thank you,' I replied, unconcerned that it looked a little short. Rising, and letting the towel drop, she helped me into it, lacing the ties and fastening the shoulder clasps. The sleeves were a little on the short side and my slippers were clearly visible but it would do. When the veil was placed on my braided hair, I hugged Nest, promising to return shortly, and followed my escort to the king's chamber.

King Edward was bent over state papers, he looked up, 'Ah,' he said, his voice thin and nasal, 'the Lady Eadgyth, do come in.'

I curtsied but to not too low, I was, after all, still Queen of Wales.

'Glad to have you come safely out of Wales, my dear. Since young Edwin's assumption of your father's lands, your brothers have been most concerned for your welfare. You are a lucky woman to have such loving siblings.'

'Yes, Sire,' I replied, thinking that there was probably a more mercenary reason for their solicitude. 'Earl Harold was speaking to me last evening of his plan to track my Lord husband down and take control of his domains.'

Edward stood up and began to pace the floor, his hands clasped behind his back. He was not as tall as he first appeared, his extreme slenderness making him seem loftier than he was. He turned to me, a hand to his once yellow beard; his eyes were rhuemy and, with some surprise, I realised he was ailing.

'Yes, he is very determined to end the strife that Wales presents,' he confessed, 'Gruffydd swore fealty to me not two years since, yet, as soon as he was safe back in his dominions, he continued to ravage the borderlands. I cannot have it, Eadgyth, I cannot have it at all.'

As he spoke he did not meet my eye and I found myself distrusting the shiftiness of his manner. He did not act like a king should and I remembered Gruffydd accusing him of letting others do his dirty business for him, a thing that my husband, for all his faults, could never be accused of.

'When is the proposed attack likely to take place?' I asked, accompanying him as he resumed his pacing of the hall. He stopped abruptly and I pulled up beside him.

'You can be sure that it will be soon, my dear, but I do not propose to impart the detail to you, who may yet prove to be a traitor.'

Dumbfounded, I could not help the impatience that crept into my voice;

'It seems whatever I do I will be deemed a traitor by someone. My Welsh kin will no doubt see my disappearance as betrayal and, should I decide to return home to *Cymru*, then my Saxon kin will brand me turncoat also. Seems my situation is one I cannot win.'

'Quite,' he replied, 'so my advice to you is to stay here and keep out of trouble until the deed be done. Your brothers are occupied on state business at the moment but will, no doubt, ride in for you as soon as they may.'

He waved me away with a limp hand but I stayed where I was.

'There is the matter of my sons, Sire, that I wished to discuss with you'

'Ah yes, Earl Harold told me of Gruffydd's sons. You expect me to redeem them and turn them over to you do you not? Tell me, Lady,' he asked, pressing his fingertips together, 'how do you expect me to believe that they will not present some future threat to this country's security? If 't were the other way about I have no doubt Gruffydd would not hesitate to have my own sons, had I any, destroyed as one would dispatch vipers in a nest.'

My mouth opened and shut as I fumbled for a persuasive answer, then, careful not to offend his fragile ego, I said,

'Sire, if my sons were raised in the Saxon court they would, in time, prove most desirable rulers of Wales for you. They could learn, under your leadership, the importance of peace between the two nations and under your combined rule England and Wales could become, at last, united.'

Edward regarded me from beneath greying brows.

'Hmm, whoever it was that said women lacked a man's capacity for policy obviously had not met you. Now, go away and leave me think on this, I will no doubt see you in a day or two.'

Turning his back on me, I bowed my head and left his chamber but, once outside the door, fear for my sons grew so strong that I lay back against it with my heart banging in my ribcage and sweat breaking out on my forehead.

A few days later I was summoned to the queen's presence. I donned the best of the gowns she had gifted me and, bracing my shoulders, took my place at the door of her bower. A faint voice summoned me in and, lifting the latch, I walked into the hall. She was not alone, the room was littered with elegant hangers on.

'Eadgyth, darling.' cried the queen bearing down upon me, 'you poor thing. My brother has told me all about it. You are quite a heroine. I for one could never have borne such indignity … but then I suspect you must be used to such inconveniences in

Wales. Mind you, you couldn't have wished for a more handsome redeemer, could you?'

I glanced from her to Harold, mentally reminding myself that he was the queen's brother. Old Godwin, in offering his daughter to Edward, had made it an offer the king could not refuse. Now, as she made it clear to all assembled that I was to be a favourite of England's queen, her voice was loaded with insincerity. Pulling back and bestowing a sympathetic grimace, she linked her arm in mine and led me about the hall. It was crowded with curious onlookers and Edith, dressed in her best, played to the crowd. The reason for such favouritism escaped me and I waited with baited breath to learn of it.

Harold and the king were engaged in their own conversation and Edward paid us little mind but I could feel Harold's eyes follow us about the room.

'My brother is so very striking, don't you think?' rattled the queen, 'Of all my brothers he is by far the best looking although they are all fine specimens. Leofwine and Gyrth, for all their Viking looks, somehow fall short and Tostig, have you met Tostig? He is my favourite brother but far too pretty for my liking. Harold, however, is everything a man should be, do you not agree?'

'I'm sure I do, Madam,' I replied, 'although, 'til now, I have given the matter little thought.'
Her laugh rang out, startling those closest to us, heads turned in our direction to see what was so amusing their queen.

'I cannot believe, Eadgyth, that a midnight rescue by a man like Harold can have had no effect upon you, why a nun could not fail to notice his most masculine attractions.'

Harold was watching us from the other side of the room with a smirk on his lips, he raised an eyebrow at me but I turned away, refusing to acknowledge him.

'My mind has been distracted with thoughts of my sons Madam, whose lives, as I'm sure you know, are in grave danger.'

She sobered slightly, 'Oh yes, your sons. I had heard something. I, of course, have no sons Eadgyth, and so I must envy you twice; once for your dashing rescue and once for the luxury of motherhood.'

Edith and Edward had produced no heir for England, a lack that could not fail to ignite the imagination of the court gossips. Various explanations were bandied about; some believed that Edith was barren and should, therefore, have been put aside years ago in favour of a younger, more fertile wife. Edward declined to do so and his lack of action prompted the less charitable of his subjects to suspect the nature of his sexual preference.

The official story was that the king's devout nature precluded carnal relations of any sort and so he had taken an oath of celibacy but, wherever he went, he was trailed by a group of sycophantic young males, all bickering hopefully among themselves and vying for the king's favour. Whether the king had any idea as to their intention is a matter for debate.

We strolled about the hall together with a group of the queen's ladies in our wake.

'Tell me, Eadgyth, would you care to join my ladies in waiting? I know you are without proper support while you await the arrival of your brothers and Edward and I thought you could join my household. Keep you out of trouble, so to speak …' she said, patting my wrist.

I could not, of course, refuse for she was right, I had no support and even my social status was questionable. I did not know if I were still a queen, or wed or widowed. I also knew that if I became her lady in waiting we would no longer be of equal status; I would be in her service. But, finding myself trapped, I took a deep breath and gave the answer I knew she required.

'Twould be an honour, Madam, I thank you. I will be glad to be of service to you, at least until my brothers or my husband come to take me away.'

'Marvellous.' she cried, clapping her hands together, making her jewelled bangles rattle. 'Edward. Harold. Eadgyth agrees to join my happy little household.' Beaming upon the company, she gabbled on, making plans and issuing orders for my meagre possessions to be moved to her apartments.

Nesta had learned to pull herself up on the furniture and one afternoon she crawled across the floor and pulled herself up on the queen's chair. Smacking her little hand on the velveted royal knee, she gurgled up at Edith in a friendly manner. The queen drew back.

'What does she want, Eadgyth?' she asked, her voice shrill with uncertainty.

'Attention, Madam, she craves attention like a pig craves his swill,' answered Æthel, sweeping Nest into her arms. I watched them from my seat at the hearthside; the queen was looking at Nest with a curious mix of longing and repugnance.

'Would you like to hold her on your knee, Madam?' I asked spontaneously.

Edith hesitated, 'I don't know, Eadgyth, babies are an enigma to me. How do I do it?' she asked. I got up and took the babe from Æthel's arms and placed her on the queen's knee. Edith placed tentative hands on the child and risked a small smile.

'There,' she said, 'we are quite comfy are we not, Nest?' although she did not sound it. Nest gurgled up at her, a trickle of dribble on her chin. She waved her arms up and down, smiling at the company while the ageing queen sat transfixed as though the jewel she held was priceless …which of course she was.

The chamber door creaked open and Harold poked his head round, seeing us gathered at the fire he came in and joined us.

'Well, well, Edith, 'tis an unusual diversion for you. Hello Nest,' he said, crouching down and taking the child's hand and pumping her arm up and down.

'Teething I see,' he said, indicating the dribble, 'have you sent to the still room for some salve?'
I raised my eyebrows at his parenting skill.

'She makes no complaint, Lord, she is blessed with a happy soul and nothing seems to dent it, not even pain …or peril.'

'Aye, she was quiet on our journey was she not? My own whelps are a different kettle of fish I can tell you. When young Gyrth was in tooth he wailed so much I wanted to throw him from the nearest window.'
A titter of laughter ran about the room. 'Seven I have, four boys and three girls, each and every one of them a monster.' he declared.

'And each and every one a bastard too,' pouted the queen, 'tis time you forgot that commoner you are hand-fasted with and sought yourself a proper wife.'

'Edith.' Harold remonstrated, 'we have been through this. Eadgytha serves me well; 'tis nigh on twenty years she has been my mistress and never once have you shown her a friendly face.'

The queen's pursed lips confirmed her age, a small frown marring the royal brow.
'tis unseemly. You should think of your family and marry well, there's no profit clinging to the old Scandinavian ways. Many a benefit comes with a wellborn woman.'

'And many an earache too, I imagine.' he cried, laughing expansively with the queen's women. 'Here, Edith, let me take the child before you drop her, look at how she has drooled all down the front of your gown.'
I blanched at the sight of the queen's brocade tunic all daubed and despoiled with dribble.

Following my line of vision Edith looked down and shrugged, 'I have other gowns,' she said, her eyes following Nest as she was borne in Harold's arms across the room.

Drinks were handed round and the company broke up into small groups. Seeking Harold, I stood before him trying not to let his personality distract me as it was want to do.

'When do you ride again into Wales, Lord?'
He looked at me from the corner of his eye.

'Straight to the point as ever, I see. Have you not discussed it with the queen?'
We both looked toward the queen who sat dabbing at the front of her gown with a kerchief.

'Their highnesses are reluctant to speak politics with me. I have yet to prove myself a loyal Saxon.'

'Hmmm,' said Harold noncommittally, taking a large swig of his ale and sloshing it around his mouth.

'I have been in conference with my brother, Tostig. You may have seen him about court, a pretty fellow, a favourite of the king. Anyway, we hope to launch the attack by the end of May, when our Welsh collaborators swear to turn Gruffydd over to us. There will be bloodshed, Lady, but I promise to have a care of your children.'

My heart thumped, loud and slow, beneath my bodice,

'And their nurses, Harold, they are my friends, one has been with me since childhood.'

'…and their nurses. Tell me,' he said quietly, leading me to a secluded corner, 'how do you find my sister? Do you not find her unbearably shallow?'

I looked to where the queen sat, leaning forward to wave at Nesta on the other side of the hearth.

'I find her sad, Lord. She seems without purpose, a situation apt to make the best of us seem shallow.'

'tis just as well Edward can't get it up, Edith would have made a terrible mother. Over indulgence breeds spoiled, insipid men and England can do without an heir like that.'

'Can't get it up?' I mouthed, curiosity getting the best of me. It was a dangerous way even for a Godwin to talk about his king.

Tipping the dregs of his vessel into his throat, he swallowed audibly and wiped the froth onto his sleeve.

'Oh yes, Edward is impotent, Edith told me years ago that he couldn't manage it. No more potent than elderberry juice. It was me who came up with the notion of piety for him and he was glad enough to take the excuse. Truth be told, he can't bear women. I blame his mother, Emma. She neglected him as a child

and unmanned him as an adult. There's usually a bad woman lurking behind a weak man.'
He fixed me with his blue eyes and I felt myself flushing. 'And your mother I presume, my Lord, was irreproachable.'

'Oh, damn yes. And she still is, Lady. Gytha, half Danish, sister in law to King Cnut. Marvellous woman, raised the lot of us and there's not a Godwin alive you can't call a man …even Tostig is like an angry bear on the battlefield.'

He strutted away and, open-mouthed, I watched him go, unbidden laughter fermenting in my stomach. I schooled my face to its usual sombre expression and turned to make conversation with the women.

Irrepressibly arrogant as the man was, it was difficult to get Harold out of my mind. The treason bubbling beneath the surface of his humour both attracted and repelled me and I wondered just how much of his loyalty lay with the king and how much with himself.

<u>April 1063</u>

The tedium of Edith's court frustrated me; the days were filled in idleness and I found the company lacked the depth and breadth of those at Rhuddlan. I had made no real friends and Edith's brittle personality grated upon my nerves. I found myself on edge and having to bite back curt retorts to her insensitive remarks. She was unable to see a situation from any perspective other than her own. If she wished to dance, we all had to join in and if she wished to listen to dreary homilies about the piety of the king, then we all listened.

I found that the poetry of the Saxon court was very different to that of the Welsh. It lacked the wistful longing of the past that I had found so touching in Rhuddlan, the Saxon poets sang of glory not of regret. And, unused as I was, to the segregation of nobility and staff at the royal palace, I made many errors of etiquette.

At Rhuddlan I had enjoyed sitting with the kitchen staff, hearing their tales and joining in their laughter but here it was frowned upon and, on one occasion, Edith even reprimanded me for thanking a slave when she brought me a fresh skein of silks from the store room.

I missed Anwen. As pleasant a girl as Æthel was, she could not begin to replace my lifelong companion and I fretted for her safety and prayed God to send her the strength she needed to care for and protect my boys. Goodness knows what perils beset them and Idwal's strained face continually floated before my mind. I knew they would worry for me for they had no way of knowing my fate and in all likelihood thought me dead.

Agitation and boredom made me snappy and I longed for the day that Harold would ride forth to bring the children safe home. It did not occur to me then that Edward and Harold may have ulterior motives for rescuing the boys and that, in securing Gruffydd's heirs they served, not just my maternal longing but, national security.

It was late April before the men were ready to ride out and I rose early that morning and prepared to see them off.

Some mornings are unsurpassable in their beauty and the day of Harold's departure was one such. The sky was so brittle I felt that, if it were possible to cast a stone high enough, the blue would shatter and fall about my feet in shards.

Birds sang and the lambs in the pasture leapt and twitched their tails in pleasure of being alive. Outside the *llys*, serfs tilled the soil ready for the new growing season and the women stood about in groups by the gates, ostensibly to take washing to the river, but in truth, enjoying the feel of the sun on their faces after the long harsh winter months.

It was early. I had my kerchief tucked at my bodice the better to wave the men off to war and the breeze whipped and snapped at my veil as I watched the chaotic scene from the steps of the royal hall.

Harold's fighting men of Wessex prepared to ride to Bristol from whence they planned to sail around the coast to attack Gruffydd from the West. Tostig and his armies would ride across the border from Chester to attack the Welsh on land.

The previous evening Harold has spoken of his intention to target Anglesey at the north-western tip of the country. I knew that Angelsey, or Mon as the Welsh called it, was the granary of Wales, the place where the best grain was grown. I was uneasy although I knew the strategic importance of hitting the enemy where they would suffer soonest. In hitting Anglesey they effectively severed the Welsh food supply, by starving the enemy their defences would weaken and the war be won the quicker. I could not but think of the innocents who would starve, my friends that would suffer and the children and old folk that would sicken and die.

I wished there were an easier way, a way to target Gruffydd alone, extricate Anwen and the children and come to some accord with the remaining Welsh princes. I had no love of war, I wanted peace and was still naïve enough to believe it were obtainable.

Biting my lips sore with anxiety, I hopped from foot to foot, eager for Harold to emerge from his quarters that I might speak to him before he left. His horse stood waiting. Harold's groom, with the hunting dogs prowling about his feet and his master's hawk on his wrist was also waiting, far more patiently than I. Horses and supply wagons filled the palace yard and began to slowly progress toward the burgh gate. Then men, dressed for battle, mounted their steeds and moved in unison through the gate.

'Where is he? Where is he?' The refrain that beat in my head and then … I saw him, emerging from a lodging across the courtyard. A woman was with him and I knew by her bearing and grace that she must be his concubine, Eadgytha of the swan neck.

She did not look especially beautiful, certainly not as fair as the gossips implied. To my eighteen years she appeared rather old and worn looking, more like an old duck than a swan. As I watched, my suspicions were confirmed and I saw him hold her close to him for a heartbeat and plant a kiss upon her forehead.

He strode away toward his horse but, at the last moment, he caught sight of me and, instead of mounting, he crossed the busy enclosure to bend over my hand. His lips were warm on my skin and when he stood up his eyes reflected the sky. I felt my insides jolt. 'My Lord,' I murmured, wishing he were not so beautiful, 'I wanted to wish you well in your quest and to bid you have a care.'

'I am grateful for your blessing, Lady,' he said, mocking me even at this crucial hour. My mouth was dry and I felt suddenly afraid for him, afraid he would not succeed, afraid he would die and my sons be lost to me. I did not know how to make him understand that it was imperative that he succeed.

Fixing my eyes on the enormous rectangular emerald brooch that fastened his cloak, I whispered,

'I beg you, bring my sons safe home, Harold.' Receiving no reply, I eventually raised my eyes to find he was regarding me with his usual teasing, lopsided grin. My stomach lurched so violently that I felt quite sick but, swallowing bile, I summoned what I hoped was a nonchalant smile,

'God b' with thee, Lord,' I said.

'And with thee, Lady,' he returned and taking my hand, placed his lips upon it again but, this time, I gasped to feel his tongue snake across my skin. He stood up, arrogant and silently laughing at my indignation. I pursed my lips and scowled at him.

'I will return, Madam,' he said and, before mounting his horse, he snatched my kerchief from where it hung at my bodice and inhaled its scent deeply before shoving it into his tunic.

'For luck,' he winked and galloped away in pursuit of the other men, leaving me outraged on the steps.

Stamping my foot and giving vent to a growl of rage I turned and swept back into the palace swearing that, once I had my children back safe, I would have nothing more to do with such a man.

For three long months we had no word and everyday at the palace was a nightmare of uncertainty.

The queen prattled on, she had engaged herself with the task of compiling a book, praising the virtue and piety of the king, her husband and, at the same time, extolling the virtues of the Godwin family.

Of course, her intention was not to write it herself but she had engaged the services of a monk from the abbey of St. Bertin at St. Omer. I sat with the other women at Edith's side, embroidering a seat cover while she enthused about her brothers and her wondrous father and the monk silently scratched notes onto his parchment. On and on she went and, sometimes, the room grew so stifling hot and my frayed nerves so raw that I pleaded sickness to escape the confinements of the hall.

Roaming the fields and woods that surrounded the settlement I could breathe. I could lie in the grass and close my eyes against the world and pretend that my life was different. My mind would drift back to my dream of being the wife of a penniless cottager, free from the cares of state. Even a bonded slave had more freedoms than a princess.

After one such afternoon I returned to the palace to find that the queen had been calling for me so, hastily changing from my muddied tunic into a plain yellow gown, I hurried to her chambers.

'Eadgyth. There you are.' she cried when she saw me, 'I suppose you have been tramping bout the countryside like a hoyden again. I wish you would not go about unattended, there are those that wish us ill you know.'

'Yes, Madam, I'm sorry but sometimes I feel so closed in that I need to go outside and breathe the open air.'

'A habit picked up from those heathens over the dyke, no doubt,' she remarked.

'Do you hunt, Lady?' asked a quiet voice and I jumped, for I had not known of the king's presence. I swept a curtsey before replying,

'No, Sire, not since I was a child at my father's house.'

Edward shuffled forward, playing with the ends of his sparse beard.

'You should try it, Lady, you would like it, there is nothing like the feel of the wind in your face and a strong horse beneath you. In my youth I was ever in the saddle but, of late, the gripes of age prevent me from riding out as often as I wish.'

'My brothers all love the hunt, Lady,' interrupted the queen, 'but, of course, you know that don't you dear, since Harold in particular is seldom without his bird on his wrist. Ooh, that reminds me, that's why I sought you out, we have a missive from Harold which I thought you'd like to hear. Come, here it is; you can read it aloud to us, we are not adverse to hearing such good news again.'

I all but snatched the letter from her hand and quickly scanned the single page of Harold's bold black script before clearing my throat and reading.

Greetings from Harold, Earl and Lord of Wessex to Edward, by the grace of God, King of England and my queen and sister, Edith, wishing you perpetual health in Christ.

This missive must needs be brief but, be assured, the message it conveys is a blessed one. After much harrying of the western coast of Wales, my ships,

combined with my noble brother Tostig's forces that struck from the east, have managed, with intervention of certain of his enemies, to subdue and overcome Gruffydd, heretofore, leader of the Welsh nation.
After laying waste to Anglesey our ships sailed south putting in at various inlets and burning all we found there. With a hold full of hostages we sailed onward ever-parallel to Tostig's forces, whose movements mirrored our own, we crushed all in our path, showing no mercy until the Welsh, in desperation, rose up against their leader and delivered him from the fastness of Snowdonia into our hands, together with various other members of his household.
Anticipating your royal wishes, my Lord King, I have placed the former lands of Gruffydd in the hands of his half brothers, Bleddyn and Rhiwallon, who have aided us in our quest. These lords have sworn fealty to the Saxon crown and pledged to serve us by both land and water should the need arise. Powys and Gwynedd are subdued and peace promised. I inform you Sire that, my task complete, I am today set upon my return journey.

May your Majesties fare ever well.

Harold

Letting the parchment fall into my lap, I looked agape at the king. 'He returns.' I cried, 'but makes no mention of my sons. He brings forth my husband but leaves my children behind. God's teeth.'

I leapt to my feet and began to pace the room, Edward picked up the letter from where it had fluttered to the rushes and poked at it with his finger.

'You mistake him, Lady, see here, where he says 'together with various other members of his household,' that must indicate he has the children safe and brings them home with his prisoners. Do not fret, Eadgyth, Harold is not a man to leave a job half done, he will return with the boys or not at all.'

'That's very true,' chimed in Edith, 'if I know my brother, he will be tucking them in at night himself and telling them stories to ease their journey. He has ever had a taking for young ones, ever since that woman of his started to produce them like a fat mouser dropping kittens.'

Edith pouted, petulantly indulging her dislike of Harold's mistress. Seeing the king and queen eagerly trying to convince me that my children were safe, for the first time I let myself believe that their show of favour held no ulterior motive.

Edith leaned toward me, a look of insipid sympathy on her face, while Edward, still scratching at his beard, stood similarly expressive beside her.

'Do you really believe so?' I cried, tears gathering on my lashes, 'after so many months of worry, do you really believe Harold has them safe?'

Edward signalled for a boy to bring wine and handed me a cup. I plopped onto a stool and drank deeply while the king stood beside me, patting my shoulder and looking to his queen for help. Uncomfortable with women, Edward made his escape as soon as he could, telling me I could keep the letter if I thought it would bring some comfort. When he had gone Edith beamed at me.

'Just you wait and see, Eadgyth,' she gushed, 'it will all be over soon, Harold will bring your boys home and you will have every cause to be grateful to him won't you? He is a fine warrior, my brother, very kind and he will care for your boys as if he were their father.'

'And what of my boy's father, Madam, what will Harold have Edward do with him?'
Edith shook her head, selecting an apple from the bowl at her side and began to slice it with her pocket-knife.

'Oh, nothing much I expect. Edward isn't a great one for handing out death sentences, although Gruffydd deserves it for breaking his treaty and pledge to the Saxon throne. Edward is far too concerned with his soul's respite to be overly harsh. I dare say he will ignore Harold's demands to have him killed and have him set in chains and locked away somewhere safe instead. Mind you, prisoners seldom live long, in my experience, it seems the lack of sun and freedom kills a man's spirit first and then his body perishes soon after. Edward was exiled in his youth you know, lived at the court of Normandy while Cnut was on his throne; he has never forgotten it. Although he was fed and clothed and among friends, he says that exile was worse than death. When he was finally able to come back and claim his rightful crown, he found he missed Normandy, his place of exile, so much that he has filled his court with all his Norman friends. I don't know, dear, there's no understanding men, really there isn't.'

Smiling dutifully at her joke, my mind wandered off, wondering if, even now, my lost family were disembarking at Bristol and whipping up the horses for the ride to the royal court.

I felt for them, they had little Saxon and would find it hard here, harder than I had when I arrived in Wales. The Saxons were far more intolerant of the Welsh than the Welsh were of the Saxons. Even I, for my very proximity to the people of *Cymru*, were shunned by some at this court. I was fearful, for my boys were such babes and the world so full of peril.

That night, when sleep escaped me, I held Nest close and prayed for her brothers' safe deliverance. I bargained with God to give up all that I had, if only he would spare me my children. If they were returned safe I would forsake all future happiness.

The king and his court celebrated victory over the old Welsh enemy with a great feast. Wine flowed and music played as the company stuffed themselves with dainties. Awash with wine, the men grew loud, the ladies tittered behind their hands as the crudities grew to such proportion that the saintly king grew shocked. His face pinched and his eyes disapproving, he clapped his hands and called for quiet and then summoned for the minstrel to recite a gentle poem.

The minstrel was from Normandy, foppish and colourful, he strutted to the centre of the hall and stood before the king's table. Strumming a note on his harp to call the attention of the hall, he began to sing the old lay of Byrhtnoth, Earl of Essex, and the famous battle of Maldon fought some seventy years ago. Although the Saxons had lost that battle, they sang its praises nonetheless, proud of the manner in which the lord had died. The minstrel's voice, rich and bracing, lifted to the smoky rafters and, in an instant, all were entranced, even I, who was so heartily sick of battle.

"Our hearts must grow resolute, our courage more valiant,
our spirits must be greater, though our strength grows less.

Here lies our Lord all hewn down, goodly he lies in the dust. A kinsman mourns
that who now from this battle-play thinks to turn away.
I am advanced in years. I do not desire to be taken away, but I by my liege Lord,
by that favourite of men I intend to lie."

The minstrel's words trailed away and the company sat up as the ornate doors of the hall burst open and Harold strode into the room, armed and muddy and seeming to have stepped straight out of the poem.

Sweeping a low bow, his sword clanking at his hip, his eyes scanned the hall. He looked as healthy as a horse, his face tanned and his hair bleached almost white from his sea voyages. Although I had yearned for his return, I felt suddenly shy and sank back in my chair so that he should not see me in the shadows. He began to speak expansively, gesticulating wildly as he performed to the crowd.

'Greetings, Sire, Madam. I beg pardon for my muddied state but I came to you straight, bearing gifts for your majesty.'

He gestured to his squires who staggered forward, grunting and sweating, to place their burden at the king's feet.

'Ooh, Harold. What is it?' asked Edith, leaning forward, her jewels twinkling in the torchlight as she clutched at herself in anticipation.

'Open it and see,' her brother replied, smirking at the greed kindling in her eye. She motioned impatiently to the squires to unwrap it and, as the layers were peeled away, the company gasped in unison. I too looked upon the offering and my blood turned cold in my veins.

It was something I had seen in better days, proudly set on the front of Gruffydd's flagship. Plated in gold and richly set with rubies, I had seen it last, cutting through the sea mist, bringing joy to our allies and striking terror in our foes. Gruffydd's figurehead, that had once borne the pride of the Welsh navy was now, cast low among the rushes of the Saxon court.

It seemed smaller, the fire in its ruby eyes was quenched and its noble expression dishonoured. I wanted desperately to flee for, as much as I hated Gruffydd, it was hard to see the father of my sons and the country I loved so degraded. Slipping from my chair, I began to move around the perimeter of the room.

Edward and Edith sat with their hands clasped before them in obvious delight at the spoils. Edith clapped in glee,

'Ooh, what else have you, Harold, what more did you bring?' Her teeth gleamed sharply as her brother smiled a slow smile and nodded his head in satisfaction.

'Oh, I have something to surpass this,' he said and turned to take a sack from his squire. I paused, half concealed by a tapestry whose sumptuous folds muffled the drafts from the passage. *What more has he garnered from my Welsh kin*, I thought bitterly and paused to watch as Harold held the sack aloft.

It bulged alarmingly and, as he swung round to show it to the king, the hessian gave way and the contents fell to the floor and spun across the flagstones. All eyes followed it as it rolled, like a ball, before coming to rest at my feet. Unable to identify it in the half-light, I leaned closer to examine it.

'Eadgyth, NO.' yelled Harold but he was too late. Unheeding, I rolled the thing over with my foot, it was slippery and mired but it moved quite easily.

The flickering torchlight leapt suddenly, illuminating the scene and a silent scream rang out in my head as transfixed I looked down upon my husband's face.

Wrenching my gaze away, I raised my arms to fend off the terrible sight but I could not shut it out. Though blackened and daubed with straw, the bloodied cheeks and the outraged mouth and distended, petrified tongue were recognisable. Gruffydd had been in a rage when he died. I staggered back, reeling, from the severed head, groping for some solid support.

Harold strode across the hall, his eyes full of self-reproach. He said something but, although I saw his lips moving, my mind could make no sense of his words. Dazed and stupid, I stood for a moment or two, unaware that the Saxon court stood witness to my humiliation, then the darkness began to gather, creeping like a blessed predator to rob me of consciousness. Blood thundered in my ears, sending me swirling into oblivion and, grateful for the encroaching dark, I plunged into Harold's waiting arms.

There are some nightmares from which it is better not to wake, for the realities of this world can be worse, far worse, than the conjurings of an abused mind.

Several times my eyes opened on the world but I closed them again, unwilling, or unready, to fight it. As I lay in my bed of feathers, swathed to the chin in softness, the words of the poem drummed in my head, bolstering my enfeebled strength.

'Our hearts must grow resolute, our courage more valiant,
Our spirits must be greater, though our strength grows less.'

And, after a few days, as if the words wove some wondrous spell, my strength and courage did return. I was able to open my eyes and sit up on my pillows to accept the nourishment that Æthel fed me from a silver spoon.

My looking glass revealed a face grown pale and eyes encircled with rings of blue. After I had sipped a bowl of thin gruel, Æthel began to sponge my skin and brush the tangles from my hair. It hurt, although she tried to tease out the knots, for in the thrashings of my madness it had become matted and snarled.

Æthel told me I had been abed a week, oblivious to the regular visits of the king and queen and the almost haunting presence of Earl Harold. 'He did not leave you for a day and two nights, Lady, but sat and watched you in your nightmare. I fear the Earl is sorely regretting his actions and swears he did not know of your presence in the hall.'

I sighed, too tired and overwhelmed by events to react.

'It makes little difference, Æthel,' I said, turning my face to the light that streamed through the small high casement. She stood at the clothes press, her back toward me, her figure a silhouette.

'He wants to see you, Lady.'

'No,' I replied 'I do not wish to see him.'

I lied. I was desperate to see him, I wanted to demand an explanation. I wanted to strike him, to scratch at him, hurt him but, as yet, I was too weak and so I refused him entry.

Later, in a strange echo of a previous time, I heard him at my chamber door. 'No,' Æthel was saying, 'she will not see you. She is sickened, Lord, and I beg you have patience.'

I heard him curse roundly and strike the closing door. 'Well, give her a message then. Tell her that I am sorry, that I need to explain. I must see her as soon as she is recovered enough; it is vital I see her, do you understand?'

I heard the door close softly and Æthel crept back into the room. She saw me watching her and smiled.

'He is eager, Lady. You will have to admit him soon.' But, turning my head to the wall, I closed my eyes and pretended to sleep.

I kept him from me for a further three days but, on the first day that I felt well enough to leave my bed, he burst into the chamber and sent Æthel scuttling to the anti room.

Hands on hips before me, he bellowed, 'No more excuses, Madam, you will hear me out. No longer will I be treated like a miscreant child.'

I surveyed him coldly, refusing to be affected by this overbearing bully. He was monstrous, no kinder, no better than Gruffydd himself.

I kept my gaze fixed on the wall and, seeing I was not going to relent, he gentled.

'How are you, Lady?' he asked, coming closer and making to take my hand but I snatched it away and kept my face turned from him.

'I am better, be it no thanks to you,' I retorted, the words issuing like dagger thrusts.

'Eadgyth, let me explain. Sit here and let us talk properly, before my journey I thought we were becoming friends.'

I kept my chin up and refused to look him in the eye.

'And so did I … so did I, but I cannot and will not be friends with a man like you.'

'A man like me? What do you mean 'a man like me?' I don't know why you are so angry. You hated Gruffydd. You know you did. Why, you told me yourself. You said you would, if you could, take my sword and strike him down. God's teeth. There is no understanding women. I had not thought you a hypocrite, Eadgyth.'

I swirled round and gave him the full force of my feelings, spitting the words.

'Do you not see it is different? I suffered indignation, humiliation and abuse, physical and mental, at that man's hand, my hatred of him was personal. I may have thought of killing him but I would never have dreamed of disabusing his corpse. How could you have decapitated him and brought his head forth as a trophy for you to show off to your king?'

'A trophy?' Harold repeated, 'Eadgyth, it wasn't me. I didn't kill him. His own countrymen, fed up with his over-zealous rule, did that. Bleddyn and Rhiwallon and that fellow Cynan ap Iago turned on him and carried out the butchery. It was revenge for years of mistreatment and harsh rule. They brought his head to me as a gesture of peace and asked me to deliver it to Edward. I was but the messenger boy. God's teeth woman.'

He was angry now, jumping to his feet and pacing the room as his words began to flow in a torrent. 'Do you know what I have been through, careering all over that God-forsaken country, up hill and down, pursuing your husband that I may redeem your children for you? I would I had not bothered, I could have sent a man to do the deed for me had I not promised you to do the job myself. God's truth. I've been beside myself these last days, waiting outside your chamber door like a love stricken fool to be allowed entry into your hallowed presence. And all so that I could beg your forgiveness. 'Tis a different reception from the one I had imagined and that's no lie. Do you not wish to see your sons, Madam?'

I raised startled eyes to him.

'What do you mean?' I whispered.

'I mean, woman, that your sons and their nurse are at my manor in Bosham and I have been awaiting your pleasure for a week or more to take you forth to join them.'

'My God.' I cried, 'why did no one tell me? What are we waiting for, Harold, have the horses saddled, we must ride today.'

I leapt from my chair and began to grab gowns from the clothes press and heap them onto the bed. Harold took me by the shoulder, halting me in my tracks.

'Hush,woman, hush. 'Tis too late in the day, we will leave tomorrow as soon as 'tis light. There will time aplenty for packing and, perhaps you should let your woman do it, I fear there is more to it than shoving a few gowns in a sack, you will look like a hedge drab if you pack like that.'

I plopped down in my chair again.

'Are they well, Harold? And Anwen and Maude, they are well? ...H...Harold, the children didn't see it did they? The murder, or have knowledge of the grisly trophy you carried all the while?'
His moustaches lifted as he emitted a sharp breath,

'God's truth, Lady, but you think me a monster don't you? I cannot vouch that they do not know of the deed itself but I can assure you they witnessed neither their father's death nor his ignominious journey here. I have children myself, Lady, and have treated yours as if they were mine own.'

'Edith said you would,' I murmured.

'Did she?' he raised an eyebrow. 'Well, the queen knows me well. Now, if you will excuse me, I have some business of my own to attend.'

I watched him stand up and make to leave but, before he could move away, I grasped his cloak as it swung out behind him. It was soft, the skin well-cured and I had the impulse to rub my face in it.

'You did not answer my question, Lord, when I asked if they faired well.'
Turning and taking my hand, he enveloped it in his for a while.

'They are well, Lady, tired and somewhat malnourished but well enough. The young one with the damn silly name, Maredudd; he has a small sniffle. Anwen has guarded them like a wolf from the night Rhuddlan burned and trust me, Lady, that is one wolf no man would care to offend, for, in truth, her teeth are very sharp.'

Bending over my hand I felt his lips, warm and dry on my inner wrist and then he was gone leaving me staring at the carved wooden vineleaves upon my chamber door.

A few months later we were all happily installed at Harold's splendid manor at Bosham in Sussex. Delighted to discover the children and Anwen had come to no real harm I, none the less, insisted that we linger in Harold's delightful home while they fully replenished their strength.

Anwen, forgetting decorum when she saw me, dropped what she was doing and flew to me, hugging and smothering my face with kisses. Maredudd and Idwal were no less demonstrative and we all indulged in a shameful display of weeping.

Harold looked on, one sardonic eyebrow higher than the other, but refrained from passing comment and instead produced gifts for the children.

He gave a small shield to Idwal's to partner his wooden sword and a lightweight helmet for Maredudd. The children accepted the gifts politely; overawed by the towering blond giant that had ridden into Wales and borne them away.

The atmosphere in the chamber relaxed and I realised I felt happy watching the children renew their acquaintance.

The boys were amazed at how much their sister had grown, for now she could toddle about the floor and scampered after them with no small skill. Soon all three were involved in a game of catch as catch can. Earlier I had thought Idwal seemed strained and worried but now he was laughing, his mouth wide and eyes bright. While they were distracted, I asked Anwen about his health.

'Oh, he has had some broken nights, Lady, but 'tis no wonder after what we all went through. I shielded them from the worst of it and we all kept as far from Gruffydd as was possible but there was fighting and unrest among the household and many harsh words spoken. The morning Gruffydd was killed we were at the stream, where I took the children daily for a walk. So mercifully we missed the attack but they could not but be aware of the danger. The skirmish was fierce but I kept them from the heat of it, I think. Worst of all was the cold and the hunger, Lady, for the food ran short right soon and, although I gave the boys half of my ration as well as their own, there were still tears about empty bellies. When the Saxons rode into camp, I was that relieved to learn that Earl Harold was your emissary and not the enemy we had thought him to be. 'Tis young Maude I had most cause to worry for, she took a fever and is not yet ready to quit her sickbed but we think she will recover fully, Lady.'

I bit my lip, thinking of the feasts I had enjoyed and the luxurious feather bed I had slept in while my children had starved in the snow bound mountains.

'I can never thank you for what you have done for them, Anwen, I am ever in your debt.'

'Oh, Lady, don't be foolish. They are like my own kin and anyone would have done the same, the poor wee things but… what will we do now you are widowed? Are we to stay here in Bosham or return to Rhuddlan, Lady?'

Unable to answer, I considered the question for some time, pondering on the fate of widows. I knew of noblewomen who had handed their children over to the king and retired from public life. Taking religious vows may suit some women but I was not yet twenty and unwilling to spend the rest of my days in cloisters. In time I could remarry but my past experience of wedlock made me reluctant to do so. I was unwilling to give up my children too, and thinking of it, I scooped Nest up and hugged her too tightly so that she squawked and tried to squirm away.

'What are you doing to that poor child?' came Harold's mocking voice. I released Nest and grimaced up at him, blushing but knowing there was little point in hiding anything from him. He could always see right through me.

'I was wondering what will become of us now. I cannot return to Wales, I know not where or even who my friends are and we cannot stay here, we have put upon your generosity for too long as it is.'

'Nonsense, Woman, you can stay here as long as you need to or, when you are ready, return to court. Edith will be glad to have you back and the children can take lessons with the royal wards. There will be no shortage of playmates, Edward the Ætheling's children, Edgar, Christina and Margaret are there and Earl Ralf's boy too.'

I pictured my sons, the sons of Gruffydd, growing up in a Saxon court becoming more anglicised as the years passed, eventually growing up more Saxon than Welsh and unloved by their countrymen. I didn't want them exiled from their homeland. Although I dreaded them becoming like their father, I would do all in my power to prevent them from becoming enemies to the land of their birth. I sighed,

'I don't know, Harold, I cannot decide what is best.'

'Well there is no hurry, Lady, you are all welcome here for as long as you wish. I have to make a journey soon, to Normandy, so you will not be under my feet. Anyway, I came to ask if you would care to walk with me a while, there is an hour or two before supper.'

Rising from my chair, I took his arm and we left the chamber and stepped outside, the sun dazzling after the dim interior.

'Oh,' I said, seeing the sunshine, 'I don't know why we were huddled indoors, it is such a lovely day. Why are you to travel to Normandy, Harold? Can you tell me or is it on the king's business?'

'As usual, madam, you are right. The king, at last, sends me to negotiate with William for the release of hostages. My brother, Wulfnoth, and my nephew, Hakon, have been in the Duke's hands for far too long … more than ten years it must be now.'

'You must be careful, Harold, I have heard William is a violent, unstable man. Do not let your own fiery temper scupper the success of your mission.'

'My fiery temper, Lady? I don't know what you mean.' he grinned. I thought for a while before replying.

'Seriously, Harold, they say that William is liable to uncontrollable rages and more than one man has met his death by crossing the Duke's will.'

The grassy path ahead grew very wet so, knowing I would not want to soil my slippers, Harold sat down on a mossy wall over looking the small harbour and patted the stones beside him, bidding me sit.

'See that church? They say that in Alfred's day, when the Vikings came, they stole one of the bells from the church tower and, lashing it to the deck, sailed away with it. Meanwhile, the monks crept back to their plundered church and, when they saw the enemy making for the open sea, they rang the solitary remaining bell. As the peals sounded across the water, the stolen bell broke loose from its moorings and replied, in a single loud note, before crashing through the ship's hull, so that the bell and the ship and the men all vanished beneath the waves. All men agree that, whenever the bells of Bosham church ring forth, the sunken one still answers from beneath the waves.'

'Ooh,' I shuddered, thoroughly engrossed in his tale, 'have you ever heard it?'

'Course I haven't, woman. Tell me, what is this womanly affection that prompts such concern for my well-being while I am abroad? Can it be that you care what may befall me? Do you perhaps hold some affection for me in your tender heart.'

My face aflame with humiliation, I looked down at my hands fiddling with the folds of my tunic. Always he must mock me. Sometimes I would like to strike him.

'You have been good to us Harold. I am a foreigner in a strange land and I value your friendship, that is all.'

'Foreigner be buggered.' he exclaimed, 'You were born in East Anglia.'
Bursting out laughing, I shook my head at him.

'You know very well what I mean. I left England when I was still a child, my time in Wales changed me, my nature is more Welsh than Saxon and I sometimes feel misplaced here, like a ship that's lost its anchor, adrift on a wild unstable sea.'

'Very poetic,' he grumbled and then, suddenly, seemed to lose his temper without cause. 'God's teeth, Woman. Let us be done with all this soft footing around, you know what I want, don't you? I can no longer be arsed with all this genteel side stepping. I want you for my wife, will you have me or not?'

Aghast, I leapt from the wall, unable to look him in the eye.

'Where on earth did that come from? I had no idea we were 'soft-footing' around each other. I am only just a few weeks widowed for heaven's sake and then, even if I did think you a suitable match, there is the small matter of your own wife.'

He pressed his lips together and scowled.

'She isn't my wife, we were handfasted twenty years since. Eadgytha is a good woman and has given me many happy years and some fine sons. I'd not abandon her but she's not the sort I'd wed; I need a gently born wife. One who can climb to the heights with me, who will grab at life with both hands and, if we go under, then will come up with me again, fighting. I say you are that woman, Eadgyth, say you will have me.'

Harold was the greatest warrior and the richest, most handsome, Earl in the kingdom and I could hardly believe that he wanted me. People said he was richer than Edward himself but, rich and handsome as he was, he still remained infuriatingly arrogant.

'I don't wish to remarry,' I said, folding my arms and turning away from him, 'I have found that marriage does not suit me.'

He got up and stood looking down at me, his arms folded across his broad chest and his blond hair whipping about his head.

'That,' he said, 'is because you were wed to an old man. I am in my prime. I am virile. I can give you more sons, Eadgyth and, the moot point is… I can give you bed pleasures that you can not begin to imagine.'

His face, suddenly suffused with desire, brought unbidden memories of Rhodri to my mind and my stomach twisted as I thought of sharing similar ecstasies with Harold.

'My brothers will not let you wed with me,' I said almost sulkily.

He put his hands on my shoulders, massaging and rubbing with his fingers.

'Rubbish. Your brothers are two of the most, ambitious, self-seeking churls I have ever met. The notion of their sister wedding the richest, most powerful Lord beneath the king will have the deal done and you wedded and bedded before the next cock crow. Think of it, Eadgyth,' he said, his tone suffused with lust, 'waking up with me beside you in your bed. I promise you, with me ploughing your furrow you'll have no cause for complaint ...'

'Stop it.' I cried, beating his chest with my fists, 'you are a monster.' All men are the same I thought as I twisted in his grip, trying to break away. All they want is to possess women, with no regard for their feelings. Held fast in his grip, I could not move though I kicked and punched at him. He relished the wrestling match until I grew weary and relaxed in his arms.

'Have you finished?' he asked and pulled me closer, covering my mouth with his, his tongue,hot and sinuous, on mine own.

My anger lasted until the third week after his departure for Normandy. He had bid me good-ye-bye cheerily, as though nothing had passed between us. I had turned haughtily on my heel and marched back into the hall without so much as a fare ye well.

But, once he had gone, taking most of the household men with him, the place seemed deathly quiet and the afternoons long. Used to his sudden arrival brightening an otherwise dreary day, my world descended once more into boredom.

He hadn't repeated his proposal and I began to question the sincerity of it. Although I tried I could not forget the sensation of his mouth on mine and the strength of his body pressed against me.

I tried to convince myself that I would as soon wed a tinker as my Lord of Wessex, but he was always the last thing on my mind at night and my first thought in the morning.

Sometimes, I walked to the ocean's edge with Anwen and the children. The choppy south coast seas sparkled more merrily than any I had seen before and I would stare across to the dazzling horizon, wondering when his ship would bring him home.

On one such a morning, as we lingered, picking up odd shells and fancy stones from the beach a messenger came to tell me that visitors awaited me at the hall. I left the children in Anwen's care and hastened back, wondering who had called.

After the brightness of the late summer sunshine the hall was dark and, although both men turned at my footstep on the stone floor, I could not discern their identity.

The shadowy figures approached and, as my eyes adjusted to the gloom, I saw that they were dressed in the finest cloth and bejewelled with the richest stones. Swords clanked in unison as they strode toward me and, as they drew close, I realised with a start that the Earls of Mercia and of East Anglia had come to call.

I had not seen my brothers since our shared exile so many years ago and glimpsing their familiar faces beneath their thick beards and fine apparel, I suppressed a sudden impulse to embrace them.

'Eadgyth.' Morcar exclaimed, taking my hand and bowing over it, 'Still fat then?' he winked. As he returned to a standing position I bowed my head.

'And I see that you, for all your finery and big boy's weapons, are still a child, Morcar.'

Edwin, ever the more amiable, took my hand next.

'We haven't come to quarrel, Sister,' he said, 'and, in truth, whether our brother cares to admit it or not, you are indeed grown into a fine woman. She has a look of Mother don't you think, Morcar?'

'Hmmm,' Morcar replied and I bowed my head again, playing the role of a gracious lady for all I was worth.

'Thank you and you both look every inch the Earl. What brings you all this way to Bosham, I should have thought you would wait to greet me on my return to court.'

'We were eager to reacquaint ourselves with you, of course, and we wanted to speak to you privately before Wessex returned …' began Edwin but Morcar interrupted him.

'We were with Wessex in Bristol the night before he left and he told us about his proposal.'

'God's grief, Morcar. Can you not be more circumspect?' Edwin interjected, 'Let me do the talking, you will do nothing but antagonise her and, remembering her temper, she will explode and we will all fall out. It is vital that we work together in this …as a family.'

Placing his arm about my shoulder he propelled me about the chamber.

'The thing is, Eadgyth, Harold said you are reluctant to commit yourself until you have sought our approval …'

'He said what?' I exploded, just as Edwin had said I would, 'Good Lord but that man is arrogant. I but used your names as an excuse, I have no wish to remarry and told him so straight but he would have none of it, so I said you would not allow it. Do not think for one minute that I give a hoot for your opinions, either of you.'

Morcar turned at my words, with a ready retort at his lips, but Edwin raised a warning finger at him and he subsided, snorting futilely before turning to look from the window, his arms folded and his jaw set.

'Eadgyth, Eadgyth, Eadgyth, think what it is you refuse. Harold is rich, rich beyond your dreams. He has more holdings and gold than your brother and I put together. He is richer than the king for heaven's sake. And I'm told women find him irresistible.'

'I care not for riches and I have had my fill of men. I am welcome at Edith's court and will make my life there, in her service.'

Edwin puffed out his cheeks and glanced at Morcar who continued to fight his rage by the window.

'Edward is sick, how much longer do you think he will live, Eadgyth? And then the queen will, no doubt, go into retirement. How will you like that, a former queen, still in the full flush of youth, living away from the court, away from the centre of things, away from your sons?'

I turned to face them again.

'What mean you the king is sick? He is sickly but not unto death when I saw him last.'

Morcar sat himself on Harold's chair, watching as Edwin continued to tempt me.

'He is ailing and old, Eadgyth and his days at an end. The witan is ever cajoling him to name his successor but he prevaricates. All men know that the Ætheling is not fit to rule and England will be vulnerable to any who wish to take her. If we wish to bar the door to Hardrada or Swegen Estrithson or William the bastard, then we need to stand firm behind the one man who is fit to lead us and the witan agree with us that there is only one man.'
Suspicion stirred in my mind and I looked from Morcar and Edwin and back again.

'Which man?' I asked, although I already knew the answer.

'Harold.' cried Morcar, coming to stand before me, 'Did you think he wanted you for your charms alone, Eadgyth? My word, you may be a fine looking woman, but it is our support he truly seeks, the possession of your luscious body will be but a bonus. Without our armies at his back he will not have the agreement of the witenagemot and England will fall to a foreigner. Think of it, Eadgyth, a son of yours and Harold's one day becoming the king of England, supporting his brother's claim in Wales, both nations united under the dynasty of Mercia. You must look to your duty, Eadgyth, and marry Harold, for the good of your family and for the good of England.'

My anger and my dignity was piqued, thinking of Harold's pretended desire for me. How could I have fallen for such carefully constructed passion?

I was loath to concede to their wishes but, in truth, I wanted him for the man he was, not for his riches or his power or his potential to become the next king but for his virile manhood. It hurt like a lash that my family connections were the only charms I held for him.

If I accepted his proposal he would think his wiles had worked and see me as a gullible fool but, if I refused, I would be denying myself the man I had come to desire more than any other. Swirling round to face my brothers I shrugged my shoulders.

'I will think on it,' I said, trying to gain myself some time to think. 'I can make no promises now.' Morcar exploded into rage.

'There is nothing to think on, Eadgyth, you have to do it. You must think of England, not of yourself…'

'Think of England? Like I was forced to think of Mercia when I was married off to Gruffydd? Don't you think I have sacrificed myself enough for one lifetime? God's teeth, you can have no idea how I suffered at the hands of that man. Not one of you gave a thought to how I would be treated, not one of you considered how I felt and I will not do it again, not for you, not for England and certainly not for Harold.'

Edwin scowled at Morcar, warning him to keep quiet and, ever the diplomat, assumed a soothing approach.

'Hush, hush, Eadgyth,' he said, stepping forward and stroking my shoulder, 'Morcar and I were but infants when Father formed the Welsh alliance; you cannot blame us for that. There is no need for a decision now and surely some calm consideration will bring you to our point of view. Harold is a good man, you know that or you would not be lodging in his house. Did he not mount a rescue and go back into Snowdonia to redeem your children for you? No man would do that did he not have your interests at heart. Think on it for a few days, Eadgyth, we will come again and surely we will reach a decision before he returns from his mission.

I thought of nothing else for the next few weeks, Harold showed no signs of returning and sent no missives or instructions to Bosham. As the weeks stretched to months, the memory of our brief passion faded and I began to wonder if I had dreamed the whole episode. Try as I might, I could not collate the picture of Harold I bore in my memory, the desperate, lovelorn Harold, with the predatory figure of whom my brothers spoke; a man who sought my hand only to advance his ambitious pretensions to the throne.

Growing restless alone at Bosham, I decided to return to court which now resided close to London on Thorney Island. The journey was not an arduous one and, once I had made up my mind, the bags were packed and we were on our way within a few days.

I had never been to the king's palace at Thorney before and was surprised to find it a substantial dwelling and noted with appreciation the modern improvements that Edward had implemented. The older shabbier buildings put up by King Cnut were used by lesser folk now although work had not finished on the new. The sound of hammer and chisel could be heard coming from the direction of the church and I knew that this must be the new foundation that the king was so proud of. From the size and splendour of the unfinished building, it was easy to see why.

I found Edward and Edith in the hall pouring over religious relics. The ladies and gentlemen of the household had withdrawn to the perimeters of the room, leaving the royal couple in the company of a clergyman who was displaying for their appreciation an old-fashioned girdle.

'They do say Sire, that the girdle, if worn by one worthy of it, will ward off the pangs of childbirth …'

His patter ceased and they all looked up as I entered and made my curtsey.

'Eadgyth. How delightful to see you.' cried the queen, rising from her chair and drawing me into their circle. 'We have missed you so, haven't we Edward? And how are your sons, Lady? Recovered from their unfortunate adventure?'

'They are quite well now, Madam, yes. I thank you for asking. It was good of Earl Harold to let us remain at his manor for so long but I feel we have trespassed upon his hospitality quite enough and I had a hankering to return to your service. That is, if you still require it Madam.'

The queen squeezed my arm.

'Of course I do. I have missed your company intolerably, haven't I, Edward? We both have. Tell me what news have you of Harold? We had thought to see his return long since.'

Hating myself for the colour that flooded into my cheeks, I shrugged my shoulders.

'I have heard nothing, Madam. I would presume his tardiness in returning is due to the extravagant hospitality of the Norman court, I've heard that the hunting is outstanding and you know what Harold is for the chase.'

'Oh yes, you are right, Lady.' chimed in the king, 'I lived as a youth in Normandy and the hunting was the best I have ever known. They have deer such as we have never seen here. How I miss it but, now, I'm forced to remain indoors for much of the day so apt am I to take a chill.'

He coughed as if to demonstrate his lack of vigour and I looked on sympathetically while Edith patted his back and beckoned to the apothecary to bring the king his remedy. I wondered how ill he really was and how much of it imagined; my brothers swore he was on the point of death but I saw little evidence of it and thought that he could continue in a similar vein for years yet.

'I saw the building work is progressing on your church, Sire,' I said to distract him from his coughing.

'It's looking magnificent is it not, Lady,' he responded. 'Later, we must all stroll about the works so that you can view it properly. It will be an abbey fit for kings by the time it is finished. I plan to be interred there myself you know, and mayhap other kings will follow, who knows?'

Queen Edith looked startled.

'That ill day is many years hence, my dear. Ooh, Tostig darling. Do you know the Lady Eadgyth, widow of the late Welsh king? Eadgyth, this is my younger brother, Tostig, I expect you have heard much of him.'

I looked down at the head of blond waves as he bowed over my hand and, when he stood up, found myself staring into a pair of blue eyes that were the exact matching shade of his brother Harold's.

'Charmed, Lady,' he drawled, without a vestige of interest and I realised that the family resemblance was only skin deep. His hands, beard and clothing was so immaculate that I felt drab in his presence.

'How d' ye do, Tostig?' asked the king, patting the seat beside him. Tostig flounced across the dais and sat himself down without ceremony, immediately launching into a discussion about the hopeless task he faced in ruling the heathens in his charge north of the Humber.

'They are impossible, Sire,' he complained, 'they take umbrage at the taxes. When I intervene in their incessant feuds they call it interfering. How I wish I could be in Harold's shoes, he never has trouble extracting the dues owed to him in his lands.'

'Wessex can afford their rents, Tostig, that's the difference,' the queen interceded before Edward had the chance. 'You can't expect people who are impoverished by circumstance to fill your coffers without complaint. Make sure you find a way of persuading them gently or you will have a rebellion to deal with and then we will not be pleased with you at all, will we Edward?'

'No, my Sweet,' replied the king, smiling up at Tostig, weakly apologetic.

'We were just about to take a stroll about the works,' he continued, 'would you like to join us.'
Tostig sighed and then, in unconvincing agreement, announced, 'There is nothing I'd like more, Sire.'

Rising from his seat he offered the queen his arm, leaving me to accompany the king. Perhaps if I had been subjected to the tour as often as the queen and her brother I should have shared their bored resignation but the newly erected abbey of Thorney Island held me transfixed. Edward's enthusiasm for his project barely surpassed my own. Unused to stone buildings, this edifice was astounding in its beauty and majesty.

'Oh Sire.' I cried when I saw it, 'It is magnificent, truly it is.'
Tostig raised a sardonic eyebrow and I was struck again by the incongruous resemblance he bore to his overtly masculine brother. He placed his hand on his sister's shoulder and, as one, we all leaned our heads back to survey the wonder of the edifice.

The lantern tower soared above us, six storeys high at least and the men who clambered about the scaffolding seemed miniscule from our perspective on the ground. On close inspection it was clear that there was much work still remaining, the completed east end at first appeared to be finished but the skeletal outline of the west end and the north transept stood stark against the sky.

Raised in Normandy, Edward had looked abroad for inspiration and employed European architects who had earned their expertise working on the grandiose cathedrals of Jumieges and Rouen. Inside, the light that was so spectacular, never had I seen a building that allowed so much exterior sunlight, the light of God, to stream in through windows too numerous to count.

'God must be in this place, Sire. I can feel Him. I swear there can be nowhere on this earth where a person can feel closer to Him.'
Edward, stooped and sweating slightly from the exertion of the walk, beamed at me.

'You feel it too, Lady? That is delightful. I feel there are those that grow weary of my building and no longer see it as I do. Have you ever heard the special tale of the first church here and how St Peter himself came to consecrate it?'

'No, Sire, I don't believe I have. Will you tell me?'
Edward cleared his throat.

'I shall try my best, Lady, but I am not a storyteller. Tradition declares that even before Sebert, the first Christian king of the East Saxons, built a church on Thorney, a temple to Apollo and a church founded by King Lucius had occupied this place. Late one night a humble Thames-side fisherman, called Edric I believe, was hailed by a stranger who asked to be ferried across the river to Thorney and back. Edric, having fished all night without success, was eager for a penny and agreed to the request. He rowed the stranger across and, while he lay idle in his boat waiting for his return, he suddenly beheld the windows of the new church spring into life. Sounds of exquisite singing issued from inside, and in the radiance encircling it arose a ladder, stretching up to heaven, upon which angels were ascending and descending. Presently, after many more wonders that I cannot now recall, the stranger who had hired his boat returned and bade Edric cast his nets into the river once more. The fisherman obeyed and was rewarded by a noble haul. Before departing, the stranger told him that he must go to the king and the bishop at the Abbey and gift them one of the salmon he had caught. He must tell them that St. Peter had already consecrated the church on Thorney as his especial property. Furthermore, he must in future give a tithe of all fish he caught to the Abbot of Westminster, and refrain from Sunday fishing for 'tis a sin. Edric did as he was bidden and, when Sebert and Mellitus asked for proof of his tale, was able to show them, within the new building, traces of holy water, crosses on the walls, signs of consecrated oil and the remains of candles used in the miraculous illumination.' Edward paused, beaming and pleased with his tale.

'Goodness, Sire, that is a wondrous story, I have never heard the like.'

My neck ached from looking up for so long but I could not stop gaping at the splendour of the stonework. Even filled as it was with workmen, rubble and dust, it was a place where God would always reside. Edward pointed to the high windows.

'All the windows will be of glass,' he said, 'some of them stained to send a myriad of colour onto the congregation and here, above the quire, where the transepts meet will hang a magnificent bell to summon all forth for prayer.'

With utter sincerity I turned my glowing eyes toward the king.

'God will bless you for this, Sire, with all my heart I thank you for showing it to me.'

'That's not all, Lady. Look here, this is to be my tomb, where I shall rest in God's bosom until the judgement.'

I suppressed a shudder, unsure if it were healthy for a living soul to be so preoccupied with his hereafter.

'It's a fine tomb, Sire, although I hope many years will pass before you come to have need of it. I'm sure you will enjoy many masses and services here in this place before it is time to lie in it forever.'

The king took my arm again and we processed further about the nave.

'Ah, you would endow me with everlasting life I know but, we must be practical, I am growing old and I am ailing. I cough at night and wake with the sweats, I know my days draw to an end and it grieves me not.

Although, in my youth, I thought myself ill-used, I see now that I have had a blessed life. It is he who follows that must concern me now…'

'Have you named an heir, Sire?' I asked.

'Nay, Lady,' he replied, 'my brother, Edmund, the one they called Ironsides, had a son who would have perhaps have been the man but he sickened and died soon after I called him forth from exile. His son, he they call Edgar the Ætheling, is yet a boy and, I fear, too feeble to bear the harsh demands that are placed upon kings. I had some hopes of Harold continuing to lead and advise him after my death but, I know the witan approves not of child kings and will seek to replace him. It is all in God's hands but I do not fret too much at that for there are no hands more capable than His.'

The sun was sinking into the horizon as we made our way back to the royal palace. The hall was filled with the aroma of roasting meat and mulled wine and we parted to prepare ourselves for the evening festivities. Tostig's chamber lay close to mine and he accompanied me part of the way. He strutted beside me like a peacock, his cloak, suspended from his index finger, tossed over one shoulder.

'Edith tells me that our brother is quite taken with you, Lady, and she has hopes of welcoming you into the family sometime soon. May I say that it is a day I look forward to.'

'The queen is mistaken, Lord. Harold assisted me when I was in distress; that is all. He has been very kind to me but, as you well know, he already has a wife.'

Tostig picked at his teeth, he looked decidedly bored and I wondered why he continued the conversation.

'Oh Eadgytha. You needn't worry about her, Harold has long tired of her and, with Edith's backing, you can win Harold easily. Our queen has no love for the concubine but has formed a rare attachment for you, my dear.'

Leaving me at my chamber door he sauntered along the corridor giggling to himself. Oh these Godwinsons, I thought as I lifted the latch, they are all impossible.

Many long months passed before we saw Harold again. No one knew why he tarried so long at the Norman court but the king grew fractious and his family speculative.

Tostig swore that Harold had formed a romantic attachment and would probably return home with a Norman bride. He cast a sly glance in my direction but I schooled my features to nonchalance and ignored him.

'It is more likely to be the hunting,' Edith objected, 'you know Harold, he has never been promiscuous has he? Oh, I know he has that Swanneck woman but, give him his due, he hasn't strayed from her as far as I know.'

'What is she like, this Eadgytha?' I could not refrain from asking, 'I've heard she is loyal to Harold and a good mother.'

'Well, she is prolific enough, I suppose, if that counts in her favour,' said Edith, not bothering to hide her dislike, 'she is just so vulgar, the way she flaunts herself as though sharing his bed gives her some status. It really is time Harold dispensed with her and took to himself a proper wife.'

I could feel the slow flush of embarrassment flooding into my cheeks for I knew that I was the 'proper wife' she referred to. Just then, the king popped his head around the chamber door.

'Ah, Edith, my dear,' he interrupted, nodding to the assembled company, 'just to let you know your mother is here and also your brothers, Gyrth and Leo…'

'Well, come in do, Edward, you are lurking half in, half out the door like a messenger boy. Eadgyth, you haven't met my mother have you? You will love her, she is a darling.'

I looked upon this darling as she entered and bobbed a makeshift curtsey to her daughter; she was tall and held herself like a queen. She was clothed in the modest style but the cloth was of the very best quality and her jewellery, although simple, was costly too. Close by her side stood two of her younger sons; the youngest of all, Wulfnoth, still held hostage in Normandy and it was his freedom that Harold hoped to negotiate with the Norman duke. Gyrth, I presumed, was the darker haired of the two; he bowed over his sister's hand after making his obeisance to the king.

'Mother,' announced Edith in her clear, high pitched voice, 'this is Eadgyth, the former wife of the Welsh king, you will have heard Harold singing her praises no doubt.'
I flushed under the scrutiny of this grand old woman.

'I have indeed. I am charmed, Eadgyth. Tell me, has Harold shown you the same lack in communication as he has his family? We find ourselves sadly at a loss to know what has become of him. He must needs return soon for the witenagemot.'

Gyrth and Leofwine greeted me and I found myself looking at two younger, slighter versions of their older brother. The strong resemblance that ran through the Godwinson family was remarkable but, this time, there was not the slightest lack of masculinity in either of them.

'There are rumours that William has been on campaign against Conan fitzAlan of Brittany, mayhap Harold travelled with him; he does like to show off his prowess on the field,' commented Leofwine. He wore his hair long like his brothers but, whereas they varied in colouring from light blond to brown, Leofwine's crowning glory was a golden red and his cheeks, that still bore the lingering evidence of freckles, were beginning to sprout a soft beard of the same colour.

'Perhaps,' he said blushing, in what I later came to realise was his habitual accompaniment to speech, 'he is having trouble persuading the Duke to release Wulfnoth and Hakon, you know Harold is not one to give up. Mayhap he is staying on to apply pressure, gently persuading the Duke that it is in his own best interest to release our kin.'

Fleeting memories of Harold's limited stores of patience made me examine the reaction of his mother and sister and their cynically lifted brows confirmed my instinct to negate this idea.

'Lord, I hope not.' cried Edith, 'If I know Harold, his methods of persuasion are usually more heavy handed than William the Bastard will care to submit to. No, I tell you, he is wearing himself ragged careering about the continent after those deer William is so fond of.'

Edward, impatient at the speculation, interrupted.

'Anyway, Gytha, can I interest you in a turn about the building works? The abbey church comes on apace and I can see the consecration being in place by next year at the latest.'

The king held his arm out for his mother in law and she bowed her head before taking his proffered elbow and quitting the chamber with him, leaving Edith and I in the company of her sons.

'Well, they will be some time. I'm right glad he did not include us in the invite, if I have to walk about that church once more this month I will scream. Leo, I have some splendid new relics for the altar when it is finished, come I will show them to you. I have a bone of Cuthbert's arm and a tooth of John the Baptist, cost me a small ransom but they are worth it and will enrich the foundation of any church.'

Gyrth offered me his arm and we processed after the queen and her brother, leaving the rest of the company to amuse themselves as they may.

Edith had been educated at the house of Benedictine nuns at Wilton Abbey in Wiltshire. During her estrangement from Edward during Old Godwin's exile, she had returned there under rather more duress and now, grateful for their care, she wished to repay them for their hospitality. She was keen that her own patronage of Wilton Abbey should not be outdone by her husband's splendidly proportioned St Peters church, which was fast becoming known as the west minster. At Wilton Edith's long purse had financed the replacing of the ancient wooden structure with a grander stone one. Various setbacks had hindered the work but the noble building was now ready for consecration and Edith, accordingly, was hunting down relics with which to bless it.

'The queen certainly loves her church,' I commented to Gyrth, uncertain of what else to say.

'She does, Lady,' he replied, flushing, 'and the relics that go with it. Did you know that a fire at Wilton destroyed a vast hoard of religious treasures she had already collected for the dedication and she had perforce to begin her search again?'

'No. I hadn't heard that. Oh dear, how awful it is when irreplaceable ancient treasures are lost. She must have been distraught.'

Gyrth poured two cups of wine and handed one to me. I took it, smiling my thanks, and sipped at it, feeling the strong flavour flow down my throat.

'When she visited the Gloucestershire abbeys, we feared for her health for a while, you know. She was collecting relics for Wilton from the abbey at Evesham and, when the shrine was opened for her inspection, as she put in her hand she was suddenly struck blind.'

'Good God.' I cried, amazed at his story, 'What happened? How did she regain her sight?'
Gyrth leaned toward me, conspiratorially lowering his voice,

'I've never heard such a fuss in all my life, Lady. The good queen, my sister, screamed like a stuck pig, weeping and wailing and casting herself onto the altar promising St Odulf never to injure the saints again if only they would restore her vision. No one could get close to her for she was quite distraught with fear but, at length, she calmed down so that the abbot could draw near enough to offer a blessing and order that her eyes be bathed. More to the point, he made no move to help her until Edith had sworn to bestow a special pall on the dishonoured shrine; after that she was miraculously cured.'

The quirky eyebrow, that seemed to be another Godwinson trait, was raised as he watched my amazed reaction.

'What do you think happened, Gyrth, was she truly blinded or was it just a fleeting indisposition?'

'Who knows, Lady,' he replied, 'my sister is convinced it was a warning from the saints and she plunders their rest no more but I will say that the shrine benefited quite royally from the incident and my sister learned a terse lesson too.'

Looking upon his cynical expression as he stood looking across the chamber, his locks flopping over his forehead, I noted how very much like Harold he was, both in thought and manner.

'You suspect some trickery don't you, Gyrth? Oh, you Godwinsons are such disbelievers. I swear I could take you all for pagans.'

'Oh never that, Lady,' he whispered, casting about the hall in some alarm, 'we all believe devoutly in the Christian teachings of the holy church.'

'I know you do, Gyrth, don't worry; I was but teasing. You are very much like your brother, Harold, you know.'

Bowing over my hand, he confirmed my comment saying, 'I shall take that as a compliment, Lady, be that as it was meant or no,' and together we began to circumvent the hall, the young women smiling adoringly up at my companion as we went.

The palace was in an uproar at Harold's return. Dogs barked as his retinue dismounted and milled about the yard and children hovered, eager to join in the excitement. He clumped into the hall and made his perfunctory greeting to his king.

It was plain he was in an ill temper and I felt piqued that he did not outcome straight to me' instead of seeking an immediate private audience with Edward. This curious behaviour did nothing to alleviate the speculation at the court and I waited impatiently with the others to hear of his exploits. Edith, her face pinched with indignation at being excluded from the audience, beckoned me to her side.

'Sit here with me, Eadgyth, that you may be among the first to greet him. Pinch your cheeks or something, you looked deuced pale.'

Dutifully I did as she bid and smoothed the front of my gown before sitting, hands clasped, beside my queen. By the time the two men issued from the king's chamber, Compline was over and the evening meal well under way. Edith was sprawled in her chair listening to Gyrth strumming on his lute; the rest of the company, relaxed and happy, laughed and talked among themselves.

When Edward and Harold emerged, silence fell upon the gathering and all eyes were turned to the pair as they took their places at the head of the table. I blushed when Harold's eyes fell on me and I found myself bathed in his warm greeting.

'Forgive me, Ladies, I had an urgent matter to discuss with the king. Ahhh,' he said, looking around the hall before bowing to the queen, 'tis good to be home.'

'Whatever has kept you from us for so long, Harold?' demanded Edith and I pricked up my ears, eager to hear his excuses too.

'You would not believe the time I have had, Madam. From the moment I disembarked I have been a man cursed by misfortune. We ran into heavy weather the moment we left port and were all but wrecked on the shores of Ponthieu and then I had the bad luck to fall into the incompetent clutches of Count Guy. I received no gentle welcome I can assure you and the fool, refusing to believe who I was, had me thrown into his dungeon.'

The women gasped and Harold, ever susceptible to female attention, warmed to his subject.

'Eventually Duke William turned up and freed me, more I'm inclined to think, to ensure my gratitude to him than anything else. We returned to his court where he made a great show of us being 'brothers' and bent over backward trying to flatter and bribe a way into my good books. Although, to be sure, I had no idea why ...d' y' know, he even offered me his daughter for wife, a tiny scrap of a thing no more than twelve years old. Coh, the nerve of the man.'

Tostig, who had been sitting on the perimeter of the group now thrust his head forward.

'There ye see, Edith, I said there'd be a woman involved.' he cried and all the company fell about laughing. Harold looked about in bewilderment,

'Ha, I see I am the victim of some joke. Laugh all you like while you can for my tale grows darker.'
We all sobered and his eyes rested on mine as he continued.

'There was no woman, although the Duke may think otherwise. I told William I was already betrothed but he would have none of it and declared that, as he had the pope in his pocket, he could guarantee that any previous alliance could be nullified.'
I felt a chill and instinctively held my hands toward the hearth to warm them.'The thing with William is that he won't take no for an answer. I kept on reminding him

that we needed to discuss the release of Wulfnoth and Hakon but he prevaricated for weeks until I was well nigh hopping with rage.'

'What of that, Harold, is he going to free them?' asked Edith. Harold's eyes flicked to his mother who dropped her swimming eyes to her lap.

'Hakon returned with me and is with his family in Winchester but the Duke hangs on to our brother, Wulfnoth, until such time as I have made good my promise ...'

'What promise?' I cried, shaken out of composure by the terrible suspicion that he was shortly to produce a Norman child bride from his retinue. He reached and took my hand, clasping it between both of his.

'Tis a long story and I could do with a drink. When I arrived, William was readying for some campaign he had been planning to put down Conan of Brittany. In the end I rode with him and William showed himself to be most impressed with what he called my prowess in battle. It was no more than a few skirmishes really, the sort of thing I am involved in all the time, but I felt as though he was assessing me or something, sizing me up as an opponent, judging if it were better to have me as friend or foe.'

A boy arrived with a tray of wine cups and Harold released my hand and took one, gulping down the contents and wiping his mouth on his sleeve as I had seen him do so many times.

'On the way back ... my 'tis a pretty country and the buildings all of stone. Anyway, I digress, we had need to cross a tidal river wherein some of his men got into difficulty and were drowning in the mud alongside. Without thinking, I spurred my horse in and whipped them out before they, or I, should be sucked under. I tell you, anyone would have done the same but William, as is his want, made a big to do about it, swearing I had acted the hero's part. On our arrival back at Bayeux he ordered an oath taking ceremony for his huscarls to swear him loyalty and, before I knew it, he was knighting me and bidding me swear fealty to him too.'

Whispered comment eddied about the hall at this shocking revelation for everyone present knew that Harold's allegiance lay with Edward.

'They do things differently in Normandy,' Harold went on to explain, 'an oath is not a voluntary thing, sworn to the man of one's own choosing. In Normandy, a man must swear fealty where he is bid. I had no choice but to kneel before the bastard and make my pledge. The hall was full of his men and Hakon and my brother held hostage to my response, I could do nought but kneel in fealty to him but I do swear now, on the queen's book,' he cried, snatching up Edith's psalter and holding it high, 'that a forced oath is a false oath and that my true loyalty lies with King Edward and with England too.'

A cheer broke out in the company and all but lifted the rafters while Harold stood smiling and nodding grimly on the crowd.

'And when will he let my son go free?' asked Gytha from her seat close by the queen.
Harold turned to her and for once, looking hang-dog and defeated, confessed,

'I know not, Madam. William swears that you promised him the throne, Edward, is that so? Did you so promise?'

Plucking at his robes, the king looked frantically from Harold to the queen,

'I don't think so, but I may have, Harold, if he was pressing me but … I wouldn't have meant it. Nobody would want him on the Saxon throne.'

Harold raised his eyes to heaven.

'Well, he took it on trust, Edward, and now wants me to turn the castle at Dover over to his care and, furthermore, to support his bid for the throne on your demise, far off may that day be. I fear that the fee for failing him in this will be the life of my brother but to that I cannot swear. I also fear that my failure to honour my pledge could result in war with Normandy and that we needs must avoid.'

The king, who had been sitting fiddling with the rich brocade trim on his tunic, cleared his throat and spoke thinly,

'I am tired of all this troublous talk now, let us make merry and praise God for your safe return, Harold. Come, harper, play and sing to us while the night is young.'

I heard a gusty sigh beside me as Leofwine turned to his brother and whispered,

'The king was ever the one to avoid unpleasantness. We needs must talk of this again, Harold, Wulfnoth cannot be sacrificed but neither can we let him be used as a fulcrum to force your hand.'

The brothers moved away to join Gyrth and Tostig close to the hearth; I followed, since my hand was still held fast in Harold's. As we drew close, Tostig moved away to join the king and Edith at the gaming table.

'I did not tell all, brothers,' whispered Harold, 'the oath I took to William was not just a simple pledge of loyalty.'

'What do you mean?'

'I mean, it was taken most solemnly, on the Holy relics of Normandy's most precious saints. I swore, before God and his saints, to uphold the Norman claim and I cannot do it, not if I burn in hellfire for all eternity, for I will *not* let that man take the Saxon throne.'

There came a loud ringing in my ears, a sign of sudden stress with which my life's misfortunes had made me familiar.

'Why did you swear then, Harold, on sacred relics? You must have been mad.' I cried, struggling to relinquish my hand and try with all my might to keep my voice within the bounds of normality.

'They had them hidden. When I said the words I believed I could foreswear honourably for, as all men know, an oath not freely given is not binding. It was not until the words were out of my mouth that the duke's brother, Bishop Odo, revealed the Holy casket beneath the cloth upon which they had placed my hand.'

'Can we avoid war now, Harold? Do you think William will let it rest? What did the king say?' asked Leofwine, and Harold, looking down into the depths of his wine cup replied,

'I did not tell the king, and no, Leo, I do not believe we can avoid war. It will come sooner or later but, I swear, that man will take this kingdom over the bones of my dead body.'

'And mine too.' cried Leo without hesitation,

'And mine.' repeated Gyrth a moment later. With dread in my heart, I stood watching as their cups kissed and all three drank to the pledge.

Much later, as the embers of the fire shifted and sank into cinders and most of the company slept where they had fallen about the hearth, Harold and I wandered into the courtyard. It was a cold, bright night, the moon riding high on a cloud-tossed, black sky.

'You gave much away tonight, sweetheart.'

'Did I?' I said, drawing my gaze away from the moon, 'in what way?'

'Oh, in the best way,' he drawled, 'your eyes lit up like yonder stars when you saw me and you revealed your care for my soul by almost weeping when you learned I would be damned to hell's fire if I break the oath.'

The intensity of his eyes discomforted me. I had missed him so much. I looked away, feigning flippancy in an attempt to return to our bantering ways of old.

'I see you have learned frenchified gallantry while you have been away, Sir,' I mocked, but he was having none of it and did not retaliate. Taking my chin between his strong fingers he tilted my head back, forcing me to look into his eyes.

'You have made up your mind to have me then, madam?' he stated, as if the question was already answered.

I licked my lips that had suddenly gone very dry and waited while, slowly, his face drew closer to mine. I kept my eyes open until his two eyes merged into one and then into nothing. My own closed and I parted my lips to receive his kiss.

We remained thus joined, gently, almost passionlessly until, at length, he broke away. I opened my eyes and looked at him, golden in the moonlight.

'Can I take that as a yes then?' he asked, smoothing a stray strand of hair from my cheek and, with tears wetting my face and unable to make any other answer, I heard myself say, 'Oh, yes, Harold, yes please.'

We planned the wedding to take place as soon as possible. Having gained the blessing of the king and bourn the overwhelming good wishes of the queen, we prepared to visit my old Mercian home so that Harold could formally request of Edwin my hand. On route we detoured to visit Waltham, where Harold had founded a church he hoped would rival Edward's abbey at the West Minster.

We were in good spirits as we rode through the golden day. Although the sun dripped through the autumn-kissed trees the sharp aroma of winter was already tingling the back of my nose and forcing me to keep my cloak wrapped tight about my shoulders.

Riding ahead of the rest of the party, Harold and I descended into the valley and I caught my first glimpse of the church tower against the bright sky. As we grew closer Harold told me that the old wooden church which had been built by Cnut's standard-bearer, Tofig, had fallen into decay and so he had ordered it rebuilt in stone. Although it still resembled a building site rather than a church, he had installed a community of secular canons with a dean to watch over them and endowed it with many sacred relics. The church was smaller than that at Thorney but still impressive, despite the thump of stone hammers and the workmen scaling the scaffolding that towered high above us. Peace did not abide here yet but the promise of tranquillity lay in the pure lines and stolid dependability of the structure.

I glanced at Harold and then, without waiting for assistance, scrambled down from my palfrey. He watched me, assessing my reaction as I moved around the building, craning my neck to absorb every angle and detail of the design, asking questions about the final plans.

Taking my arm, he guided me through the stone entrance at the west end and along tiled floor toward the high altar. He told me of the splendid cathedrals in Normandy. The sunlight streamed in through the window openings, illuminating the cavernous space yet leaving intimate, half lit corners, like small secrets as yet undiscovered. Pigeons fluttered high up in the roof space, sending feathers and other, less savoury offerings, scattering to the floor.

The rough voices of the workmen drifted away, insignificant in such splendid surroundings and, forgetting the chaos of the building site, I felt Harold and I were alone in the holy place. Although God, I am sure, was watching.

'Will you lay with me here, Eadgyth?' Harold asked quietly. Aghast at his suggestion, I turned startled eyes upon him, unable to find my voice.

'Harold.' I exclaimed at last, flushing red. His sudden loud burst of laughter echoed about the nave, turning workmen's heads toward us in curiosity.

'I didn't mean that, sweetheart. Although I must confess the idea does have its attractions.'
Doubling up again, he clutched at himself until, seeing I was not amused, he fought to quell his mirth and, straightening up and spluttering a few times, added,

'I meant, will you lay with me here in the hereafter, as my wedded wife. 'tis such a tranquil spot to spend eternity, I thought we might share it.'

Looking at the light and shadow of the interior and, in my imagination replacing the sound of hammering with plainsong, it did strike me as a good place to rest until the day of judgement. Smarting with embarrassment and reluctant to climb down from my high horse, I responded,

'tis a good thought Harold but, until such time as I may be your wife, I think 'tis an indelicate discussion.'

Turning on my heel, I marched outside, hearing him swear as he stumbled over a wheeled barrow that had been left unattended near the door.

'Eadgyth.' he cried, joining me by the horses, 'What has happened to your sense of humour this morning?'

'No one likes to be laughed at, Harold,' I said, 'The children and Anwen are here now. Why not go about your business while I stroll about here in the sunshine? No doubt by the time you return my temper will have righted itself.'

Bowing over my hand, he walked away without looking back while I turned to greet the children as they came running toward me across the greensward.

'Mother!' cried Maredudd, reaching me moments before his sister. Nesta clung to my knees, her face beaming up at me, aglow with love.

'We sawed a fox, Mother.' Maredudd cried, 'a great, big red one.'

'You *saw* a fox, my sweet,' I corrected, stroking Nesta's black hair back from her white brow. No matter how hotly the sun shone, Nest's skin never tanned but retained the opalescent paleness. Anwen and Maude joined us, Idwal clutching his nurse's skirt.

'Greetings, Mother,' he said, bowing from the waist as he had been taught. He was a quiet boy, often seeming troubled, although he continued to grow like a weed.

'Have you been inside the church?' he asked, craning his head back to look up at the top of the tower.

'I have, Idwal, but I want to see it from the other side, Harold says that the crossing tower can be viewed better from there.'

Taking his hand and hoisting Nest onto my hip, we walked together around the west range, passing what would soon become the new monks' quarters. A wall, flanked by a row of clean square arches with stone benches, was set back from the breeze providing an area for quiet, monastic contemplation. Anwen's leg, that still vexed her from time to time was making her walk with a dip, so I bade her and Maude to wait for us in the quadrant.

Settling them beneath an arch, I took the children with me to examine the church exterior. Pointing out the gargoyles that hung impossibly high on the stonework, I watched their responses, enjoying their unique view of the world.

'Why did Earl Harold wish to build a church, Mother?' asked Idwal from my side. He held my hand while Maredudd and Nest tumbled in play on the grass.

'I think, Idwal, that he wanted to show his appreciation of God and to secure a place in heaven.' Idwal was silent for a while as we walked on.

'Perhaps, Mother,' he hesitated for a moment, '... perhaps it is to seek God's forgiveness for all our kinsmen that he murdered.'

Looking down at his white face I knew not what to say so, instead, I knelt in the grass and hugged him. I had hoped he had forgotten or perhaps not comprehended the relevance of our wild ride that night but, as I held him, I realised that he had understood all too well.

I wondered then, what his sojourn in Snowdonia had been like for him; how fearful had he been? What horrors had he witnessed? What conversations had he overheard? Anwen swore that he had not seen Gruffydd's murder but he must have learned of it all the same. I wondered if the knowledge troubled him very much and wished for a more suitable location to discuss it with him.

'It was war, sweetheart. Earl Harold is a soldier, Idwal, and soldiers must do bad things. All soldiers do bad things, each one believing their own motivation to be the moral one, the one that God supports. We cannot decide which act is God's will and which is not, that is for him to decide. All human beings are flawed, my son, we come into the world that way and can only seek perfection. Some men manage to commit offences in God's name and maintain their moral fibre and ... others do not. I think, for all his offences, Harold has managed to keep God's grace.'
Idwal looked blankly into my eyes,

'Is that why you are going to marry him, even though he murdered my father?'

'Oooh, sweetheart, you do not understand the truth. Harold did not murder Gruffydd, twas our own Welsh kin that did so, to free themselves from him. He was not a gentle king, he suffered much as a youth and was a man who did not manage to keep God's grace. The Welsh suffered under Gruffydd and, in surrendering to England, you lost your inheritance; in marrying Harold, I hope to redress that loss. His position as Earl of Wessex means that he has power and influence with King Edward and may well be able to reinstate you in Gwenydd when you reach a man's estate. Harold can help all of us regain some of what we have lost and he can help you to learn to be a just ruler and the people of *Cymru* will welcome you home. We need Harold to help us.'

Chewing at his lip, Idwal continued to look at me, blinking as he tried to absorb my words. I felt a pang of remorse for I had but told him the half-truth. Harold could possibly help me to reinstate my sons in their Welsh cantrefs but the real reason I had agreed to wed with him was because my body burned for him as I had never expected it to burn for a man again.

Clutching the hilt of his wooden sword, Idwal looked across to where his brother and sister were playing.

'Who are they talking to?' he asked suddenly and, glad to change the subject, I followed his line of vision to see a group of children sitting in a circle with Maredudd and Nesta on the damp grass.

'Let us go and see,' I said, glad of the distraction, and taking his hand, we walked together to join the others.

'That's a curious name,' a golden-haired girl was saying, 'I have never heard the like before have you, Magnus?'

'No,' Magnus replied, 'and the name Nesta is strange too.'

Maredudd stood up to acknowledge my presence.

'We are Welsh,' he said, 'my name is well known in Wales and so is the name Nesta. My father was the king of all Wales and I am a prince, and Nesta is a princess too.'

'Welsh.' the strange children exclaimed in unison, 'How far you are from home. We have never met a Welshman before, have we, Magnus? What are you doing here in Waltham?'

'Looking at this church. My mother likes churches, the ones in Wales are made only of wood and we had never seen a stone one until we came to England. Have you been to the king's new abbey church at Thorney? I think 'tis bigger than this.'

'No,' the girl replied, clearly put out that the Welshmen were so much better travelled than she. 'We rarely travel abroad, my elder brother has travelled far and has his own manor toward the south coast; we haven't been to the king's court yet but we shall when we are older.'

They all looked up as Idwal settled himself beside them on the grass.

'Hello,' I said, 'isn't it a lovely day to visit the church. This is my son, Idwal. Maredudd and Nest are his siblings,' I smiled at them, encircling my children with a sweep of my arms. 'My name is Eadgyth, what are your names?'

The girl stood up and curtseyed, she was simply clad in cloth of the finest quality and I hoped she'd not get into trouble for the grass that marred the front of her tunic. She regarded me with large blue eyes before replying,

'I am called Gytha and this is my brother, Magnus. He cannot rise easily so I hope you will excuse him, he was crippled from birth but my father says has the finest mind he has ever known in a child.'

I smiled my pity on the boy but he shrugged it away so I continued without comment.

'Do you live close by? We are travelling from the King's lodging at Thorney to my brother's holdings in Mercia and stopped here to view the church, although it is much out of our way.'

'Our home is about a two mile walk from here, tis not far. It is a pleasant property, my mother is there with our sister, Gunnhild and our brother, Edmund. My father is away a lot but we see him whenever his business allows and he always brings us presents. Last time he bought me a psalter and an ivory comb fashioned into the likeness of a shell but it is sometime now since he has come.'

The girl sat down again with us and shoved at her brother, forcing him to lift his backside from the grass,

'Magnus, sit on my cloak for the grass is damp and Mother will scold if you should catch a chill.'
Obediently the boy lifted his buttocks so she could feed her cloak beneath him, then we all settled down to talk again. Nesta climbed onto my lap and began to suck upon her thumb.

'Father gave me a pony with a special saddle so that I should not tumble from his back into the dirt,' announced Magnus, 'now I can ride out and canter if I wish to without coming to any hurt.'

'How wonderful.' I exclaimed, glad that the boy had such a doting father for many men would disown such a son. 'I used to love to ride when I was your age. I followed the hunt too and there is nothing like the feel of the wind in your hair and the thrill of the chase…'

'Our father hardly thinks of anything but the hunt, unless 'tis war. He rarely goes anywhere without his hawk on his wrist.'

Far off a woman's voice called but we took no note of it. Suspicion began to nibble at the edges of my mind. I looked at the children more closely, noting their flaxen hair and blue eyes. Gytha was returning my stare with a determined, chin set expression that I knew well, and suddenly I recalled that Harold's mother's name was Gytha too.

I scrambled up, needing to get away, wanting to run, anywhere, as far and as fast as I could. Spinning round, I saw a figure outlined in one of the arches; it was a figure I had seen before. I recognised the graceful sweep of her neck and the passive, almost saintly demeanour. It was Eadgytha of the swan neck, Harold's concubine.

Her children saw her at the same time as I and rushed to her, hugging and leaping about her as gleefully my own children had greeted me.

'We did not hear you call, Mother.' they cried, but she did not look down at them but instead locked eyes with me above their heads.

'We have made new friends, Mother,' Gytha was telling her, 'they are Welsh and have the strangest of names, Nesta is the little girl but I misremember the boys' names and their lady mother has the same name as you, Mother, isn't that the strangest thing?'

The three of them drew nearer to me and I stood, unable to move, until she was before me in the sunlight. I should have been glad that the unfriendly sun revealed the fine lines about her eyes and mouth and highlighted the grey streaks in her hair, but I was not glad.

She was too beautiful and would be unto the grave, even her bones were lovely; she exuded a grace and refinement that made me feel both stout and awkward in her presence. We stared at each other, each disliking what the other saw.

'I knew not who the children were,' I apologised, 'I had no idea you lived close by.'

'It is of no moment,' she replied, as gracious as she was graceful, 'It is like Harold not to have told you.'

His name spoken between us at last made me break into a sweat. I cast about me, wondering where Harold was and, reading my thoughts, Eadgytha answered my silent question.

'He is with our son, Edmund, trying to explain why he must marry. He is a sensitive boy at heart, for all he is a man grown. I always knew it would happen one day and was prepared for it but … the children … well, it is harder for them to understand.'

Swallowing deeply, I was suddenly aware of the awful crime I committed upon this woman. In her eyes she had been wed to Harold for nigh on twenty years, hand-fasted and accepted, by all but the church, as his wife. Now, because of me, she must step back and allow him to announce me to the world as his church-wed wife. I saw now the reason for her red-rimmed eyes and realised that her outward serenity did but conceal inner turmoil. I knew I should never be so passive were the tables turned.

'You are very brave, Eadgytha,' I said, sincerely wanting to make it easier for her. She raised her chin and gave a semblance of a smile,

'I must be brave so that it is easier for the children. It is they who must not suffer, I have had twenty years of bliss and now,' she shrugged, 'tis time to pay the price. Harold will look after us, see us warm and fed; there are worse ways to suffer.'

We parted after that, not as enemies but not as friends either and, half hour or so later, Harold appeared from the cover of the woods, cantering toward the party that waited ready to ride onward on our journey. I kicked my mare forward before he could catch up with me and rode with my chin up and my back erect.

Once he was beside me I refused to look at him. Tears ached at the back of my throat but I would not give in to them. He tried to engage me in conversation, remarking upon the changing terrain. When I made no response, he began commenting upon the splendour of his church and asking my opinion on its design. For a while I was able to ignore him but soon my irritation grew to proportions so unbearable that I spurred my mare forward into a canter and, as soon as the way was clear, galloped ahead, hearing him start off behind me in pursuit.

The wind tore at my eyes and I let the tears spill, feeling them dashed coldly from my cheeks by the speed in which I travelled. A small wood loomed and I saw, from the corner of my eye, the green blur of the undergrowth. Harold, on his superior mount, drew closer behind me and, at last, he caught up and almost overtook me. Grabbing the bridle he forced my mount to a halt. I was breathless with exertion and anger. The air wrenched from my throat in gasps.

'God's teeth, Eadgyth.' he panted, 'Whatever is the matter with you today?'

'You Goddammed, lying bastard.' I screamed, using words I had only ever heard my brothers use.

'You have lied to me constantly, since we first met. You lied about the reason for our marriage, you lied about wanting me for myself and you lied about the reason for stopping at Waltham. I hate you, you ill-formed, disease poxed, ditchscum.'
I panted for breath, dashing annoying tears from my eyes before I continued,

'I have met your wife, Harold, and I have met your charming children. And all I can say is that you are a heartless, goddammed rotten bastard that doesn't deserve them.'

'Eadgyth.' he exclaimed, obviously shocked at my fluency in gutter tongue. Had I not been so angry I would have thought his outrage funny.

'Oh don't, Eadgyth me.' I cried, trying to disengage his hand from the bridle so I could ride on. The horses began to sidestep together along the woodland path, it was uncomfortable to be jogging along in such a fashion so, at length, we fell into step and moved along at a slow walk.

'It isn't as if I hadn't told you about them, is it?' he asked and I knew he was right, he had been open about his situation from the start …all but the fact that, up close, her beauty was unsurpassable. I had liked the children but now, having seen Eadgytha face to face, I felt both jealous and guilty at the pain I was inflicting.

'I don't know how you can think of hurting them so, Harold. The fact that you have no conscience about your actions makes me wonder if you are the man I believed you to be.'

I refused to look at him but I could tell from his voice that he was rattled enough to have abandoned his usual casual, mocking manner.

'Eadgytha and I were happy for many years. I was little more than a lad when we met and she a maid. I have treated her well, and our children, and will continue to do so. She knew that our union was not recognised by the church and she also knew that, should it be required of me, I would have to marry a church-wed wife. 'Tis the way of the world, Eadgyth, if she can accept it, why can't you?'

He sounded so pompous that I lost control again. 'So, you would wed with me simply because it is required of you. How do you think that makes me feel? What was it you once said? That you wanted *'a woman who would grab at life with both hands with you and if you went under would come up fighting'* or some such similar pretty words. You lied to me, Harold, you led me to believe that you wanted me for myself but, in truth, you only want me for the power my brother's support can provide you in your quest for Edward's throne. I've been pawned in marriage once before and do not wish to be so again.'

He reigned in the horses.

'Get down.' he ordered, barely waiting for me to disengage my feet from the stirrups before dragging me to the ground.

'What is it that you want, woman. I've asked ye to be my wife, I've told you how I feel about you and I've tried to explain about Eadgytha and the children, yet you obviously require some other proof of my sincerity.'

Taking my wrist, he dragged me to the side of the road and pushed me against a tree, where he leant against me so that I felt the hardness of his body against mine. He kissed me, refusing to stop although I pushed against his chest with both hands. The kiss went on and on. The rough tree bark dug into my back. Hardly able to breathe, my heart banged and my head whirled as his tongue thrust between my lips. My nose was filled with his odour and my mouth with his hot, livid lust and I stopped fighting, vanquished by a will stronger than mine own.

Mercia 1065

It was strange to be in my grandfather's house again. I looked in delight around the carved high hall where I had spent so many happy times. Edwin, proud of his inheritance, greeted us with enthusiasm, his wife standing in the background waiting for an introduction.

'Harold.' Edwin cried, 'so, I am soon to call you brother?'

They slapped each other effusively on the back while my brother's spouse and I exchanged shy glances and the children scampered off in search of mischief.

'Well, Eadgyth, you decided to accept Earl Harold's offer after all. It pleases me much, does it not, Gunnor? Oh, you have not met my wife have you? This is my sister, Eadgyth and this, Harold of Wessex, of whom you will have heard and this is Gunnor, soon to be the mother of my son.'

She dropped a small curtsey and ushered us toward the hearth where a tray of victuals awaited.

'Just to take the edge off your appetite,' she assured us, 'a meal will be ready 'ere long.'

I bit into a honey-filled wafer.

'Mmm, delicious,' I murmured as Nesta flung herself at me, embracing my knees with delight. Harold swung the child into his arms and she squealed with glee, grabbing at his moustaches with her pink, starfish hands.

'Your children are delightful, Lady,' commented Gunnor, 'and I think you have found them a loving step father.'

I watched Nest snuggled contentedly in Harold's arms and could find no argument with Gunnor's words.

'And your child, Gunnor, when is he expected?' She flushed, 'In March, God willing. Edwin is beside himself with joy, like a cur with two tails.'

The men were laughing at something, it pleased me to see them getting along so well, Edwin barely topped Harold's shoulder but was his equal in rich attire and I recalled that he had ever been concerned about his apparel in his youth.

'Did Edwin tell you that Morcar will be joining us tomorrow?' Gunnor asked, 'We thought we should mark your betrothal with a proper family feast. Both of your brothers are delighted at the match.'

'Well, I am not surprised, an alliance with the mighty Godwins can do us no harm and Harold benefits equally. Our marriage will mean a family foothold in each of the Earldoms now. His brothers, Leofwine and Gyrth, hold much of the south and east and Tostig is Earl of Northumbria; now, with this alliance with Edwin, Harold strengthens his position further.'

'I'm sure that isn't his only reason though, Lady Eadgyth, it is obvious Earl Harold holds you in high esteem.'

'Hmmm,' I answered, 'Gunnor, we are sisters are we not? Eadgyth is my name. Now, would you accompany me on a stroll about the manor, I used to visit here as a child and would love to see it all again. My grandmother, Godgifu, had a wonderful flower garden, is it still here? Would you show it to me?'

Gunnor put down her goblet.

'I should be delighted. Shall I call the children to come with us?'

We quit the hall, the boys running ahead, calling out to me as they discovered the secrets of the manor. Nest was fractious so Anwen carried her; she sucked her thumb and tucked her head into the hollow of her nurse's neck. Outside, we perched on the edge of a stone seat, making the most of the last autumn sunshine.

'Do you see much of Morcar?' I asked, 'I have only seen him the once since I returned from Wales, he seemed to have changed little but I am surprised he remains unwed.'

Idwal brought me a small posy he had picked. I smiled my delight and held them carefully on my lap.

'He comes from time to time,' Gunnor answered, 'but they closet themselves away so I have not really become acquainted with him. Edwin says he is unsettled and needs a wife to soothe his restless spirit, I think he has a suitable match in mind.'

I laughed.

'Oh, they teased me terribly when I was a child. I grew up thinking myself fat and ugly because of their constant taunts, but I have since learned that I do hold some charm … for at least a few men.'

'Brothers are like that. I have five and each and every one of them tease me remorselessly, even though I am a woman grown with my own household. Mind you, should any mistreat me, they would be up in arms about it.'

'Harold's brothers are all very much like him, have you ever met them?'

Gunnor shook her head.

'No, I haven't, although I have heard much. Is not one of them … Tostig is it? Is he not troublesome to his father?'

I watched Maredudd pick up a small pebble and toss it into the ornamental pool, Idwal followed suit until Anwen got up from the bench. 'The water will soon be like a midden if we foul it with rubbish.' she scolded and the boys slunk away in search of further mischief.

'Tostig was a trial in his youth, the father is dead now but Harold has told me that Swegen was the worst of them all. I believe he found himself in disgrace when he abducted an abbess and refused to release her. She was quite ruined by the matter and bore him a child in the end; when he tired of her he just abandoned her and the babe.'

'But that's scandalous.' cried Gunnor, 'Edwin didn't tell me that, the poor woman. I am quite certain he told me it was Tostig who was trouble, said the folk under his rule in the north couldn't abide him, that he was too harsh and his greed had led to the murder of some good men.'

Exchanging looks with Gunnor, whose face was pinched with disapproval, I wondered at the truth of her words and made a mental note to enquire of Harold.

'I don't know, I have only met him the once. He is a fine looking man. Gyrth and Leofwine are brave looking men though, they seem tall and godlike until you see them next to Harold and then they pale to insignificance.'

Gunnor smiled. 'That's love speaking I think, Lady,' she said, but I was bending over to examine a flower that Idwal had brought me and so made no reply.

The betrothal feast was planned for three days hence and, with the arrival of Morcar's entourage, the holding was at bursting point. The place took on the atmosphere of a king's court, albeit not so pious as that of Edward.

There were games and dancing, contests and bards. Harold and I were the centre of attention as everyone wished us good fortune. The king and the queen were not present for Edward had been unable to resist an invitation from Tostig to hunt with him at Britford. Part of me suspected that Tostig, ever jealous of Harold's favour with Edward, had been attempting to spoil our celebrations but, since neither Harold nor I minded that the royal couple stayed away, it was a plot that failed. As fate decreed we did not need Tostig to spoil things for fortune had already ordained otherwise.

Our festivities were well-advanced, our cups brimming and the dancers building up a healthy sweat, when a messenger arrived, hot foot from Britford, summoning Harold to the king's presence. To my dismay he began to make his preparations to leave at once.

'Oh, Harold, must you go?' I cried, over the clatter of the celebrations. ' How unreasonable for Edward to summon you when he knows we mark our betrothal.'

He took my hands in his, looking so contrite I almost believed he was as regretful as I.

'I'm sorry, sweetheart, but you know that when the king calls, his serf must obey.'

Devastated to be so let down on our special day, I did not smile at his likening himself, the richest earl in the realm, to the peasantry. There was little he could do but I felt dour nonetheless. 'Shall I accompany you?' I asked.

'Nay, sweetheart, you will only hinder me. I shall hasten back as soon as I may.'

And so, taking only a few huscarls with him, he cantered into the night leaving me watching with Edwin at the hall entrance. My brother looked pensive.

'Mayhap I should go too,' he said, 'I suspicion there is trouble looming for Edward to call Harold forth from a private gathering.'

'Oh no, Edwin, stay here with us, he will return as soon as he can, he promised, at least, to send me word should he be delayed.'

As good as his word, Harold was back in three days but only to relate the news to us and bid me farewell 'ere he rode forth again. We gathered about him in the hall and waited while he gulped a cup of ale.

'Ahh,' he gasped, wiping his mouth on his sleeve, 'I needed that.'

Unable to wait any longer, I asked the question that everyone longed to.

'What did Edward want?'

Harold looked about the thronging room.

'It is not good news, sweetheart. Trouble had broken out up north,' he said. 'It seems the thegns have risen in rebellion against Tostig. They have ridden on York and broken into his residences, stolen his treasure and murdered his huscarls. His retainer, a fellow called Copsig, managed to escape and raise the alarm. The king is calling it treason. Although the thegns swear they ride soley against Tostig and not the king; mind you, it amounts to the same thing when a man is as deep into the king's pocket as my brother.'

'What has Tostig done?' I asked, as soon as the room grew quiet again. Harold perched on the edge of the mead bench and put his foot on a stool; the company was hanging on his every word.

'Things haven't gone well since he was given the blasted earldom. I've told him he can't tax the northerners as though they are as prosperous as the south but he would never listen. Since the very beginning there have been whispers against him and, as his brother, I have ever believed only the good. I never got to the bottom of what happened at his house when Dolfinson and Ormson were murdered. He pleaded innocence then which was enough for the king and he escaped punishment even though their blood still stains the floor of his hall. I tried to advise him then but he wouldn't listen.'

I held up my hand, halting his speech.

'But, Harold, I don't know anything about that; who were these men and how could Tostig have had a part in their murder without any repercussions?'

'Because he is the King's friend,' Harold continued, 'they had some sort of a grievance and went to discuss it with Tostig, apparently at his invitation. They were given hospitality at first but, when they could not reach an amicable agreement, Tostig had a couple of his heavies slip out of concealment and slit their throats.'

I spun round to look at Edwin and then back to Harold.

'But how could that happen?' I cried, trying to equate cold-blooded murder with the languid young man that had teased me at court, 'it can't be true. Edward would never condone a crime like that.'

Edwin moved to Harold's side.

'Edward is a weak man, Eadgyth. He ever takes the route to an easy life, he buries his head and refuses to see what lies before him,' For once Edwin looked deadly serious, I regarded him for some moments before continuing with my questions.

'What was their grievance? Surely it could have been sorted out. I can imagine no circumstance that is worth such bloodshed.'

Harold took a mouthful of ale.

'Tostig imposed an increase on the Northumbrian tax rate, raising both his income and the king's. So, thegns like Gamldbearn for instance, who owns about sixty carucates, saw his taxes rise from twenty shillings to thirty. Dunstan is expected to pay twenty-four instead of sixteen and Gleniarain nineteen shillings and six instead of thirteen. The demands could not be met and it is these three thegns that are leading the rebellion. 'Tis no surprise really.'

I could not find it in my heart to blame them, for such demands were extortionate. It was an earl's duty to protect his thegns in return for their service, not ring the life's blood from them. Harold had not finished his tale.

'Then at Westminster, last Christ's mass, when Gospatrick was killed. You will remember the brawl in the king's hall? Well, the northerners pointed the finger at Tostig but, again, Edward protected him…'

'I heard the queen was behind that,' interjected one of Edwin's retainers, forgetting that she was Harold's kin.

'I'll have no talk against my sister,' Harold said, his face white and set, his eyes staring hard into the face of the speaker. 'Tis treason to speak ill of your queen.' The fellow backed down, red-faced and edged his way to the back of the crowd and Harold picked up his story where he had left off.

'Yesterday, Tostig was beseeching the king to call out the fryd but I declared, there and then, I wouldn't authorise my men to fight and Gyrth and Leo backed me up. Gyrth is usually Tostig's firm ally but even he could see that civil war must be avoided, we need unity in these troubled times. The thegns ...' he said, with a glance in my direction, 'are demanding Tostig be stripped of his position and replaced with our Lord Morcar here.'

All heads swivelled to my brother who was paring an apple with his knife; he stopped with the blade halfway to his mouth.

'Indeed?' he cried, 'Ha, these northerners show some sense after all. I'm certain I can accommodate them.'

Gentle laughter broke out among the gathering but Harold quelled it with a raised hand.

'I can hardly depose my own brother in favour of my brother-in-law, I do have some family loyalty.'

I remembered then how Edwin had spoken to me of Harold's need to increase his power base and knew that the temptation to support my brother must be great. If Morcar were Earl of Northumbria then, should Edward die, support for Harold's claim to the throne would be absolute. I wondered if he had overlooked that fact but, by the look in his eye, I could see that he waged an inner battle between loyalty to Tostig and his own, personal ambition.

'And what does the king ask you to do?' asked Edwin, who stood with a hand on Gunnor's neck, one finger stroking her bare skin where it disappeared into her tunic.

'I am to ride north and try to make peace between them. They are heading for Oxford and the king and Tostig are at Salisbury. I can't let them get their hands on Tostig or they will rip him limb from limb and then war will be inevitable and my mother would never forgive me.'

Managing to smile at his feeble joke, I caught Morcar's eye. He looked petulant, like a child that has been offered a sweetmeat only to have it snatched away again.

'When do you leave, Harold? I will ride with you if I may?' asked Edwin, releasing his grip on Gunnor and signalling to his huscarls to make ready. Harold raised his voice above the hubbub made by the scraping of stools as the men drained their cups and prepared to leave.

'As soon as we can make ready, brother, but 'tis a peaceful mission so only bring your household militia. Eadgyth, I am so sorry our plans are altered, I will endeavour to sort out this disarray as soon, and as peacefully, as I can and return to you unharmed.'

He kissed the top of my bowed head and strode off across the hall, calling for his master of horse. I felt bereft, my high hopes for feasting and festivity dashed by the onset of war. They would leave at first light.

Later that evening Anwen was braiding my hair when the chamber door flew open and Harold roared in.

'Did you know what was afoot madam and think to keep it from me?'

'What?' I stammered, trying to hide my modesty behind a bed curtain, 'I have no idea what you are talking about.' I yelled, my anger matching his own.

He stalked toward me, the air he disturbed lifting his long hair from his shoulders.

'Your brother, Madam. Morcar has ridden out to join the rebels. By God, I should have kept my mouth shut, I even told him where they were mustering. He will have himself at the head of the dissenting army in no time at all.'

I relaxed. 'Why would I know of Morcar's plans, Harold? I am not in his confidence.'

Dropping the curtain, I moved to the table and, pouring two cups of wine, handed him one. Harold took it and smiled wryly as his body relaxed.

'I'm sorry, Eadgyth, I am so on edge I would no doubt yell at the Pope were he here. You are right to be angry. I am just so damned annoyed that our week has been spoiled.'

He sipped at his drink, watching me above the rim of the cup. Slowly his expression changed and the first twinklings of lust crept into his eye.

'Did you know, Madam, that the light from the brazier makes that nightrail quite transparent.'

I tried to slip back behind the curtain but he caught my wrist and pulled me onto his knee.

'Good God,' he cried, 'tisn't as if it's the first time I've seen you in your nightgown. Didn't we ride back from Wales with you similarly clad and, all the way, my cock nudging you in the back like a battering ram?' His big laugh rang out as I struggled to get up.

'Harold. You are outrageous.' But he was nuzzling at my neck and I could not maintain my displeasure; just as the attention was chasing away the last of my resistance, Anwen came back into the room.

'Lady!' she exclaimed, and Harold hastily ceased his attentions.

'It's alright, Anwen, don't worry, I must away,' he said, getting up suddenly so that I had to stumble to find my feet. 'I will be back to finish what we just started when I have sorted out your damned brother.' And, with a lingering kiss for me and a brisk salute for Anwen, he quit the chamber.

Our cavalcade wove its way through the Oxfordshire countryside toward Salisbury where Edward held court. Far off in the distance, pluming smoke betrayed the path of the rebel army who had lain waste to much of Northampton. We passed burned-out holdings and settlements devoid of life. I wondered where the people had fled to. As I followed the cavalcade I pondered the tragedies of the poor that are never realised by earldormen and kings; warbands ride across country, destroying crops and burning farmsteads without considering the monumental cost to the peasants. Famine and death would be inevitable now.

I had no idea of Harold's whereabouts but I harboured hopes that he might be found closeted with the king when we reached Britford, close by the abbey of Wilton. Word had reached us that Morcar had joined with the rebels and agreed to become their earl. Tostig stood not a chance against the huge united armies of the north and Edwin was applying pressure to convince Harold that Morcar would make the better lord of the north. He had no real choice but to agree for Tostig had treated his people badly. Now all that remained was for Harold to persuade King Edward to that fact.

My lower back and buttocks were sore of the saddle when at last we rode into the royal lodge. I slid gratefully from the saddle as a boy appeared from nowhere and came running to take my horse. The children were tired from the journey so Anwen took them straight to the royal nursery where they would lodge with the royal wards. I entered the hall, brushing the dust of the road from my cloak and all but collided with the queen.

'Eadgyth.' she wailed, 'You must persuade him, he will listen to you. Harold is refusing to take Tostig's side in this stupid rebellion and the two of them have been fighting and saying unforgivable things. Edward is distraught. Come, come with me, they are within; you must stop them before 'tis too late.'

Voices were issuing from the council chamber and, without knocking, she thrust open the door and we were both inside. Tostig was empurpled, leaning forward across the table jabbing his finger beneath Edward's nose. He paused and all three men looked up as we entered.

Harold was pale, his face set as he attempted to control ungovernable anger. The king looked as if he was going to weep.

'There, Harold,' cried the queen, 'Eadgyth is here to talk some sense to you. Tell him, Eadgyth, family comes first, he must support his brother.'
She looked from me to Harold and back again, waiting for me to take her side. Totally out of my depth, I knew not what to say. Had Edith quite forgotten that in asking me to champion her family, she was asking that I betray the interests of my own?

'I …I,' I stammered, floundering badly before Harold came to my aid.

'This is not women's business, Edith, I have told you. We cannot risk civil war just because we love our little brother. Sire,' he continued, turning back to his king, 'we cannot afford to fragment our strength at this time. England is in peril, William awaits his chance overseas and at the first sign of unrest he will come, we cannot defend England on two fronts.'

'But, Harold,' whined the king, 'Tostig is my faithful servant, should I not show my gratitude for that?'

Harold put his head back, mouthing unspoken words at the vaulted ceiling,

'No, Sire. Not if it puts all England at risk. I have never advised you wrong and you know I would never go against my kin unless it were imperative. I beseech you, my king, give Northumbria to Morcar, Tostig can have other lands.'

'East Anglia or Wessex?' sneered Tostig, and Harold turned on him, his face white and his lips clenched,

'Hold your tongue, Tostig. For the love of God, have pity on your king, look at what you are doing to him.'

Edward was hunched on his throne, plucking at his sparse beard, his watery eyes darting back and forth between the brothers. He fixed his gaze on Harold and swallowed before announcing,

'You decide, Harold, you have ever guided me right, I leave it all to you.'

Tostig whirled on his king,

'You weak-livered, coward.' he screamed, 'I put up with your whimpering, cloying ways for all these years and now, at the first sign of trouble, you abandon me. I am leaving, do you hear me, old man? You will not see me again.'

Evading Edward's clutching hands and shouldering Harold out of his way, he strode from the chamber; we heard him calling his men to horse as he stormed along the corridor. Edith burst into tears,

'How could you, Harold? I swear I will never speak to you again. Never, never.' she cried, rushing in pursuit of her other brother. Edward began to sob into his kerchief,

'Christ.' Harold cursed. I put my arm about the king's shoulder.

'Do not fret, Sire,' I murmured. 'Shall I call your man to help you to bed? You are unwell.'

Edward clutched at my arm, and we shuffled toward his sleeping place, calling to his servant, Geraint, as we went. When he was passed into safe hands I returned to find Harold sitting on the king's table with his head in his hands.

'Christ's wounds, Eadgyth, what have I done to deserve this? I have lost a brother and a sister this day and all for want of a competent king.'

'Hush, Harold,' I murmured, stroking his bowed back, 'You did what was best for England, you were right to avoid civil war at all cost and the king knows that.'

He sat up and span round on his buttocks to face me. His usual arrogant expression was marred by stress.

'Your brother, Edwin, joined the rebels last week in support of Morcar's claim to the earldom, the combined northern armies are vast; Edwin even had some Welsh with him. They have laid waste to vast tracts of land and, had we wanted to, we would have been hard put to beat them. No, Eadgyth, I backed your family for a number of reasons. We would have been hard pressed to win against them, and losing would have made it difficult to maintain our marriage agreement.'

He leaned forward and I felt him grow calmer in my arms; he kissed me.

'I suggest we appease your brothers, make sure Edward reinstates the laws of Cnut and get ourselves wed as soon as we may.'

Bosham November 1065

I woke early and lay quietly for a few moments, wondering what had disturbed my dreams. Slowly, as the dullness of sleep wore off, I recalled that it was the day I would become the Lady of Wessex. The King was unable to shake off his melancholy and sickened, his lingering illness precluding the huge wedding due to us as the Earl of Wessex and his lady butI was glad to be spared the fuss. I had no wish to be made an exhibition of. Instead, Harold had organised a small intimate joining at the ancient church at Bosham with only our families present. The queen refused to attend and refused to be reconciled with Harold so only Gytha and Harold's sisters and brothers and Edwin and Morcar were coming and of course Anwen and the children would be there.

I sat up, stretching my arms, becoming aware as I did so, that my bed was strewn with winter garlands, woven ivy and holly, bright with berries. Leaning forward to draw back the bed curtain, I noticed I was not alone and gave an involuntary cry. Harold waited, wide-awake, by the window.

'Good morning, madam, I come bearing gifts,' he grinned, 'I had not realised you were such a slug-a-bed. Had the season been more clement I would have

smothered you with posies but these evergreens will have to suffice, my page had a devil's job collecting them.'
He came over to the bed and handed me a cup of ale from the nightstand.

The sun was just beginning to lighten in the east, so I knew that the household would be abroad.

'What time is it?' I asked, 'and where is Anwen?'

'I sent her forth,' he grinned, 'much to her disapproval. Do you know, I don't think she has taken to me.'
I sloshed the ale about my mouth, freshening my breath before swallowing.

'She has a natural Welsh instinct to mistrust Saxons and she worries that you may sample the wares before you've paid for them.'

'How well she knows me,' he laughed, leaning forward and trying to peer down the neck of my nightgown.

'Are you ready for your *morgengifu* now?' he asked, drawing a small package from the folds of his tunic. I had forgotten the Saxon tradition of a gift to the bride on the morning of the wedding. I sat up, reaching to take the parcel from him and he kissed me on the side of the mouth,

'Of course the real gift will come later,' he whispered and for once I did not blush at the inference of his words.

The package was wrapped in a soft covering and tied with ribbon. I untied it, discovering within a psalter so small that I could conceal it within my palm. Its tiny size did not mean that the artistry of the book was less fine. The cover was wrought with gems and gold and, inside, the lettering and illumination was vivid and beautiful. I had lost my old psalter during the attack on Rhuddlan and Harold, knowing how I mourned it, had ordered this one made for me especially. There was a dedication to me on the first page and the scribe had noted that the prayer book commemorated the union of Eadgyth Ælfgarsdóttir and Harold Godwinson of Wessex. Tears misted my eyes, it was so much more than I had expected.

'Thank you, Harold,' I croaked, 'it is more than I deserve.'

'No, it isn't.' he exclaimed, 'Look, I have this for you too. I can't have you coming to the altar without proper adornment,' and he draped a chain of gold about my neck. It was heavy and I looked down, lifting it to allow closer inspection.

The goldsmith had worked tiny, multicoloured enamel squares into separate leaves of gold that lay flat against my neck. It was joined by links of gold to form a chain. I had seen nothing like it before and Harold said that he had picked it up from a goldsmith near York while he was organising the instatement of Morcar as Earl of Northumbria.

I slid from the bed and stood barefoot in the rushes, tiptoeing to kiss him on the mouth. 'Thank you, Harold.' I whispered.

It was the first time I had initiated an intimate gesture and he drew back a little with a quizzical expression.

'Had I thought you so easy bought I'd have given you gifts sooner,' he teased. Then he turned to leave the room, slapping my rump, naked beneath the flimsy nightgown. 'See you in church, sweetheart,' he winked from the doorway, 'and don't be late.'

When I was a girl I had dreamed of a wedding upon which the sun shone and the birds sang. Instead, as at my first marriage, soft rain fell, soaking everything and turning the ground beneath our feet into a quagmire. Harold's mother, Gytha, had come for the ceremony. She was quietly proud of her son and glad that he had, at last, found himself a church-wed wife. Kissing me on the cheek, she welcomed me to the family, admired my dress and tickled Nesta on the chin, finding a silver coin in her ear and pushing it into her fat, little fist.

'For the alms box,' she told her, as Anwen hoisted her into her arms to bear her to church. Then taking Leofwine's arm, Gytha sailed off at the head of the wedding party and assembled in the churchyard ahead of my arrival. In between showers, my women and I dashed from the manor, our gowns making a splash of colour on the grim scene.

The birds were silent and the sun did not show his head at all but the church door stood open and BoshamBosham's single bell rang out to let the world know that it was a special day. Harold, clad in warm soft leggings and a plush blue tunic, met me at the church door and we all stood in the rain while the priest said the holy words over us and joined us as man and wife in the sight of God. Afterwards, when the deed was done, everyone gathered round, kissing me and slapping Harold on the back and I was no longer dowager queen of Wales but the Lady of Wessex.

Our household was a merry one as we hurried back to the hall for the nuptial feast. Inside, the cheer chased away the grey weather. The walls were lined with tables, piled high with pastries and meat and the leaping firelight reflected in the gleaming cups. As we crossed the threshold the bards lost no time in tuning their instruments and Harold and I took our places at the head table to smile benevolently upon the gamboling host.

The lilting tunes of the harpist took me back to Alys' wedding at Dinefwr so long ago. What a child I had been then, full of girlish ideals; unspoiled, as yet, by the cold reality of Gryffydd's debauchery. I smiled, recalling how Rhodri and I had laughed together after I'd caught Gryffydd rutting with the serving wench.

'What are you finding so amusing, wife?' Harold broke into my reverie so that, startled, I slopped some wine onto my lap.

'Clumsy.' he teased, mopping me with his kerchief.

'I was thinking of when I was a girl, the harpist reminded me of a friend's wedding that I attended long ago.'

Sliding onto the bench beside me, he looked about the hall.

'Grander than this, I'll warrant,' he said.

'Well, it probably was, and a lot more crowded too, but I don't mind. I'm not one for grandeur; in fact, my dream has always been to live in a small cott, married to a simple cotter with a garden for vegetables, some chickens and maybe a house cow. Riches have never bothered me …'

His big laugh cut off my speech.

'…and here you are married to the richest man in England. However will you endure it?'

'I'm sure I will manage,' I laughed and then sobered a little. 'Don't you ever tire of it though,

Harold? The demands of your position, all the pretence and the pomp of court?'
He looked about him at the frolicking company.

'Tell the truth I haven't given it much thought. I can't imagine a different way of life, this is all I know … it's all I've ever known.'

'I wonder how the king is?' I said suddenly, 'he was looking so frail when we left. I hope Edith doesn't think it too selfish of us not to wait until he was recovered enough for them to attend.'
Harold filled our goblets with more wine.

'At least it saved her the satisfaction of refusing the invite. She hasn't spoken to me since the upset with Tostig but she was ever one to sulk. I suppose Edward's sickness will take the minds of the chroniclers from our wedding too, the fusty old fellows will be hunched over their inkpots writing about Edward's illness and the northern rebellion and forget all about us.'
Sloshing the deep red liquid about my goblet, skilfully keeping it within the rim all the while, I thought for a moment before replying.

'Well, I for one don't care. You have the parchment to prove it legal, don't you? Just so long as our children are legitimate, it doesn't matter one bit.'
At my words a scurrilous expression spread across his face.

'How many children are you planning, sweetheart, four or five?'

'Oh, I thought six or seven at least, my Lord.' I replied, refusing to be disconcerted. Placing his hand beneath the table and caressing my thigh, he smiled wickedly.

'The sooner we get to it then the better, I say,' he murmured and I buried my face in my goblet and took too large a gulp of wine.

'Choke up, Sweetheart.' he cried, thumping me on the back as I coughed and spluttered.

To concentrate my mind away from the feel of his hot hand upon my thigh, I pretended interest in the maids and swains who were dancing, skirts twitching and boots thumping on the wooden floor before the dais. Maredudd and Idwal ran, darting in and out of the dancers, with a couple of terriers barking at their heels. Leo and Gyrth were involved in a game of high jump, leaping over the flames of the central fire while the company squealed and clapped with appreciation.

'Watch your balls, boy.' cried Harold, laughing as his youngest brother all but scorched his breeches. Harold's head was thrown back and his big laugh echoed about the lofty hall. Reaching for a wafer filled with honey and currants, I noticed Harold suddenly grow still and following his gaze I saw that the doors had been opened to admit a stranger.

Harold put down his goblet and wiped his mouth, standing up and waiting as the young man approached the high table.   He was not much more than a boy, nineteen or twenty perhaps, his fair hair lifted on his shoulders as, his chin high and gaze direct, he made straight for the high table. I could not place where we had met before. He bent his knee before us, not looking in my direction but fixing his gaze on Harold all the while. Harold held out his hand in friendship.

'Godwin,' he said, 'you are well come, my son, I am glad you could make it. I would like you to greet my wife, Eadgyth.'

My eyes swivelled from Harold to rest upon his firstborn.

'Godwin,' I murmured, 'I have heard so much of you, it feels we are already acquainted.'

This was not true. Harold hardly ever mentioned his family and I don't know why I lied. Godwin bowed and I felt his breath, although not his lips, on the back of my hand.

'Madam,' he said, without feeling, 'I could hardly miss my father's wedding, I am only sorry I was not here in time for the churching.'

Offering him a goblet of wine, Harold sat down again, indicating that Godwin should follow suit. The boy perched on the edge of the table and gulped his wine. I felt for him as he wrestled conflicting loyalties to his mother and his father.

'I came by way of court,' he said, looking about the thronging hall, 'the king is sinking and my Aunt Edith would barely look me in the face. She is sore upset at you, Father.'

'I know, but how else could I have acted? I cannot have the country up in arms just to please the whims of my brother and sister. What of Edward, does he not rally at all?'

Godwin shook his head.

'No, I spoke with his physician who says he is weak and chilled all the time, no matter how high they stoke the fires. He says there is a sweetness to his water and that he suffers an unquenchable thirst.'

With a quick smile of regret Harold put down his drink.

'We must return to court tomorrow so that I can consult with the physician myself. I had thought he would be recovered 'ere we returned but, if he is ailing and like to die, he must name a successor. Young

Edgar will be no good at all; the country will fragment beneath his rule, like ice beneath a hot sun. A fine Christ's mass this will be with an ailing monarch and a stubborn, vindictive queen. Can you make ready to travel on the morrow, sweetheart?'

And so, where I had hoped for a month at Bosham, Harold and I had just one night and we were determined to enjoy it.

The rain continued to fall and after dark the wind got up to howl and moan about the hall, lifting the tapestries and belching smoke back into the company. As soon as was seemly I kissed the children and took my leave of the family; Godwin looked on tight lipped as my husband and I, accompanied by the usual nuptial jokes, escaped to our chamber..

'That went well, sweetheart,' Harold commented as he dismissed the servant and stoked the slumbering fire back into life himself, 'Godwin seems to accept you.'

'No, he doesn't, he hates me, Harold. How can you be so blind? Did you not see his tight lips and bitter eyes.'

Struggling to loosen a knotted thong on his shirt, he said, 'He might not like it much but at least he has shown he will make an effort to accept the marriage. I know him well, sweetheart, it is a good sign that he came. If we meet with him half way he will come round. Anyway how can any man fail to be won over by your charms?'

I struggled playfully in his arms for a moment.

'I think it more to do with his wish not to lose his father than any wish to welcome me as his mother.'

'Hush, Eadgyth,' he whispered, lowering his mouth to mine, 'you chatter too much. The time is come for silence.'

Alone in our bed, his tongue licked my soul, nibbling and kissing my psyche, changing me and moulding the molten wax of my heart to his will.

Shamed at first, I tried to resist but soon, I gave in and lay back, delighting in the forgotten thrill of the right man's lips upon my secret places. We rolled back and forth, wrapped in the shroud of my hair, while he stroked and kneaded and I wept, pulsing and drunk upon the skill of his craft.

He discovered and opened something within me that that had previously lain fallow and upon his lathe I was turned into someone new.

Thorney Island January 1066

Christ's mass was a drear one that year. The king was sick unto death and the palace in gloom, we crept about as joyless as the grave. The court was more crowded than was usual, even for Christmas, for men had come forth to attend the consecration and dedication of Edward's church of St Peter's. Too ill to attend the ceremony, the king had wept, exacerbating his malady and filling us all with anxiety. The Christmas celebrations were kept minimal, the mood subdued as we waited fearful in the royal palace.

As soon as I laid eyes upon him, it was apparent that the king was not long for this world. It was only a few days since I had seen him last but, in that time, his skin has yellowed and his breath, when one drew near, was rancid. My old cook Envys, had she smelled it, would have said that spectres were dancing on his tongue.

He was tetchier than ever. The court hastened to do his bidding, trying to tempt his palette with sweet morsels and bringing liquid to quench his insatiable thirst. Edith, stony faced and horrid, barely spoke to me although I had taken no part in Tostig's downfall. She sat at her husband's side and held his chilly hand, willing him to live, afraid of what would befall her after.

The witanagemot, summoned to the Christ's mass court, looked helpless upon their stricken king. It was a large gathering. The five earls, Harold, Leo, Gyrth, Morcar and Edwin, two archbishops, Stigand and Ealdred, together with eight bishops and all the leading thegns of England, stood helpless and knew not what to do. A successor must be named but still the king prevaricated.

The outside temperature had dropped and many braziers burned in the king's apartments, supplementing the roaring fire and depriving the room of oxygen. I watched our shadows leap and eddy on the wall as, like mummers robbed of lines, we waited for Edward to utter his last words and so provide our cue.

'Go and refresh yourself, my queen,' I whispered into Edith's ear, 'I will sit with the king.' After a few moments, she rose and left the room without speaking. I sat beside the bed and took the king's hand. He stirred, some instinct informing him that it was no longer his queen that wept beside him. He opened his red-rimmed eyes.

'My Lady of Wessex,' he croaked, remembering, even in his extremity, my new title. 'Tis good of you to come.'

'I am honoured to be here, Sire,' I replied, grief tearing the back of my throat. He fidgeted his legs.

'My feet and legs are so cold,' he said petulantly, 'and, did you know, I missed the consecration of my church, Eadgyth; after all my work and waiting, I was too ill to attend.'

Tears of pain and disappointment crept from beneath his eyelids.

'I attended the ceremony though, Sire. It was splendid. Would you like me to tell you all about it?'

For the remainder of the chill afternoon I whispered into the king's ear a description of the splendid consecration and dedication ceremony at St Peter's, the west minster. He closed his eyes; the only indication that he still lived was the grip he maintained on my fingers. When the torchbearers came to replace the dimming lights, Edith returned and I rose and curtseyed.

'He says his feet are cold, Madam. Shall I request extra blankets?'

'I know he is cold, he complains constantly, but there are already so many coverings on him.'

Sitting at the foot of the bed, she put her hands beneath the blankets and rubbed briskly at his feet and lower legs.

'Bring the king fresh stockings,' she ordered and Edward's servant scurried off to find a pair. On his return, Edith stripped off his old ones and threw them, damp and stained with sweat, onto the floor and replaced them with soft, woollen ones. Continuing to rub his feet, she glanced up at me and, overcoming her resentment, said,

'I thank you, Lady, for the care of him, I was in need of some respite. The king ever had much regard for you.'

She did not smile but I took heart from her words nevertheless, wanting to heal the breach between us.

'Madam, any time you ever have need of me, you have only to call,' I said before curtseying again and retreating from the chamber.

Alone, I waited long into the small hours. Wrapped in furs against the cold, I sat and looked out at the black sky. The stars stood out, stark upon their backdrop and the moon hung low, a great opaque orb, just above the horizon. It was quiet, the kingdom waiting breathless. Far off a dog barked, a night bird shrieked and then, all was quiet once more.

I drew my furs closer about my shoulder and wrapped my arms about my body to warm myself, wishing Harold were with me. Wondering what was happening in the king's chamber, I rose and fetched a drink from the nightstand and added some charcoal to the brazier. My eyes felt crusty and heavy with sleep but my mind writhed with regret for Edward, sympathy for Edith and the implications the king's passing may have upon my future.

Anwen had stayed at BoshamBosham with the children so, unwilling to summon a stranger to help me disrobe, I began to loose my braids, brushing and brushing until my hair leapt and crackled like a living thing. Then, slipping out of my gown I hurried into my nightrobe and back beneath the bed furs. I must have dozed because, quite suddenly, I became aware of movement in the chamber and opened my eyes. I saw that the candles had burned low and were guttering in a pool of grease.

Turning over on the bed, I saw Harold sitting beside me staring into the slumped embers of the fire. It was not until I placed my hand on his shoulder that he realised I had wakened.

'Eadgyth,' he said, 'I'm sorry I disturbed you.'

'I have been sitting up waiting so there is no need to apologise. How does the king?'

Harold ran his hands through his hair. 'He has gone, sweetheart,' he whispered, 'peaceful at the last. He gave Edith and the country into my keeping but still did not specifically name an heir.'

Tears gathered and dropped onto my cheeks. Although I had known his passing was inevitable, he had been a friend to me. An inadequate monarch, better suited to the church, but a good man nevertheless and he would be sadly missed.

'What will happen now?' I asked at last and Harold turned to me and took my frozen fingers, rubbing the warmth back into them with his own.

'The witan met directly the king had gone. As the man most suited to rule they offered the crown to me. There was none who disputed it, Eadgyth, and I am to be crowned on the morrow, at the West Minster, after the king has been laid to rest.'

'The king is dead, long live the king,' I murmured.

'Tis what we expected to happen, 'tis what your brothers wanted.'

'I know,' I groaned, 'but it will change so much, Harold. We have been wed such a short time 'twould have been nice to have some space to enjoy it. There will be no peace now, no leisure, no private time. Now we will be at the beck and call of everybody.'

Harold began to remove his clothes, throwing his boots into the corner far from the bed so that the stink of them should not sour our sleep.

The moonlight crept into the room and glistened on his torso, his skin shimmering in the opalescent light. His muscles rippled and stretched as, stripping off his tunic and braes he threw them near the brazier where they would retain some warmth. Then he strode across the chamber and climbed into the high, wide bed beside me.

I lay my face on his shoulder and traced with a lazy finger the scar of a long-healed axe wound that trailed like a woodland path through the forest of golden hair. That night I lay with my Lord of Wessex for the last time. The night after, and for every night hence, I would lie with Harold, the chosen king of England.

West Minster 6th January 1066

The slab of Edward's tomb stood out stark, the mortar around the edges still wet. I could not take my eyes from it. I pictured him lying there, wrapped cold in his shroud as his erstwhile subjects continued with their lives as though nothing had happened. A few hours before dawn they had closed his blind eyes and, early this morning, we had laid him to rest. Now, some three hours later, we assembled again at the minster to crown Harold king.

Cloaked in unreality, I sat like one cast in stone as the ceremony was carried out. Flanked by Archbishop Ealdred of York and Stigand of Canterbury,

Harold, dressed in his finest, processed through the aisled nave that thronged with the cream of England's nobility. All those who had come forth for the Christmas witanagemot and stayed to bury their king, now delayed their departure further to witness the kingmaking of Harold Godwinson.

Quire monks sang the *Te Deum* 'We praise thee, O God,' their voices rising high and clear to the vaulted roof, where pigeons fluttered, indifferent to the exulted company. Next to me Gytha, Harold's mother, shredded her kerchief in her lap; overwhelmed with pride at her son's achievement, she could not stem her happy tears. Leo and Gyrth sat further along but, of the dowager queen, there was no sign. Edith, no doubt, remained in her chambers, her future uncertain and her emotions in turmoil. I wondered what she would do now, her break with Harold would make it difficult for her to stay at the court and I could not imagine her shutting herself away in cloisters. Perhaps she would retire to her Winchester holdings.

Archbishop Ealdred was speaking so I sat up straighter, paying the attention the occasion required. He asked if the people accepted Harold as the right man to rule over them and the congregation rose to a man.

'We do.' they cried out, 'We do.'

When the clamour of their cries died away, Harold spoke, promising to uphold the laws of England, to protect the people, without favouritism or regard for rank or class. Detached from him, set apart in the crowd, he seemed a stranger to me. There was no crooked smile or quizzing frown and no hint of derision in his voice. For once he was perfectly sincere and I knew that his promise to rule justly was an honest one, given from his heart.

I was numb from sitting for so long and needed to get up and move around, to bring the blood and warmth back into my frozen feet, but I did my duty and sat unmoving through the lengthy service. There were further prayers and psalms and then more hymns, in which the archbishops asked God to help Harold maintain his oaths. They prayed for peace and protection from enemies in his time and, all the while, the ethereal voices of the choir rang out, scattering goose pimples across my body. When Harold finished speaking, the congregation stood again and shouted, '*Amen*' and I joined in, tears on my cheeks, swept away by the emotion.

The anthem, the same sung at the anointing of King Solomon, began while the Archbishop Eldred stepped forward and anointed the kneeling figure of the new king with the sacred chrism. Then another prayer and Harold was helped to his feet and garbed in the royal vestments, the robe, coat and stole. The coronation ring was placed upon his finger and the sword fastened about his waist and then, finally, the crown was placed upon his brow. The anthem *May the King Live Forever* burst forth and Harold stepped from the altar down into the welcoming throng.

'Vivat rex in aeternum.' his people cried.

I stood apart as first while his brothers and then his sons by Eadgytha made a knee to him. As soon as she was able to reach him, his mother fell to her knees but Harold stooped and raised her up, kissing her on both cheeks before drawing her to his side.

'You will never kneel to me, Mother,' I heard him say and then I saw him look about the nave, and I knew he was looking for me. Our eyes met above the milling heads of his subjects and he smiled, his mouth crooked and one eyebrow raised in the old familiar way.

Part Four
Beneath the Hoaréd Apple Tree

Thorney Island-March 1066

Early one morning, seeking the solitude of the surrounding fields, I walked from the palace. Rising from my empty bed, I looked in on the children. They slept, curled like a litter of pups, the covers tossed and rumpled, their faces pink with the flush of sleep. Leaving the door ajar lest the squeaking of the hinges waken them I crept away. Anwen or Maud would hear them should they stir. It was a rare escape now that I was queen and I could not recall the last time I had wandered abroad at will.

The March wind whipped my cloak, tugging it back against my throat and teasing tendrils of hair from beneath my cap. I wrapped it around me and mounted the hill, growing breathless from the exertion. At the top I stood, looking down upon the river as it snaked, serpentine across the valley floor. I wondered if Harold would return that day. Too often of late had I woken to find myself alone.

There was no doubt that state business kept him busy from dawn but I could not help but wonder how many nights he spent at Waltham, wrapped in Eadgytha's arms. The early weeks of his reign had not been easy and an anxious, overwrought expression replaced his usual cheer. Left alone at the royal palace, I seemed to do little else but worry about my ability to hold my husband's affection. My second marriage was proving as discontented as the first but, this time, it was not because I despised my husband but because I loved him too well. I could not tell him how I felt or explain my irrational female moods for he would laugh, lift that eyebrow in derision and no doubt discuss my insecurities in the softness of Eadgytha's bed. I could not blame him for returning to his former love in these hard days, for she was undeniably more beautiful and understood his needs far better than I could ever hope to. But soon I would be even less equipped to compete with her. My belly would rise, my ankles and fingers swell and I'd offer not the slightest temptation to a man of Harold's tastes.

Kicking at a loose stone, I held back my hair and turned my head to look downstream to where a trading vessel had become stranded on a sand bank. From the distance I watched men clambering over the deck, trying to unload the cargo before the craft became swamped in the incoming tide.

No noise from the town reached me on my lonely hill, the only sounds I could hear was the cawing of rooks as they spiralled and turned in the brittle skies, and the slow tolling of the Terce bell. The children would be rising and the servants bringing my breakfast and, knowing the palace would be thrown into panic at my unexplained absence, I reluctantly turned and made my way back toward the hall.

As I had suspected, the wooden shutters were thrown wide and Anwen hung out of the window, still in her nightrobe, her braids hanging like bell ropes from the casement.

'Lady.' she cried when she saw me, 'the entire household is searching for you. Where have you been? Look at the hem of your gown, all soiled and dirty. Tut,

tut, tut, I don't know. Come, break your fast, the king has sent word that he returns this day.'

'Will he bring presents?' asked Idwal, hearing her words as he emerged from his sleeping chamber, rubbing his eyes. 'I hope so; he does bring such good things. Do you think he remembers that he promised us a pup, Mother?'

'I don't know, sweet one,' I replied, kissing the top of his head, 'now he is king he has so many other things to remember so we shouldn't mind if we are overlooked from time to time.'

Anwen shot me a sharp glance and I sat down and began to spoon the porrage into my mouth. I did not feel like eating but couldn't face the consequences of her disapproval should I try to avoid it.

'The king rides from Winchester, Madam, the messenger said he should be another hour or two on the road.'

'About time. It has been a long three days since he left.'

'Well, Madam, pardon my saying so, but if he returns to see the dismal face you are wearing this morning he may not wish to tarry long.'

I put down my knife and burst into tears. Idwal sat with his spoon in his mouth, his eyes wide while Anwen scurried around the table to take me by the shoulders and lead me to my sleeping quarters.

'Whatever is it?' she asked when we were alone. I rubbed at my nose with my cuff and dabbed my tears on my apron.

'Oh, I don't know, Anwen. I'm afraid. Suppose I cannot keep Harold's affection? I know I could have if we had stayed at Bosham but, now that he is king and we are apart so often, I fear I will lose him. And now there is to be a child …'

'I knew it!' cried Anwen, hugging me and planting a big wet kiss on my cheek, 'Oh Lady, he will be so pleased. You have wasted no time at all in proving your fertility. How can he fail to be delighted with you?'

'Delighted with a bloated pig of a wife? How can I hope to keep him away from the swan-necked Eadgytha now? And he has sons already, what makes you think he will want mine to follow in his stead when he has young Godwin proving so able a prince?'

Anwen sat down beside me, taking liberties the other ladies would not have dared.

'Now, now, now,' she crooned, 'tis naught but that babe making you testy. These early months, they sour your porrage and salt your honey. Just you wait 'til the king gets here and you give him your news. I swear he will be beside himself with joy. Why, the promise of an heir will secure his seat on the throne and chase all his foes away.'

Sniffing, I raised my eyes.

'But, Anwen, when I tell him I am with child he will have all the more reason to find his comforts elsewhere. This child may prove to be the final breach between us.'

Anwen got up and began rummaging through my clothes press.

'I think you misjudge him, Lady. He adores you, that is plain to see. You shouldn't judge this man by your last. Come let's dress you in your finest, give him a taste of what he has been missing.'

When Harold strode through the door and flooded the chamber with his charm I could not help but be glad.

'Anwen!' he cried, opening his arms, 'me true darlin. Come and sit on my knee and let us discuss whatever arises.'

Anwen threw her apron over her head and ran, shrieking, from the room. Still angry with him, I smothered my sudden smile.

'That got rid of her,' he grinned and, in two steps, was across the room, planting a kiss on the back of neck. I hunched my shoulder against it and pulled away.

'Look, what I have for you,' he cried and, producing a sack, poured a heap of coins into my lap.

'Harold.' I exclaimed, 'this is a small fortune. Whatever do I need so much money for?'

'Tisn't just any old coin, Sweetheart. Take a close look at it.'

Picking up a fresh-minted silver piece I held it to the light, twirling it between finger and thumb.

'Is that supposed to be you, Harold? You look like a Roman emperor.'

He laughed.

'You are right, I do. And why shouldn't I, hey? They are to be minted and distributed throughout the land, 'tis important that the coinage of the realm is centralised to put an end to counterfeiting. What do you think? I bet you never thought to see my handsome features on a silver penny.'

I certainly had not and it pleased me. It was good to see he was concentrating on aspects of kingship that meant much to him. Although he had long played the part of Edward's right arm, he had ever been at his king's bidding and unable to govern as he saw fit.

I looked to where he sat on the window seat, one foot on a stool. He was grinning at me as if he had not a care in the world, displaying no guilt at having spent time with his mistress. It took him some time to note my silence and, at length, he sighed, getting up and coming to stand close to me.

'You seem out of sorts,' he said, brushing my hair back from my shoulder the better to see my face. 'What's the matter?'
The resentment plain in my voice I cried, 'Where have you been, Harold? 'tis three nights and four days since you rode out. I had expected you sooner.'
He let out a long breath.

'I've been being a king.' he cried, 'ruling the kingdom, what do you think? I've met with Archbishops and taken advice of the witan. I've decided to give Tostig's lands at Northampton to young Waltheof, the son of Siward. He deserves some reward for his loyalty and neither your brothers or mine are in need of more land.'

He was so casual, so seemingly innocent; how could he lie to me like this? Unable to restrain myself I took a deep breath. 'And how are Eadgytha and your children?'

Immediately I wished the words unsaid but it was too late. He swivelled on his heel and glared at me, the blood draining from his face and anger replacing his former high spirits.

Answer that if you can, my Lord. I thought and then jumped as he kicked savagely at the stool, sending it flying into the hearth where soon it would begin to smoulder.

'So that's what's been hanging in the air like a putrid fart,' he yelled, 'I thought you knew me better, madam.' He made to leave the room but, before he reached the door, changed his mind and came back, grabbing my arms and all but dragging me to my feet. I hung on tiptoe before him, his enraged breath gusting into my face as he bellowed. 'Let me tell you, madam that, should it please me, I would indeed take a mistress but it would not be Eadgytha. She is a good, virtuous woman and my respect for her is too great to expect her to resort to impropriety. I would not ask it of her. Eadgytha was my handfast wife; that does not make her a whore. She is the mother to my children. When I visit them, I will tell you, although I don't see why I should, but when I do visit it will not be to sate my lusts, it will be out of gratitude and affection. Is that clear now, Eadgyth or should you like me to set it down in letters?'

Tears were on my cheeks, my mouth was dry and from the sudden, loud ringing in my ears, I knew I should soon faint.

'What on earth is going on?' came Anwen's outraged voice from the door, 'We can hear the rumpus all the way to the kitchens. And what do you think you do, my Lord, treating my Lady so in her condition? Leave her be and go cool your head.'

Harold released me as if I was contagious and I would have fallen had Anwen not been there to support me. She led me to the bed and helped me lie upon it, removing my slippers and loosening the neck of my gown, fanning my brow ineffectually with her kerchief. Harold remained unmoving before the hearth. Anwen turned to face him, hands on hips.

'Well?' she enquired, all respect for her king forgotten. Harold shuffled his feet.

'What condition?' he asked, 'you said *'in her condition'* what condition would that be?'

'Well. When you've calmed yourself perhaps you can ask her that yourself.'

Pushing past her Harold approached the bed where I lay back on the pillows. He took my limp, sweating hand.

'Are you with child, Eadgyth?' he asked, all rage subsided, and I nodded, tears rolling into my ears, for now I knew he would now no longer come to my bed.

But, instead of shunning my company as Gruffydd had he scooped me into his arms, his breath hot on my neck.

'Oh, may the Lord be praised,' he wept.

Thorney Island April 1066

'Well, I managed to find most of what you asked for' said Harold, coming backward into the room with a laden tray. 'The strawberries you will have to do without but I have the rest ...even the salt herring.'

He deposited the tray on the nightstand, beneath the flickering torches and climbed onto the bed. I reached for a honeyed wafer and a gull's egg. 'I don't know,' he continued, taking off his boots and throwing them across the room, 'the household sleeps while the monarch and his queen are forced to find their own sustenance. Even the night guard have dropped off, I could have slit their throats had I so wished. By rights I should have them hung but I am too soft.'

'I could not wait until breakfast,' I said, biting into a pasty, 'I'm starving.'
Helping himself from the odd assortment, he ripped the leg from a chicken.

'Maybe its all the night-time activity we've been enjoying, do you think we should stop?'

'NO.' I cried, 'certainly not. I am well and happy, my Lord, abstinence will do neither of us any good.'

'Hmm, just as long as you are not saying that because you fear I will take my needs elsewhere.'

Thoroughly chewing the meat and vegetable pasty before swallowing, I helped myself to a goblet of wine, well watered down, as my condition dictated.

'Truly, Harold, do you not think that if the good Lord did not intend us to make love while we were pregnant he would have it impossible for us to do so?'

'Oh, you don't have to persuade me, Sweetheart. I am happy to oblige just so long as it suits you.'

I threw a cushion at him and he lifted the bedcover, climbing in beside me and snuggling up, the chill of his body striking cold through my thin gown.

'What do you make of that strange star in the sky, Harold?' I said, licking chicken grease from my fingers. 'They are saying it is an omen, do you think it is? And is it a good omen or a bad? Never have I seen ought like it and it is there without fail, every night, like a great fiery dragon belching forth flame.'

Pulling the neck of my gown wide, exposing my breasts, Harold cupped them, delighting in their increased size and density. 'I think 'tis a sign that my reign will be a great one. Together we will bring all England to prosperity and peace.'

I gasped as he began to pull, slowly and steadily on my nipple. Fighting for concentration, I continued.

'What about William? And there's Tostig too, what is he doing all this time? Where has he gone and what are his plans? Do you think he allies with Normandy?' Harold propped himself up on his elbow and looked at me in exasperation.

'Do shut up, woman, you have no sense of timing. I will deal with William just as soon as he sets sail and, as for Tostig, well, if he steps out of line, he will be made right sorry. Don't worry, the country will be safe from invasion by the time this little one comes to rule. I shall make it my life's work. Now, have a hush, I'm busy.'

So I lay back and enjoyed the feeling of his moustaches tickling the taut skin on my stomach. His hands cupped my womb before moving lower, stroking, tickling and probing. All other thoughts vanished.

The strange haired star remained in the sky, moving imperceptibly, a bright blaze in the night and even remaining just visible during the day. We eyed it askance, uncertain what it meant. The people spoke of omens and evil portent, of the inevitability of failed crops and famine and its silent presence spread disquiet throughout the land. Although it was May, the weather clung to the winter season, wet, bleak and windy. The children ailed and tempers were short.

Harold had cast his net of spies far and the news from Normandy was that William, in a frenzy of rage at the perceived betrayal, was building ships and summoning armies to ride against the *oath-breaker* as he had dubbed Harold. Leaving the children in Anwen's safe hands, I accompanied the king to the Isle of Wight where, as a precaution, he had set his fleet in the channel under the command of Eadric the Stearsman, a loyal and trustworthy man who would watch, undaunted, for signs of William's coming.

We stood together on the chalky cliff top, looking across the choppy grey seas toward the empty horizon. Above us seagulls soared, lamenting the world's end while a skirmishing northerly wind set my skirts thrashing at my ankles and whipped my hair from its bands. For too long Harold stood still, staring unblinking across the seas. I slipped my frozen hand into his, which was warm and dry, and he looked down at me.

'Come, Madam, I keep you in the cold too long, let us go back, my stomach growls for want of food.'

His arm about my shoulder, we walked together back to the camp and, as we drew close, the smell of roasting meat teased our noses and set our juices running. A group of burly warriors cleared a path for us as we moved toward our pavilion.

'How worried should I be, Harold?' I asked sometime later, sinking my teeth into a juicy hank of mutton, 'You can beat William's army, can't you?'

'Course I can,' he scoffed, breaking the bread in two and handing me half. 'I've not met an army yet who can best a Saxon shield wall.'

He chewed diligently for a few moments, 'and anyway, God is on our side, he will not allow the Norman bastard to even get close to our land. I have put the fyrd on alert and your brothers are mustering their armies in the north. By the time William's ships draw nigh our shores, we will be ready and waiting. I'll wager not one Norman foot will venture from their decks.'

The tent was warm, the braziers hot and, snuggling to his side I grew drowsy, and he bid me lay down for a while; there was no need for me to go outside with him again. Wrapped in furs, my belly full and my fears sated by his brave words, I lay on the bed and let the crying of the gulls and the rhythmic flapping of the tent lull me to sleep.

West minster -summer 1066

We returned to the mainland certain that England was safe. The fyrd were on standby, ready to ride out at the king's command and Eadric the Steersman stood vigil in the channel. Safely back at West minster, when the first threat did come, it caught us unawares for it came, not from Normandy, but from Tostig.

Embittered and irate, he launched a sea attack upon the Isle of Wight, burning and slaying all who attempted to stand against him and press-ganging the survivors into his service. Harold, furious at his brother's perfidy, called out the fleet and the Wessex fyrd and sent word to the earls to stand ready for battle.

The precious bulge of my stomach was just visible beneath my draped tunic. I placed my two hands protectively over it while I waited anxiously in the palace compound. The mustering army grew by the hour, great armoured warhorses milling and jostling while, on their backs, Harold and his huscarls made ready to ride forth beneath the belching flag of the Wessex dragon.

The banner rolled and unfurled in the wind, its trailing tails snapping like a living beast, the red and gold thread glistening in the sulky sunshine. The sight of it reminded me of Gruffydd's flag *Y Ddraig Goch,* a dragon too, and the memory of an old Welsh refrain Rhodri had often sung jangled annoyingly in my head. I stood alone, bereft at Harold's imminent departure, unable to ask him to stay.

Harold, armoured and armed, was mounted on his warhorse, clothed in battledress; looking, in fact, just as he had when I first saw him. He removed his helmet and the horse pranced, snorting hot breath into my face. I found myself incredulous that I had been brought from Wales on that very same beast. I tiptoed across ground that was trodden into mire, to stand close to the stirrup, dwarfed by the massive horse. Harold smiled down at me, his lopsided grin lending boyish appeal to the deadly façade.

'It will be over soon, sweetheart, so keep my bed warm.' he called and I saw Godwin, who rode beside him, blanch and set his jaw.

Anwen was urging me to step back from Harold's stirrup, declaring the compound to be no place for a pregnant woman.

'One kick could kill you, Lady, or the slightest jostle abort your child,' she cried and, obediently, I retreated with her to the steps of the hall. I raised my kerchief and smiled wanly at Harold's ironic salute and, with a great cry and an answering bellow of fury, they clattered over the bridge in a swirl of dust and chaos.

The palace dogs chased the cavalcade, barking and leaping about the horses' feet, snatching at their tails. Small children cheered and ran after them, only returning at their mother's behest.

Silence settled with the dust and I returned to my chambers, hearing but not listening to Anwen's cheerful chatter and the clamouring of the children. There was nothing to do now but pray for him, to entreat the Lord to look kindly upon England's king and send him home safe …and soon.

Edward's church stood out against the wet summer skies and, pushing wide the carved door, I shook the raindrops from my hood and approached the altar. It was deserted within, the vast space magnifying the sound of my footsteps. An extravagance of candles burned on the altar and I lit another, saying a prayer for Harold's safe return and also asking God's blessing for the late king who lay beneath the nave.

'Oh Edward,' I thought, 'if only you had been strong enough to name a proper heir, none of this would be happening. If only your weakness hadn't led you to promise everything to all men, England would have continued in peace.'

On my knees I prayed again, for Harold, for Edward, for my children and for all England that trembled beneath the threatened violence of the dragon in the sky.

It was not until the end of June that I received a missive from my husband, it was a much-crumpled parchment by the time it reached me, tossed and jostled and passed from hand to hand on its journey. Breaking the seal and unrolling it, Harold's words were revealed, written in his own hand.

Well beloved (he wrote)
May this find you in God's keeping and bearing our child with great care. My brother, Tostig, after harranging and bringing a scourge upon the people of Wight, sailed on to Sandwich, where he recruited more men, most against their will. Our army, together with the fleet, chased his scyps off northward where he raided along the coast of East Anglia. He now heads for the Humber where 'tis hoped your brothers lie in wait. Where trouble goes, so must I follow and this is to tell you that my return will be delayed. Have faith that, as soon as this matter is dealt with, I shall return to you at Thorney and recommence our nuptials.
Look to yourself and the children.
Harold rex.

I still have that letter, here in my pocket and I treasure it, for it is the last he wrote me. Edwin and Morcar, together, drove Tostig from their lands and made it too difficult for him to continue to wreak his vengeance. As the weeks went by his men began to desert until he was left with just twelve ships where once he'd had sixty. In the end, forsaken and demoralised, he fled to the court of Malcolm of Scotland where he lurked like a spider, spinning and plotting, all the summer long.

I spent my time watching from the highest hills around Thorney. Longing for the first glimpse of the dragon of Wessex or Harold's banner of the fighting man. After many days I eventually saw, in the distance, the dust thrown up by the cavalcade and, leaping upon my pony, I rode forth to meet him, cantering ahead of my escort and not stopping or heeding anyone until Harold was before me on the road.

Panting for a few moments, I watched his approach and as he drew near I slipped from the saddle, covering the last few yards on foot. He swung me into his arms, breathing hard into my neck and squeezing the breath from my lungs. 'Oh, Harold. I am so glad you are back safe, I have not had a minute of peace, I swear.'

Pulling back, he looked me up and down.

'Well, you look good on it, sweetheart. For a while there, so swift was your approach, I thought we were under attack. Come, let us walk a while, my arse is sore of the saddle and I would hear all your news before I am swamped with state business.'

Later that night, when all his business was done, we ate a meal together in the comfort of our chamber. He fell upon his food while I feasted my eyes upon of him. In the bob and dance of the candlelight he looked drawn and ailing and I resolved to restore his former vitality. I told myself that a little love and rest would soon have him back in full fettle. Yet, in the weeks that followed, all the cosseting and loving I heaped upon him couldn't restore him to his normal self.

He blamed the worries of state. The tedium of kingship and the constant coming and going of messengers, couriers and spies drained his energy and sapped his enthusiasm. As we waited for William, our nerves raw and our tempers frayed, his face and demeanour remained dour.

I was poor company for Gytha, who had come to be close by when the child came. But she made no comment on my distracted mood and, instead, played with the children and gossiped with my women while they stitched tiny garments for the coming babe. I had no patience with needlework at this time, all I could think of was William waiting, just the other side of the narrow stretch of water, to burn our palaces and slaughter our children.

Harold was in a similar vein, with no time for hunting, his forced incarceration brought pallor to his face and his former rapacious appetite decreased. I grew fretful in the small hours and lonely in my bed, waiting for him to come to me while he signed charters and permissions until dawn. As daylight was beginning to show in the east, he would come creeping, cold and exhausted, beneath my bedcovers to fall straight into a deathlike sleep.

William set sail in July; the news came as we broke our fast on a Friday morning. Harold threw down his knife and rode away with barely a word of farewell. I wept, certain he would never return. 'Come, Lady, do not fret. Look, the children have come to show you the pup that Harold gave them.'

I sat up and wiped my eyes on my sleeve as the children approached. I must be brave for their sake, as Harold would expect. Idwal regarded my red-rimmed eyes and thrust the puppy at me,

'He will cheer you up, Mother,' he said, 'He is small now but the king says he will grow as big as a horse in no time.'

The pup clambered up my chest and tried to lick my nose and I made a watery attempt at a smile.

'He likes you, Mother.' laughed Maredudd, 'he wants to kiss you.'

'Hmm, I am not sure that I wish to kiss him though, Maredudd. Come sit on the bed with me, you are making me feel better all ready.'

The pup bounded about, leaping from one child to the other, trying to lick their faces, delighted with his new friends.

'What have you named him?' I asked, stroking the rough grey coat of the young wolfhound.

'Puppy.' announced Nest, lunging forward and patting him roughly.

'Ooh gently, Nest.' I cried, 'you must be gentle-like-a-lamb with baby creatures.' Her touch gentled and she beamed up at me, 'like a lamb,' she repeated, her soft cheeks glowing in the torchlight.

'I wish it would stop raining,' sighed Idwal, 'its ages since we played outside, bathed in the stream or made camps in the woods. Do you think it will rain forever, Mother?'

'Well it never has before,' I replied, stroking his hair, 'It has to stop sometime soon.' He ducked his head from beneath my hand and slipped from my reach,

'I'm not a baby, Mother, I am nigh on seven years old.'

'I'm sorry, sweet one. It is easy for a woman to forget her son is all but a man. Harold complains that Grandmother Gytha treats him like a ten year old.'

They laughed, Idwal throwing his head back as he had seen Harold do. Was it truly seven years ago that I gave birth to him? I remembered the companionable cooking hall where Rhodri had chosen both my boys' names.

I wondered which name he would have chosen for his daughter given the chance, would he have approved of the name Nesta? I sighed, sure that he would have. We had been so young. Sometimes I tried to recall his face but it was dim in my memory now, superimposed with the jaunty, moustached face of my new husband.

Now that I was so in love with Harold, a man entirely different from my first love, I recognised the immaturity of that first tenderness and I wondered if it would have lasted had he lived.

The old people used to say that three women, known as the Norns, wove human fate. They sat in the roots of a great, spreading tree, spinning the fragile threads of destiny into the complex fabric of life.

When they grew peeved they worked misfortune and despair into the pattern. I sighed. My own fate trailed behind me like a worn petticoat, patched and mended with good intentions. What, I wondered, would those three women make of my future.

Drawn from my reverie by the children's excited chatter, I exchanged glances with Anwen and indicated with a nod of my head that she should bring forth some sweetmeats I had laid away in a cupboard. The children fell on them and, for a while, there was no sound but the appreciation of honeyed wafers.

'Will the king be away long do you think?'

'Let us hope not. Let us pray that he will defeat the invaders quickly and send them home with their devil tails tucked between their legs.'

Maredudd's eyes were huge, 'Do they truly have tails, Mother? I had thought that was just a story.'

'Horns too, I've heard, beneath them helmets,' chimed in Anwen, sending the children into squeals of laughter. The fun intensified when the pup who, for want of a better name, was still referred to as Puppy, sauntered over to where Harold's favourite cloak was draped over his chair and lifted his leg up it.

Our hilarity spread like his puddle of pee but it was the kind of laughter you hear at a funeral. I have seen it often, the grim reality of death countered by the relief of simply being alive. Hilarity is the best weapon for warding off our own mortality, a reality often too terrible to contemplate. I joined in with them, forcing my anguish into joy but I expect I fooled no one, least of all myself. At bedtime they clustered at my knee to kiss me good night before trailing after Maude to their beds.

It was a few days before the clouds thinned enough to allow the sun to break through and we were able to walk across the water meadows toward the river's edge. The ground was soggy underfoot.

I felt the damp seeping into my slippers and knew the hem of my gown would never come clean again. However the sun had shone too rarely of late, so I ignored the damp ground and, taking Nesta's hand, helped her negotiate a drier way through the mire.

The boys ran ahead, the pup splashing through puddles behind them. They waved their wooden swords in the air while their happy cries mingled with that of the birds that wheeled and soared in the blue sky.

At the edge of the river, waterfowl stepped through the mud and, as the boys approached, a heron flew up and flapped, calm and aloof, away from the furore.

An ancient willow provided a handy seat where Anwen and I propped ourselves while we loosened the neck of our gowns, protesting that it was too hot. It had been so all summer, dark, dull and chill until the sun burst forth in all its glory to roast us in our winter woollens.

Maredudd and Idwal dabbled at the water's edge, looking for fish and frogs, Nest tried to follow but, unskilled as she was in rivercraft, she sat down in the mud and cried out in protest at the sudden cold on her nether regions. I watched, laughing, as Anwen picked up the sopping child and stripped off her muddied gown, she would do better in her shift and be cooler too. Promising to keep a watch on Nest, Anwen moved away a little, leaving me to lie back on the fallen trunk to look at the scudding sky and doze in the sun. Just as I was drifting off, a cry came from the direction of the bank as Maredudd flicked a fish onto the bank.

'Got one.' he cried, watching the tiddler flounder in the grass, 'Harold said all I needed was patience and he was right. I just crept up on it slowly, hardly moving at all until I was beneath it and flipped it into the air. Ha ha. I bet the fish was surprised to find himself flying like a bird.'

'Well done, sweet one,' I called, lying back again but another call brought me upright again.

'Who is it who comes? I think 'tis our step brother, Godwin.'

My heart beat sickeningly as I watched Harold's son ride closer. His horse sloshed through the wet grass and came to rest a few feet from us. Godwin slid to the ground and stood before me, shy and hesitant. I knew he had come to tell me Harold was dead, I just knew it and every cell in my body cried out against it. Inside my head was screaming, long, high and loud.

'Tell me.' I cried, closing my eyes and tilting my head back, 'just say it, go on.'

'Nay, Lady.' he answered, reaching out to steady me, 'tis good news I bear … well, not as ill as you imagine anyway. The king is well, he sends me to bring you to him for he plans to make camp on the coast. The bastard set sail as was reported but was thrown off course by the wind. According to Eadric, his fleet has been beached close to St Valery harbour. He is stuck there until the northerly winds allow him to leave.'

All the strength deserted my body. 'God be praised.' I cried, sinking onto the tree trunk again, 'tis good news indeed, Godwin, I thank you for it. 'Twas not what I expected to hear.'

'I guessed that, Madam, forgive my clumsiness. Now by your leave, I must ride forth to my mother who also waits for news. I will return tomorrow to convey you south to the king if that is your wish.'

He rode away, his back erect and his legs long in the stirrups; the further he rode the more he resembled his father. I felt a renewed surge of resentment for Eadgytha, who had enjoyed so many years of trouble free happiness with Harold while I, his church wed wife, knew nothing but fear.

September 1066

Strung out along the south coast of England, Harold's army waited, with scarce a free-drawn breath, for William's ships to appear on the horizon. The tents and paraphernalia of war made a cheerful splash on the green cliff top, but there festivity ended, for faces were tense and conversation muted.

We were all worried and overwrought with waiting. The men of the fyrd, already out for longer than their allotted time, were eager to get back to their farmsteads where crops awaited harvesting and animals needed slaughtering and salting for winter. Should the Normans not come at all, England still faced a bleak winter season if the crops be left to rot in the fields.

I walked among the men, safe and confident in their midst, for they loved Harold and had taken me as a lucky talisman. Passing a group of rough soldiers who sat ringed about a fire honing their new-shafted axes, making ready for war, I nodded and smiled.

'Evenin' Madam,' they murmured, pausing in their work to watch me pass by.

I felt for them, far from their homes and families and knew myself fortunate indeed to share my anxious days with the king and, each night, snuggle with him in the warmth of our bed furs. As secure as this seems, there was no respite from the tension, no leisurely laughter or time to relax. We just sat and waited, too anxious to stray far from camp and too restless to find much joy in each other's company.

The leaves were beginning to turn, the summer almost over before it was properly begun. It was mid September and I was due to give birth in December. I wondered where we would be by then? What if William defeated Harold? What would become of us all? What would become of the babe I carried? Sitting high upon the pillows, I stroked the neat bulge of my stomach and could not sleep. There were so many questions I could not answer. Did I carry the next king in my womb?

Would I be safely delivered of a boy or, like so many women, bear the wrenching pain of childbirth to produce only a dead prince? My other pregnancies had run smooth and the births had been easy; even the fiasco of birthing Maredudd in a damp, cold cave had been straightforward but there was no guarantee that this birth would be so.

Harold stirred beside me, his own loud snores waking him. His breathing slowed for a few moments and then he blinked and stretched out an arm for me.

'Why are you awake?' he asked, 'lie down with me, you will catch a chill.'

'Tis not cold, Harold, although the rain falls and the wind blows like 'tis March. I am restless that is all, how can it be otherwise? This uncertainty is driving us all to madness.'

He swung his legs over the edge of the bed and, finding the pot, pissed loudly into it, yawning and scratching his head. I watched the clenched cheeks of his bare rump as he emptied the last few drops from his bladder before crossing the chamber and scrambling back beneath the covers.

'Come, Woman, warm me up, I am frozen.' His hands were like ice on my body but I did not flinch from his touch, instead I wound my legs about him and drew him closer.

His face burrowed into my neck, hot breath on my skin. When he began to love me, I was not eager but, knowing that the morning might bring war and chaos, I opened myself to suggestion and let his desire melt my reluctance away. His hot mouth and the soft probing of his tongue sent shivers of awakening pleasure through my body. Lazy fingers, idly teasing and caressing, developed into insistence and, their spell working, I soon lay beneath him panting, wanting him as much as he wanted me.

He reared above me, his scarred chest gleaming in the torchlight as he prepared to enter. Gasping and clutching at my pillow, delight began to melt my bones. Breath came short. Harold, his jaw set and his blue eyes looking deep into mine, kept firm control, monitoring his movements with mine, our bellies bumping, our hips grinding, pleasure flooding, threatening to drown us.

A noise outside. The tent flap opened, bringing in a blast of night air, 'No.' I groaned and, still inside me, Harold turned his head toward the intruder,

'Get the hell out of here!' he yelled and the messenger fled.

Eyes screwed shut and my mouth wide I panted, urging him with my muscles to continue but, our moment spoiled, he withdrew reluctantly, kissing me gently before getting out of bed and dragging on his breeches to cover his dwindling fervour.

'I'll kill the bastard.' he said as he stormed from the tent and I rolled onto my stomach, biting the pillow and cursing all messengers.

A few moments later Harold burst into the tent again. 'Get up and get dressed, Eadgyth,' he said curtly, 'we ride back to Thorney, now.'

'But, Harold, it's dark. What has happened? What about William?'

Sitting on the edge of the bed pulling on his boots, he didn't look at me.

'The north wind, that has kept William from us, has blown trouble instead onto our northern shores. Tostig has landed in the shire of York. He has allied himself with Hardrada who thinks to lay a claim to this land himself. Apparently they mean to take York and set Hardrada up as king there in opposition to my rule. Over my dead body, do you hear?'

Passion forgotten, I scrambled from my bed and began to struggle into my clothes, my fingers refusing to tie the lacings.

'But, Harold, what about William? If you ride north you leave the door open for the Bastard in the south.'

'Aye, sweetheart, I know, but what can I do? Let Tostig and Hardrada make free with my northern properties? They won't stop at York. Even now they range abroad looting and burning. At my crowning I swore before God to protect and serve the people of England …all of the people.'

Grabbing a comb, I began to drag it through my hair.

'But will Edwin and Morcar's armies not be strong enough to defeat the invaders?'

'By all accounts the invasion force is large, and I am sick of inactivity. I have the urge to kill these pretenders to my throne; look how my hands shake with the rage that surges through me. Kill them, I must.'

He threw back the tent flap and disappeared into the lightening dawn.

Thorney- September 1066

Leaving his brother Leofwine in charge of the court, Harold rode away again, his set face and squared chin filling me with fear. I knew he would stop at nothing to defend his kingdom, even if it meant he die in the attempt. I needed him. I wanted to hold him back, strike him unconscious, anything to prevent his departure.

Instead, I sought and found the courage to summon a watery smile as he leaned from his saddle to leave a kiss on my hair.

'Farewell, Sweetheart,' he said, but I had no voice to reply. Mutely, I watched them ride away, a bright cavalcade of hope on the dull September day. Idwal, who had crept away from Anwen's watch, slipped his hand into mine, sharing his own small store of courage. Turning away, we re-entered the hall, my throat closed and tears stinging my eyes.

An agony of waiting followed. It is the lot of women to sit idle at home while their men take their chance on the field of battle. Unable to rest or concentrate, I paced the confines of the palace, tetchy and miserable. I could not recall ever having felt so when Gruffydd rode off to war; I can never even recall asking whence he rode. In those days I was concerned only with myself and spared him not a thought, apart, perhaps, from an unspoken wish that he should not return.

With Harold, however, it was different; each hoof beat or footfall had me leaping from my chair, although I knew he could not possibly have returned so swiftly. Had I not been carrying England's heir I would have taken up a sword and ridden into battle alongside him, as the queens of bygone days. Boudicca, Gwynhyfyr and Æthelflaed, had not borne the tortuous task of staying home but had fought valiantly for their country on an equal footing with their menfolk.

But I did not want to fight, I wanted peace, time to enjoy my husband and nurture my young in domestic tedium. Since the day we were wed we had enjoyed scarce a moment of quiet and Harold's promise that, once all invaders were driven from our shores, we would wallow in self-indulgence seemed no more than a dream. All I could do was wait his return. Throughout the long, dark nights I lay wakeful and moved, like a ghost, throughout the long, dark days that followed. Time seemed suspended, those last weeks dragging by until the very last day of September.

The day was a wet one and the children and I were confined to the palace, playing a game of Taefl in my chambers. Nest sat near the hearth with Puppy, her apron crumpled and coated with dog hairs. I was not really concentrating on the game and was horribly outnumbered. My king was in real trouble and the assailants, in Idwal's hands, triumphant. The boy crowed with delight at his easy conquest but Maredudd was not fooled, 'Mother, you weren't concentrating; Idwal can never usually beat you.'

'Mayhap my game improves.' cried his brother, 'Shall we play again, Mother?'

'No,' I said, vacating the seat, 'I have the headache. Maredudd, you play in my stead.'

Pushing the shutter wide for some fresh air I looked out. The rain had ceased but heavy, dark clouds threatened to burst upon us again at any moment. I could see the full expanse of the palace yard gleaming in the watery sunshine. Everything was as it should be. Leaning my arms on the sill I watched the ducks dabbling in the pond. The poultry, scratching about in wet straw, clucked in alarm when the goatherd scurried toward the gate with his charges running, tails up, before him.

My attention was taken from this domestic scene by some commotion at the gate and I saw a horse, mired and sweating, being led toward the stables, his head low and his coat steaming. He had obviously been ridden hard and long. His rider hurried up the hall steps with his head lowered against another sudden shower. The door was thrust open as I reached it and I almost collided with Anwen who was rushing in.

'Oh Lady.' she cried, 'pardon my haste but young Godwin has ridden in with news from the king.' Before the last words were from her mouth Godwin entered, muddy and wet, sprinkling drops of rain onto the chamber floor. He bowed over my hand, his face flushing; 'Lady,' he said, 'forgive my disarray but I have news from my father.'

'Yes, yes,' I cried, signalling Anwen to fetch refreshment, 'tell it to me straight. Does the king live?'

'Aye, Lady, the king is well. He prepares to ride home even now. He sent me forth to set you at your ease but, I would warn you, my news is not all good.'

'Just tell it, boy. Stop prevaricating.' I cried, sounding like his father.

Godwin perched on the table and, twisting his gauntlets in his hands, began to tell his tale.

'We had not ridden sixty leagues from here before news reached us of a great battle. Your brothers, Edwin and Morcar, together with the fighting men of seven shires had met with Hardrada and Tostig at Foul ford gate outside York. They say that the fighting was fierce and the casualties many; they were beaten Lady, some say they were out numbered, some say 'twas the earls inexperience in battle. Your brother Morcar was wounded, but not killed, he will fight another day. Hardrada and his army had taken York with much slaughter. My father, the king, was furious and we rode forth fast and, without respite, night and day, day and night until the site of the battle was reached. 'Twas a sorry sight we found there, Lady. 'Tis my first experience of bloodshed and there had been great violence.'

He took a swig of ale and wiped his mouth on his sleeve before continuing, 'Saxon bodies lay all about, dismembered, hacked about where they had fallen. Good men drenching the ground with their blood so that the waters of the flood plain ran red. Your brother, Edwin, met us there with his thegns, almost spent as they were. He was injured also, but not badly and he joined with us when Father ordered the mustered army to march on toward the camp of Hardrada and Tostig.'

I watched his young face trying to compose itself before he went on with his tale, trying to recall what he had seen and relay it forth in a manner fit for my womanly ears. 'We marched, it was fierce hot but we were not permitted to remove our armour. You know what Father is for discipline. Edmund and I were supposed to stay with the baggage train but Father called us forth to ride beside him.'

Here Godwin stumbled over his words, flicking his eyes from me to Anwen, 'He ordered us not to fight at the forthcoming battle but to look to ourselves so that, should he not prevail, we could seek vengeance for his slaughter. He also bade us, if the day went ill, to look to you, Lady, and … to our mother.'

My lips tightened at the mention of Eadgytha, I imagined her waiting as I did and I wondered if her serenity wavered now. Did she weep as hopelessly as I against the fate the Norns wove for us?

Godwin's polite cough pulled me back to him and he continued. 'So swiftly had we travelled that Hardrada's army were not expecting us for some days and, from our position above the river, we saw them at leisure. The day was so warm that some of them had disrobed and were swimming in the Derwent river. My uncle Gyrth advised that we should fall on them while they were in disarray, slaughter them in their unarmed state and your brother Edwin backed his suggestion. Father would have none of it and insisted that we parley with the enemy first. He rode forth with twenty huscarls; I went with them, at my own request, but was told to keep to the rear should there be any trouble. When we met with the enemy, my Uncle Tostig rode forward with a man taller than any I have seen, even though he be mounted. I guessed him to be the Norwegian king, Harald Sigurdsson, known as Hardrada, the hard ruler. They stopped a short way from us and Father greeted my uncle, not warmly but reasonable when I think he had every reason to slay him then and there.'

Godwin licked his lips and drank again, striving to retain his composure. 'Go on, Godwin,' I murmured.

'Well, Father hailed them both and offered my uncle his old lands back, that land lately given unto Earl Morcar, plus a third of the country for his own rule if he would only return to our side and fight with us against the Norwegians.'

My mind darted from Harold, desperate not to have to kill his own brother, to my brother, Morcar, whom I knew would be equally desperate to keep his northern lands. It did not bode well for future peace but, although it came as a shock that Harold should jeopardise the balance of peace between our two families and make so free with my brother's properties, I knew that he did so out of desperation and with some thought for his mother. Poor Gytha's heart must be broken at this enmity between her two sons. I wondered if Harold had been in earnest or if he had simply been attempting to lure Tostig away from Hardrada.

Godwin was speaking again. 'I am unsure if Hardrada understands the Saxon tongue very well for Tostig seemed to relay the message to him and the big man laughed and said something in his own tongue. Tostig then leaned forward in his saddle and asked Father if he, Tostig, accepted the bargain what would Father offer Hardrada. A great murmur of disquiet rumbled about our men at that but Father, a wicked gleam in his eye and that eyebrow of his raised in that particular way he has, said loudly, so that all should hear. 'I shall give Hardrada just seven foot of Saxon soil or as much more as he is taller than other men.' Our army laughed aloud at this, the uproar reaching Hardrada's assembled force, unsettling them and setting their feet shuffling. He is a brave man, my father, to laugh and make jokes at such a time; I was proud to ride with him.'

I pictured Harold astride his horse, encouraging his men to ridicule the massively built man who had come across the wild ocean to slay him and take from him everything he owned. I could not help but smile, so clearly could I visualise his quirky raised eyebrow, his fair moustaches glinting in the sun.

'Then what happened?' asked Anwen, impatient to know more. Godwin blew out his cheeks, his blue eyes full of the incredulity at what had followed.

'Then,' he said, 'all hell broke loose. I have never seen battle before, never truly understood what it meant when men spoke of the killing rage and the chaotic camaraderie of fellow warriors. The Norwegians retreated back across a bridge and formed their shield wall there and the two armies began to hurl insults at each other, as is the custom. I heard more abuse and foul language on that day than I have ever heard. T'would make you blush, Lady, should I repeat it. My brother and I stayed by the baggage and were happy to do so for the fighting was ferocious. At the start, a big fellow, even bigger than their king, took up a position on the bridge and none could best him to clear a passage through, although many died trying. Arrows were flying thick in the air and the clash of sword on shields was enough to burst your ears, so eager were the men to engage. At length, one of the men crept from the shield wall and, unseen by the enemy, put out on the river in what appeared to be an old swill tub. Once beneath the bridge, under the very feet of the giant, he lunged up with his spear and, into his nethers, pierced him through.'

Anwen and I pulled a pained face at each other but Godwin continued, growing more eloquent as he warmed to his theme. 'Then, once he was down and the way cleared, our armies thundered across the bridge and engaged the Norwegians in battle. Slashing at their legs and chopping their way toward where Hardrada fought beneath his standard; the land waster, a black raven that flapped and snapped in the wind above the best of his archers. I could see Father's fighting man banner above the furore so I was able to keep an eye on his position, unable to take my eye from it lest it fall.'

Godwin wet his lips again, his blue eyes, so like his father's, earnest, the fearful experience of war returning as he retold his tale. 'It is difficult for me to tell what happened, 'twas all chaos and screaming for what seemed like hours. Although Hardrada was slain in the early stages of the battle, the enemy would not accept quarter and they fought relentlessly on, beneath a cruel sun, until late in the afternoon when, to all our surprise, Norwegian reinforcements arrived. They had run across country to redeem their king in his losing battle but, although they arrived too late, they fought anyway and with great vigour, some of them dropping from exhaustion and despair. When, at last, all was quiet, we crept through the piles of dead and wounded until we found the body of my uncle Tostig, his head spliced in two, still clutching his bloodied sword.'

A hush fell as each of us remembered Tostig in happier times, before greed and ambition had turned him from the heart of his family. I recalled him riding forth with Harold, brave brothers in arms against

Gruffydd, defeating him and bringing my children safe home.

I remembered him sitting fragrantly at King Edward's feet, laughing at some joke of the queen's. He had been so alive, so vibrant. How had he come to this; a corpse, traitor to king and country, defeated by his own brother's army? I had never felt comfortable in Tostig's company, had not disliked so much as distrusted him. He had disturbed me but he was my husband's brother and I knew the pain Harold would be feeling and the lengths he would go to hide it from his fellows. I knew him to be in torment, yet he was too far away for me to offer comfort.

'And your father took no bodily hurt?' I asked, offering Godwin a plate of chicken. 'No, Lady, only a few scratches,' he said, stripping the flesh from the bone with his strong teeth. 'I was amazed to see him walk from the fray unscathed; it was all I could do not to rush up and embrace him but, Edmund has not my reticence and he hugged him hard enough for us both, wept too with relief.' The boy laughed in recollection. 'Father all but threw him aside and told him not to be so mawkish. Then he hollered for ale and spent the night carousing with the men. The next day they prepared to clear the battleground of valuables and deal with the prisoners. Father sent me hence on the Tuesday morning and it has taken me this long to reach you, I lost my way twice but, after asking direction, I found the road again.'

It sounded as though Harold was fully restored to his normal self, the sharp edge of inactivity dulled by battle. I smiled and took Godwin's hand, 'You have done well Godwin; Harold will be proud, very proud.'

At last, warmth and friendship surged between us and he returned my smile, looking away again, shy at our newfound alliance. 'Now, get thee hence to Waltham to tell your mother the news,' I said, getting up and opening the door for him.

'That I will, Lady,' he cried, and was gone, forgetting the solicitations due to his queen, but I did not mind, I felt accepted, like a mother.

Heartened by the news, I helped Anwen tidy the chamber. 'Lady, 'tis not your place to be helping me.' she scolded but I ignored her, folding the linen and placing it in tidy piles on the bed. If only our lives were so easily ordered, our emotions and relationships neatly stacked, ready to be taken from the shelf and unfolded at will.

When all was in readiness for the next day, Maude brought the children to say goodnight; Nest in her nightgown, plump and rosy from the hearthside snuggled on my lap while the boys sat at my feet, telling me of their day. Puppy foraged in the rushes for interesting smells and dropped titbits.

'Mother, do you think Arthur was as brave a king as Harold?' asked Maredudd. The boys had been hearing stories of Arthur and Gwynhyfwr from Maude and Anwen, whose Welshness remained undimmed by the everyday realities of Saxon England.

‘I don’t expect so, sweet one, although he seems to have had as many foes as Harold. I like to think …’

A rumpus in the courtyard interrupted my train of thought. ‘Whatever is happening, Anwen?’ I cried, leaping from my chair, almost letting Nesta fall in my haste.

‘I will find out, Lady, stay you here. Maude, look to the little ones.’

In a flurry of skirts she swept from the room while I went to peer through the shutter into the gloom of night. The habitual quiet of the evening was shattered. Horses milled about, the voices of their riders shouting, torches blazing, dogs barking, footsteps running.

The memory of Harold’s attack on Rhuddlan Castle came rushing back and I cast about me looking for somewhere to hide with the children. Maude, beside me at the window put her hand on my arm, ‘Do not worry, Lady, I think they be friends. Look, is that not Earl Leofwine’s mark?’ My heart banging, I focussed on the men that clamoured in the yard.

‘I think ‘tis so, Maude. Oh my heart. It beats like a drum.’ I laughed in relief. The children were clinging to my skirts when Anwen burst through the door followed by Leofwine and the messenger. Anwen’s face was stark white, her eyes wide.

She tried to stutter her news but, for once, she was bereft of speech. Leo stepped forward, as white faced as she, clearing his throat he said, 'I have news, Lady, that has flown the court into panic. You must ride at once to safety, the Normans have landed on the south coast, at Peven sea and even now, are looting and burning a swathe across the country.'

All summer long we had been prepared, we had waited with pennants flying, armed to the teeth, ready to take on the Norman armies when they came. Now, we were cast into disarray by their untimely arrival. The fyrd had disbanded to see what could be salvaged of the harvest, our armies were scattered and Harold, our king, at the other end of the country. Messengers were dispatched to the four corners of the realm, one to Harold to summon him back in haste, the others to muster the fighting men, the earls and thegns of England.

Soon the militia began to ride in; the good men of Berkshire, Essex and Kent arrived first, their morale strengthened by the news of Harold's success against the Norwegian king. They put up in tents, waiting for instructions. Our spies told us that maybe seven hundred ships had landed on our southern shore; ships, bristling with spears and laden with men and horses. Immediately on landing, the invaders had scouted the area, burning, killing and stealing livestock and produce. Further reports said that they then set to building themselves a makeshift fortress, a wooden structure from which to defend their position.

Leofwine strode about the palace, his face darkened with responsibility. Without waiting for Harold, he sent his fighting men to ride forth to contain the Norman's in their makeshift stronghold by the seashore.

'You must go, Lady,' he told me, 'ride to Waltham or Bosham, somewhere you will be safe should they break through our defences.'

'I will not,' I replied, 'I will wait for Harold and do as he tells me to do.' I stuck out my chin, determined to see Harold before he rode off to fight again. Leo raised his arms in despair at my obstinate refusal to do as I was told.

'On your own head be it, Lady,' he growled, 'and if Harold threatens to take my head for it, be so good as to intervene on my behalf.'

'That I can promise to do, Leo,' I smiled, as he rushed off, distracted by the weight that had fallen upon him.

It was an exhausted band that arrived, foot sore and hungry a week or so later. As the weary men dispersed, Harold slid from his horse and kissed me, keeping his arm about my shoulders as we entered the palace. The stench of the road clung to him, his clothes were mired and his face filthy.

'You, my husband, need a bath,' I observed, as he threw his stinking cloak at a passing slave, unleashing the odour of his unwashed body.

'Tis a drink, I need more, sweetheart,' he said taking a wine jug and emptying it down his throat. 'Jesu, I'm as dry as an old woman's crotch.'

He wiped his mouth on his sleeve and grinned at me, his exhilaration showing through a face grey with dust and exhaustion. 'Well, Eadgyth, we trounced Hardrada and, those we didn't kill, we sent back across the North Sea with their tails between their legs, now all that remains is to do the same to William.'

Kneeling before him and pulling off his boots, I examined them and decided they were only fit for disposal. 'Godwin told me the full story. He said Morcar was hurt, not badly I hope.'

'Not mortal hurt, but he will not be fit to do battle for a while; Edwin has gone to muster more fighting men and meets with us at the hoaréd apple tree tomorrow.'

I looked up aghast, 'Tomorrow? What are you thinking? You are exhausted and your men too. You cannot possibly march again tomorrow? You need food and rest, Leofwine can keep the Normans at bay for a day or two surely.'

He got up and began to pace the room. 'I cannot tolerate that man on Saxon soil for one day more. If you could have seen how we vanquished the Norwegians, Eadgyth, you would understand that my blood lust is up and I cannot rest until I have slaughtered the Normans too. I need to strike while the iron is hot.'

'You should listen to your wife, Harold,' said a voice, and we turned to see Gytha standing by the door.

She seemed to stand out, a lone figure against her surroundings, as if set apart from the rest of us by her terrible grief. Harold put down is cup and swallowed audibly, 'Mother,' he said, wetting his lips with his tongue. Gytha came forward, her face white, and stood before him,

'How are you, my son?' she asked after a pause, surveying his strained face. For a few silent moments they stood close together, each looking for answers in the other's eyes.

So delighted had I been to see Harold come safe home, I had momentarily forgotten about Tostig. Now, witnessing their private torment, I remembered her terrible sorrow and realised that I was intruding. Making an excuse, I hurried from the room. As I closed the door I saw Harold slump to his knees before his mother and clasp her knees, sobbing his repentance while, with her head bowed, she stroked his dirty hair.

When I returned an hour or so later, Gytha had gone and Harold lay across the bed, his head back and gentle snores issuing from his open mouth. I crept to look at him.

He seemed vulnerable and small, his larger than life personality quenched by sleep. His hair, still grimy from the road, had fallen back from his face and the strong bones of his jaw were slackened; the bristly skin pallid and his eye sockets hollow from exhaustion. He looked, in fact, as he would look when he became an old man.

I pondered briefly upon the joy with which we would fill the intervening years. The homes we would build, the children we would raise. Then Harold stirred in his sleep drawing me from my reverie and I saw it was coming on dark so, disrobing and finding a coverlet to throw across us, I climbed onto the bed beside him. The fire had sunk low in the grate and the chamber chilly. As I eased myself beside him he seemed to sense my warmth and rolled over, tucking an arm across me; soon we both slept.

The next morning the children were riotous with excitement so I instructed Anwen to take them for a walk to the river to feed the royal swans.

They set off, armed with stale bread, their cheerful voices floating to where I stood watching them go. Back in the chamber I made myself busy, one ear tuned to Harold's snores but it was close to noon before he eventually awoke. As soon as he began to stir I sent Maude to organise water to be heated and the wooden tub to be brought to the chamber. My husband was to take a bath, whether he felt he needed one or not.

Complaining that he had better things to do, he reluctantly began to strip, scattering his clothes about the chamber. I followed him about the room, gathering his garments up and handing them to Maude. 'Take them to be burned,' I told her, 'they are not fit for a beggar.' Then I turned to my husband, armed with a scrubbing brush and scented soap.

'NO.' he cried, when he saw my approach, 'I can do it myself, woman.' but, undeterred, I began to soap him all over and scrub him, the soft bristles stimulating his blood and bringing the life back into his skin. My sleeves rolled up like a dairymaid and elbow deep in the king's bath-water, I rubbed away the grime of battle.

As the water discoloured and the warmth soothed his aches he ceased his complaints and lay back allowing me to continue with my administrations. I chattered of inconsequential things, the children's progress, our forthcoming babe, Maude's recurring toothache …anything but the imminent battle.

He was watching me as I rubbed in slow circles, covering his stomach in suds and watching his wet belly hair undulate in the water. So ingrossed was I in my task that I was unprepared when he grabbed me suddenly and pulled me into the tub, submerging me, veil and all.

A wave of water surged over the sides and slopped into the rushes and I came up breathless, my veil lost and my hair stuck to my head. My mouth opened in shock as I gasped for breath while he roared with laughter at me, delighted with his revenge.

'Harold.' I yelled, 'what the...' but he silenced me, engulfing my mouth with his and tugging my encumbering skirts out of the way of his questing hands. His moustaches tickled my nose as I gave up the fight and relaxed against him to easily let him win the fray.

Afterwards, while he shaved his chin, I cleansed myself in his cooling bathwater and found a fresh gown, unwilling for Maude or Anwen to guess at what had passed between us. He watched me as I adjusted my hose and tied my garters. 'Eadgyth,' he said, spoiling the quiet intimacy of the moment, 'I must ride to Waltham today.'

His words doused me like cold water and I felt my stomach turn. Anger surged unbidden and I heard myself saying; 'I would have thought you would have had more urgent matters to attend on the eve of battle than a visit with your mistress.'

'For God's sake, Eadgyth, why do you persist in this? She is not my mistress, I have explained that and, if you had allowed me to finish, I was about to say that I wish you to accompany me?'

I had not expected that. 'Whatever for? I do not wish to be in her company for a moment so do not invite me along and think I will exchange niceties with her.'

My face felt hot with jealousy and I fought hard against indignant tears. I knew I was behaving like a child but I could not quell my instinctive dislike for the woman. Harold softened.

'Come here,' he said and I went to him sulkily and he sat me on his knee and twiddled my fingers. 'Listen, sweetheart, these are difficult times and, as king, I must do things I would rather not do. We all must, for the sake of England. Ordinary men have left their homes and families to fight a battle from which they may not return, women have watched their husbands and sons march away without a word of recrimination, although they may never be back. My men have marched the length and breadth of the country, to fight and now must fight again. We cannot let the Norman's win and in order to ensure it, I must ask all my subjects to do as I request without exception…even you, Eadgyth.'

'Me?' I said, startled out of my sulk, 'I will do anything, Harold, anything you ask.'

He let out a long, audible breath. 'Well, that's good to hear, sweetheart, because I have to ask you to do something you will not like, and I am trusting that your sense of duty will help you do it with dignity.'

'What is it?' I asked, my blood chilling. Harold's blue eyes did not falter as he looked into mine and explained;

'I need you to come to Waltham with me, to bring the children and Anwen and remain there, with Eadgytha, while I go to fight William. When I …'

'You must be mad.' I screamed, 'Why on earth do I have to go there? Why can I not wait here?' Leaping from his knee, I snatched my wrist away as he tried to catch it. He regarded me coldly, his lips tight, then he stated,

'You said you would do anything.'

'Anything but that, Harold, how can you ask it of me?'

'You might consider my position, madam, and the fact that I am asking a similar favour of Eadgytha. I have the confidence that her answer will be more accommodating than your own.'

When I looked at him I saw only his disappointment in me and I hated him for it. I hated the Swannecked woman and I hated myself for acting in such a detestable way. I could see quite clearly that my hurt pride was preventing me from becoming the generous person I had always intended to be.

'Eadgyth,' Harold was saying, 'Think of me. I have two families to protect. Mother has agreed to join Edith in Winchester but you, sweetheart, need to be in safe hands too. In your condition you are made all the more vulnerable. Eadgytha is a good woman, she will not show prejudice toward you or your children; she will care for you for my sake.'

My sense of inferiority increased at his words and I dissolved into tears again. He gentled and pulled me onto his knee again, tucking back my hair and kissing my cheek. His faith that she would do the right thing, made me seem mean spirited and I knew he was right The swan neck would care for me but, were I in her shoes, I would not do the same for her.

'I suppose I have no choice,' I said, and he smiled, satisfied that I had given my word. Patting my knee, he spilled me to the floor and began to shout for the grooms to make ready our horses.

'Your boxes can be sent after, right now all we need is to get you and the children to safety. In the next few days you must all ride to Chester in the company of Eadgytha's household. There, you will all be safe should ill befall me. At all costs, sweetheart, you must not fall in to William's hands. Should I be slain, you carry the rightful king in your womb.'

The pain in my throat became unbearable when he so casually mentioned his own death. I made to call him back but he had already hastened from the chamber and was bellowing out orders in the bailey.

I was silent on the journey, sickened by the trial that lay ahead. I fought angry tears, dreading him comparing my own awkward bulk with Eadgytha's elegance. Oblivious to my discomfort, the children chattered as we rode, pointing out a darting fox and exclaiming when a buzzard swooped for its prey. My eyes remained on Harold's back, broad and straight, before me on the road and I wished we were journeying any road but the one that led to Waltham. I wanted to explain how I felt but I did not know how to make him understand. Each opportunity for me to break the silence passed and, as the sun reached the tail end of its downward journey, we turned the last dusty corner and there was Eadgytha standing with her children in the dusk.

I absorbed the domestic scene. Poultry scratched in the yard and the hedge bordering a pretty kitchen garden was strewn with washing. Eadgytha stood, poised and beautiful, while Godwin, followed by a brood of siblings, rushed to engulf our party in welcome.

'Father.' exclaimed the small girl that I remembered from our previous encounter at Waltham church. She ran to Harold who swept her into his arms and kissed her happy cheeks. I took my time dismounting, unwilling to witness Harold's tender greeting of his family. I made some pretence of fiddling with my stirrup before allowing Godwin to help me to the ground. He steadied me, squeezing my arm to indicate his support, then, brushing the dust of the road from my skirts, I waited while Harold, with his hand on Eadgytha's elbow, led her forward to greet me.

'Eadgyth,' Harold began, 'this is Eadgytha…' I interrupted him.

'We have already met,' I said, watching my rival with a critical eye as she executed a sweeping curtsey. She smiled, seemingly unmoved by our encounter.

'I remember you.' said the fair-haired child at her side, 'We met you at the church. You didn't tell us then you were going to marry our father.' The child pouted, looking from me to Harold and back again. I recalled they had named her for Harold's mother, Gytha, in an attempt to win her approval.

'That, little lady, is because it was none of your business,' cried Godwin and I flashed a grateful glance at him, glad that our newfound friendship extended to him defending me against his family. Eadgytha must be proud of her tall, golden boy, I thought as I watched him gather the little ones together.

'Come,' he said, 'let us go in and refresh ourselves, you must be thirsty after your ride.'

Idwal hung back. Magnus however, felt no such fears and, his twisted gait no obstacle, fell in beside him, admiring Idwal's wooden sword and comparing it with his own. 'There is to be another great battle you know,' I heard him saying, 'but Father will win, he always does. I'm certain that, had he been in time for the battle of the foul ford, the Norwegians would not have beaten us. You have only to listen to the tales of Stamford Bridge to know that. I have heard, already, that the bards set the day to rhyme.'

Idwal, with Maredudd at his side, nodded his head.

'Yes, my uncles were there too; Uncle Morcar took some hurt but will fight again…'

Their voices trailed away as I passed into the hall and accepted the goblet that Eadgytha offered me. Looking around the hall I noted, with a pang of envy, the rich hangings and the bright armoury above the high table. *So, my lord keeps his light o' love in good comfort,* I thought, sipping at my cup of wine.

My heart sick within me, words froze on my lips and I stood silent until the awkwardness threatened to swamp us. Godwin sought to put us at our ease.

'Look, Madam,' he said, indicating the finely worked embroidery of the hangings, 'Tis my mother's work. Your own needlecraft is very fine too; you will be able to spend the afternoons working together. Mother, the queen has sewn some sumptuous covers for Father's chambers.'

I doubted I would ever be able to work alongside Eadgytha but, grateful for his felicity, I cleared my throat and spoke out, breaking the silence between us.

'It is very fine,' I said, and, indeed, the fine crewelwork was delicate and the colours bright, 'I shall look forward to working with you, Eadgytha.'

She flushed, 'You are very kind, Madam, but I fear my son is biased, my work is no more than adequate.'

Her manner was so gracious, I felt sickened. Circumstances meant that our dislike must be mutual yet she plastered on that ridiculous expression and pretended love for me. I looked away, wishing I were anywhere else on earth.

Harold, slapping his knees, stood up and said,

'Let us show the queen her chambers, then she can settle in a while before supper.'

Eadgytha nodded her ascent and I stood up, stroking my belly and unstiffening my back. She ushered me from the hall toward the women's quarters, a cluster of separate bowers set apart from the great hall.

The chamber was dark. Anwen threw back the shutter and light came streaming in revealing a richly carved bed with thick tapestry hangings and a table and chair set mid way between the brazier and the window. Refreshments were heaped on the table, nuts and fruit and wine. The floor was strewn with fresh rushes and herbs and the bed looked freshly stuffed and inviting.

'Thank you,' I said, 'You have done me proud.'

'Tis only for a few days,' said Harold, 'you must both travel to safety at Chester, just until I have dealt with William and then you will be straight back at court. Anyway, sweetheart, you must rest awhile now. Anwen, make your mistress comfortable and Maude, keep the children away so the queen can sleep.'

Then, ushering Eadgytha from the room, he left me alone with Anwen, dismissed from his presence as if I were his subject.

Resentment surged through me, jolting in its intensity. For a few moments I listened, with compressed lips, to their dwindling footsteps. I could hear Harold's voice but not discern his words but I imagined they were tender. Once they were out of earshot, I rose from the bed.

'I'm buggered if I'm staying here like an errant child.' I announced to an astonished Anwen and, opening the door, I marched down the walkway back in the direction of the main hall.

My footsteps slowed with my dwindling courage and, as I reached the open door, I hesitated on the threshold, hidden from those within by the screen that redirected the winter drafts. Through a chink in the tapestry I could see them. Harold was perched on the corner of the table close to where Eadgytha sat in a high backed chair. Her head was down and she fiddled with the ends of her veil while Harold spoke earnestly to her.

'Tis not for long, Eadgytha, and there is no one else I can trust. I cannot fight if one part of me is worrying for the safety of those I care about. You must travel with the queen to Chester and wait events there. Should I not win the battle…'

Eadgytha looked up then, her face protesting, she tried to speak but Harold silenced her with a hand on her shoulder. Envy twisted my guts.

'Should I not return,' he continued, 'you must help her escape into Wales. Should William capture her, her life will be forfeit for she carries my heir. Besides, I would have you and our children safe too. You can be sure he will let none survive who may threaten his cause.'

She nodded but did not look up.

'I knew I could rely on you,' Harold said, lifting her to her feet and kissing her brow, 'you are a good woman, Eadgytha, the best of women. I am grateful for your acceptance. Many would have wept and wailed against what fate has dealt you these last months yet you remain strong and noble in the spite of everything.'

My heart pounding, my breath grew short but still I did not move. How could he help but compare her composure with my filthy temper? How many times had I berated him, pelted him with insults or slapped his face? She was graceful in a crisis while I raged against it. She was slender and refined while I was too tall and fat. I knew that I could never compete against her goodness.

My heart breaking, I watched as Harold's kiss extended for too long to remain brotherly and he drew her to him and held her, her bowed head beneath his chin. I turned and ran blindly back to the chamber and, throwing myself on the bed, gave vent to jealous tears.

He did not come to my chamber until almost dawn and I was sure he had been with her all that time.

Unable to look at him or school my sulky face into pleasing lines, I kept my head low until he grew angry, spoiling our last hours before he rode away.

'Why must you be like this, woman?' he yelled at me, 'This is hard for me too. Do you think I want to go and fight? You think I'd rather risk all in the shield wall than lay idle in your chamber all my life? Grow up, and do what you must do and with good grace, as your betters do.'

Tears flooded my cheeks, collecting beneath my chin, the sobs rending me but I could not tell him the reason for them. I could not tell him I had witnessed his last tender moments with his concubine. All too soon the messenger came to tell him his mount was saddled. Harold sighed and stood hands on hips looking down at me and I sensed he fought against steadily rising anger; he seemed to win the battle. He knelt before me, the king of England on his knees in the rushes at my feet.

'Eadgyth,' he said, coaxing me to quit my weeping, 'I must go now. Let our leavetaking be tender. I need you to take care, of yourself, of the children and of our young prince.' He touched my stomach, a moment's contact with his unborn son, before continuing.

'I know you don't want to, but you must promise to do as Eadgytha says; she will cherish you for my sake. I have her promise and, now, I ask for yours.'

All I could do was nod. I had no words. Harold stroked my hair,

'Eadgyth,' he said, 'I will return. Remember that you bear England's prince and keep him safe for me.'

Then he was gone, a gust of wind, a slamming door, a shouted order to move out, the sound of hooves ...and he was gone. By the time I reached the door all that remained was the dust settling, like rain, in the yard. Eadgytha stood beside me, silent.

'He has gone,' I said, 'and I never told him that I love him.'

Eadgytha smiled encouragement.

'Do not worry,' she said, 'if I know Harold at all, it will not have occurred to him that you may feel otherwise.'

And, together, we walked back into her hall.

Waltham, 1066

'I'm not going to Chester, Eadgytha.' I cried and she turned from where she and Anwen were folding garments and placing them in a travelling box.

'Of course you are, Lady.' exclaimed Anwen, placing her hands on her hips and preparing to do battle.

'No, I'm not. I cannot do it. I am going to follow Harold. Supposing he is wounded? He will need me.'

'He needs you to look after his child.' argued Anwen and I saw Eadgytha glance at her, surprised at such insolence. They stood, shoulder to shoulder, ranged against me and I stuck out my chin.

'I don't care what you say, I am your queen and it is for you to do as you are told ...both of you.' They glanced at each other but Eadgytha remained silent while Anwen refused to be cowed.

'And what about the children?' she cried, 'What of your duty to them as their mother? How can you think to expose them to the rigours of a battlefield and how can you risk the king's unborn son too?'

'I don't care.' I began to cry again, my already sore nose beginning to run.

'Come. Lady,' crooned Anwen, trying a different tack, 'tis just the babe making you act peculiar. Harold will be back in a day or two and all this upset will be as eggs an' moonshine.'

'And if he doesn't, I will live with regrets for the rest of my days.' I sobbed, 'I am going, Anwen, whether you like or not, so pack me a separate box please and cease wasting your breath on arguments.'
Torn between her natural common sense and her loyalty to me, Anwen looked to Eadgytha for support.

'What do you think, Lady?' she asked.

Continuing to fold Gytha's nightgown, Eadgytha smoothed the linen and then placed it in the box.

'I think,' she said, 'that we should do as our queen commands. I think that you, Anwen, should accompany the children and travel with all speed to Chester, while the queen and I follow the army. Harold asked me to look after her and so I have no choice. Wherever the queen goes, there must I follow.'

My mouth fell open in surprise, I was not altogether pleased not to be rid of Eadgytha's company but, clapping my hands together, I cried,

'Yes, that's it. You can take the children to Chester, Anwen. They will be safe with you, and Eadgytha and I will join you there after the battle, as soon as we can.'

'Oh no,' frowned Anwen, 'I'm not having that, I am coming with you. When I was taken off into Snowdonia with Gruffydd I swore I'd never leave your side again. You take me with you, Madam, or I follow behind you like a stray hound. Maude can manage the children with the help of the under-servants, tis you and that young'n you carry that I must look to now.'

Without waiting for my consent she began to burrow into the already packed boxes and separate our belongings from the children's, piling her clothes in with mine. Eadgytha shrugged and I raised my eyes to heaven. It seemed Anwen was to have her way.

Later, when we broke the news to the children, there were tears. Gytha climbed onto her mother's lap and buried her head while Magnus tried to look resigned.

Godwin and Edmund had ridden forth with their father, leaving just three of Eadgytha's children behind. Her elder daughter, Gunnhild, was a noviate at Wilton abbey where, it was hoped, she sent fervent prayers for her father's victory. When they heard the news, Idwal bit at his underlip, trying to maintain his composure. Maredudd, eager for adventure, hastily checked he had his sword and helmet and then challenged Magnus to a playtime duel.

Nesta, too young to understand, just sucked her thumb, sensing some threat to her security. I would miss them but I felt driven to follow Harold, to speak to him before the onset of battle and to tell him that he was more precious to me than the stars in heaven.

A lively wind whipped about us as we waved Maude and the children off. I snuggled Idwal's cloak about his neck and bade him be brave, sensing his fear and knowing he recalled his last flight from danger.

'Be of good cheer, my son.' I told him, 'this time tis but a short parting and, before we know it, we will all be back together.' He attempted a plucky smile and allowed me to place a kiss on his forehead. Nesta opened her mouth and gave vent to a huge roar as they rode away, leaving no one to doubt her feelings. Maude pulled her close and the wagons and horses moved off, Maredudd and Magnus waving their swords and issuing war cries as they went.

Eadgytha surreptitiously wiped away a tear and I felt a pang of guilt at parting her from her children. She had confided the previous evening that they had never been separated before and at that moment I knew exactly how she felt. Quelling the impulse to rush after them and call them all back, I placed a hand on her shoulder and we went to complete our own preparations for the journey.

My mare stepped daintily through the mire of the road that led to Caldbec Hill and the site of the hoaréd apple tree. Eadgytha and I looked about us in wonder at the constant stream of foot soldiers who trod the same path as we.

'The whole country has turned out.' I exclaimed, 'I had not thought there would be so many.'

'Harold is a good king,' Eadgytha replied, 'and no man wants to live under Norman rule.'

Anwen followed, one pace behind, open mouthed at the spectacle but, for once, adhering to the demands of etiquette and forebearing to make comment. The way was thronged with fightingmen; huscarls, thegns and fyrdmen armed with wooden shields and bristling spears, axes swinging at their belts and swords at their hips. Bowmen with their quivers stuffed full with arrows. Abandoning their harvest, farmers and ploughmen marched grimfaced, girded with scythes, pitchforks and hammers.

We saw grandfathers with clubs, and young boys with slings. We even passed a group of monks, shuffling in single file behind their abbot who led them in a rousing psalm. Women followed in lumbering carts, bringing bandages, food and other comforts for the soldiers. Eadgytha and I looked about us, our throats tight with gratitude.

'God bless you.' we cried to them as we passed by and they saluted us although they knew not who we were.

The apple tree, tortured by decades of wind, stood proud on its ridge, the slopes beneath it bright with Harold's mustered armies. Pavilions, brilliant in the sun, flew pennants that fluttered and snapped in the breeze.

I spied the dragon of Wessex straight away and, a moment later, Eadgytha pointed out Harold's personal banner of the fighting man; his club raised and his prodigious cock erect. Armed men sat stolidly sharpening their weapons, honing the blades to a deadly edge. Minions and servants scurried to and fro with messages and a few women intermingled with the men, bringing food and drink.

The royal pavilion stood brave in its royal colours and I made toward it but Eadgytha held me back.

'Nay, Madam, stay a while. The time is not right. Remember, he will be angry that we have disobeyed him and we should not distract him from his task. We came to watch over him, did we not, not to provide him with further cares?'

Although I was desperate to see Harold I agreed, she was always right. We guided our mounts away from the royal camp and presently joined a group of women on the ridge who had set up a makeshift infirmary. Already they treated ailments of the arriving force, soothing the footsore and dosing the sick. In our homespun tunics nobody guessed we were of noble blood and, without revealing our identities, Eadgytha offered our services and set to bathing the bloodied feet of a young bowman.

I sat rolling bandages while listening to the tale of his fifty-mile journey from the home where his mother, young wife and baby waited 'twill be a poor harvest this year, Lady, no matter what,' he was saying, 'but, if we can send the Norman back whence he came quickly enough, I may still be home in time to bring in the barley and collect the apples from the orchard.'

Eadgytha was murmuring assurances that he would do so when I heard my name and, on turning, saw Godwin fighting his way through the throng until he stood aghast before me, his face flushed and angry. He had not seen his mother at the bowman's feet.

'What are you doing here? Have you no sense? Father will be furious.'

Standing up, I led him away from the tent, dodging the darting messengers, and walked with him to the edge of the hill

'I had to come, Godwin, I could not just wait and wonder. I meant to come alone but they would not let me, believe me, I wanted them to go on to Chester without me.'

He turned, his quizzical expression slowly turning to realisation.

'You mean, Mother is here too. God's grief, Madam. Are you both mad? I hope to Christ you had the sense to leave the children at home...If things should go ill tomorrow...'

Placing a finger over his lips to silence him, 'Hush' I said, 'hush, do not even speak of that and, don't worry, the children are safe on the way to Chester.'

'As should you be.' he cried and then, smiling ruefully, 'Father will be spitting mad Eadgyth, if he finds out.'

'Oh, I know and he will find out, for I mean to visit him as soon as dusk has fallen.'

'More fool you then.' he grinned and I knew he had overcome the worst of his anger, 'perhaps you could escort me, Godwin, I should not care to walk through camp unaccompanied.'

'I will be honoured, Madam, but I fear I must abandon you at the entrance of the tent for I'm not heroic enough to want to risk Father's wrath.'

Much later, when the sun had almost gone and scudding clouds were darkening an already dreary evening, Godwin came to escort me to Harold's pavilion. As he went to lift the flap we heard voices within and hesitated, not wishing to intrude. Leofwine was speaking, his tone edgy.

'Harold, I think you shouldn't fight. You are exhausted, man, you have had nothing but strain for months and now think you can fight a battle when you are still stiff and worn from the last.'

'Don't be ridiculous,' came Harold's voice, 'have you seen these men that have come to fight for me? Men that have marched the length of England; men who have left their ploughshares and their hearthsides to fight for a man they do not know? Are they not weary too? How then can I plead tiredness and sit in the sun while their good blood is spilt? Nay, brother, I fight tomorrow and I will not rest until William is dead or fled.'

Another voice, lighter and younger than the last and I realised it was Gyrth; the three remaining sons of Godwin were together on the eve of battle.

'They can't flee, for the duke ordered their ships burned to prevent such a thing happening.'

'Then they can swim home,' snarled Harold, in a voice I had never heard him use before. Gyrth broke through the forced flurry of laughter.

'But Harold, what if the day goes against us? Should we not preserve our king to fight another day.'

'Nay, lad,' replied Harold, 'we finish them tomorrow, I will not fight another day. I will end it tomorrow or die in the attempt…'

'And where will England be then, without a king?'

'You will have a king, boy.' he roared, so loudly that, all around, heads turned toward the royal tent. 'The queen rides to Chester with the next king tucked safe within her womb. If it goes ill for me then you must rule, Leo, until my son is of an age to do so and you, Gyrth, must aid him. Godwin too, for all his youth, is a good boy, and will stand by his half-brother.'

Outside in the cold, Godwin and I, heard his words and stared at each other, realising that our presence could only undermine the king's confidence in his plans. With a brief shake of his head, Godwin backed away, beckoning me to follow him and we slipped away into the steady drizzle that had begun to fall.

Senlache Ridge 14 October 1066

Despite their exhaustion few slept well that night but a hush fell upon the camp as darkness fell. The men sat at their campfires, watching the glowing embers, wondering if tomorrow's battle would bring victory or death. Godwin had commandeered a tent for Eadgytha and I, where we both lay sleepless until the first notes of dawn confirmed that day had come. I rose from my bed, stretched my aching limbs and crept outside. I thought Eadgytha slept but, a few moments later, I found her at my side, as crumpled and weary as myself.

A white blanket of mist covered the land but, as the morning wore on and the world kicked off its bed covers, a white, nondescript sky was revealed. The day was neither dull nor bright, neither warm nor cold. Anwen produced a rough breakfast of honeyed milk and coarse porrage, which we both ate, more from gratitude than hunger. As the morning wore on and noise in the camp increased, Godwin appeared, pale from lack of sleep. At first, by his height and bearing, I thought he was Harold and my heart gave a little leap.

'Good morning, Madam,' he said, 'and to you, Mother. The day looks fair set for battle; father says that these white skies are better than sun that dazzles a soldier's eyes and saps his strength. It is better too than rain, that turns the battle ground to a quagmire and obscures the vision.'

We both smiled but made no reply until Eadgytha broke the silence.

'How is your father this morning, my son?'

'Oh…anxious… preoccupied. He has no idea you are here and it will be best if we keep it that way. He is closeted now with the earldormen, Edmund is with them but I made my excuses and came to find you, to see if you have all you require. You must both stay well clear of the battle and, should things begin to go wrong, you must flee from here, do you hear?'

We both nodded mutely and then Eadgytha said,

'I have been praying that the Normans would creep away under cover of night but, I suppose they are still there.'

Godwin gave a snort, 'They are and, rumour has it, that they carry the papal banner. With Rome on their side they will feel themselves invincible.'

I placed my empty porrage bowl on the table.

'They have won the pope to their cause with lies,' I said, spitting out my words. 'They declare your father an oath-breaker but they are the ones without honour, Harold would have sooner died than pledge allegiance to William over holy relics.'

'We know that, Madam,' soothed Eadgytha, staring out across the undulating land, 'but we must have faith that God knows this also and so sends us victory over our enemies. Should things go wrong, England will be changed forever. Our customs and language lost and our children's children will be as Normans.'

'Then they must be stopped,' I cried, 'and Harold is the man to do it.'

'Amen,' said Godwin, 'Amen to that.'

The camp fully awake, the noise and activity of battle preparation took our minds from the enormity of the moment. My rising panic was doused by small emergencies; a young serf with a badly scalded foot came to be salved and bandaged. He was no more than eleven summers, his face white, both from the shock of his injury and worry that he would miss the battle.

'I can still fight, Lady,' he declared, 'bind it well and I will fight for the king 'til I drop.' I smothered a desire to ruffle his hair. He was little older than Idwal. Instead, I washed his scrawny foot and smothered it liberally with goose grease before binding it. He wore no boots and I suspected the dressing would soon work itself free.

'I thank you, Lady,' he cried as he limped away, armed with just a rusty axe, some relic of the ancient wars. I wondered what he would say if he realised it was the queen of England that had just bandaged his grimy foot.

The country was depending on men like him, torn from their families by duty and honour. When he was gone, Eadgytha and I fell to helping the other women put the infirmary into some order, for, even if the day went well, there would be casualties, there are always too many injured …and killed in conflict.

It was still early when we watched the men take their positions on the hilltop. We knew nothing of Harold's plans and could only hope that he had some winning strategy to finish the day quickly. They lined up across the ridge of Santlache hill, an impregnable wall of muscle, their shields locked and their axes and swords honed. Harold's fighting man banner snapped in the skies along side the dragon of Wessex and the flags of Leofric and Gyrth. The Godwinson brothers stood ranged together for battle. The fighting men of England were backed up by the hoards of untrained ploughmen, blacksmiths and grim faced monks; their flanks ungirded, and armed only with clubs and maces. To one side the archers stood ready, their arrows stuck into the ground around them so that they could let fly a rapid succession of deadly missiles. England waited, determined to stop the invader and to spill without mercy the Norman blood upon the Saxon shore.

Scanning the massed army, I searched for Edwin's banner, sweeping my eyes twice or thrice across the hillside.

'Where is my brother Edwin?' I asked, 'why is he not come?'

Eadgytha shrugged.

'He has much ground to cover and many men to muster. He may be held up but there is time yet. Don't give up on him, the day is young.'

I felt that he should be here; his tardiness was letting all England down, letting his king down, letting me down and bringing dishonour upon the name of Ælfgarsson. But I could not ponder his whereabouts for long, for my attention was snatched by an outbreak of unholy noise.

From where we stood we could not see the ranks of William's army but we could hear them shouting insults, trying to break the resolve of our shield wall. In response our men stood firm, clashing their weapons against wooden shields and roaring, 'Ut. Ut. Ut.'

Eadgytha clutched my arm, our petty dislike forgotten in the face of shared fear. Not only Harold but Godwin and Edmund were out there among the fighting men and we both prayed for them, vulnerable and untried in battle as they were.

All at once there came a hail of Norman arrows, they whispered through the sky before spiralling softly to the ground, short of the target. Our men let lose a stream of derisive abuse, thumping their shields again, enticing the enemy into action while our archers let fly their arrows in retaliation. The Normans crouched beneath their raised shields and we knew from the screams that some of our archers had reached their mark. First blood, the day had begun.

Their next volley was more precise and we heard the stuttering thud of a multitude of arrows imbedding into our raised shields. So thick did they fly that some found a way through the close linked shields and men fell, struck down screaming, only to be hauled from the front ranks from behind to be quickly replaced by another warrior.

After that we were forced away from the scene for the wounded began to arrive at our tent in a steady stream, some limping, some carried; those we could were bound up so they could fight again but others were too badly hurt. There were those for whom we could do nothing but offer them comfort, hold their hands and croon soft words to them as they cried for their mothers. Every so often, one of the women would abandon her post and run to the edge of the hill to ensure that the fighting man banner still flew proud above the furore.

Anwen rallied the wounded, teasing them and making light of often horrific wounds, squeezing together the torn flesh before binding it tight and sending up a silent prayer that they might recover. The lilting of her Welsh tongue barely ceased but Eadgytha and I worked more quietly, each with half our minds upon the battle that clamoured so close by; our hands soiled with good Saxon blood and our tunics soaked in gore.

A monk was brought in with an arrow through his throat and, swallowing nausea, Eadgytha knelt at his side, his fingers clasped within her praying hands, while I bathed his forehead and waited helplessly while he choked slowly to death on his own blood. When his gurgling breaths ceased I gently closed his eyes and stood up, signalling to a servant to bear the body away as another was brought in to replace him.

'Take a rest, Madam, you look exhausted,' begged Anwen, 'we shall manage without you for a while.'
The boy she tended was not mortal hurt. She bent over his skinny torso prising an arrow from his shoulder.

'This will smart a bit, *bach*,' she said, 'so grit your teeth and let's get it out.' He fell into a swoon as the barbed blade was ripped from his flesh, bringing a further torrent of blood. 'That's better, lad, now I can work without fear of hurting you further.'

She looked up at me, flicking her black fringe back from her eyes, 'Are you still here, Lady?' she cried, 'go on, outside, take the air and see if your Lord's standard still flies.'

The noise from the field was incredible. Screams, taunts, trumpets, the thump of twenty thousand swords on twenty thousand shields; shrieks of the dying and the roar of rage issued from the battle while closer, in the camp, the cries of the wounded mingled with the shouted orders of the those tending the fallen. I hurried closer to the edge of the hill and looked across to where Harold's shield wall still held strong against the foe; his pennant blowing strongly in the wind.

Beneath it I could see him rallying his men, bolstering their courage from the rear. His mouth wide and his fair hair flying beneath his helmet, he whirled his axe about his head and shouted to his men to stand firm.

All eyes in the shield wall were fixed in one direction; I turned my head to see what held their attention and the breath caught in my throat. William's army, four ranks deep, were approaching on foot, swords raised and spears pointing forward. At first they marched but soon they broke into a jog, roaring insults and obscenities as they came. Their ferocity was such that I feared our lines would never stand firm, but they did not so much as falter as the vast hoard bore down upon them. My heart stopping, I watched as they came.

'Sainte criox.' they bellowed, 'Holy cross.' our ranks hollered back,

'Godemite. God Almighty. Olicrosse. Holy Cross.' and 'Ut. Ut. Ut.'

The Saxons let lose their spears into the approaching army, felling them as they ran, but the Normans barely faltered. Our men, fixed like oak trees to the ground, gripped their battleaxes, ready for the onslaught. With a mighty roar the two sides met, a human wave crashing onto rocks and all I could do was look on in horror as they slashed and struck with axe and sword.

Fresh blood fountained into the air and I saw heads severed and gaping holes smashed into armoured chests, but as each man was felled so did another take his place, unflinching in the face of certain mutilation.

I turned and fled, swirling back into the tent where Eadgytha was binding the bloodied stump of a frydman's arm. My heart thumping, I snatched up a bowl of soiled bandages,

'The battle grows worse.' I cried, 'prepare yourself, Eadgytha, for I fear our task is about to become harder.'

'Harold lives still?' she asked, helping her patient from his chair and conducting him to sit with the other wounded outside. The wounded awaiting our care were groaning, some screaming. Eadgytha thrust her hair from her face with the back of her wrist, exhaustion writ clear on her face.

'The banner still flies,' I replied, 'I have never seen battle before, I tell you, men make light of it in their mead hall boastings.'

'This is a battle…'began Anwen but her words were interrupted as one, desperately wounded, was carried in and dumped upon the table.

'Oh, my good Lord, have mercy.' cried Eadgyth, her face white, 'tis Harold's uncle Ælfwig …oh, Eadgyth, he is sore hurt.'

Judging from the gore, this was an understatement. Grabbing my knife I began to cut away his clothes.

'These are monastic robes and he wears a hair shirt.' I exclaimed.

Anwen slopped a bowl of water before me as Eadgytha replied, 'He is the abbot of Winchester. Godwin told me yesterday that Ælfwig had brought the youngest of his brethren to the fight. Oh God, he bleeds so, we will never save him.'

She was right, his wound was so severe that all our ministrations were useless and his breathing grew shallower as his blood seeped steadily away without him gaining consciousness. We all wept freely as his portly body was shrouded and borne away. He was the first we had tended who was noble kin, a Saxon prelate, torn by loyalty from the peace of his abbey to die amid the horror of war. It was my first taste of despair that day and it was not to be my last.

After that they came in droves, thegns, farmers and ploughboys, cut so deep and wide that there was little hope that, even could we halt the flow of their blood, they would not take the fever and die. We battled on, weary and sickened, staunching, stitching and soothing as best we could. And then came Godwin with blood on his brow and an arrow in his thigh. Eadgytha screamed when she saw him and we both rushed to him, leading him, limping, to a chair.

'I'm alright, Mother,' he said whitely.

I cut his leggings and wiped the blood away while his mother fussed ineffectually, kissing his face and trying to smooth his hair.

'tis not lodged so very deep,' I said, 'but it will hurt, Godwin.'

Eadgytha mopped his head, examining the source of the injury.

'This is but a flesh wound; thank Jesus. Heads always bleed profusely. Oh, my son …' she sobbed, suddenly overwhelmed by the trauma of the day and the fear that, like all the others, her son too would slip from life beneath her hands. Putting her head on his shoulder she let the tears flow while I worked at the arrowhead.

'How goes the battle?' I asked to distract his attention from the bloody knife I wielded.

'I don't know,' he replied, 'it was going well and they had not so much as dented the shield wall. The slaughter was great, far more falling on their side than on ours. But, of a sudden, the Bretons who fought against us on the right flank suddenly faltered and began to retreat, at first backing up slowly but then turning and running full pelt down the hill. Father yelled for the wall to stand firm but the fryd closest to them thought it a rout and ran after them howling their derision. Ow, Eadgyth. Watch you don't sever my manhood.'

I grinned up at him, 'Sorry, I'm sorry, I am being as gentle as I can.' He nodded and, after a moment, continued his story, breathless with pain.

'The fryd, sensing victory, chased the Bretons past the marshland and straight toward the Norman camp. Hundreds of them, screamed after the fleeing foe like demons, overwhelming them and striking many down as they went. For a while it looked as if the triumph was ours.'

I grasped the stump of the arrow shaft and tugged it. The arrow jerked from his muscle followed by a crimson jet of blood that spattered across my face.

'God's teeth, woman.' he yelled, sounding exactly like his father but when I looked up to apologise I saw he had fainted clean away. Eadgytha, in an agony of panic, splashed water on his face while I staunched and bound the wound. Moments later he regained consciousness and was watching me, his eyes still bleary,

'If the Norman's get too much for us to handle we can set you on them, Madam,' he said before slipping into unconsciousness again.

Later, he concluded his tale and we learned how William, foreseeing the total collapse of his infantry, led his men in a decisive onslaught, blocking the retreat of the Bretons and crashing into the Saxons, slashing with their swords and trampling the defenders into the ground. We lost many men; those who tried to return to the shield wall were pursued and hacked to the ground while the shield wall looked on.

'Just after that,' continued Godwin, 'Father noticed my head wound and sent me to have it tended, there was no arguing with him and he hadn't even noticed the arrow jutting from my leg.'

'At least you will fight again, my son,' said Eadgytha, 'and I am shamed I was so little help when you had need of me.'

Before Godwin could answer a group of men stumbled in, their faces and torso's bloodsoaked and we fell straightaway to tending their hurts.

'What is happening on the field?' I asked of a be-whiskered farmer.

'They rode on horseback into our shield wall. Can you believe that? They did battle with their horses, used them as a weapon against us.' the old fellow uttered with bewilderment on his face. 'I have never seen the like. The Normans have no honour. The Saxon shield wall has always stood firm against everything but … horses it cannot withstand.'

I dabbed at his face, most of the blood didn't seem to be his and he confirmed that he had sliced the head from an oncoming horse before the rider had slashed his shoulder with his sword.

'And the king, he lives still?' we asked, again and again of the wounded and they answered,

'Yes, he lives, as far as we know, he still lives.'

Trumpets sounded and the next wave of injured told us that there was a lull in the fighting. The wounds that we tended now were different, if anything they were less severe, for so fierce had the fighting become and the injuries grew so brutal that more of the maimed died before they could be brought from the field. There was no rest for the women and during the break in the violence our nursing continued feverishly, our fingers hurrying to patch up the wounded so they may return to the fight. Eadgytha, hearing her son, Edmund's voice, turned to greet him and assure herself that he was unscathed.

'Edmund.' she called and he looked up, appalled at finding her there.

'Mother? What are you doing here? We thought you far from danger…' his voice trailed away and all heads swivelled as Harold strode into the tent.

'I am come to discover how Godwin's headw…' he stopped mid-sentence and glared at Eadgytha, unable to believe his eyes.

'What in God's name are you doing here?' he bellowed. Eadgytha blanched at his anger, bowed her head and did not answer. Harold, gory from the fight, stood, hands on hips before her,

'I asked you a question, Madam' he bullied, 'I entrusted a job to you and I would know why you abandoned the task.' Still she did not move and I could see her trembling.

Suddenly I saw Eadgytha as Harold must see her, daubed in gore, lank hair stuck to her forehead and her rough gown covered in wet patches. She was a mess and I knew I must look the same. I stood up from behind the patient I was bandaging.

Harold's eyes flicked past me unseeing, and then back again. His features froze, the blood drained from his face and I knew he was angrier than I had ever known him. I clenched my fists and looked him in the eye,

'I am to blame, Harold. I refused to go to Chester and Eadgytha would not leave me because she had given you her promise.'

'As had you, Madam,' he growled and, his grip tight upon my arm, he marched me from the tent. Briskly he all but dragged me away from the curious throng of people toward the edge of the hill, close to the place from which I had watched the battle. Glancing across I saw the field littered with the dead and dying; strewn with remnants of banners like the fields around Thorney after the day of the spring fayre. Anwen hovered a little away, out of earshot.

'Well?' he spat, 'explain.'

How could I explain? It all sounded so childish now. I wanted to risk my own life, and that of Eadgytha and my maid, because I had been too proud to tell you how much I loved you and I was afraid you would be slain and die never knowing?

I could not say that and so I said nothing, hoping he would understand and just take me in his arms and hold me as I craved. The silence stretched on until it became overwhelming.

'I was afraid,' I said at last, 'I thought you may need me, if you were wounded. I couldn't bare to think of you injured… or worse and myself far away and of no use to you.'

Hollow eyed, he looked away; I thought he couldn't bear to look upon me.

'Eadgyth, your duty is to do as I say. You need to put our child before everything else, if he is safe then there is hope, but if you are taken then he is taken and Saxon England is lost. You will go now, under escort, to Chester and there will be no argument. Do you understand?'

I nodded, my throat a knot of pain. He made to walk away but just as I was about to call him back, he turned and pulled me close. He held me, my head beneath his chin; he smelled dreadfully of blood and sweat but I did not flinch from it. For a long moment we stood upon Caldbec Hill and there was nothing but us two with the solid earth of England beneath our feet and the Saxon sky above our heads. When he released me and began to walk away I rummaged in the pocket that hung at my side,

'I wanted you to carry this, Harold,' I said and offered him my kerchief, 'for luck.' He came back toward me and took it, examining the fine embroidered edge before handing it back.

'I don't need it, sweetheart. I have this, look,' and from his jerkin he pulled a crumpled, grey rag. I took it and, after a moment, smiled a brilliant smile.

'It is my kerchief, or what is left of it. It's the one you stole from me on the day you rode into Wales against Gruffydd.'

'tis the very one,' he grinned, 'I keep it by me always and hasn't it ever brought me luck?'
Throwing myself into his noxious embrace again, I held him tight, 'Be safe, Harold,' I cried.

The bodies of the dead and wounded lay scattered about the camp, some calling for water. Anwen was trickling water between the lips of a dying boy, pretending she was his mother so that he should die in some comfort. 'You've always been a fine son,' she was saying, 'and I love you dearly.'

When his head fell forward she lay him back and covered his face with his torn jerkin. I stood beside her for some moments before she stood up and handed me the jug; I drank deeply and then looked about me, wiping my mouth on my mucky apron.

'Oh, Lady,' she whispered, close to tears, 'to think we should ever see such sadness.'

Together we looked across the hillside, at the living tearing the armour from their dead comrades for protection in the coming fray, at the wounded dragging themselves back to the field to fight again, and at the dead staring blank eyed upon a world gone mad.

'Nothing is worth all this,' I said, 'maybe we should surrender. Normans can't be as bad as they say.'

'Don't you believe it, Madam, I've heard tell those devils eat young babies and there's not a woman in the realm who'd be safe from them should they prevail over us. We must all fight, man and woman, girl and boy, and to our last breath.'

Eadgytha strode from the tent toward us, glancing up at the sun. To my surprise I realised it was not yet noon.

'Harold has ordered Godwin to take us to Chester without delay. The boy is spitting mad but has given his word. I don't know about you, Lady, but I feel I am needed here. I have asked Godwin if we can find reason to delay our departure.'

'Eadgytha.' I exclaimed, 'are you telling me we should disobey our lord king …again?'

She flushed, quite exquisitely. 'I am, Lady, we cannot leave these dying men and, should things turn very bad, there may still be time to get away. Godwin has horses ready in yonder copse so our escape can be swift.'

The shield wall was lined up once more and, as before, flights of Norman arrows rained down upon them and the noise of battle resumed. I stood beside an ancient oak tree, its twisted trunk rough against my hands, and watched the fighting recommence. Although I had heard the tales told of the previous mounted attack I had not really believed the ferocity of it until I saw it with my own eyes.

A large band of horsemen, led by whom I assumed to be William, bore down upon the men of England. Our wall stood firm until the huge beasts were almost full upon them. They hacked the horses down with their axes; the screams of the animals almost worse than those of the men who were mutilated as they fell from the saddle.

I saw a horse roll headless from the fray and slide downhill in a river of his own gore, his slaughtered master prone upon his back. I heard the Saxon war cries and I saw my husband with the killing rage upon him; on foot amid his huscarls he cut about him with his axe, dispatching Normans and horses as I had seen him swat fruit flies in our chamber.

Time and motion seemed slowed and the clamour of battle drifted away as I watched him from afar. I felt I did not know the fighting man who laid waste all before him, who took life without a qualm. Although the figure was familiar, the blond hair flying, the moustaches glinting in the sun, his actions were appalling and I was sore afraid. Just then a hail of projectiles rained suddenly from the skies, clattering as they fell useless or thumping dully as they found their mark. The papal banner that swirled above William's head floated to the mired ground and a great cry went up.

'Le duc est mort. Le duc est mort.' they cried and I had enough of the Norman tongue to know that Duke William was dead.

Whirling around, I saw Godwin limping toward me, a makeshift crutch beneath his arm; his face was sulky at being banned from the fray.

'Godwin, Godwin.' I cried, almost jumping up and down with delight, 'William is down, he is dead, we have won the day.'

I leapt at him, flinging my arms about his neck, my hard pregnant belly tight against his stomach. He pushed me away, blushing, and went to my vantage point the better to see. We stood side by side looking toward the battle, with hope in our hearts.

The Normans were in disarray, the death of their Duke, diminishing their arrogant bravado. They began to disengage from the conflict and back off down the hill, a stream of Saxons in their wake.

'They are running, Godwin, but there is nowhere for them to run. We have trounced them, just as Harold said we would.'

'Wait, Eadgyth' he said, with a hand to my arm, 'look, what is happening, there by the marsh.'

Together we looked with increasing dread as a figure emerged from midst of the Norman infantry and clambered upon a fresh horse. Removing his helmet, he waved his arms and called out to his men, his absurd hair cut and hefty build marking him as their Duke.

Our hearts sank, hope dwindling as with his standard bearers beside him, William rallied his army, reassuring them that he was unhurt. I turned and wept onto Godwin's shoulder while he stroked my hair, as despairing as I.

For hours the Normans continued to attack our shield wall, it went on for so long that I grew immured to the bloodshed and no longer flinched at every falling axe or severed limb.

Transfixed, I watched as William continued to send his forces to attack again and again, with both infantry and cavalry. The Saxons fought on, weary but determined, refusing to let the shield wall weaken. At one end of the ridge our men were cutting down the attacking invaders.

Suddenly the Normans seemed to falter and then back down, in retreat down the slope. Like a snapping bowstring one end of our shield wall broke forth and ran in pursuit of the fleeing foe. The far end of the defending wall was weakened, something that did not escape the Duke's eye. When the pursuers were too far to retreat, the Norman army turned, driven onward by the Duke, cutting the Saxons down and breaking through our ranks. The cavalry poured onto the hilltop.

'Oh my God,' I screamed, 'they have gained the ridge.'

The Norman horse was charging across the hilltop to where the Saxon royal standard fluttered in the breeze. The shield wall shifted, blocking the path to their king and preparing to face off the invaders once more. Gyrth and his huscarls stood between William's men and Harold's standard. Godwin grasped my arm.

'We should go, Eadgyth,' but I shrugged him off and turned back to the battle just in time to see the chevaliers smash into Gyrth's fightingmen.

The Saxons, mown down by the mounted force, stumbled and fell, the cries of the trampled reaching us at the malformed tree. I watched as Gyrth fought valiantly for his brother's kingdom, hacking and slashing with his battleaxe. Then, screened from my view by the surging enemy, Gyrth's standard fluttered for a while before wavering and finally falling to the ground to be crushed beneath the hooves of the Norman cavalry.

'Oh, Gyrth,' I wept. Tears wet my cheeks but I did not move and I was not aware when Godwin left me. A few moments later I realised that Eadgytha and Anwen were beside me. 'Gyrth has fallen,' I sobbed without turning my head, 'and Leo too. I saw him smite down a charging cavalryman and then he fell, taken down by another from behind.'

Eadgytha and I stood handfast, looking upon the scene while behind us, Godwin and Anwen beseeched us to flee.

The horsemen sped toward where Harold and his huscarls had made their stand; his men clustered about him, their battleaxes flying. I saw the Norman horses fall and I heard the thunk of blades cutting into flesh and I heard the screams of the dying. I saw my husband, his mouth open in a scream of rage I could not hear, lay waste to all who approached him. And then, quite gently, a swarm of silent arrows flew overhead to descend in sweeping destruction upon the ridge.

So thick were they that they shadowed the sun, making our men glance upward. I saw Harold put a hand up to his head before he stumbled, his standard swaying, the fighting man banner staggering before his final collapse. Edgytha and I fell to our knees.

'Harold!' Our screams rang out as one as the mounted men moved forward and, drawing back their lances, smashed them down onto the prostrate body of the Saxon king. Godwin and Anwen were tugging at my clothes, both sobbing as they tried to drag me to the horses to make our escape but Eadgytha and I stayed upon the ground and gave vent to our terrible hatred.

Domesday

<u>October 15th 1066</u>

I willed the sun not to rise the next morning but it did, just as if it were like any other morning. The dawning light slowly chased back the dark to reveal the horror of the cream of England's youth and vigour stricken in the dirt.

They lay in piles; rigid, blood-drenched, corpses, eyes wide to the rising sun. Soon the carrion birds came, great kites and buzzards swooping down to join the crows to feast upon our dead. As cold as death itself I clutched the trunk of the oak tree and saw the Normans come again and, scaring away the birds, begin to strip the corpses of their wealth.

The Norman dead were carried from the field but the Saxons were left, naked beneath the October sky, for the birds to peck and the worms to chew until all flesh was gone and their bones began to bleach in the sun.

The disturbed birds retreated to the perimeters of the field, watching and waiting for a chance to return to their banquet. A light rain began to moisten the air and Eadgytha stirred beside me. I don't know if she had slept or, like me, had spent the night in wakeful misery.

'We must find him and take his body,' she said dully, looking at the scene, 'we cannot leave him for carrion.'

Other women moved with us among the dead, wives and mothers turning torsos and lifting helmets to reveal the ravaged faces beneath. The ridge was silent after the clamour of the day before, the peace broken only by the keening of the bereaved as they fell upon the corpse of the man they were seeking.

They all looked the same, bloodied and blackened cadavers, their staring eyes and faces frozen in horror at the moment of death. Eadgytha and I lifted our skirts and tiptoed, slipping and skidding through the mire. We did not look like noble women now, our bedraggled state blended us invisibly with the peasantry.

At the top of the ridge a group of Norman's sifted through the Saxon slain, turning the corpses with their feet, their alien voices strident in the hush, their laughter an insult to our sorrow. We paused, uncertain if we should continue, Harold's warning to stay clear of the enemy prominent in our minds, but they saw us and shouted something too rapidly for us to understand.

We turned and made to move away but they pursued us. Eadgytha faced them, bracing her shoulders and pushing me a little behind her, shielding me from their sight. The men approached, gesturing widely and shouting so that we may better understand their heathen tongue. They indicated that they were seeking the body of the Saxon king and asked if we could identify his body among all those that lay piled around.

'I can identify the king, should he be found.' Eadgytha stated loudly, 'my maid here, and I, will find him for you on the condition that we be allowed his body for burial.'

I pulled Anwen's cloak close about my body to shield my pregnant belly from their gaze. The men huddled together, gesticulating with their arms while they conferred. At length, one of them turned and said in halting Saxon,

'You may 'ave the oathbreaker's body if you show us where 'e lies.'

They watched us as we moved about the hilltop, close to where we had seen Harold fall. The remains, both of man and horse, were piled thick here and we grew weary in the sun, turning corpse after corpse, each time dreading that it may be him.

It was Gyrth that we found first, his naked body intact apart from a great gash that laid his chest open. His intestines spewed forth to soak the battle standard that draped across him like a shroud. We wept over his body and tried to cover it with the banner and the Normans, seeing our grief, made to come near but Eadgytha waved them away.

'It is not the king,' she told them and, after a brief prayer, we rose and continued our search.

Gyrth's was the last body we found that was not entirely dismembered. As we grew closer to where the standard had flown we found only pieces, trailing innards, severed limbs and heads. It seemed to us that most of the damage had been done after death, even their genitalia had been sliced away in a savage desecration of manhood.

I espied the banner of the fighting man before Eadgytha. The coloured flag, bloodied and twisted among the bodies of the huscarls. Clasping hands, together we moved toward it, the pieces of what had, yesterday, been hot-blooded men, thick about our ankles.

Close to the fallen standard we climbed over the body of a horse, its throat had been severed and its entrails unravelled on the grass, the bulbous eyes stared glassy in the sunlight. Here the ground and the corpses upon it were bristling with arrows and we knew we came close to where Harold had fallen.

Beneath the sun, in that great landscape of slaughter, we hesitated, afraid and not knowing which way to turn. Hand in hand, we scanned the bodies for a sign, a clue, that might indicate where Harold lay; compelled to discover him yet reluctant to do so …and then I saw it, a scrap of crumpled lace kerchief fluttering in the gentle breeze.

Together we moved toward it and looked down upon a torso, no head, no limbs, no genitals, just a broad, muscled chest that had once been the vessel for Harold's beating heart.

The sun had dried the blood so that it lay thick, congealed in the once golden hair. Our feet slipping in gore we kneeled beside it and, taking the wine skin from her waist, Eadgytha began to wash the blood away. A thin scar, trailed like a road winding through a golden forest and, when I saw it, I sat back on my heels and knew how it felt to stop living.

'It is Harold,' we said in unison and, so deep was our sorrow that our tears could not fall.

The Normans came, indifferent to our grief, and shouted at us, trying to make us understand. They asked if this was the body of the oath-breaker and, when we nodded, they pushed us out of the way and began to manhandle his remains.

'What are you doing?' Eadgytha cried, trying to shield the body from them, 'you said you would give us the corpse.'

'We tell a small lie,' one of them said in bad Saxon, 'the duke does not want the grave of the oath-breaker to become a shrine so he will be buried in obscurity.'

I could not believe what I was hearing, had Normans truly so little honour? I could not comprehend the ignominy of refusing an anointed king a proper burial.

'Wait,' Eadgytha cried, 'I will give you his weight in gold if you only let us have his body. We will inter him in secret and let none know where he lies …but, please, oh please, let us have him.'

'Non, non,' they replied, 'our duke is waiting to see the body, it is for him to do with it as he pleases.'

They picked him up and began to bear him away. I watched in detached horror as Eadgytha threw herself across Harold's body and one of the Normans lay hands on her and threw her to the bloody ground.

Later we saw the duke come to watch them bury him on the beach, beneath a simple cairn of stones, facing out to sea. The bastard laughed and spat.

'Now the oathbreaker can guard the Saxon shore for all eternity.'

The world seemed empty and silent, as if it held its breath in horror at the king's passing. That night we began a long, sombre journey to Chester. On the way we passed smouldering settlements and holdings, devoid of life; even the sheep and pigs were gone, slaughtered to feed the ravaging army.

The wayside was littered with the dead and so we sought the old pathways, trodden for generations before the Romans had brought better roads. A twisting, winding network that took us away from the main byways that the enemy travelled. England was silent. The nation hushed, no wind or rain and no birdsong, as though the country knelt in eloquent respect for the passing of its king.

When it grew too dark to ride forward, we found shelter in an abandoned shepherd lodge, it was squalid, the floor of earth and the thatch of sod, but it was dry and warm. We huddled together about a miserly hearth, speaking little, all at a loss to understand how to carry on without our lord.

Godwin killed a hare and we stripped its charred flesh and ate it, meagre though it was, burning our fingers and wiping them on our skirts. Then, after hours of silence, Godwin's voice jolted us all from our private thoughts.

'I cannot believe all are lost; there must be some who survive to fight again. There are your brothers, Edwin and Morcar, they are not slain. I could seek them out and join with them, we can form another army and drive the Normans from our land.'

'How can we without Harold?' My grief spat bitterly from cold lips, 'Do you know where to look? Edwin was reported to be bringing men but he never arrived. For all we know he saw our cause was lost and betrayed us. He could be breaking bread with the enemy even now. He may be my brother but I'd not put it past him.'

Anwen came clattering through the door, bringing in water from the well. She stopped at my words.

'Lady.' she cried, 'do not speak so. You know that Edwin would do no so such thing. He may be a fool but he is no traitor. I'd lay down my life against his loyalty.'

The resentment I felt against my brothers was strong. I was so angered by their failure to support us that I would have felt better had they lain dead at Harold's side.

The horrors of the last few days surged in my mind and I could not shift them. The strain of the battle, the dreadfulness of seeing Harold fall and the discovery of the cruelly maimed body was scpred permantantly behind my eyes. And wherever I looked I saw them again. Images as clear as the paintings on a church wall.

Eadgytha had not spoken for hours, throughout the ride remaining silent, eating little and drinking only enough to staunch the worst of her thirst. White-faced she moved like a woman in a trance and none of us could reach her.

Suddenly she put down her cup making us jump with the suddenness of her movement.

'We cannot leave him there,' she announced, 'buried forever in a kind of exile, far from his home and loved ones. It is not where he should be, Harold was a king, anointed by God.'

'He wanted to lie at Waltham,' I said, a memory stabbing me of the day he had asked me to lie there beside him

'And so he shall,' vowed Godwin, standing up so that his frame was silhouetted by the firelight. So determined was his expression that he could have been Harold. 'I swear to you, ladies, on my father's soul, that I shall return one day and take his body home to lay him where he wished to rest.'

We all nodded but with little hope. That would be good day should it ever come but, in the strange unreal world we now inhabited, who knew what would come to pass.

The trials of the last weeks had matured Godwin, turned him from boy to a man so that we all looked to him for leadership. He was suddenly noble despite the raggedness of his clothes and I thanked Christ that he was there.

I suppose horror has a way of jolting one from adolescence. I, myself, felt aged, an aching crone in a burdensome body, although I had not yet seen one and twenty summers. Looking back on my girlhood that had been snatched away almost ten years ago, I felt I had lived a lifetime of insecurity since and God alone knew what would become of me now.

It was a perilous road we followed. We knew that the enemy rode abroad, ravaging the land so we travelled stealthily, our mood sombre. The weather began to draw in, biting through our thin clothes and, as the nights drew in earlier and earlier each evening, we were forced to seek shelter before we had travelled but a score of miles.

On occasion we passed families, cast from their homes and fleeing from Norman injustice into the forests. They told us tales of an England caught in the grip of terror but those we spoke to were not cowed, they swore to fight against the bastard's rule, to burn the Normans in their beds until there was not one left alive. 'Amen,' we said, 'Amen to that.'

It was early November before the outline of the burgh of Chester stood against the darkening skyline. Our family fell upon us with tears, both grievous and glad. Maude had cared for them as if they were her own and they were warm and wellfed but none of them had known if we were alive or dead.

We were a sorry party, forlorn and bewildered at what had befallen us and, like everyone else in England, afraid of what would happen next.

The Saxon tongues spoke of burnings and killings, of insurrection and a determined refusal to accept the Norman bastard as our king. Small factions fought back. We heard that in London, Edwin and Morcar, who to my relief remained loyal after all, had declared Edgar the Ætheling as rightful king, although he was not crowned.

Godwin rode away to join them, promising that as soon as the opportunity arose, he would restore his father's body in secret to the abbey church at Waltham. The farewells were tearful. I kissed him, his chin dimpling in a rueful smile as his eyes burned into mine. Eadgytha clung on to his arm, reluctant to lose the only man remaining to her.

Only those who have risen high can fall as low as Eadgytha and I fell then. We were alone and without an influential friend in the world and in our meagre lodging that barely kept out the December cold, I gave birth, after much trevail to Harold's twin sons.

Eadgytha and Anwen, with the birthwaters still dampening their gowns, stood afterwards at the foot of my bed, each bearing a swaddled babe in their arms. They smiled ruefully; smiles full of 'if only' and the 'might have been.' And my own heart cleaved afresh when I beheld Harold's boys; he would have been so proud.

Eadgytha was sworn as God-mother to them when, in the stone cold chapel, we named the eldest Harold, and the second, born just twenty minutes later, we christened Wulf.

Both boys, to our shared delight and sorrow, are cut in their father's exact image. Their blond hair is the same shade and their eyes shine as brightly blue as the summer sky

The Hereafter

Chester –1070

It is four years since my sons were born. Four years in which the conqueror has ravaged all England, laying waste vast areas of the country and punishing all who will not surrender to his rule.

Saxon landowners are no more, we are reduced to lowly things and the country is divided as spoils for William's supporters. Violence and hatred simmers and the Saxon people are churlish and edgy.

Now, the conqueror has come to Chester to wreak his hatred and Edgytha and I must go elsewhere. Idwal and Maredudd are ten and eleven summers now although it seems but yesterday they were swaddled in my arms. I sent them, for safety, over the dyke into Wales to the court of their uncle Bleddyn where they are training to be fighting men. I plan to join them there, to introduce their new twin half-brothers and reunite them with their sister, Nesta.

My Nest is eight summers now and growing into a beauty, unfashionably dark like her father and with skin like the purest snow. In Gwynedd we will make ourselves a proper home, raise her in the Welsh way and find her a good husband. Perhaps, when her brothers have regained their own status in Wales, they can raise an army to aid Harold and Wulf in their quest for the English throne.

There is nothing in my life now but my children and, as Eadgytha and I sit, knee to knee before the fire and the children tumble in play, there comes a rapid knocking on the door.

We all jump, exchanging anxious glances. We get no callers here. Anwen takes a poker and creeps to stand by the door while Eadgytha and I grab the children and cower in the darkened corner, afraid that we are discovered.

'Mother,' comes a whispered voice, 'it is I. Open the door.'

Anwen does so and Godwin creeps in, smiling in sheepish delight upon us. It is long since we have seen him and he is some inches taller and with a full man's beard upon his chin. My heart wrenches as he strides, so like his father, across the room to hug his mother. Then he turns to me to leave a kiss upon my wrist.

Scant news has filtered through to us here in Chester but we know that Godwin has not been idle. Two years ago he raised an Irish force and attacked Bristol but was driven back and, just last year, he raided the West Country, rallying men to his standard. His army cut a swathe across the land until the Norman forces overwhelmed them and forced them back across the sea.

Since then we have had no word and can scarce believe he is here with us, when we had thought him lost. 'Godwin.' Eadgytha sobs, overcome and Godwin hushes her,

'Do not weep Mother, he says, 'look, I have brought Edmund home.'

And, in the doorway stands Eadgytha's second son, whom we had all thought slain on Senlache Ridge, and she falls upon him too, finding a fresh supply of tears.

Anwen slaughters our last hen and we celebrate, ignoring the shrivelled status of our family that had once been the highest in the land. When we are settled and our bellies full, Godwin leans back with his jug of ale and begins his tale.

'I have been everywhere, Ladies. Norway, London, Ireland, the West Country and, wherever I go, I recruit men who will fight our cause when the day comes. And it will come, we will vanquish the Norman's though it takes the rest of our lives.'

We smile but say little; we women are tired of fighting and happy just to savour the look of him as the firelight seeks out the brightness of his hair. Edmund is smaller than his brother in every way, a shade less fair, a shade less handsome and retentive in contrast to Godwin's volubility.

'We are returning to Ireland soon, where King Diarmait has promised us more aid. Tis money we need most, all our followers are in the same boat as we and have barely a coin in their pockets.'

I remember the goodly hoard that Harold had buried at Thorney and Gleawanceaster before leaving for his last battle but I do not tell Godwin of them for fear he will venture into danger to retrieve it.

I am weary of unrest and long for the life I have always dreamed of. I crave peace like a drunkard craves his wine. Even if tis only to scratch a living in a woodland cott. Edmund catches my eye and smiles at me warmly, the last of the Godwinsons to accept me and, looking about the shrunken circle of my family, our faces shiny in the firelight, I feel certain that Harold is looking down from his heavenly seat and thinking it good.

'Father would have liked this,' Edmund says, as if reading my thoughts, and we all murmur our agreement, nodding our heads and smiling. Eadgytha stretches out her hands to the flames, happy to be with her sons again.

'Tis strange to think how we all disliked each other at the beginning,' she says, 'but now, Eadgyth, you are my foremost friend; you have become the sister I never had. I shall miss you when we part.'
Reaching for her hand, I clasp it.

'Tis not forever, Eadgytha, when young Harold has won his throne, I will call you back to court where you will take your rightful place as the mother of the king's siblings and we shall all live in right royal state.'

As if in response to his name, in the corner young Harold stirs on the straw mattress that he shares with Wulf and I rise to quiet him. I turn him onto his side and the familiar touch of my hand soothes him and he soon sleeps again.

When I stand up I find that Godwin has followed me and we move together, away from the slumbering children. 'You look well, Eadgyth, it does my heart glad.'

'Tis but the flush of youth,' I reply, 'It has been a sore time and inside, I am far beyond my years.'

'As am I,' he grins and I remember, with a start, that he is of an age with me, just four and twenty summers.

'What do you plan to do next?' he asks and I shrug, looking up at him.

'We return to Wales. I was happy there once and I would like to be with Idwal and Maredudd as they grow to manhood and, when she is of an age, I would seek one good enough for my daughter to wed. A Welshman or a Saxon, I do not want her staying here to join with a Norman for they treat their women poorly.'

'That is why the priories are overflowing with novice nuns. My sister Gytha is safe in Denmark and set to make a fine match, did Mother tell you? She is to wed the Grand Duke Vladimir of Russia.'

Impressed at her good fortune, I nod.

'I wish her well.' I murmur, waiting for him to continue,

'and Gunnhild is happy in her convent and Magnus, my brother, has entered orders also. He is not cut out for the life of a layman and Father always said he was possessed of a brilliant mind.'

I smile, remembering the crippled boy with a fascination for weapons.

Opening the back door we see that the moon throws down its silvery light, beautifying the midden and the barn. A fox slinks, soft foot across the yard in search of chickens and we watch him sniffing hopefully at the corner of the empty roost.

'How things change,' I say, 'how strange that, even when all is lost, we can still find beauty in simple things.'

He stands behind me with his hands upon my shoulders, both of us looking up at the sky. A sky that reminds me of the night that Harold returned from Normandy and asked me to be his wife.

'Resilience is what keeps us all from madness,' Godwin says, 'if we didn't have the power to heal, to move on and overcome our grief, the human race would not survive.'

I turn, twisting in his grip to look up at him,.

'You are very profound this evening, Godwin,' I laugh and he rubs his nose and confesses he is quoting his brother, Magnus' philosophy. We are laughing together softly, when he sobers and, suddenly speaking urgently, says,

'All is not lost, Eadgyth. Don't go back to Wales; come to Ireland …with me.'

I am surprised and yet, not surprised. I ponder his offer for a while and feel a gentle tremor where my heart once was. It seems I have been here before, as though I have waited all my life to hear him speak those words. He is so tall and earnest that I know I can love him. I am sore tempted, but the memory of another stepson pledging his self to me stirs and I remember all the sorrow that love brought with it.

I thrust temptation away. I need to forge my own path and decide upon the direction of my own feet. Steeling myself, I make my reply.

'I cannot Godwin, not yet, although 'twould be a fine thing. I must help my sons win back their properties and status, both in Wales and in England. And you, Godwin, you must keep on fighting too. For the sake of your father's memory you must return to Ireland and live to do battle again.'

He opens his mouth to speak but I place my finger on his lips.

'Hush,' I say, 'speak no more of this now, but perhaps one day, when our work is done, you will travel into Wales and find me and, who knows, when all the strife is finally over, we may then begin to salvage something from our broken lives.

Author's Note

Although I have poured for many months over historical sources, *Peaceweaver* is primarily a work of fiction. The records of the Anglo Saxon period are incomplete, and those detailing the lives of women few and far between. This offers great scope for the novelist but it can also make the job harder.

I have sifted through the muddle of fact, legend and fantasy to craft a story for Eadgyth that I hope my readers will enjoy. My main aim is to provide a voice for her and to illustrate, from a female perspective, what the years leading up to the Battle of Hastings may have been like. I plead forgiveness for any blunders I may have made.

Eadgyth appears fleetingly in the historical record, even her name is written variously as Aldith, Eadgyth, Aldgyth and Eadgifu. The Anglo-Norman historian Oderic Vitalis, writing in the early 12th century, states that Ælfgar's daughter, Ealdgyth was wed to Gruffydd ap Llewellyn to secure his alliance with her father, the Earl of East Anglia. She is barely mentioned again until 1065 so I made it my job to fill in those missing years.

The main characters in the first half of *Peaceweaver* are factual, although it is not possible to trace their movements exactly. Anwen is a fictional character, a companion forged to move through the story beside Eadgyth, to protect her and also act as an outlet for Eadgyth's innermost thoughts and feelings.

The servants at Rhuddlan, Heulwen, Maude and Envys, are imaginary also but Llyward and Tangwystl are the recorded names of Gruffydd's chamberlain and his wife. Gruffydd's brothers and sons are on the historical record but Alys and Rhys at the *llys* of Dinefwr are my inventions.

Young Rhodri, I am afraid, is a figment of my imagination also. I wanted to provide Eadgyth with some romantic joy in her early life and I cannot believe that she would have held any tender feelings for a husband so many years her senior. Rhodri's murder at his father's hands was an authorial device to accentuate Gruffydd's ruthlessness.

Gruffydd was, by all accounts, a brutally efficient ruler, undoubtedly clocking up resentment and dissent among his fellow countrymen in his quest for power. It is widely recorded that, while under siege in Snowdonia, he was killed by his own men but the chroniclers offer no detailed explanation of their motive to do so.

The Welsh, under Gruffydd's half-brothers, Bleddyn and Rhiwallon, then capitulated to Harold. Gruffydd's severed head was delivered to Edward's court as proof of a job well done. We do not know why Gruffydd was betrayed but, for the sake of fiction, I felt constrained to make him as unpleasant a character as possible.

I stumbled across the story of Gruffydd's encounter with his first wife in an obscure journal and was compelled to include it in his story. It may be the stuff of legend but it suited my purpose to use it. We do not know the manner of her death but, since the major cause of female death at this time was childbirth, I thought it a credible demise.

Harold's attack on Rhuddlan is well documented; it took place just after Christmas. What became of Eadgyth during the raid is not detailed in the sources but we do know that, either just before or just after his coronation, she married Harold. Eadgyth gave birth to his son, or possibly twin sons, in the December following the battle at Hastings in 1066.

Whether Eadgyth and Harold really enjoyed the love match I have provided for them is doubtful, the records do not speculate upon tender feelings. There is no doubt the marriage was politic but the love angle adds a little spice and poignancy to my tale.

After having suffered the experiences with Gruffydd, I for one, would have fallen at Harold's feet. He was a good match; powerful, rich and even the Norman's allow that he was a good-looking, heroic figure. One article I read made a connection between Harold's banner of The Fighting Man with the Cern Abbas Giant on the hillside in Dorset. I found this so intriguing that I have included it in my story.

Harold was around forty-four when he was killed. I have made his relationship with Eadgyth volatile and highlighted her insecurities for the same reason that I make her conscious of her failings as the *ideal* woman. She was a child thrust into a terrifying world and I wanted to illustrate the pressures put upon all women to adhere to preset expectations that, even in this day and age, can only have a negative effect.

As her story progresses it is easy to forget that she is so young. Her resilience in the face of the troubles heaped upon her evoke a much older woman. Eadgyth was just 21 years old at the Battle of Hastings and, by the end of the same year, she had given birth to five children and buried two husbands. It makes one stop and think.

In the second half of the book, set at Edward's court, most of the characters (apart from the servants

Ethel and Mary) are historically recorded. There has always been speculation as to King Edward's reasons for not consummating his marriage to Edith and his reluctance, or refusal, to provide an heir. Victorian historians were content to accept piety as an explanation but modern day scholars tend to dismiss this. Several theories have been put forward, impotence and homosexuality among them so, unwilling to commit myself, I have hinted at both without being conclusive.

It is Queen Edith, to whom we owe thanks for the manuscript *Vita Edwardi Regis.* It provides invaluable information about her family, the Godwinsons, and also King Edward's reign. (Or perhaps I should qualify that and say, as much as Edith wished us to know.)

In *Peaceweaver* she is rather shallow and unfulfilled, none of which is historically based. I feel that, in an age when a woman's prime responsibility was to provide children, a queen in her position may have been made to feel inadequate. She did have many royal wards and the evidence tends to go against the scene I have written which suggests she was uncomfortable with children. I feel she was, more probably, a woman who suffered her barren state deeply and sought compensation in religion. After the battle she capitulated to William and was allowed to remain on her properties in Winchester.

I have tried to adhere to the battle sequences as best I can, bearing in mind that it is reported through the eyes of a woman with no knowledge of strategy or warfare. I was also keen to show the women fighting their own, rather different battle along side the men at Hastings; attempting to save lives rather than take them.

Anglo Saxon chroniclers were infuriatingly vague about women and the little they did record tantalises and teases the imagination. We can never glean the real truth from their faded script.

Most surviving records of the Battle at Hastings were written by Norman scribes but a few survive that were the work of Saxon hands; many of them written long after the battle date. None are unbiased so I have tried to cut my pathway somewhere through the middle.

We do not know for sure the place where Harold was laid to rest. Norman records state he was buried on the shore watching over the channel but others say he was moved to Waltham. Some claim he lies at the church at Bosham, where a body of the correct date was discovered. The remains of blond hair and bones showing signs of violence lead some to believe it is Harold.

However, there are other more likely possibilities. It could the body of his father, Godwin, who is recorded as being interred there or, perhaps, one of his brothers, or even his cousin, Beorn.

After Hastings, the Saxons did not roll over beneath their Norman masters but for many years fought on against them. Some of the characters in *Peaceweaver* are documented fighting on in the resistance to the new regime; others fade from the record.

Of Eadgytha Swanneck we know nothing more, even the legends have not bothered to speculate on her fate. Many women rushed for safety's sake into nunneries at this time and we know that Gunnhild, the daughter of Eadgytha (Swanneck) and Harold, was in the nunnery at Wilton.

It seems that the religious houses were not as safe as we are led to believe for, in 1093, Gunnhild was abducted by a Norman named Alan the Red. Alan had recieved Eadgytha Swanneck's lands from William as a reward for his support. Harold and Eadgytha's other daughter, Gytha, did indeed marry her Russian Duke and gave him many children.

In 1067, Harold's mother, Gytha, fortified and held Exeter while William was absent in Normandy. As soon as he returned to our shores he turned his attention to Exeter, one of the largest towns in England. She held out against him for eighteen days, destroying many Norman soldiers in the process. It is believed Godwin and Edmund (and some records say Magnus) may have been present.

Godwin and Edmund went to Dublin with their huscarls to seek aid from King Dairmait. In the summer of 1068, after trying unsuccessfully to take Bristol, they invaded the West Country with a large Hiberno-Norse force. There followed a large battle with many losses on both sides but the brothers managed to escape. In 1069 they returned again with a fleet of sixty ships and attempted to take Exeter but were foiled by the large garrison and newly implemented fortifications. Later they raided Somerset and Cornwall until defeated by a large Norman force led by Count Brian. They returned to Ireland with just a remnant of their army. Their ultimate end is not recorded.

Of their brother, Magnus Haroldsson, nothing is known, some say he died in battle in the West Country but, there is a tiny chance that, perhaps he didn't.

Near Lewes in Sussex an inscription of that date records the presence of a Prince Magnus, who came of the royal northern race. It may be the stuff of legend but some suggest that this is Magnus Haroldsson and that he lived on in Sussex which had long been the home of the Godwin family. Legend says that he lived as an anchorite until his death.

In 1068 William appointed Robert de Comines as Earl of Northumberland in place of Earl Morcar. The men of Northumberland, unhappy with his decision, massacred Robert and nine hundred of his men in Durham. Edgar the Ætheling was thus encouraged to come from his refuge in Scotland but William, hearing of his movements, marched north, surprising the rebels and slaughtering hundreds of them before torching the city of Durham.

On the Welsh border, a local thegn, later to become known as Eadric the Wild, allied with Gruffydd's brothers, Bleddyn and Rhiwallon, attacked the castle at Hereford and devastated Herefordshire as far south as the River Lugg. They then retreated to the Welsh hills and carried out guerrilla warfare against the Normans.

In 1072 the Scots began to muster men to Edgar Ætheling's standard but William took an army across the border and forced King Malcolm to back down and make peace. On his way to Scotland to join the mustering armies, Edwin, Eadgyth's brother, fell into a dispute and was slain by his own followers. It was after this that Morcar joined Hereward the Wake as a fugitive.

Hereward the Wake together with many of the survivors from earlier uprisings plagued William from his hiding place in the fens. The events that took place under the command of Hereward in the Isle of Ely have become legendary.

More than once William lay siege to them but they could not be moved from their stronghold. The eventual betrayal of the rebels by the monks of Ely led to the breakup of the rebel army but Hereward escaped, continuing to harrass William for many years.

There is some discrepancy over the identity but a man named Morcar was captured and imprisoned by the Conqueror in one of his castles in Normandy until pardoned by William on his deathbed in 1087. Some chronicles say that following his release he was immediately re-arrested by William's successor, William Rufus, finally dying in captivity in 1092.

When Harold beat Gruffydd ap Llewellyn in 1062 he divided Wales between Gruffydd's half brothers, Bleddyn and Rhiwallon ap Cynfyn. When they obtained sufficient strength, Eadgyth's sons, Maredudd and Idwal ap Gruffydd contested for their Welsh lands at the Battle of Mechain. Maredudd and Idwal were defeated, one slaughtered during the battle and the other perishing shortly afterwards. Rhiwallon was also slain, leaving Bleddyn to rule alone.

I must apologise to little Nesta, and her descendents, for suggesting that she was not the legitimate daughter of Gruffydd. I can only restate that *Peaceweaver* is a work of fiction and it suited my purpose to make the inference. The real Nesta married Osbern fitz Richard of Richard's castle in Shropshire and had at least two children. Hugh FitzOsbern and Nesta fech Osbern.

Eadgyth gave birth to Harold's son, Harold Haroldsson at Chester in December 1066. (Some records state that Harold had a twin named Wulf or Ulf). One record claims that Eadgyth fled to Ireland with her son(s) and I have hinted at this possibility.

There is little mention of Ulf in the historical record although some say that he spent the whole of the reign of William in prison. The records may be confusing Ulf with his uncle Wulfnoth who spent most of his life a prisoner. Ulf gained his freedom and William's eldest son, Robert Curthose, who became Duke of Normandy after his father's death, knighted him. It is possible that he fought with Robert in the First Crusade.

As a man, Harold Haroldsson journeyed to Norway to the court of King Magnus and, according to William of Malmesbury, was well received because of the mercy King Harold had shown at Stamford Bridge.

It is believed he may have fought with Magnus against the Norman earls of Shrewsbury and Chester where Earl Hugh of Shrewsbury was killed by an arrow. After that Harold Haroldsson fades from the record although a Norse saga tells of a King Harold living as a hermit near Chester.

In the tale this king speaks to King Henry I, and some believe that, the King Harold referred to in the legend could be Harold II's son, Harold Haroldsson.

Lightning Source UK Ltd.
Milton Keynes UK
UKOW05f1900030114

223971UK00004B/214/P